I0746429

ETCHED IN GOLD

UMA SRINIVASAN

Published in Australia in 2025

Uma Srinivasan Books

Copyright © Uma Srinivasan 2025

I write from the land of the Wangal people, clan of the Eora nation. I acknowledge the traditional owners of the land and give my love and gratitude to elders past and present and emerging.

A catalogue record for this book is available from the National Library of Australia

ISBN: 978-1-7637653-1-3 (Paperback)
ISBN. 978-1-7637653-2-0 (ePub)
ISBN: 978-1-7637653-4-4 (ePDF)

Cover Design
Kavitha Amarnath

Editors
Cathie Tasker
Robyn Hooper
Laura Boon

To
AMMA

Who sent me on a journey to Tanjore
Where I found

AMBA

PRAISE FOR ETCHED IN GOLD

Etched in Gold transported me to a distant place and time, and made me feel like I belonged. Highly recommended.
    --Pamela Hart, Award-winning Historical Novelist

I identified with Maya in contemporary Sydney who struggled with her craft of music. Maya helped me understand Amba in Tanjore in 1610 who was facing similar creative and personal struggles.
    A wonderful character-driven book.
    --Cathie Tasker, Editor and Creative Writing Teacher

Etched in Gold is a song across centuries—bold, beautiful, and quietly subversive. Srinivasan revives a forgotten legacy with grace and power.
    --Shankari Chandran, winner of the Miles Franklin Literary Award 2023

CHAPTER 1

MAYA

Sydney, Australia, 2010

I couldn't hit the high-octave notes in the shower that morning. It was as if my vocal cords had lost the ability to expand at will. I ignored the tightness in my throat, mopped my damp face as I got out of the shower, then pulled on a grey jumper and headed out to work.

As I hurried through the cold June air across to my office, a health tech start-up overlooking the Parramatta River, I pined for the world I had left behind in warm Chennai, India. That world had nourished my music and showered me with awards and accolades. Sydney had smothered my voice. Now, living in a joint family home with my husband Deepak and his parents, the soundscape was dense with the crackle of TV. Sports commentators yelled out footy or cricket scores for Deepak and his dad Vikram. My familiar sounds, the temple bells, *ragas* with their unique melodic patterns and songs that filled my ears when I grew up in Chennai were gone. My singing was confined to my time in the shower.

Sitting at my desk at work, while a part of my mind tried to find patterns across rows of numbers on a spreadsheet, my fingers tapped a rhythmic pattern, a ten-beat *tala* of the song that had changed my life.

Three years ago, when I had stepped on to the platform at the centre of the large stage of the Chennai Music Academy, wearing a placard with my name––Maya Murthy––I was drawn into the comforting world of traditional South Indian Carnatic music. Then all I had wanted was to be a musician and that was my chance to be recognised as one.

The auditorium was packed. My mother, Viji Ma, was there, smiling and blinking away her tears, waving to me from the third row. Had my Appa lived one more year, he would have been sitting next to Viji Ma, his face glowing with pride. My father was my first music teacher and my ardent champion. He came from a family of Tanjore musicians and scholars and had inspired me to pursue advanced music lessons along with my maths degree.

It was a competition for young musicians, a two-hour vocal concert. Well-known senior instrumentalists had accompanied me at the concert, playing the violin, *mridangam*, the horizontal drum, and *ghatam*, the clay pot. The dais offered a cosy space for our ensemble of four to sit down cross legged as south Indians do, and be visible from every corner of the large Chennai Fine Arts auditorium. Winning this competition, held during the busy December music season, would set me up for life. Lucrative sponsorships from record labels and corporate sponsors would follow, and I would gain YouTube followers around the world. Many avenues would open if I won a prestigious event like this.

Vinayak, the violinist, spectacled and serious, sat to my left at an angle, facing me and the audience. He tucked the curvy end of his violin on the crook of his ankle and fine-tuned the strings. Placing his *mridangam* across his lap, Manoj, the highly-respected percussionist, sat on my other side, at right angles to the audience, so his prancing fingers would be visible as they hovered over the stretched membrane of his drum. Nimble-fingered Ganesh set his *ghatam*, against his bulging belly and tapped his fingers on the gleaming surface, instantly lifting my spirits. Senior percussionists like Manoj and Ganesh could make or break a concert. For them this was a concert like any other. But for me, it was the start of my music career.

I still remembered the *sari* I wore that day. Maroon silk, with a thin gold border, to match the sparkling gold earrings that dangled if I moved my head while singing. My hair, while not too short to raise conservative eyebrows, was short enough to be noticed by the traditional Chennai audience, too used to female performers coiling their long hair into oily plaits or tight buns decorated with strings of jasmine. Rather than wear bangles that tinkled when my hands moved to keep the *tala* rhythm, I had chosen a bracelet with embedded with garnet, modelled on temple jewellery. It was the one piece of jewellery I still frequently wore, a talisman that linked my bleak present with my bright past.

I followed the traditional Carnatic concert structure. The first song was about the Elephant God Ganesha, highlighting the devotional aspect in *raga 'Hamsadhwani'*. I followed my teacher's dictum and added my interpretation to the song. Combining long-short notes with the original beats allowed me to present tonal and rhythmic variations to depict Ganesha's head nodding from side to side as he walked through the temple archway. The violinist followed my lead, accentuating the trills and lilts in my voice. The percussionists added their unique rhythmic tempo to the seven-beat *tala*.

Towards the climax, I adjusted the lyrics to fit into seven beats, then fourteen, and finally twenty-eight, before slowing down to the original seven beats.

As the last note faded, the audience broke into spontaneous applause. A stranger in green T-shirt sitting next to our neighbour Jaya Aunty clapped long and loud, even after the others had stopped. His wide-eyed expression proclaimed loud and clear that he was new to the environment of classical music connoisseurs.

The finale was a fast-paced composition by Kshetrayya, the famous sixteenth century Tanjore scholar. The lyrics and the beats depicted dancers swirling in rapture around Krishna. As the song concluded, I allowed the melody to fade note by note into a deep silence.

Before I could emerge from that meditative space, my ears were filled with the loudest applause I had ever experienced.

The words of the judge, Mrs Jayam, praising my energy and unique improvisation, reverberated in my ears. 'A rare quality in youngsters,' she had said when she handed me the award.

The award, a rosewood plaque with a *tanpura* etched in gold, now sat on my dressing table in our bedroom, one of five bedrooms in Deepak's parents' house in Castle Hill while I spent my days with numbers and the clatter of keyboards in a health technology start-up. There was no way to foresee the demise of my music when Mrs Jayam was raving about my performance.

At home the TV was on. The sports commentators' voices rose and fell with every goal or catch, as Deepak and his father bonded over sports. Deepak's mother, Neetu, and I, both too exhausted to chit-chat after a long day at work, spent our time cooking dinner. In the evenings in Chennai, my mum and I would talk about a *raga* I had practiced that morning or a new song we had heard. But here, music doesn't even creep into the sound space. As I rolled out the dough for yet another *roti*, my thoughts flew back to that evening in Chennai.

When I'd walked out of the concert hall, the green T-shirted stranger hovered behind our neighbour Jaya Aunty who introduced us.

'Maya, meet my cousin, Neetu, and her son Deepak, a software engineer. They are visiting from Sydney.'

Neetu's smile was as graceful as the rest of her. Grey hair cut stylishly short, raw silk *kurta*, black pants, high heels. She stood apart from the ladies with their oiled hair, draped in bright silk *saris*. And even his stubble, did not hide the deep dimples that appeared when her tall son smiled. My hands unconsciously brushed my shoulder length hair, so my dangling ear rings were visible. I felt my face grow warm. My heart was beating to an unfamiliar rhythm.

'Hello Maya.' Deep dimples. NRI attire. Expensive sandals. Like most non-resident Indians, he too wore his status on his sandals. Every auto driver in Chennai identified them and charged them double fare.

'Hi Deepak.' We shook hands. He held mine longer than I expected. I didn't pull back. When I finally let go of his gaze his voice turned hoarse.

'You have an amazing voice, Maya. You were brilliant.'

My entangled emotions assumed my dreams were his when Deepak praised my voice. When he invited me and Viji Ma for dinner with his mother and aunt at the exclusive Tanjore restaurant, my head got caught in the clouds.

I ignored the fleeting frown that crossed Viji Ma's brows.

'Maya, are you okay to go out tonight? Aren't you tired after the concert?'

I was exhausted. My blouse stuck to my sweaty back. The

deodorant under my arms had long evaporated. My body needed a cold shower. But my mind wanted to hear Deepak's voice.

'Viji Ma and I will meet you at the restaurant,' I said, smiling at Deepak. 'Their hot pepper soup, *rasam,* will be soothing for my voice.'

Deepak's lips drew a crooked grin.

'A drop of red might be better. It will relax your whole body.'

Neetu rolled her eyes. Jaya tapped him on the shoulder. Viji Ma hid her smile behind her handkerchief. It was amusing to watch the seniors squirm at the mention of wine.

I grinned. 'Good attempt, Deepak. *Rasam* is all I can handle today.'

When we reached the restaurant, a tall doorman with an ankle-length maroon coat studded with gold buttons ushered us through the ornate doors of restaurant Tanjore. Tiny brass bells embedded along the length of the doors tinkled as we entered the marble lobby.

Deepak pointed his thumb and whispered, 'Did the doorman walk out of the Maharajah painting in the lobby?'

'Perhaps,' I chuckled, 'but he forgot to get the shoes off the painting. Did you notice the *chappals* on his feet?'

A hostess in a beautiful orange silk *sari* welcomed us and handed out strings of jasmine.

'Namaste.'

Deepak took the flowers to his nose. 'Beautiful fragrance. What am I supposed to do with these?'

She glanced at me and smiled. 'You can give it to your ...'

Deepak's hand brushed against mine as he handed me the flowers. I wound the flowers around my wrist like a bracelet.

'It's rare to see multi-layered jasmine like this in Chennai. Where do these come from?'

'We get them from Tanjore, Ma'am. This eight-layered jasmine is an heirloom variety.'

The aroma of spices and sandalwood incense greeted us when we entered the dining area. Tall brass lamps, bronze bells and sculptures carved on gleaming teak pillars conjured up an image of a glamorous palace of a bygone era.

Soft Carnatic music floated in the air. I heard the notes of my favourite *raga 'Thodi'*. Four musicians playing the veena, violin, the long bamboo flute and the *mridangam*, were seated on raised floor cushions between two carved teak pillars. The music was mellow to allow conversations at tables. Did these artists enjoy playing music when people talked? I would not want to perform to talking heads and clattering dishes.

The welcome drink of cold buttermilk laced with salt, pepper and lemon cooled my throat and stomach. I held the frosted glass to my forehead and stretched out my feet under the table. I couldn't wait to taste the ten-course banquet.

A waiter in a maroon *kurta*, white cotton *dhoti* and matching shawl woven with a thin gold border, brought a tray with a large silver bowl of palm-sized *papadums*. Five tiny matching crucibles, filled to the brim with multi-coloured chutneys were arranged around the white *papadums*.

He recited in a sing-song tone. 'Green coriander, red chilli, white coconut, yellow lentil, brown tamarind.'

Neetu inhaled the flavours. 'What a feast!'

Jaya had a jolly expression on her face. 'Welcome to Chennai!'

As the main dishes arrived, Viji Ma and I got into our usual game.

I tasted a spoon of the spinach. 'Fenugreek.'

Viji Ma replied, 'Coriander and aniseed roasted together.'

Neetu took a spoonful of the *avial* and smiled. 'Coconut, ginger, green chillies, sour cream.'

Jaya chimed in, 'The cauliflower curry is unusual, north Indian flavour. Star anise and cinnamon?'

The four of us continued identifying every ingredient in every dish. Deepak stayed out of the game. Was it deliberate or did he not have a nose for these things?

When the dessert, the *kulfi* ice cream arrived, Deepak took a spoonful and raised his thumb. 'Mango.' His eyeballs grew round like a little kid tasting ice cream for the first time.

'Finally,' I grinned. I was relieved.

The waiter brought the bill on a small silver tray and hovered. Before any of us could react, Deepak picked up the bill, glanced at it, extracted his credit card from his wallet and placed it on the tray.

Viji Ma was all smiles. 'Thank you, Deepak.'

When we were ready to leave, an elderly couple came to our table and gave me a warm smile. 'We were at the concert today. Congratulations.'

Deepak whispered, 'You are a star.'

His aftershave was headier than the fragrant jasmine. The hostess at the door folded her hands and gushed.

'Ma'am, if you liked the food and the ambience, please like us on Facebook. Coming from you, it will be noticed. We have worked hard to create an atmosphere of ancient Tanjore and its music.'

'Hello, Maya.' My colleague's voice broke my reverie––and took me away from Tanjore and its music.

CHAPTER 2

AMBA
Tanjore, India, 1610

Amba wove through the crush of people hanging around the courtyard of the Big Temple, Periya Kovil, after the morning *puja*. Gliding through the sea of shiny *saris* and colourful turbans, her mother, Paru Ma, was right behind her, puffing and panting, trying to keep up with Amba. The air was dense with the pungent odour of sweat mingled with jasmine. Tanjore women rarely went out without jasmine entwined in their hair. Amba's stomach churned as she tried to shake off Paru Ma's tight grip on her elbow.

They were headed to the music palace, Indira Mandira. It was easily accessible from their tiny house, tucked in a narrow street behind the western arch of the temple. Rather than walk on the muddy streets, gathering a border of brown dust on her ankle-length, yellow silk *pavadai*, Amba cut across the paved temple courtyard and exited through the eastern gate. Her long frilly skirt billowed around her waist as she twirled around and entered the main street leading to the music palace.

They walked past the huge monolithic sculpture of the mythical bull Nandi and entered the festive-looking main street. Orange and yellow banners embossed with Shiva's Nandi fluttered on top of tall wooden poles lined on either side of the road.

Earlier that morning, while Amba hooked gem-studded hair pendants along her long plait, Paru Ma had walked in with the dreaded strands of jasmine strung together with banana fibre.

'Let me decorate your hair with this eight-layered jasmine from the temple garden.'

Amba jerked her head. 'No. When I walk on the street, smelling like a flower, men turn their heads and stare.'

'Why do you care?' Paru Ma said. 'Enjoy the day instead of worrying about men and their stares.'

Amba snapped. 'Maybe you are used to them; I am not.'

Paru Ma's eyes clouded. She muttered in a soft voice, 'A temple musician does not care about men. Our duty is to God alone.'

But Amba never felt devotion to the temple as she did to music. With a touch of remorse, Amba blinked away her tears and hugged her mother.

Paru Ma shrugged and did not insist further on the jasmine. 'Amba, before we head out, offer your prayers to Goddess Parvathi to bless you with inner strength and courage.'

Paru Ma applied the holy ash and a small dot of red vermilion to Amba's forehead, convinced that this would protect her daughter from the evil-eye. She handed Amba a small bowl. 'Eat your *prasad*.'

Amba had nibbled a handful of raisins and guzzled a cup of warm water laced with ginger and cardamom earlier in the day. She mentally thanked her guru's wife, Mami, for her advice. The ginger had cleared her throat, and the cardamom kept her breath fresh.

Amba pushed the four green bangles she had worn over each wrist until they sat firmly in the middle of her arms. If she wore any more, they would jingle and interfere with the rhythmic beats when she performed. She took a deep breath and turned to her mother. 'Let's go.'

A tremor ran through her body. This was her moment to take on the snooty scholars of Tanjore and challenge their notions about temple musicians being amateurs. She'd make them sit up and listen to her compositions. Her jaw clenched with determination as they approached the gates of the music palace.

Amba shot ahead with long strides, determined to reach the palace well ahead of her mother. She did not want to be boxed in like a *devadasi* or tamed and fettered like the temple elephant.

Amba was here to win the Tanjore Music and Literary competition and gain the freedom to enter the world of scholars. Freedom to compose and to perform beyond the boundaries of the Big Temple, away from the constant clang of temple bells. Every devotee who walked into the Big Temple yanked the rope tied to the clapper for God Shiva to fulfil their demands. At times, Amba wished she could shove little balls of cotton in her ears and block the reverberating sounds that hung in the air long after the first toll.

But this morning, for the first time, she felt the vibrations of the bells resonating like the strings of her guru's perfectly tuned *tanpura*. For ten years, she had followed his every instruction.

Guru lived in the *Agraharam*, the *Brahmin* neighbourhood where houses had stone floors, thick walls, and beautifully carved wooden doors set in brass frames. Her mother, Paru Ma, could never live there, as she was not a *Brahmin* scholar like Amba's Guru.

Amba loved Guru's wife Mami. Her smile was brighter than her shiny gold chain. Mami had a sweet treat for Amba whenever she was exhausted after a strenuous music lesson. Guru's stern voice never allowed Amba's attention to wander. 'Inhale, pause, exhale and chant OM. Make it a slow and steady hum that travels through your veins. Each OM should be longer than the previous one.'

In the morning, music lessons were held in the central hall, which had wooden pillars carved with lotuses reaching up to the ceiling. In the afternoons, Guru sat in the courtyard, cooled by coconut trees, and talked about languages, poetry, and composition. This had been her routine ever since the venerable scholar Govinda Ayya had heard Amba sing with her mother at the temple.

Amba had a vague memory of Ayya patting her head and talking to her mother. 'Paru Ma, even at her young age, Amba is able to compose and improvise in Sanskrit, Telugu and Tamil. She needs formal training to reach her full potential. I will talk to Guru Chengala. He will be a good teacher for Amba. He and his wife Mami will treat her like the *daughter they never had.*'

Guru showed her how musical notes combine to create a unique *raga* with its own name. Guru personified every raga. One day he'd say, 'Let us take *"Kalyani"* on a journey today. *"Kalyani"* is a complete *raga*, and all seven notes contribute to its melodic patterns.'

Guru sang the scale accentuating the fourth note *ma* and the seventh note *ni*: 'Sa re ga *ma* pa da *ni* sa. Sa *ni* da pa *ma* ga re sa.

'Did you hear the transition from the fourth and the fifth? Use your voice to express the emotions of those notes. Hum the scale. Follow it up with an improvisation segment set to an eight-beat rhythmic *tala*.'

Guru sat back with half-closed eyes and invoked a meditative mood. 'We will explore the emotions expressed by composer Kshetrayya in this song.'

Guru narrated the story behind the composer's inspiration. 'When Kshetrayya visited God Vishnu's temple, he found Vishnu's smile was ethereal. "Where is Goddess Lakshmi?" the composer wondered. "Shouldn't she be with her husband Vishnu when he is radiant?" Kshetrayya searched for Lakshmi all around the temple, but she was invisible. Suddenly, the composer visualised Goddess Lakshmi hidden deep inside Vishnu's heart. Her presence made Vishnu glow.'

Guru never stopped singing the praises of his composer friend. 'Kshetrayya's lyrics provide a creative space for the musician to explore both the *raga* and the emotions embedded in the words.' How Amba wished she could compose a song that would make her guru proud.

One day, Guru said, 'Amba, you are blessed with a melodious voice. Make sure every word you sing touches the emotions of everyone who hears the song. Only then can you be a true *devadasi*, a temple musician like your mother.'

Amba wanted to scream, *I don't want to be a devadasi. I want to be a scholar like you,* but she lacked the courage to spill out her thoughts.

Guru taught Amba the technique of projecting her emotions through her voice. He made her improvise over and over until he was convinced that Amba had glimpsed Lakshmi's presence in Vishnu's heart.

On days when Amba was drained from the vigorous training, Mami invited her inside for a snack. The polished stone floors of Mami's kitchen were a stark contrast to the mud floor in Amba's house. Mami gave her a banana-leaf cup filled to the brim with cardamom and nutmeg-flavoured pudding, *kesari*. After eating it,

Amba loved leaning against the carved wooden pillar on the veranda, feeling the gentle breeze through the coconut palms cool her warm cheeks.

At midday, Mami served Guru his lunch first. Later, Amba and Mami ate their lunch in a leisurely fashion on fresh banana leaf plates from the backyard, which was dense with coconut, mango and neem trees. The banana leaves added their own aroma to the *ghee*-infused white rice, yellow lentil *rasam*, and cumin-flavoured spinach on the side.

The moment Amba finished her rice, Mami always asked, 'More rice?' in such a kind voice, Amba could never refuse. She ate every morsel on her leaf. Mami's face reflected a sense of peace, unlike Amba's mother, Paru Ma, whose face was creased with frown lines.

After a heavy lunch, Guru let out loud belches and then snoozed on the stone bench in the open courtyard. Just when Amba thought she could get Mami to tell her a new story, Guru would set her a task.

'While I take a nap, compose four stanzas of poetry in Telugu and Sanskrit. If you want to be a scholar, become a multilingual extempore composer.'

Amba loved composing. She raced through her task, wrote out the verses on palm leaves, and then coaxed Mami to narrate a story before Guru woke up. His snores and the swish of coconut fronds provided a rhythmic background for Mami's stories. Mami knew many stories about poets and musicians, kings and queens, gods and goddesses. The ones Amba loved most were stories about strong women who made men notice their talents.

Mami often said, 'Guru won't be happy if you spend your time listening to my stories. You are here to learn from him, not me.'

'Mami, you know what I learn from him, but he does not know how much I learn from you.'

'Big words, little Amba,' Mami smiled.

Over the years, languages became Amba's friends. She composed in Telugu, Tamil, Sanskrit and its derivative Prakriti. If a language shared a root with Sanskrit, she learnt to interpret that language.

The day she turned sixteen, after a particularly rigorous practice session, Guru unfurled a silk scroll, his face beaming with joy.

'King Raghu Nayaka is pleased to invite your student, Amba, to the annual Tanjore Music and Literary Festival.' Guru placed his palm on her head, in a gesture of blessing. 'This is the very first time the king has invited women to take part in this festival.'

Gruelling months of practice followed. Whenever Amba's voice turned coarse, Mami handed her a tumbler of warm ginger water.

When she met all the challenges Guru had set, he patted her head and smiled though he seemed more sad than happy.

'Being invited to this event is itself an achievement, Amba. Many aspiring musicians, poets, and scholars come to Tanjore from neighbouring towns seeking the king's patronage. Not many succeed.'

Guru did not spare her the bitter truth. 'As a woman and a young one, you have to be far better than the best man who turns up for the competition to win.'

What an unfair world! Hot tears streamed down Amba's cheeks.

The stench of jasmine yanked Amba's thoughts back to where she was—the gates of the music palace. The ornate central dome painted in red, gold and yellow reached the sky, blending with the evening colours of the sun.

Tall, symmetrical stone pillars around the courtyard were carved with figures of mythical gods and goddesses holding various musical instruments. The mythical bull, Nandi, appeared on another pillar with his *mridangam*. Yet another pillar had God Krishna playing his flute, with dancing women twirling all around him. On another pillar, the Goddess Saraswati, holding her ornate *veena* upright, appeared larger than the male gods. The fingers of her right hand hovered over the strings, and her left hand curved around the long fretboard. Amba bowed in reverence to Goddess Saraswati, the custodian of music and knowledge.

Excited whispers broke into her reverie. 'Did you hear women are singing today?'

And another voice: 'The king plans to attend the competition. He wants to see the women perform.'

Amba clenched her fists and strode through the archway, her mother right on her heels. An elderly attendant recognised Paru Ma.

'Welcome. Are you singing today?'

Before Paru Ma could respond, Amba interrupted. 'No. I am.'

The attendant ignored Amba and politely directed Paru Ma to the visitor's gallery. Amba stood still before entering the central hall. It didn't matter that the attendant ignored her. The ornate arches stretched out their arms and welcomed her into their world.

Large chandeliers holding hundreds of tiny oil lamps hung from high ceilings, ready to dazzle. Stone pillars on both sides of the hall were etched with elaborate carvings of leaves and flowers at their bases while the middle sections were carved with musical instruments of all shapes and sizes. Amba's gaze moved up. Paintings of women in various dance postures sprawled across the vaulted ceiling, reaching out to mythical figures. Elephant-headed Ganesha, monkey-faced Hanuman, and Vishnu with a boar head. Whatever the sculptor conjured from mythology was carved in stone.

The alcoves between the pillars were covered with clusters of colourful bolsters woven in silk and gold. Attendants in yellow tunics, green vests and red turbans flew around like lost parrots in and out of the ornate areas arranging silk cushions. Female attendants wearing pink and orange *saris* guided Amba to a separate section of the hall. And there was her friend Vani, seated on a thick silk mat, invisible behind a pillar.

Vani chimed. 'I expected you here.'

'Vani, I didn't know you were coming.'

Vani was born to sing, but she was not a composer and, therefore, not a threat to Amba. They both sat at the farthest end from the dais, invisible to the male scholars and musicians assembled in the front rows. The visitors' gallery was rapidly filling up. Paru Ma, swathed in shimmering pink and seated in the front row, was a comforting presence.

All chatter ceased when Prime Minister Govinda Ayya, renowned musician and mentor to three generations of Nayaka kings, entered. He stood tall and erect, his salt-and-pepper hair pulled into a traditional top knot and a forehead smeared with *vibhuthi*, the holy ash. Govinda Ayya was ageless, like God Shiva. The yellow shawl wrapped around his shoulders created a halo as if the sun illuminated his brilliant mind.

Everyone stood up and hailed in one voice, '*Namaskaram*, Ayya.' They had shortened his name––Ayya––out of respect and love.

Ayya returned the gesture, a gracious smile lighting up his face.

Years ago, Guru had taken her to Ayya's concert at the Rama temple. 'You are here to listen to Tanjore's legendary musician Govinda Ayya. He composes his own songs as he sings, while simultaneously playing the *veena*.'

Ayya's sonorous voice penetrated through her thoughts and every crevice of the hall, as if to wake up the mythical figures. 'As in previous years, the program will have two segments. *Sangeeta*––the musical component and *saahitya*—the literary part.'

Ayya glanced at Amba and Vani, a gentle nod acknowledging their presence.

'Choose a composition in Telugu, Tamil or Sanskrit. Sing the complete song in the specified *raga*. Then, pick one verse to illustrate the emotional elements in the lyrics. Use your imagination and improvisation techniques to highlight the composer's intent.'

Amba rubbed her sweaty palms against the border of her skirt.

Ayya cleared his throat. 'For the literary section, you will be given a theme. You can compose in any of the three languages: Sanskrit, Telugu or Tamil.'

Ayya's gaze swept over the audience. 'For the first time, young women, our hidden gems, whom you have not heard before, will present their talents to Tanjore musicians and scholars. King Raghu Nayaka, himself an excellent musician and a *veena* player, will also be joining us this year.'

Excited whispers grew into loud chatter. Heads turned, and piercing eyes pricked Amba's face. She ducked her head. She did not want to return their stares—not yet.

When I become the best musician in Tanjore, I will look them straight in the eye, she promised herself. Her cheeks burned as she thought about her mother's resilience. Temple musicians like Paru Ma had never been allowed by *Brahmin* priests and scholars to perform outside the temple premises. As if their music was sufficient for temple audience, but not good enough to be performed at court and concert halls where scholars performed. *I will not be constrained like my mother*, thought Amba.

The shrill sounds of the seven-hole reed pipe, *nadaswaram*, announced the king's arrival. Amba's hands went up to her ears. She could never get used to the piercing notes reserved for ceremonial occasions.

The king entered, his head jutting forward like a peacock, balancing the weight of his gem-studded crown against the trailing golden robe pulling him backwards. His attire was a comic contrast to the pure white *dhotis* of the scholars.

Ayya waited for the king to take his seat. 'I expect participants to be conversant with the rules of composing lyrical poems in Telugu, Tamil or Sanskrit.'

Ayya's eyes glinted like the tips of sharp arrows. 'The judges will provide a few keywords for the participants to come up with thematic improvisations. The style, metre and rhythm of the lyrical composition should follow the grammar and syntax of the language chosen.'

Amba blew out the momentary panic that parched her throat. Guru's training had prepared her for this moment. Up in the gallery, Paru Ma's mouth was wide open. Perhaps she could not follow what Ayya was saying. Amba caught her mother's eye and nodded. She had it under control.

Chin resting on his palm, the king was listening with rapt attention.

A tiny smile played on the corner of Ayya's lips when he glanced at the king. 'Yes, few people fathom the complexity of these rules. However, I am sure our talented young musicians and scholars are ready for this challenge.'

Ayya introduced the judges. 'To my right is musicologist Venkata, the judge for the musical segment.'

Venkata was perhaps in his twenties. *Too young to be a judge,* thought Amba. His short, stout neck made his head look like an inverted brass pot stuck in the middle of his shoulders. His frosty expression highlighted his confidence, but the moment the king appeared, Venkata's face softened with reverence.

What an actor! Amba's jaw tensed when she looked at Venkata and saw the way he covered his arrogance in the king's presence.

Ayya's tone was full of warmth when he welcomed the visiting poet. 'We are honoured to have renowned poet Daasarati as our judge for the literary segment. His poems and plays are widely popular around Tanjore.'

Amba wriggled her bottom and settled on the soft silk mat. Years ago, Daasarati had visited her guru when she was learning the rules of Sanskrit poetry. The poet had explained the art of composing *champu*, a unique way of combining prose and poetry to dramatize lyrical compositions. Then he had asked her to compose a couple of extempore verses. Would he recognise her now?

Ayya sounded the ornamental bronze bell, and the competition commenced. The theme was devotion.

After a tepid performance by male scholars, it was Amba's turn. She walked to the podium, hiding her nerves under a sure-footed stride. Her yellow skirt with its green border and the matching half-*sari* and blouse filled her with confidence. Yellow was her lucky colour. It sparked her imagination. Amba sat down, looked straight ahead and pushed her four green and gold bangles away from her wrists till they were taut around her forearm.

Amba recalled her guru's words and allowed her inner self to take over.

She selected a song by the well-known composer Kshetrayya. She loved how the artist used different rhythmic patterns to bring out the devotional element in the lyrics.

With her whole heart in unison with the composer's vision of the goddess, Amba fitted the words into a sixteen-beat rhythmic cycle to convey the full range of emotions felt by a devotee yearning for God's love.

Eyes half-closed, the scholars in the front rows listened with rapt attention. The audience in the gallery tapped their fingers and kept time with her rhythmic *tala*.

The literary segment was pure joy for Amba. In the time it took most participants to compose one verse in one language, Amba improvised verses in three languages. She was delighted to see Ayya acknowledge her performance. The king, too, flashed her a smile, but not thick-neck Venkata. His displeasure ran down his cheeks, fusing his chin and neck.

Daasarati summed up the performance of participants. 'Amba's fluency with languages, coupled with her knowledge of grammar and prosody is remarkable––far beyond her age. She is indeed a rare gem in King Raghu Nayaka's court.'

Just as Amba savoured the sweet words of poet Daasarati, Venkata rose to his full height. 'Amba may have a flair for languages, but that does not make her a musician. She reduced Kshetrayya's devotional composition into a song of erotic connotations.'

Venkata spewed out his venom like a scorpion. 'Amba lacks the serenity and devotion required to bring out the aesthetic and meditative elements of music.'

Amba's fists crunched her skirt. How dare he. Thick-necked Venkata will acknowledge me and my music – one day.

CHAPTER 3

MAYA
Sydney, Australia, 2011

When I walked into the house after work, father and son were arguing over the umpire's decision on TV. A wicket had fallen. Vikram supported the visiting Indian team, and Deepak rooted for the Australians. Neetu was in the kitchen preparing dinner, seemingly oblivious to the deafening sounds. I could never tell if Neetu's silence was due to bored indifference or meek acceptance.

I felt like grabbing the remote and muting the space around me, so I could take up my *tanpura* and practice music. You would think that a large house like this would have some quiet space. But the open plan, which all three of them were so proud of, offered no respite from the cacophony of voices in and around the TV. Evening music practice, a constant in my life in Chennai, had vanished. I was striving to fit in and be part of this family and now my voice refused to traverse the higher octaves.

Had I known then what I know now, could I have resisted Deepak's advances? That was a heady time; I had won the competition for young musicians and was all set for a career in music. Here was this handsome man, oozing charm as we walked along Chennai's Marina beach, taking in the sound of the waves, the honks of autos, and the caw of crows swooping down for the food scraps. While we held hands, waiting for the waves to drench our feet, Deepak compared Chennai's Mariana Beach with Sydney's Bondi Beach. He had convinced me that Sydney was the most charming city in the world.

The TV theme music announced the 7pm news. As always, Neetu had come home from work before the others and had cooked dinner. I set out the plates and cutlery and brought the bowls of cumin rice, *dal*, and zucchini curry to the table. Neetu stacked the *rotis* in the hot case, yanked off her apron, and sat down heavily.

I said, 'Sorry I am late Neetu Ma. You had to cook and make fresh *chapatis*. You must be tired.'

Neetu's eyes turned moist as she looked up. 'Maya Beti, I am used to this life. But I don't expect you to cook with me every evening. You didn't grow up cooking every evening. It'll be exhausting for you.'

Deepak sauntered in. 'That's right. Maya's mum had a cook and a maid in Chennai.'

I felt like wiping that snide smile off his face. 'Deepak, you have grown up with a wonderful mother cooking and cleaning dishes every day while you sit around and turn up to eat as if it's a restaurant. You are totally spoilt. Do you ever notice when your mum is tired?'

Deepak's eyebrows creased into a frown. 'Mum, why didn't you tell me you're tired? I would have ordered take away.'

Are you going to order take away every day? Get away from the TV and help your mother. I wish I had the courage to voice my thoughts.

Neetu let out a loud sigh and sank further into the chair. 'What about your father? You think he'll eat takeaway and not complain about wasting money on bad food.'

All discussion died when Vikram walked in and took his seat as the head of the table. He said, 'Maya Beti, is there any leftover of that tomato chutney you made last week?'

Neetu's face lit up with a nostalgic smile. 'Remember the chanting of the waiter at that Tanjore restaurant in Chennai? Green coriander, red chilli, white coconut, yellow lentil, brown tamarind.'

Seeing Neetu's love for Chennai chutneys, I had asked my mum for the recipes. Now, coconut, coriander, or tomato chutney spiced up our meals every day. Deepak's parents loved the chutneys. But I missed my mother's special touch. She could infuse aromas into food with any herb or spice she had handy.

Deepak reached out and took my hand. 'Maya brings Chennai to Sydney.'

I muttered, 'But not the sounds of Chennai.'

'Don't tell me you miss all that noise. Auto rickshaws that rev up all night, and when they finally fade, you close your eyes, and the temple bells shake you awake,' Deepak said.

Vikram joined in. 'See how quiet Sydney is.'

I'd rather have noise outside the house than inside, I wanted to say, but instead, I stayed silent.

Months passed, sports seasons and teams changed, but my life remained mute, without music.

One Saturday, I had the house to myself. Deepak had a work barbecue, and his parents were attending a *puja* at the Krishna temple. I removed the dust cover from my *tanpura*. When I strummed, all four strings were out of tune. I twisted the knob of the first string, and it snapped. Even my tanpura didn't want to hear me sing. Uncontrollable sobs choked my throat. I had become that woman who had allowed marriage to erase her dreams.

I had vowed it would never happen to me the morning after the concert in Chennai. Viji Ma was browsing through the morning newspaper, *The Hindu,* a staple in every home in Chennai, while I was sipping my morning coffee on the balcony.

Viji Ma's finger tapped the photo of the legendary octogenarian musician, Mrs DKP.

'Women like DKP are rare,' said Viji Ma, her voice mellow with nostalgia. 'In those days, no matter how talented they were, women were never allowed to sing outside their homes. Your father's sister, Sarada was a brilliant musician. She and Mrs DKP had the same guru. But Sarada got married to a family who hated her music. So, she stopped singing altogether, and the light disappeared from her eyes forever.'

I remembered how angry I was when I heard my aunt's story. That's when I vowed. 'I'll never allow that to happen to me.'

That same day Deepak invited me to go for a morning jog on the Marina beach in Chennai. I put on my bright pink sneakers, blew a flying kiss in Viji Ma's direction, and ran down the two floors to the front gate.

Deepak was talking to the watchman in English. 'Is it always hot in Chennai?'

The watchman's head bobbed up and down as he answered in Tanglish. '*Romba* hot, Sir.' Everyone in Chennai understood this unique mixture of Tamil and English.

Deepak caught on and imitated the watchman's nod. '*Romba, romba* hot. Verry, verry hot.'

As I approached, Deepak said, 'The coolest part of Chennai is you.'

I grinned. 'Not hot?'

Before Deepak could reply, I hailed an auto going past the gate. 'We'll be at Marina Beach in ten minutes.'

As soon as we got into the auto-rickshaw, the jerky acceleration and wide u-turn sent Deepak sliding towards me, his thighs brushing against mine. I moved my leg away without being too obvious.

Marina Beach was crowded, even at 7am. Hawkers trundled their carts, selling ice blocks, or roasted peanuts in their shells. The more enterprising vendors had gas stoves on their mobile carts and served steaming *idlis* and deep-fried *vadas* smelling of curry leaves and fried onions.

I pulled up my jeggings and strode ahead. 'Let's get away from the crowd.'

As we sprinted towards the water, Deepak's feet left deep marks on the sand next to me. Rolling waves thrashed our ankles as we waded through the wet sand. At some point, we held hands. His grip was strong and reassuring. My whole body was tingling, a sensation I had never felt before. My fingers wanted to caress his arm, but I drew them back into a clenched fist. I had never been attracted to any of the boys in college like this before.

Deepak flashed a gorgeous smile that lit up his eyes.

'Your name suits you. Maya––magic.'

'Maya also means invisible power.'

Deepak took my hand and held it with a gentle grip.

'I saw that power in your voice at the competition. How long have you been singing?'

'Ever since I can remember. Since I was seven, I think.'

'Did you study music in college?'

'No. Music was in the air I breathed. Carnatic music was part of my soundscape: the radio, TV, a neighbour singing the morning prayer, the temple priests chanting in the distance. I learnt the names of *ragas* when I was seven. Don't recollect how I learnt them. That's when my parents decided, I should get private lessons in music, outside my school and college hours.'

'Vow! What did you study in college?'

'Pure maths. Music and maths hold the same magic; order, pattern, progression.'

Deepak passed his hand over his stubble. 'Fascinating. I thought arts and science were too far apart to meet.'

I burst out laughing. 'Music and maths have much in common. Notes or numbers, their sequences are elegant and hold hidden patterns.'

'Never heard that one before. How are you using your maths? Do you work somewhere?'

'No. Since I graduated two years ago, I have spent all my time learning and practicing advanced music. This competition required a lot of work.'

Deepak was silent for a while. 'If you were to choose a profession, what would you choose? Music or maths?'

'Music, of course.' I walked ahead. 'By the way, your question sounded like a job interview.'

Deepak mumbled, 'Sorry, I didn't mean to pry.' He then talked about his job as a cybersecurity specialist at one of Australia's largest banks. I remember thinking my Chennai college friends would have called it a dream job.

But then when he talked about his high pay, I thought his voice carried a touch of arrogance. It made me wonder if he loved the money more than his job.

I steered the conversation away from jobs and money. 'Do you folks come to India often?'

'Mum and Dad visit their parents in Ahmedabad every couple of years. They used to drag me along when I was in school. But I stopped coming once I got into college.'

He rolled his eyes and made a face as he explained why he hated visiting India. All because he caught Delhi belly that one time he went along the Golden Triangle. He went to Delhi, Agra and Jaipur to visit the Red Fort, the Taj Mahal and the Jaipur Palace.

Would he make that face if he fell ill in Sydney? Deepak must have caught my frown. He kissed his fingertips and placed them between my eyebrows as if to erase my frown, sliding my unruly tendril away from my eyes.

'This time, when mum decided to visit her sister, Jaya, in Chennai, I tagged along as I have not visited South India. My aunt Jaya is the cool one in our family. She rebelled and married a Tamilian, outside the traditional Gujju community.'

I still remembered how shocked Deepak looked when I mentioned that many of my cousins in the US had married non-Indians. 'Ours is an international family,' I said.

Deepak had asked. 'Would you marry a foreigner?'

That was such a strange question for someone who'd grown up in Sydney. It never crossed my mind that he or his family could be conservative.

'I would if he was the right person.'

'How would you know the right person?' Deepak asked.

'I'll know when he turns up. A cheerful man who loves my music.'

'Who wouldn't be stunned with your music?'

Looking back, I wondered if I had imagined the admiration in his voice.

That entire week we went for a morning jog at one of Chennai's beaches. I wanted him to see Chennai's colourful beaches. The iconic Marina Beach, lined with statues of Tamil poets and politicians; Elliot's Beach in Besant Nagar, dubbed by locals as the NRI beach, where non-resident Indians who had worked overseas jogged or walked wearing shorts and branded shoes. After our jog one morning, I took Deepak to my favourite coffee bar in Besant Nagar, that boasted over fifty different coffee roasts and blends in its menu.

The day before Deepak was scheduled to head back to Sydney, he said, 'If jogging on the beach is your thing, we have the world's best beaches in Sydney. Have you seen pictures of Bondi Beach?'

'You mean the nude beach?' I chuckled.

'It's a pity they've marketed it that way. The walk along the sand, the rocks, the cliffs – it's the *best* in the world.' There was an edge to Deepak's voice.

I tapped his arm. 'I didn't mean to poke fun at your precious beach.'

Deepak seemed to relax. 'You'll love Sydney. Come for a visit.'

My answer was spontaneous. 'I'll come to Sydney if I'm invited to perform at a music festival.'

A week later, I received a text from Deepak in Sydney. 'Miss you. Can I be your reason to visit Sydney?'

I tapped a smiley emoticon in response.

Over the next six months, our weekly Facetime turned into daily chats. Sometimes, Deepak asked me to sing. Some nights, he fell asleep as I sang *'Neelambari'*, a *raga* meant to induce sleep. I would fall asleep clutching my phone.

One Saturday, I had a performance at Kalakshetra, the renowned school of dance and music. I couldn't talk to Deepak that day and the next day. Later when I called Deepak on Facetime, he frowned and didn't meet my eyes. I hung up.

He called back instantly. 'Why didn't you pick up when I called?'

'I was working,' I said, 'Would you pick up if I called you while you were at work in your bank?'

Deepak retorted. 'But you don't work.'

I was annoyed and wanted to hang up again. His words should have rung alarm bells. But I was more worried about smoothing his ruffled feathers.

'I'm the lead *veena* player for a ballet choreographed by a famous Indian dancer. I don't take calls when I am with the orchestra.'

A few days later, Deepak called again. 'Do you often play with an orchestra?'

'Two or three times a year during their dance festival season.' I paused. 'But this is big. The choreographer is a national award recipient from the President of India. The next few weekends will be extremely busy with rehearsals. I won't have time for long chats.'

Deepak persisted. 'How about weekday evenings? That'll be after 8pm in Sydney, and I'll be back from work.'

I felt uneasy. 'I am not sure about this long-distance relationship.'

Deepak's reply was swift, as if he had expected this. His tone turned bright and chirpy. 'It doesn't have to be long distance. I am sure you'll love Sydney.'

I laughed out loud. 'Is that a proposal?'

'I wanted to send you flowers first and then propose. But I couldn't hold back when I heard your hesitant voice.'

'Wait, this is all too rushed,' I said. A tightness gripped my chest, like when you walk into an exam hall unprepared.

That's when Deepak turned on the video on his phone and went down on one knee, like you see in movies.

'My darling Maya, will you marry me and move to Sydney? It's the most beautiful city in the world. People are friendly. Mum and Dad have a lot of Indian friends. You won't miss India.'

How would he know? He didn't grow up in India.

My head was spinning. I was an only child, and my mother was my closest friend. I would miss her immensely if I moved so far away. And then there was the prestige and recognition that came with winning the Music Academy competition.

'I may not miss India, but I will miss my music.'

'We'll find a way. There's a huge Indian population here in Sydney. I'm sure there'll be plenty of people interested in Indian Carnatic music.'

His smile was the widest I had seen, and his dimples grew deeper. I felt a warm glow caress my face His love was genuine. Perhaps, I could find a way to keep my music alive.

And then Deepak added, 'With your maths background, you can get a fantastic job.'

My jaw dropped. *Job!* That was not my plan. I should have caught on at that instant. Deepak had worked it all out, but I hadn't.

Deepak was gorgeous, he was fun, and he loved me. But.... 'Deepak, I need time to think through this.'

A few days later, Deepak's aunt Jaya was at our door with a large red and gold box filled with *laddu* and *burfi*. Handing the box of sweets to Viji Ma, Jaya said, 'Did Maya tell you that Deepak has proposed to her?'

Jaya gave me a hug, as she often did whenever she came over for a chat with my mother. But in that instant, my body tensed, unable to respond to her warmth. Had Deepak asked her to bring me that glittering sweet carton or was it all her own doing? What did he tell her? I had not yet said yes. It was all moving too fast. Yet another part of me was thrilled. *What a mess!*

A fleeting frown seemed to cross Viji Ma's face as she accepted the sweets. But in the next instant, she turned to me with a beaming smile.

'When did Deepak propose? I didn't realise you had decided!'

I wish I had spoken with my mother before Jaya arrived. I hadn't expected Deepak to talk to his mother and his mother to Jaya before I had time to think things through. Viji Ma knew of our frequent Facetime calls and knew I was sort of interested in Deepak. But I hadn't yet told her about Deepak's proposal, because I couldn't make up my mind. He was charming and attractive, but something was holding me back. I couldn't put my finger on it at that time. Looking back, perhaps I should have listened to the little voice that was nagging me.

Once sweets were exchanged and parents got involved, there was no turning back. Viji Ma's enthusiasm rubbed off on me eventually. Wedding invitations embossed with a gold Ganesha went out to relatives and friends.

Three months after our first date, a wedding hall in Mylapore, Chennai, was decorated with mango leaves and marigold buntings. Deepak's family was from Gujarat. His entire clan from Ahmedabad and Baroda landed in Chennai three days before the wedding. Between visits to *sari* shops and jewellery shops, I barely had time to chat to Deepak. And then they organised the great *garba* dance. Every Gujarati, men and women knew how to perform the group dance. They clapped and they danced in small groups and large. That type of dance was new for me, but it was a simple rhythm and I happily joined in the fun. But Deepak stood apart and looked perplexed the whole evening. After much coaxing from Jaya Aunty, he joined me for a dance and that was fun. Later he confessed he could dance the *garba*, but didn't like to dance in a crowd.

On the actual day of the wedding, a huge placard displayed our names in neon bulbs: Maya weds Deepak.

Neither Deepak nor I had any say in the garish decorations.

Decked in silk *kurtas* and *Kanjivaram saris*, reeking of colognes and perfumes mingled with sweat, every relative and neighbour turned up for a free meal, kids and extended family in tow. The actual wedding ceremony lasted about an hour with the priest chanting Sanskrit mantras. I had attended weddings of my college friends in Chennai and knew the routine. We all accepted that Indian weddings were orchestrated by the parents. The bride and groom show up and do what they are told. Deepak and I hadn't talked about the ceremony; it was easier to go with the flow.

After the chaos and commotion of Chennai, when we flew into Sydney, the landscape around the airport was like a stretched canvas of earth, water and sky, glistening like wet paint. It was 6am when our flight circled the waterways around the airport.

'That's Botany Bay,' Deepak said, leaning over and kissing me. Botany Bay shimmered like the tiny Swarovski crystals on my bracelet —Jaya Aunty's wedding gift. She had been buzzing around organising everything as if it was her own daughter's wedding. More than a mere neighbour, Jaya was Viji Ma's closest friend. She was around every day, consoling her after my father's sudden death. Viji Ma and I had grown closer, more like sisters than mother and daughter, after Appa's death. She would miss me. I wiped a tear from the corner of my eyes.

Deepak put his arms around me and whispered, 'Welcome home. I'm sure you'll love Sydney.'

Sydney was eerily quiet as we rode in a taxi from the airport to Deepak's parent's place in The Hills district of Sydney. No traffic sounds. Even large trucks did not blow their horns. They didn't carry placards that said 'Horn OK Please' as trucks did in India. The sky was the bluest I had ever seen. With no dust, the heat had a sharp sting I had never felt in humid Chennai.

We drove through streets with large houses and beautiful gardens. But where were the people? They had built these humongous houses, drawn their blinds and disappeared. Not a soul on the street, such a far cry from Chennai, where even people with large houses hung out on the front veranda talking to neighbours.

Deepak's parents, Neetu and Vikram, had organised a welcome reception for us in their large backyard. The space was filled with sparkly *saris* and flashy jewellery, which South Indians like me scorned. But the sounds of laughter and chatter, warm hugs from aunties, and 'Welcome, Beti' from uncles gave me a sense of comfort. It was like being back in India. But when pizzas and pasta were served alongside *samosas* and *pakoras*, I felt like a confused *desi*.

'Some kids don't eat Indian food.' Neetu Aunty made a face. 'They prefer pizza over *pakoras*.'

It was a carefree first year while I waited for my spouse's visa. On weekdays, Deepak and his parents went to work, and I had the house to myself. Vocal and *veena* practice in the mornings, frequent FaceTime with Viji Ma, never-ending chats with cousin Preeti in the afternoons, and long nights with Deepak. I couldn't have asked for a better life. Our bodies danced to a new *raga* each night. Deepak was gentle and kind and listened to my body and mind while making love. We had decided we were in no hurry to become parents. Too many parents with kids were stressed.

On weekends, Deepak and I walked along Circular Quay under the sails of the Sydney Opera House. We laughed at a startled woman when a seagull swooped and snatched her burger. The white paint on the didgeridoo player's body reminded me of *vibhuti*, the holy ash used by Brahmin priests. Sydney Harbour was grander than what I had seen in Bollywood movies. At first, I was too shy to kiss or be kissed in a public place. Then Deepak said, 'Maya, this is Sydney; nobody is going to judge you. You won't bump into friends and family here. Relax.'

My spouse visa arrived earlier than we had anticipated. Our love that night was like a *raga-maalika*, a garland of *ragas*. Relief flooded me as I rolled over and snuggled under his chin.

Deepak kissed my forehead and remarked in a casual voice. 'Darling, I know you want to be a musician. But Indian classical music has zero value here. You can't earn a living with music.'

My head jerked away from his neck. My cheeks flared as though he had slapped me hard. Tears burnt my eyes. I ran to the bathroom and squatted there, stunned. My body rocked with sobs I couldn't control.

When I came back to bed with puffy eyes, Deepak was fast asleep.

A week later Deepak came home with a glossy brochure. Bold letters proclaimed, Invent your career in bits and bytes.

'Maya, Western Sydney Uni offers a part-time course in Data Science. With your maths background, it'll be a cakewalk for you. Since the course is part-time, you'll have plenty of time to practice music.'

How I wish it was a course on theory of Western classical music instead of data science. Was there a course that said: Invent your career with musical notes?

All along, Deepak had dropped hints that I had to earn my keep; something my infatuated mind had not picked up. Served me right for boasting I was good at maths. Deepak latched on to that.

I didn't want to be perceived as the lazy laggard when all three of them worked. Getting out to the university and studying maths, which I loved, was better than feeling guilty although the first few months were a struggle.

The Australian university system was different to India's. In

Chennai, the teachers compelled us to do the assignments, a far cry from the relaxed approach of Sydney universities. My classmates were from all over the world. Everyone spoke English in class, but the moment the lecturer walked out, a cacophony of foreign words filled the sound space. My ears longed for loud discussions in Tamil and English, mashed into Tanglish.

I never had such low grades as I did that first semester. I was a natural with numbers; equations were my friends. Yet, I couldn't latch on to the system.

At night, when I grumbled about my low grades to Deepak, he said, 'Why do you waste your time cooking and cleaning with Neetu Ma after dinner? I never did when I was a student.'

I snapped back. 'I didn't either when I was in Chennai. My mother had a maid who took care of the cleaning. But here, when there's no domestic help, how can all three of us expect your mum to do all the housework? Like the rest of us, she too works during the day.'

Deepak shrugged and mumbled, 'Your choice.'

I continued helping Neetu in the kitchen in the evenings. One evening, I had a huge assignment to complete. As I was rolling out *chapatis*, I said, 'I need to spend more time at the library to improve my grades. That means I won't be around to help you in the evenings. Is that okay?'

Neetu's answer was a beautiful smile. 'Beti, that you ask me shows how much you care. That's enough for me.'

'Neetu Ma, why don't you ask Deepak to help you some evenings?'

Neetu rolled her eyes. 'He's his father' son.' *Meaning men didn't help out in the kitchen?*

Soon, I had high grades and graduated with honours. There was a collective sigh of relief at the family dining table the night I got offered a job at a health-tech start up in Paramatta.

I was out the door at 8am. I loved the challenge of analysing data to find anomalies in the cost and quality of healthcare services, but the long bus commute from Castle Hill to Parramatta left me drained at the end of the day. I was too exhausted to practice music once I got home.

I couldn't, even if I wanted to. Deepak and Vikram argued around the TV every evening. On occasions, when it got unbearable even for Neetu, she would glare at her husband Vikram, and he would pipe down. But she never stared down her son, even when his arguments were baseless, and his voice grew louder than his father's.

Once we were in bed, no matter how tired I was, Deepak's gentle, sensuous touch melted every pore of my body. I snuggled into his arms and fell asleep like a baby.

But when I woke up, I felt a part of me was eroding away.

CHAPTER 4

AMBA

Tanjore, 1611

A year on, and nothing had changed. Amba was back at the temple, only now she didn't have to be her mother's shadow. Paru Ma allowed Amba to sing her own compositions during the evening *puja*.

Standing in the inner sanctum of the temple, palms together, Guru's words echoed in Amba's ears. 'Rise above your own likes and dislikes when you compose music for the temple.'

Eyes closed, Amba chanted the primordial mantra OM. The sound rose from her navel, susurrated through her throat, echoed through the sanctum and floated away with the incense burning in a corner of the shrine.

The red and gold *sari*, tucked in to fit the small bronze figurine of Goddess Parvathi, enhanced the curves of her bulging breasts, waist, and hips. The expressions on the goddess's face changed with the movement of flames from the oil lamps hanging on either side of the statue.

Amba felt transported to a space filled with peace and oneness in the company of her divine goddess. She had composed a new song about Goddess Parvathi in the *raga 'Hindolam'*, which described Parvathi's beauty, serenity, and strength. Amba concluded the last stanza, coaxing the notes to fade away into a poignant silence.

With her eyes half-closed, she stayed in that secure space for a while. Here, she and her goddess shared the same sacred sounds. She could feel the audience responding to the devotion expressed in the song.

But at the competition, the judges had misjudged her devotional interpretation of Kshetrayya's composition. How dare that arrogant Venkata and his *Brahmin* cronies dismiss her music as frivolous, erotic, and lacking depth. The memory of the insults hurled at her last year came crashing back. Those self-proclaimed scholars had no clue about divinity and devotion that existed outside their privileged world. Entitled by birth and supported by the king, they remained cocooned in their secluded *Brahmin* township, their *Agraharam*. They could not get past her social status and reach her music.

Amba's eyes clouded with tears, blurring the figurine of the goddess. Noticing the priest approaching, Amba patted her eyes with the corner of her sari and pretended as if the incense smoke had gotten into her eyes. She accepted the temple *prasad* of coconut and banana from the priest and slipped out of the inner sanctum.

As she hurried along the outer courtyard, Amba heard an unfamiliar voice.

'*Namaste*, young lady.' His tone was raspy, but respectful.

Standing tall under the shadow of a stone pillar, the man resembled one of the many large carved figures in the temple courtyard.

The filtered evening light played hide and seek with the intricate carvings, and Amba could not see his face clearly. She was in no mood to exchange pleasantries with a random stranger.

Yet, his words stopped her. 'Your voice made me experience Goddess Parvathi's divinity today.'

Still smarting from the rejection of the Tanjore scholars, Amba's heart warmed to his compliments. 'Thank you for your compliments, sir.'

Amba folded her hands in a *namaste* and looked up. The man's eyes were hidden under the shadow of a huge turban. The curly moustache and the thick beard concealed his features further. Why wasn't he coming out of the shadows? Sweat beads trickled down her neck and back.

'I don't remember seeing you before.' It came out more like a statement than the question she had intended to ask.

His raspy tone sounded like a whisper. 'I am from Gingee. My wife and I visit this temple often.'

'Gingee?' What had Paru Ma said about Gingee? Amba scratched her ear.

As if he read her thoughts, the stranger stepped forward and grinned as he smoothed his oily moustache. *What a disgusting gesture.* Was he asserting his position? Amba shuffled, ready to move on.

'Your mother, Paru Ma, is well known in Gingee. You have inherited her talents.'

How did he know her mother's name?

He smiled, revealing large front teeth stained brown. *Too much betel chewing, perhaps.*

He said, 'We would like you to sing in our temple. It's smaller but older than this temple.'

A small temple hall would never have the reverberation of the hundred-pillared hall in the Big Temple. But the echo of a smaller space would be different, and the audience would be different, too.

With a polite nod, Amba said, 'Thank you for the invitation. I'll talk to my mother. She will be waiting for me at home.'

Amba hurried through the western gate and entered the narrow street behind the temple. The smell of roasted cumin and coriander seeds greeted her as she entered her house.

'Paru Ma, I could smell the *rasam* from the other side of the gate.'

Amba went to the backyard, drew a pot of water from the well, washed her face, hands, and feet, and returned to the kitchen.

Paru Ma fetched two banana leaves from a stack piled on a wooden rack in the corner of the kitchen, sprinkled them with a few drops of water, and wiped them clean. Amba sat down in front of her leaf plate and said in a chirpy voice, 'You know people come from out of town to hear me sing.'

Serving Amba a large ladle of *rasam* over steaming hot rice, Paru Ma asked, 'How do you know they are from out of town? Who has been talking to you?' Deep lines of worry appeared on Paru Ma's forehead.

Amba mixed the rice and *rasam* with her fingers. 'Don't look so worried. There was this man with a kind voice at the temple today. He said he and his wife come often to listen to my music.'

'What is his name? And where is he from? What did he say?' Paru Ma's tone grew sharper with every question, suspicious of praise even when it was well deserved.

'He didn't tell me his name. He said he was from Gingee.'

Paru Ma's hand froze as she clutched the ladle. Her stony expression revealed more than it concealed.

Amba bent her head and slurped the *rasam* and rice. She glanced at Paru Ma with an innocent expression and asked, 'Have you been to Gingee?'

'Yes, a long time ago. It is a small town beyond Tanjore and has a small temple. And those people, too, have small minds.' Paru Ma's voice spat out her hatred.

'The Governor of Gingee is venomous vermin. He plots with Portuguese mercenaries and instigates riots in the region. Our king keeps a close watch over his movements and treats him like a snake—best avoided.'

Paru Ma's eyes started turning as red as the steaming *rasam* she served. 'Stay away from strangers who turn up at the temple and talk to you in private.'

Spiced with Paru Ma's anger, the *rasam* tasted sour.

On any other day, they would have discussed the lyrical verses Amba had composed. Today, they remained silent throughout the rest of the meal, each with her own thoughts.

A few days later, the moustached man appeared again after the evening prayer. This time, a stout middle-aged woman wearing a purple *sari* stood meekly by his side—perhaps his wife. He showed Amba a decorated scroll from the Governor of Gingee. They stood by politely as Amba unfurled the invitation.

His tone was gentle. 'The Governor would be overjoyed if you composed a song on God Rama, the residing deity of our temple. It would be an honour for our people to hear your devotional music.'

The woman's head went up and down like the temple bull nodding to its master's tone. 'How about Wednesday? The day you don't sing here. Perhaps that's the day to visit our temple.'

How did the woman know her schedule? Perhaps she asked the temple priest about Amba's free evenings. Amba nodded a consent and headed back home. She was in the midst of composing a song on Goddess of Learning Saraswati and forgot to mention the invitation to Paru Ma.

One Wednesday a few weeks later, Amba was at the bangle markets, trying out the new green and gold bangles that sparkled and tinkled as she tried it on.

A familiar voice called out her name with a greeting in Tamil.

'*Vanakkam*, Amba.'

It was the Gingee woman, wearing a red *sari* this time. She pointed to a palanquin at the end of the street. 'The Governor has asked me to accompany you to our temple.'

Amba had not expected the Gingee folk to return. Should she go home and inform her mother? No, Paru Ma would never allow her to leave the temple markets. But these people seemed so keen to hear her music. It would be rude to refuse.

This was Amba's opportunity to show Tanjoreans that people beyond their borders recognised her talents. Amba placed the bangles back where they belonged. It was late afternoon, but there was enough time to go to their temple, sing a couple of songs and return home before sunset.

With firm resolve, Amba climbed into the palanquin and moved over to let the woman in. The woman shook her head with an apologetic smile.

'I have a couple of errands here at the markets. We don't get the same type of brass utensils in Gingee. I will buy them and join you by the time you come around to the southern gate.' With a nod, she disappeared into the market crowds.

The palanquin bearers, two in the front and two at the back, synchronised their movements as they trotted through the crowded streets around the temple. They passed the southern gate of the temple. The lady must have finished her purchases. Any moment now, the palanquin bearers would stop and pick her up. But they kept moving, and their pace grew faster. Soon, the calls of vendors, the aroma of mangoes and the fragrance of jasmine faded away. They reached the outskirts of the city, and there was no sign of that woman. Could she have conveyed some secret message to the palanquin bearers before they picked up Amba?

Sweat beads trickled down Amba's blouse. *A little praise, and I have lost my head.* Amba stuck her head out from the side of the palanquin and asked one of the bearers, 'Where is that lady? How long will it take to reach the Gingee temple?'

One of them answered, 'Not long.'

They moved along at a steady rhythm. The sun was rapidly losing its heat, and the cool breeze made Amba shiver. She tucked herself deep inside the palanquin and checked the curtains were drawn on both sides. Familiar sounds faded into an eerie silence as they moved on.

A distant rumble turned into a clop of hooves galloping towards them at great speed. The palanquin hit the ground with a thud as Amba parted the curtains and stuck her head out. A hooded horseman towered over her. She screwed her eyes and took in the unfamiliar surroundings of the narrow street.

'Don't panic, Amba.'

She knew that voice. *The moustached-man!*

He removed his mask with a menacing grin. His white teeth and red eyes gleamed like fireflies in the dark.

'You! What's the hood for? Who are you?' demanded Amba as she stepped out of the palanquin and adjusted her *sari*.

A loud guffaw. 'Would you have come if you knew who I was? I am Thimma, and your king hates me.'

He pointed to his accomplice. 'My friend here wanted to meet you.'

The 'friend' was a white man, sizing her up. Amba felt a thousand ants crawling down her hands and legs. Paru Ma had warned her to stay away from Portuguese soldiers.

Amba glared at Thimma. 'How dare you come to the temple and lie to me! The goddess will pull your tongue out.'

Thimma sneered. 'All I had to do was praise your music, and you fell into my net like a fish.'

Before Amba could utter another word, Thimma pinned her hands against a rough surface, turned his head and nodded to his white friend. It was a narrow street. There was no one around. Amba felt the sharp pricks of a thatched wall on her lower back, poking through her *sari*. The stench of cow dung hung in the air. Amba opened her mouth to scream, but the Portuguese soldier stuffed her mouth with his dusty handkerchief. His rough hands and sour breath were revolting. Amba tucked her belly in and, with every ounce of her energy, kicked him hard below his belt. He had not anticipated such an action and staggered a few steps before he fell on his back.

A sharp slap across her cheek caught her off-guard. Thimma covered her face with his huge hand and dug his nails under her jaw. She could feel the blood trickle down her neck. She bit deep into his wrist, aimed a long kick straight at his groin and ran to the palanquin. The bearers had disappeared. She grabbed the long bamboo pole on the side of the palanquin and charged at the groaning figures rolling on the ground.

'Goddess Parvati is with me, you scoundrels!'

Yelling at the top of her voice, Amba charged at Thimma with her pole. He lunged forward, catching the free end of the pole, and dragged her towards him. She held on to the other end and shoved the pole straight into Thimma's eyes. He screeched and let go.

The white man was groaning, doubled up on the ground,

holding his groin. Amba yanked the pole back and thrust it again into the man's groin. Tucking the loose end of her *sari* around her waist, Amba ran out of the narrow street, turned a corner and slammed into a woman.

The woman dragged Amba into an alleyway around the corner and pushed her through a narrow door into a dark house. Amba's heart thumped so loud she thought her ears would explode. Her mind was in a whirl; she could barely keep her eyes open. Who was this woman? Was she their accomplice?

The woman put her forefinger on her lips, signalling silence. The sound of hooves gradually faded. Had her attackers galloped away? Amba doubled over rocking back and forth. She tried to hold her vomit, choked and then threw up.

Finally, the woman spoke. 'Amba, I know who you are. You are lucky that your goddess sent me in time to rescue you.'

Amba caught sight of an earthen pot in the far corner of the room. Her throat was parched. She could barely focus on the face that spoke to her.

'The vermin have disappeared.' The woman's voice was bitter. 'We need to act fast.'

A barrage of questions stormed through Amba's mind. She blurted out: 'Who are you? What's your name? How do you know Thimma?'

'It's a long story. My name is Selvi. I know Thimma––too well. You'll have to trust my word. I am not his accomplice. Every time I hear his horse thundering down these cobbled streets, I know that a young woman has fallen into his trap.'

There was a sense of urgency in Selvi's tone. 'My son will be here soon. He will take you back to Tanjore on his horse. God knows how long we have to keep doing this to save Thimma's victims.'

What did the woman mean? Who was her son? How Could Amba trust this strange woman? Her eyes closed.

The woman's voice seemed to come from a great distance. 'My son's name is Govinda. You don't need to worry about him. Women hold no interest for him.'

Amba sensed a hand mopping her face and neck gently with a damp cloth. 'Wake up.'

Eyes glistening with kindness, Selvi handed her an earthen cup. 'Drink this glass of buttermilk. You'll feel better soon.'

Amba cupped her hands around the cool earthen bowl. All that bile was burning her throat. Amba took a big gulp and felt the cool liquid trickling through her throat. Her mind was awake. She turned to Selvi. 'Why don't you inform King Raghu Nayaka about Thimma?'

'It's complicated. Thimma is not a Tanjorean.'

Selvi handed Amba a black robe. 'Wear this. Neither my son nor anyone else will recognise you.'

Selvi was right. Govinda didn't glance in Amba's direction. Selvi hoisted her on the saddle behind Govinda and they galloped off. Soon, they were at a street corner near her house. Without removing his hood, Govinda helped Amba get off the horse. Before she could thank him, he had disappeared into the darkness.

The sun had set, but the heat remained. The air was thick with the scent of incense sticks burning next to the flickering oil lamps, lighting up the entrance to every house on the street. Amba's armpits were sticky with sweat. The stench of vomit was like an invisible veil around her face. She felt a shiver run through her insides when she entered her doorstep. Her mother would surely sense something was wrong. Paru Ma believed people's worst qualities rise when the sun sets. Home before sunset was a rule Amba had to abide by.

Just as Amba expected, Paru Ma was waiting inside the door, eyes spewing fire like the fierce sculpture guarding the temple entrance.

Without meeting Paru Ma's eyes, Amba ran to the backyard well. She scrubbed and scratched her face and hands to wash away the men's stinking stares. She retched and vomited till there was no more bile to burn her throat. When Amba staggered back into the house, Paru Ma was sitting in a corner of the kitchen, rocking with sobs and hiccups as if she was the one who had been assaulted.

Following the Thimma debacle, Paru Ma refused to allow Amba to sing at the temple in the evenings. Over the next year, Paru Ma's voice grew gruff, and she went off-key on several occasions when she sang at the temple. When Amba offered to take her place and sing in the morning after the *puja*, Paru Ma let out a huge sigh of relief. She would go to the temple in the evenings and sing a few short songs.

The new arrangement worked well for Amba, too, as she had the evenings free, alone at home, to work on her own compositions. She wanted to finish this particular piece of writing before the evening light faded. Amba applied a thin layer of dye with a cotton rag on a stack of palm leaves resting on the floor next to her small writing desk.

Paru Ma bustled in as she lit an oil lamp and placed it next to Amba's desk. Paru Ma's grace and smile, which had disappeared last year after that unpleasant encounter with Thimma, were back again.

'Will you sing with me on the night of the *Shivaratri* Festival?' asked Paru Ma.

As the temple's chief *devadasi*, Paru Ma organised the music and dance program. *Shivaratri*, the temple's grandest festival of the year, was due to take place in a month. On this night, God Shiva performed the symbolic nocturnal dance of creation, preservation, and destruction.

Amba took her time to respond. Then, she wiped the dye with a dry cloth, and watched as the calligraphy sprang to life. 'I am not keen to sing in the evening, Paru Ma. We both know that evening visitors come to *see* the performers, not to hear them.'

Paru Ma's eyes softened, and she pleaded. 'Amba, my daughter, this is a special event. Nobles who normally don't come in the evenings, will be present at this special festival for Shiva. Don't you want them to hear you sing?'

Amba wrinkled her nose. 'Those nobles don't come to listen; they come to socialise. I want connoisseurs of music to *hear* me. I want them to enjoy the melody and rhythm in my compositions.'

'Amba, music is not exclusive to connoisseurs. Tanjoreans like to experience the devotional aspect of the song. Let us pick a song composed by a Tamil saint. You are good at bringing out the devotional element.'

'I am not interested in singing for people who can't identify the name of a *raga*.'

Paru Ma let out a loud sigh. 'It's up to you. I am going to the temple. I have a lot of work to do.' Paru Ma was happiest when she was busy with festival arrangements.

Amba said, 'I am going to the market with Vani. I'll ask her to sing with you.'

Vani was an excellent musician, and her Tamil diction was flawless. Paru Ma and Vani would form a good team and keep the evening crowd happy.

Vani waved to her from the corner of Bangle Street, their favourite place to meander, touch, and feel the glittering bangles. They were arranged by size and colour on bamboo tubes spread out on old saris.

Vani tried out a pair of red bangles. 'How's Paru Ma? Has she picked any new dancers and musicians to perform this year?'

Amba reached out to her favourite colour and tried on a pair of green bangles. She said, 'Paru Ma wants me to sing with her on the final evening of the festival. I flatly refused.'

Vani turned around, rotating her hand to hear the bangles tinkle. 'Why did you refuse your mother? I would have jumped at the offer.' Vani continued in a wistful tone, 'If my mother was not a governess but a musician or dancer like yours, I would be performing with her all the time.'

'Vani, I sing with Paru Ma all the time. I am tired of it.'

'But the festival will be a different experience.' Vani repeated Paru Ma's words.

Amba snorted. 'I don't want to be my mother's mouthpiece.'

As they walked back to the temple Amba asked, 'Vani, would you like to sing with my mother?'

'Would Paru Ma allow me to sing with her?' Vani's eyes were dancing.

'I am sure she will be delighted. Paru Ma wants to sing a Tamil composition this year. Remember the Tamil song you sang at the competition? If they had judged on music alone, you should have been the winner, not the Madurai man.'

'I don't understand how they completely ignored you, Amba. You were better than any of us; you composed in three languages!'

Amba gritted her teeth. The pain rankled.

They entered through the eastern gate, the main entrance to the temple precinct. All around the large temple courtyard, people were waiting for the *prasad*, the special offering distributed to all visitors after the evening *puja*.

Vani asked, 'What's for *prasad* today? I can smell ghee and cardamom.'

'Sweet *pongal* with lots of *ghee* and *jaggery*. I already had two helpings. If I go there again, they'll shoo me away,' laughed Amba.

Amba and Vani waited for Paru Ma to finish her discussions with the palace official.

'Hello Vani, how are you?' Paru Ma's tone was kind when she spoke to Vani.

'*Namaste*, Paru Ma.' Vani's eyes were full of respect and admiration.

'I have been practising poet Nayanar's Tamil compositions on Shiva. It would be an honour to…'

Before she could complete her sentence, Paru Ma cast a rueful glance at Amba. 'Did Amba put you up to this?'

'No, Paru Ma. I always wanted to sing with you but was too scared to ask.' Vani said, clearly in awe of Paru Ma.

At the *Shivaratri* Festival, Paru Ma and Vani sang the first song of the evening. Amba stood away from the crowd at a vantage point where she had a good view of the stage.

A hush fell when King Raghu Nayaka turned up just before Shiva's cosmic dance recital was scheduled.

Did Paru Ma know the king was going to turn up? Was that why she tried to coax Amba to sing? It was too late now. With a deep sigh, Amba moved closer to the stage to get a better view of the king, who sat on an ornamental chair placed in the centre of the front row.

Paru Ma's young students sang the invocation song on the Elephant God Ganesh. Vani sang the next song in Tamil. The lyrics described Shiva as the divine essence hidden in all creations, visible and invisible. As the song continued, a young male dancer strode onto the makeshift platform to the rhythm of drums and cymbals. His powerful movements depicted Shiva's energy, his fiery third eye flashing on his forehead--it could destroy all evil in men. Clad in deerskin, hair piled in matted locks on the crown of his head, and wearing cobra around his neck, the male dancer was the epitome of God Shiva. He was one of Paru Ma's students. Paru was a temple dancer in her young days and now choreographed the dances of her young students.

The music and dance concluded to a thunderous applause.

King Raghu rose from his seat. In a spontaneous gesture, he removed the long string of pearls around his neck and presented it to Vani. He pulled out an ornate sword from his waist and handed it to the male dancer. The king raised his hand and a palace guard walked in with a tray full of silk garments and gold coins. The king took the tray from the guard and presented it to Paru Ma.

In all these years at the temple, Amba had never seen such a public display of wealth showered on performing artists. Had Amba sung this evening, she would have certainly caught the king's eye. Instead, she had been foolish and ignored Paru Ma's request, and now Vani was basking in all that glory.

Yet, a small corner of Amba's mind whispered, 'I want to be recognised as a music composer, not as a temple performer.'

CHAPTER 5

MAYA

Sydney, 2012

If I wanted to ever perform again, I would have to practice, not in the shower, but with my *tanpura* on my lap, tuned to my pitch.

Over dinner that evening, I suggested that Deepak and I move to a rented apartment near Parramatta station. I could save my commute time and use it to practice music instead.

Deepak's mouth flew open. His right hand froze in mid-air, a piece of *chapati* dangling from his fingers. His eyes became piercing pins. 'Why do you want to move? Life is good here.'

I patted his left hand. 'Deepak, this is your parents' home, not yours. I need to practice music in the morning and evening, which I'm not able to do here. It's not fair to expect Neetu and Vikram to change their habits to suit my needs.'

Father and son were grumpy for the next few days. Neetu, the peacemaker, came to my rescue. 'Every woman needs to make her own home.'

She looked at Vikram, kindness and love shining in her eyes. 'Didn't we leave our parents and come to Australia to build a new life?'

Over the following weekends, Neetu took me to furniture outlets and kitchen stores and helped me assemble the essentials to set up my own home. Deepak didn't join us for the window shopping, but later he caved in when I insisted he should be around to select our bedroom furniture.

The day we moved to the new apartment, Neetu placed a small statue of God Ganesha on the sideboard next to the dining table and I lit the tiny silver oil lamp my mother had given me as a wedding present. Vikram purchased *Gulab jamuns* from the Indian restaurant in Harris Park. We offered the sweets to the God Ganesha and chanted a prayer seeking his blessings for a happy married life.

Moving to a rental apartment in Parramatta saved several hours of commute, which left me energetic at the end of the day. Deepak was a passionate yet a gentle lover, and we enjoyed the freedom of real privacy at night - not worrying if Neetu and Vikram heard our nocturnal grunts and groans. I got up early, and before heading out to work I practiced music for an hour in the morning. Over the next few months, I could once again hit the high notes without stressing my vocal cords. I often missed my mother Viji Ma, with whom I would analyse the songs and improvisations I had practised. In Sydney, I had no south Indian friends with whom I could talk about Carnatic music.

Deepak was blunt about his views. 'People in Sydney don't care for Carnatic music.'

I usually reached home before Deepak, which gave me enough time to cook dinner. I sprinkled a dash of roasted cumin powder and added a sprig of mint, bringing the tomato and cucumber salad to life. I carried the colourful plate to the dining table, humming '*Hindolam*', my favourite *raga*.

Deepak walked in from work and dumped his backpack in a corner of the living room. He changed into casual clothes and straight away reached for the remote and turned on the TV.

I said, 'How was your day?'

Deepak didn't bother answering, and I continued humming. With an annoyed expression he thrust the remote at my face. 'Mute. Stop humming.'

My hands went numb. The glass plate crashed on the kitchen tiles.

Deepak's voice rose above the din of the TV.

'This wouldn't have happened if we had continued to live in comfort with Mum and Dad, but Princess Maya didn't want to live with my parents. And now, I'm stuck in a tiny unit.' He added after a pause, 'With no break from your non-stop humming.'

After that, coming home late from work became a habit with Deepak. At first, I was upset, but I soon got used to a new routine that gave me even more time to practice in the evenings before he got home.

One night, I had finished my practice, and Deepak was not yet home. I stood on the balcony watching the sunset over the Paramatta River; dark clouds were pushing away the remaining streaks of purple and pink. The harsh tone of the huge white cockatoos screeching their way home had become familiar. The familiar sounds I had grown up with, the sounds of temple bells, pressure cooker whistles from neighbouring apartments blowing out whiffs of rice and *dal* and the constant flow of Carnatic music on the radio had all vanished from my life.

Ping. Text from cousin Preeti. 'Come to Chennai and see me off.'

My fingers flew over the phone. 'To where?'

'US of A. I'm going to do a PhD.'

Lucky Preeti.

Ping. 'Tell me you'll come.'

'Are you crazy? I am in Sydney, remember?'

A minute later, Preeti's boisterous voice boomed over the phone. 'Of course, I know you're in Sydney. How's your hero, Deepak? Is he so hot that you can't take a break, even after three years? You haven't been home since your wedding.'

'Airfares are expensive.'

'Didn't you say you have a job now?'

'Yes, but we are saving to buy a house.'

Preeti was insistent. 'I'll be finished with my Bio-Tech degree in three months and have to vacate the Tanjore University hostel. We'll use that as an excuse to go on a road trip around Tanjore before I head to the US.'

'Will your parents let you go to the US without getting married first?'

Preeti's snort crackled through the phone. 'I have a scholarship. I'm not seeking their permission. I'm informing them, and marriage is definitely not on my agenda.'

'Lucky you,' I muttered under my breath.

Preeti changed tack. 'Don't you want to see your mother? Viji Ma will be thrilled if you visit her.'

The vision of Viji Ma quietly listening to me practice each day and our discussions about the *ragas* I had sung had faded into a distant dream.

The front door clicked.

'Deepak's home. I'll call you later.' I hung up quickly and went into the kitchen.

Deepak went to the washroom before returning to reach for the TV remote. 'What's for dinner?'

'*Dal*, cauliflower *bhaji*, salad, *roti*.'

Deepak mumbled. 'Same food every day.'

I wanted to say, so why don't you cook something else? But given his recent grumpiness, I let it pass and set out the food on the dining table. Instead I said, 'How was your day?'

'Exhausting,' Deepak groaned. 'We had a team building work-shop. The HR manager played a video clip of a rugby game – as a great example of teamwork.'

'Sports, even at work? That should make you happy.'

Deepak tore a piece of *roti* and dipped it in the *dal*.

'The fun didn't last, thanks to Gita, our software architect. She's a proper Indian aunty.'

'Why do you call her an aunty? Is she old?'

'That's not it. She behaves like a *pukka* Indian aunty. Says rugby is a violent game and insists we should use a different team model, like an orchestra.'

I punched the air with my fist. 'What a wonderful idea! I can see where she's coming from.'

Deepak muttered, 'I thought you would.'

I said, 'Gita's spot on. Members of an orchestra come with different skills, play different instruments, and together create some-thing unique. No individual can bring out the sound of an orchestra.'

I served Deepak another hot *roti* dabbed with a large dollop of *ghee*. That's how he liked his *rotis*.

'Is Gita married?'

'She's married to an Aussie bloke, Dave. Yet, she has no clue how to blend in with the team.'

Blend in! What did he mean? Not voice your views if they were different to the team leader's? Or did he mean, being a woman, a brown woman at that, Gita ought to agree with the white people around her?

Thank God, nobody at my work said such things to me.

Later, when we got into bed, I said, 'My cousin Preeti called this evening.'

'What about?' Deepak grunted in a sleepy voice.

By the time I could collect my thoughts and words, Deepak was snoring. When I closed my eyes, discordant *ragas* floated all around me.

Preeti called again a week later. 'Have you booked your flight?'

'Chennai's not a hop, skip and a jump from Sydney. I have to ask Deepak.'

'Don't ask. Tell him you need to go to Chennai to see your cousin off, your mother misses you, and she's unwell or something. Tell him...whatever.'

Preeti's voice grew stronger, emphatic. 'Where's your gumption gone? Didn't you declare that marriage would never stop you from doing what you wanted? Fares are cheap if you book in advance. Text me your date, and I'll plan the road trip. We'll go see some ancient forts and temples around Tanjore.'

It was Sunday, the day we often went to the beach. But there was a footy game on, and Deepak was glued to the TV. I sat next to him, my leg brushing against his. 'I want to visit my mother in Chennai.'

Deepak pressed the pause button with a jerk. 'I thought we agreed to save for a deposit on a house.'

'You don't have to fund my travel. I have saved enough for a cheap return ticket.'

'I expect your savings to also contribute towards our house.' Deepak's tone carried authority, as if he owned my life.

A steely resolve crept into my voice. 'I haven't seen my mother in three years. I miss her. You don't understand because we see your parents every week. Have you ever been away from your family?'

Deepak stormed off to the bedroom.

Lying in bed, that night, Preeti's voice kept going round and round in my head. Don't ask him, tell him.

Next morning, I cooked Deepak's favourite breakfast, a tomato and cheese omelette, and set it out on the dining table. The kitchen was filled with the aroma of Lavazza coffee. Deepak liked his coffee super-hot. He came out of the bedroom, showered, and dressed. He scowled at the omelette and shrugged his shoulders before grabbing his backpack.

'I have an early morning meeting,' he muttered on his way out.

Couldn't he have mentioned this last night? I had seen his father ignore his mother, and now Deepak was following in his father's footsteps. But I was not Neetu and had no tolerance for rudeness. I tossed the cold omelette into the bin, got dressed and rushed to work.

We had a tight schedule to deliver a software module for a client, a health insurance company that wanted to compare healthcare costs across hospitals. I had to test the software and complete the documentation before Christmas break, barely a month away.

I was late getting home that evening. Deepak wasn't home either. I ordered a pizza, ate half and left the other half for Deepak. I had tried to be a model wife, but Deepak had crossed a line. He was my husband, not the manager of my life.

I searched for an online no-frills fare and booked a return flight during the Christmas break. Sydney to Chennai and back again in two weeks.

The calls of vegetable vendors and the clang of temple bells were what I needed to stop the silence creeping into my heart, ready to throttle my voice.

CHAPTER 6

AMBA

Tanjore, 1615

There was no way Amba, living right behind the Big Temple, could sleep through the morning gongs. Just as she stretched her hands over her head and relaxed into the sounds, the pungent odour of cow dung, followed by the herder's call, broke the spell.

Amba had settled into a regular routine at the Big Shiva Temple. She enjoyed singing as soon as the early morning *puja* concluded. The ambience at the temple evoked a sense of peace and oneness with the divine. Incense fragrance wafting through the dimly lit inner sanctum channelled her deepest emotions to flow into her compositions.

The morning visitors to the temple were genuine devotees who came to experience God's presence. Their eyes were mostly closed in prayer instead of piercing her body. Priests steeped in noisy rituals chanted the morning hymns with a sense of peace, their devotion taking precedence over mindless reciting of jumbled-up words. Amba was happy she had managed to escape the evening cacophony and the roving eyes of men who came to ogle women.

That morning, Amba sang one of her own compositions written in Sanskrit. The lyrics described God Shiva, who took the form of the dancing Nataraja to please his goddess wife, Parvathi. Amba arranged the eight verses of the song, each verse composed using a distinct *raga* to depict the wide-ranging emotions portrayed in the eight verses. Her voice reverberated through the thousand-pillared hall encircling the inner sanctum. She transitioned from one *raga* to the next, and towards the end, she elaborated the cosmic dance that shook the whole world.

Amba repeated the final verse, and the audience joined her in a chorus. With a soft tap of hands, they followed the rhythm of the last two lines. She concluded with a soft humming that allowed the notes to fade away into a blissful silence.

With a sense of peace and tranquillity in every pore of her body, Amba accepted the *prasad* of bananas and coconuts from the priest. She then climbed down the steps of the inner chamber.

'Namaste.'

A turbaned man wearing the palace uniform bowed his head and handed her a large silver tray loaded with pearls and jewellery.

'King Raghu Nayaka sends his compliments. He was moved by your music and wishes to thank you.'

Amba stepped back. What if this was another of Thimma's tactics? 'I did not see the king. Was he present this morning?'

'Sometimes the king remains incognito. He wants to experience the divine presence like a common devotee.'

The messenger had the Nayaka emblem on his turban. He bent

his head low, a sign of respect. 'Shall I bring the gifts along to your house, my lady?'

Would Paru Ma approve? Amba did not want the guard to see her narrow house on a narrower street.

'That won't be necessary. Please thank the king and let him know I hope to see him in person when he visits the temple next time.'

A few days later, a palace messenger arrived at their door with a tray full of pearls and a silk scroll sealed with the palace insignia. If Paru Ma could read, she would have snatched the scroll from Amba, but as she could not, she waited impatiently for Amba to read the message aloud. The king had invited both Amba and Paru Ma to the palace.

The king's message transformed her mother into a singing bird. Paru Ma went about the house, humming songs and chanting prayers in a voice that had grown gruff with age. Expectations clouded Amba's head and heart. Did the king recognise her as a talented composer and a scholar? Would he reward her the way he rewarded *Brahmin* scholars? A house in the *Brahmins'* quarters, perhaps? That would release her from the temple and give her plenty of time to compose poetry and music that would be fit to perform at the king's court.

The evening before their planned visit, Amba rummaged through her cane basket and selected a cream silk *sari* with a thin orange and gold border. It would go well with the coral necklace and matching earrings she had bought at the temple market. Paru Ma pulled out her trunk, which was tucked away in the far corner of the storeroom adjacent to the kitchen. As a kid, Amba had spent many hours exploring the trinkets wrapped in silk pouches. Paru Ma had been a temple dancer in her younger days, but Amba had never seen her mother dance. Paru Ma selected a pair of silver anklets for Amba to wear.

At the crack of dawn, the palace palanquin was at their door. The sky was pink, and the sun was in no hurry to leave the horizon. Four palanquin bearers bowed low as Amba and Paru Ma came out of the house. Paru Ma's smile was brighter than the resplendent purple silk sari she wore.

Amba went in first and moved over for her mother to climb in. She closed her eyes and let her mind wander as the palanquin rocked and swayed with the rhythm of synchronised feet. Paru Ma, too, was lost in her thoughts—none of the constant chatter of advice Amba had expected.

Two young maids greeted them with a platter full of sugar crystals, a sweet welcome. The girls massaged their palms with sandal paste, sprinkled a few drops of rose water on their heads and offered strings of jasmine to decorate their hair. Amba took the jasmine to her nose; the smell was not overpowering, so she tucked it into her plait. Paru Ma smiled graciously, a touch of pride brightening her eyes. The front door of the visitor's palace was decorated with mango leaves and colourful flowers. A large colourful *kolam* motif covered the floor of the front veranda.

The girls led them to a large room with a woody scent, a mixture of polished teak and sandalwood. Ornate chairs with silk upholstery and cushions lined the long walls of the room, which were covered with paintings of beautiful women and men entwined in convoluted postures.

Guru had said the king was a scholar. Would a scholar surround himself with such erotic paintings Amba wondered?

The king strode in, his gem-studded gold robe trailing heavily behind him. He looked younger than Amba had expected. She thought he was short and stout when she had seen him at the *Shivaratri* festival. Before meeting Amba's eyes, the king went straight to Paru Ma, bowed low, and took her blessings.

'*Amma*, I am a great fan of your daughter. Her compositions have an extraordinary capacity to invoke the divine presence––a rare talent in someone so young.'

Paru Ma was all smiles and no words. Her tongue seemed stuck to her palette in front of royalty.

Amba felt a shiver run through her body. She had never seen the king this close. What if he thrust his heavy body on her? Was he truly a musician, as her guru had said?

As if he heard thoughts, the king smiled at Amba. A real smile reached his eyes, but he addressed Paru Ma and not Amba.

'I would like to play Amba's compositions on my *veena*. I seek your permission for Amba to become my musical consort. She will be treated like a queen. With your blessings, we can release her obligations to the temple.'

The king had said, 'She will be treated like a queen.' He did not say she would be a queen. *Does he want my mind or my body? What does he expect from me?*

Paru Ma's eyes sparkled like twin stars on a round face that glowed like the full moon. Clearly, Paru Ma's dream was being fulfilled, but was this Amba's dream? She was not sure.

A month later, Paru Ma met the temple astrologers. They calculated Amba's astrological birth chart, matched it with the king's and came up with an auspicious date for a ceremony that would remove her knots from the temple and tie her to the king. They had a brief ceremony in a private temple within the palace precinct. Paru Ma handed her over to the king as his musical consort, and Amba moved into her own private chambers at the courtesans' palace.

Paru Ma gave her a small silk pouch when she left. 'Myrrh and castor seeds, pleasure without being burdened,' she whispered. Amba could not see her expression.

The king showered Amba with gifts and jewellery and was gentle when she allowed him the use of her body, exactly as specified in the *Kama Sutra*.

Amba had few friends in the palace, not that she cared. The queens were snooty because they came from royal families, and the courtesans were foolish and would do anything to gain the king's attention. She did not belong in either camp.

Mornings with the king were the best part of her day. She composed the lyrics, the king improvised the *ragas*, and together they developed a shared repertoire of Carnatic music *ragas* and songs. She scribed them on palm leaves every day after the morning session. Music in the morning, literary pursuits during the day, evenings in the garden, and nights with the king, her life was full.

One evening, while walking in the garden, Amba stopped to admire a huge orange hibiscus that stood out among a row of smaller red ones. As she caressed the unusual flower's petals, she heard the rustle of feet and turned around.

'*Namaste*, my little Amba.' Old gardener Muthu was grinning from ear to ear.

Childhood memories came flooding in, vivid memories of Muthu carrying her on his shoulders. The passage of time had given him a slight stoop. His legs were crooked spindles sticking out of his dusty brown *dhoti*. The large turban could not hide the brightness of his eyes and his wide, toothless mouth.

'I am not little anymore, Muthu.' Amba came forward and held his hands. His rough calloused skin did nothing to hide the warmth of his heart. 'How lovely to see you after so many years!'

Amba said, 'Do you remember once my mother left me here to play with you? You were patient with me, even when I was impatient.' With a twinkle in her eyes, she asked, 'Did that mango seed grow into a tree?'

Muthu's smile got even wider. 'Amba Ma, you used to pull it out every other day to see if it had grown. Your curiosity never gave it a chance!

'Do you want to visit that mango grove?' he asked. 'We have many varieties of mangoes now.'

Amba said, 'I would love a tour of your beautiful garden, Muthu.'

Muthu limped with her to the mango grove and showed her the different varieties. Some were grown especially for pickles, some for their sweet pulp, and others for their flavour, size, and colour. Tiny flies swarmed around some mangoes with a golden hue. The sweet smell made her hungry, and Amba took a deep breath, inhaling the scent.

Muthu went to a corner of the garden and brought out a long stick with a small hook tied at one end and a cane basket tied to the other. He lifted the hook end and deftly tugged at a ripe orange mango hanging on a low branch. Before it could hit the ground, he swiftly turned the stick around and caught it in the cane basket at the other end. Muthu cut up the mangoes and gave them to her in a banana leaf cup.

Amba spoke, her mouth full of juicy mangoes: 'Remember how I used to squat on the ground eating the mangoes, and my mother Paru Ma would scold me for dirtying my skirt?'

Muthu chuckled and brought a clay bowl with some water, and she washed her hands.

'Shall we go see the flower garden?' Muthu led her through a cool, perfumed pathway formed by a canopy of jasmine clusters.

Lifting her chin up, Amba took a deep breath. 'I never used to like jasmine when I was young, but now I like the fragrance of the layered jasmine.' She brushed her hand across the green and white velvety wall. 'How did you grow this?'

Muthu explained, 'I started with one plant and kept adding cuttings to form a hedge.'

Pointing to the wall of the canopy, he continued, 'I weaved thin bamboo strips into a lattice to provide a support for the plants to climb and grow freely.'

The crevices of his weathered face were moist with sweat. But Muthu didn't seem to notice the heat. His eyes shone when he talked about his beloved plants.

When they reached the spot where Muthu had found her, he pointed to the hibiscus flowers.

'These plants grow all year round; they like the heat and humidity here. This orange variety you were admiring is new in our garden. I got the cutting from a gardener who came from Jaffna.'

Amba pointed to a shady corner of the garden. 'Muthu, will you help me establish my own flower garden in that far corner? I promise I'll be patient.'

'How can I refuse my little Amba?'

'I want to make this a heavenly garden, Muthu, with flowers from everywhere.'

'You have not changed much, have you? Remember, it takes time to grow a beautiful garden, and not all flowers grow in our soil,' warned Muthu.

'From where do you get your seeds and cuttings? Do you have regular suppliers who bring new varieties of plants here?'

Muthu had answers to all her questions.

A constant stream of traders came to visit Muthu, bringing their handcarts loaded with plants. Muthu had established a barter system.

Moghul traders from the north brought seeds and bulbs to grow marigolds, lilies and tube roses. In exchange, they took back cuttings of jasmine, seedlings of mangoes and bananas. Jaffna traders from the south brought cuttings of hibiscus, magnolia and roses and were happy with the many varieties of jasmine that Muthu bartered with them.

Soon, Amba started spending her evenings in the garden tending to her plants. Months passed, and her garden became a colourful bouquet of fragrant flowers that inspired new compositions.

Every morning Amba woke early and composed songs about one of the goddesses; the beauty of Goddess Lakshmi, the energy of Goddess Parvati, and the serenity of Saraswati, the Goddess of Knowledge.

CHAPTER 7

MAYA

Chennai, 2013

I walked out of the aircraft and into the lobby of Chennai airport. Ornate arches, intricately carved on aged teak, welcomed visitors to the land of temples.

Joss sticks burning under a bronze statue of Goddess Saraswati gave off jasmine-scented perfume that mingled with the stench of sweaty underarms. Fortunately, it didn't take long for my red suitcase tagged with a purple ribbon to arrive.

Viji Ma's faithful driver, Gopal, was waiting outside the green exit gate, a tobacco-stained smile lighting up his rheumy eyes. Loud honks, flavours of curries––Chennai never changed. What had changed were the ad campaigns on the back of the public buses. The bus in front of us showed a young girl telling her father she knew where her future lay––in IT training!

When Viji Ma opened the door, the glow in her eyes was so much brighter than the dim bulb in the living room. My voice choked as I greeted and hugged my mother. It was 2am, but Viji Ma was wide awake, and our discussion jumped straight to music. She had bought tickets to a few concerts during the music season.

The 'season', as the locals call the annual December music and dance festival, is the time when Carnatic music lovers from all over the world throng to Chennai. It was at this time, three years ago, that I won the music competition for young artists. Throughout December over a thousand artists would perform in over two hundred concerts every day. Concert venues ranged from the grand Music Academy to humble school auditoriums and even temporary marquees set up around temples in every suburb. It was also the unofficial time to display the latest silk *sari* designs. Thankfully, I had packed a few *saris* which never got aired in Sydney.

I guzzled a full bottle of cold water from the fridge. Even in January, at the height of summer, Sydney never grew as humid as Chennai.

I hugged Viji Ma again. 'Who's singing tonight?'

'Your favourite artist, Sampath. The Mylapore Fine Arts Society is celebrating a retrospective of the sixteenth-century composer Kshetrayya. As his music is popular with both musicians and dancers, there'll be plenty of concerts featuring his work this week.'

We had reserved seats in the second row, as Viji Ma was a life member of the Mylapore Fine Art Academy. Vocalist Sampath sang a Telugu composition in *raga 'Kalyani'*, a *mela raga* with all seven notes. He improvised extensively around the fourth, fifth, and seventh notes to emphasise the devotional element of the song. He followed it up with a Tamil song about Shiva, the cosmic presence who inspired the

Chola king to build the Tanjore Big temple. I felt a sense of peace I had not felt in months.

As we were driving back, Viji Ma asked, 'How's your music going? I hope you have time to practice.'

I turned my head and avoided Viji Ma's scrutiny. How could I tell her that Deepak thought my music had no value and that my job left little time or energy to practice? There was no point in burdening Viji Ma with my problem.

Preeti breezed in early the next morning and gave me a bear hug. 'Maya, you've lost weight,' Preeti exclaimed. 'Bet you are fed up with your own cooking? Does Deepak cook?'

'Fat chance.' It hit me that I had never asked Deepa to help me in the kitchen. I felt ashamed to tell Preeti that all Deepak did was watch TV when I cooked.

Preeti opened the lids of the bowls on the dining table one by one. She let out a loud whistle. 'Wow, Viji Ma, what an elaborate breakfast for your darling daughter!'

Viji Ma tapped Preeti's cheek. 'And for my naughty niece too.'

I scooped a spoonful of the rice and lentil *pongal* and inhaled the aroma of pepper and cumin tempered in ghee.

'Chefs say we eat with our eyes first, but Viji Ma, your cooking has to be admired with the nose first.'

Preeti chuckled. 'I can't believe you are raving over the humble *pongal*.'

'Deepak isn't a fan of *pongal*. I have neither cooked nor eaten it in three years.'

Preeti said, 'So what if he doesn't eat it? You should cook it for yourself.'

Viji Ma dished up another spoon of *pongal* onto my plate.

Preeti turned towards Viji Ma. 'Did Maya tell you I'm dragging her away on a road trip? I am taking her to a secret destination first, then to Tanjore. She'll give me a hand to pack my stuff at the university hostel.'

I served myself another spoonful of *pongal*. 'Viji Ma, we'll be away for a week. I'll be back for the concerts. I don't want to miss any of them.'

I thought Viji Ma would object as I was visiting for just three weeks.

Surprisingly, her smile was full of love. 'I am sure you two girls want to have fun away from prying parents.' Viji Ma wangled her fore finger. 'But...,' and then she laughed.

'Don't worry, no advice, but I do need a favour. I'm writing a series of articles for the Tamil magazine *Kalki*. I need some Tamil reference material from the Saraswati Mahal Library.'

I gave Viji Ma a high five. '*Kalki* has a huge circulation. How did you manage to get in?'

'I have my ways,' Viji Ma grinned. 'Remember my friend Sujata, the poet? She attended your wedding with her three kids. Her brother is a journalist with *Kalki*. We got chatting, and now he wants me to write a series of articles on the Tanjore Nayakas.'

Viji Ma served Preeti a spoonful of coconut chutney. 'So, where's this secret location?'

Preeti blinked her eyes rapidly, like a kid about to be caught red-handed. 'It won't be a secret if I tell you, will it?'

Viji Ma's mouth drooped in a mock expression of disappointment.

I burst out laughing at their exchange. As if it didn't want to be left out, the street corner temple bell tinkled with my laughter.

Viji Ma said, 'Coffee? I have brewed a fresh decoction.'

Preeti stood up. 'I'll make the coffee.' She glanced in Viji Ma's direction. 'Mug or *dabara* tumbler?'

Viji Ma smiled. '*Dabara* tumbler. Filter coffee tastes better when the aroma wafts out of the tumbler. Mugs are for tea.'

Preeti grinned at me. 'I bet you, too, want the traditional utensils?'

I smiled and gave a thumbs-up.

My heart swelled as our chat brought back memories of my father. Drinking filter coffee and flipping through the pages of the newspaper, *The Hindu,* was his daily routine for as long as I could remember.

I stretched my hands above my head and let out a deep sigh. My taut nerves unwound of their own accord as I sank deeper and slouched back into the chair.

'Sleep early tonight. Driver Gopal will pick you up at 5am tomorrow.'

'So early? I'm jet-lagged!' I groaned.

Preeti gave me a peck on my cheek as she got up. 'It's a seven-hour drive, princess. You can have your beauty sleep in the car.'

And that's what I did. Slept all the way till Preeti nudged me awake.

I stepped out of the air-conditioned car and hastily extracted my dark glasses from my handbag. Even before my eyes could adjust to the white-hot glare of the midday sun, Preeti got out from the other side of the car and flung her hands wide open as if revealing a new painting. 'Welcome to the mystery fort.'

Washed by sun and sand, the faded walls of the fort hugged the shores of Tarangambadi—the town of singing waves. The locals used the Tamil name for the town, but most people called it by its European name—Tranquebar.

There was a rusty signpost at the entrance to the fort: Dansborg Fort built by Danish settlers in 1640 AD.

The rugged walls rose and fell with the ebb and flow of the tides. Did the foundations go under the sea? They must have had highly skilled architects and engineers. I wonder if they were Danish or Indian.

I stepped onto a low-lying rock jutting out to the sea and scanned the beach. From where I stood, the Tarangambadi townscape was an ad promoting multi-cultural India. The spire of a Shiva temple stood right over the waves in one corner of the rocky beach. Further inland, the dome of a church covered the skyline, and a bit further to the right, a minaret with a crescent moon stood tall among the coconut trees, oscillating with the waves.

The Danish fort stood apart at the far end of the beach. A few fishing boats lay toppled on the sands.

Preeti waved to a tall European girl who strode towards us.

'Sofia, meet my cousin Maya from Sydney.' Turning to me, Preeti said, 'Sofia's a part-time tour guide and full-time PhD student studying Danish history in India.'

Sofia's head of blonde hair was a stark contrast to the dark hair of everyone else around. But her clothes were what most young women wore, cotton kurta over loose pants.

'Nice to meet you, Maya.' Sofia's accent was more European than British, but she had acquired the sing song inflexion of the Tamil tone.

Sofia extracted two bottles of water from her cotton shoulder bag and handed them out.

'Thank you,' I swallowed the cold water in one big gulp. 'That's thoughtful of you.'

The sentry standing guard smiled at Sofia and waved us in

without checking our entry tickets. Sofia smiled back and folded her hands in a *namaste*.

'He knows me now; I bring visitors here all the time. Let's go see the centrepiece of the museum first.'

Three flights of dusty stone steps lead to the main hall of the museum. A long flat wooden cabinet with a sloping glass front stood at the centre of the hall. The base of the cabinet was lined with velvet. A long gold foil etched with Roman and Tamil alphabets was stretched out on the faded maroon fabric.

Sofia pointed to a tarnished brass placard nailed to the side of the cabinet.

'This gold foil is a replica of the trade agreement signed on the 19th of November, 1620 AD, between King Raghu Nayaka of Tanjore and King Christian IV of Denmark. The original is preserved at the Copenhagen Museum in Denmark.'

I peered through the thick, dusty glass front. I could recognise a few Roman alphabets but could not read the words. The Tamil letters were familiar, but the words smudged. Lines curled into themselves, making it impossible to read. Perhaps the script was an older version of Tamil? The writing sloped downwards towards the right. Some lines ran into each other rather than staying parallel. Whoever scribed those lines must have struggled to write on the metal surface. Some parts of the third and fourth lines had tiny holes.

I asked Sofia, 'Have you seen the original? What language was it written in?'

'Yes. I saw the original years ago when I was in high school. I believe it was written in both Portuguese and Tamil.'

A dusty frame displayed the translation of the texts etched on the gold foil:

We, the Royal Highness Raghunatha Nayaka, send this message to the ambassador of the King of Denmark on the 22nd day of

Chitrai in the year *Raudri*. We are prospering here. Kindly despatch the news about Raja Nayaka's prosperity. We are pleased to learn the news of that place brought to us by Captain Roeland Crape …

…It has been resolved that we should not entertain distinction between our country and yours. We order that the people from your country could come and settle in this place …

As I continued to read, Preeti's grin grew wide. 'Now you know why I call this a mystery place.'

Sofia pointed to the last line on the gold foil. 'That's king Raghu Nayaka's signature sprawled across several text lines. We don't see King Christian's signature here, but the original in Copenhagen has his signature.'

I conjured up a gold-turbaned king struggling to write on the gold foil. Maybe King Raghu signed it first and then sent it to Denmark for King Christian to sign.

I asked Sofia, 'What got you interested in Tranquebar?'

'Two of my mother's relatives are buried here. My great, great, great grand-uncle from my mother's side, Ove Gjedde, maintained a diary of his travels, and he mentions the trade agreement.'

Sophia pointed to the gold foil. 'It's that piece of history written in gold that sparked my curiosity.'

I said, 'What an amazing journey for you, far from home living in this hot town.'

Sofia stretched her hands. 'I see a fragment of my history here. This, too, is home.'

Far away from her home in Denmark, Sofia seemed happy in this remote, hot little town. *Was I a wimp to complain about my life?*

We wandered through the museum's smaller rooms filled with exhibits of coins, weapons, and other artefacts from seventeenth-century Tanjore.

As we came outside, I said, 'Let's take a selfie with the fort in the background.'

The photo captured three smiling girls on an adventure. I uploaded it to my Facebook page and sent a message to Deepak. 'Dansborg, a Danish Fort in a remote South Indian town.'

The prompt ping from Deepak caught me by surprise. 'Miss you, love you.'

My thin *kurta* stuck to my sweaty back, and tiny paper tissues were useless in this sweltering heat. My cotton *dupatta* came in handy for mopping my brows.

Sofia led us to a cyclist selling tender coconuts and signed with her fingers. Behind the rider's seat, a cluster of coconuts hung on either side of the carrier. It was a miracle the cycle did not topple under the weight of its load. With a deft twist of his sickle, the coconut seller chopped the head off a coconut and poked a hole in the soft centre. He gently inserted a straw and gave one to Sofia first, and then prepared two more for Preeti and me.

I guzzled the sweet liquid in one go and handed the empty shell back to the man.

He asked, 'Do you want the pulp?'

I nodded. He sliced a corner of the outer green fibre with his sickle and fashioned a spoon out of it. One end was narrow and the other was wide enough to scoop the tender coconut. With another swift sleight of hand, he split the coconut right down the middle. I scooped out a large chunk of the moist fruit with the eco-friendly spoon. The smooth pulp was soft and tender and melted in my mouth, like the first kiss I had experienced with Deepak. Was he really missing me?

A bus unloaded a group of schoolchildren in blue and white uniforms. Their teacher, a plump, *sari*-clad woman with hair tied in a bun, got out of the bus and admonished the children to form a single line before entering the fort.

I chuckled. 'Reminds me of school kids I once saw at the Sydney Aquarium. They kept sticking their noses to the glass enclosures and the teachers kept drawing them back.'

Sofia asked, 'Do you like Sydney? I want to go there someday.'

'Sydney is beautiful.' I paused. 'But for me, it's not yet home.'

I pointed to the distant temple.

In the distance, there was an ancient temple. Half of it was submerged underwater, and the other was perched precariously on rocks hugging the waves. 'That temple appears to be drowning.'

Sofia nodded. 'Part of that temple was submerged and then re-emerged after the 2004 tsunami. More than eight hundred fishermen from this town died while they were at sea. It was a miracle the fort survived. That event got the Danes to wake up to their heritage, and the Friends of India Society raised funds to help the local people here. My mother was an active member of that group.'

We walked around the temple and headed back to our Air BNB which Sofia recommended. 'You get the best home-cooked food in Tranquebar here.'

It was lunch time and we were served turmeric and lemon rice, coconut curry made with white pumpkin and *papadums*.

Preeti's hand went straight for the crisp *pappadum*. She said, 'Our families have lived around the Tanjore district for generations, yet I had never heard anyone talk about Tranquebar or the Danish presence in India.'

A tiny bit of pepper in the curry tickled my throat. 'It's amazing to think that pepper motivated sailors from all over Europe to venture so far across the seas.'

Sofia reached for more *pappadums*. 'The story goes that a Danish ship accidentally landed on the southern coast. Ove Gjedde, the captain, got lucky because King Raghu Nayaka of Tanjore was a friendly king who welcomed him with open arms.'

Preeti chuckled. 'Tanjore's our next stop.'

Sofia said, 'I, too, plan go to Tanjore next week. I have a meeting with a history professor at the university.'

Turning to me she said, 'I would love to travel to Sydney someday.'

'It's a beautiful city. Let me know when you plan to come.'

We exchanged contacts and promised to stay in touch.

CHAPTER 8

AMBA
Tanjore, 1620

The cool morning air was thick with the perfume of magnolias. Amba took a deep breath as she hurried through the garden of the music palace. The damp grass under her feet stretched out like a soft, cool carpet. The full moon hanging low behind the magnolia tree was in no mood to leave the beautiful palace garden, but the sun was in a great hurry to paint the blush of morning blooms.

'My beauties,' Amba whispered as she brushed aside an insistent jasmine creeper that tugged at her floating *sari*. 'I can't pause and chat with you now. I am late, and the king must be waiting to play his morning *raga*.'

Her maid Kamala had not turned up that morning to set out her clothes. Amba selected the first *sari* she could lay her hands on: pink silk with sequins and silver embroidery. She snapped on a pair of pearl earrings and a matching pendant as she hurried to meet the king at the music palace.

Amba wanted to be on time to present her new composition on the Goddess of Wealth Lakshmi, whose seat of meditation was a lotus, according to mythology. The pink petals of a lotus opening up to the sky from a small pond in her garden had inspired Amba to compose a song on Goddess Lakshmi.

Sculptures of women with voluptuous breasts were carved into the stone pillars of the music palace, Indira Mandira. The sculptures were King Raghu's addition to the magnificent seven-storey structure his grandfather, King Sevvappa Nayaka, had designed.

As a ten-year-old, on her way to her guru's house for music lessons, Amba had watched the sculptors at work. Her mother would point out, 'See those stone masons chipping away patiently, creating what's hidden in their minds.'

Amba had been more interested in the mythical animals the boys carved on the lower end of the pillars.

Humming a verse of her new composition, Amba climbed up the whirling staircase to reach the innermost chamber of the music palace. She gently opened the heavy wooden door, making sure the entry bells did not tinkle.

She stopped midway and her whole body froze. The king was hunching over the long fret board in what looked like a painful posture. The fingers of his right hand were in a frenzy when he plucked the strings. The left hand moving over the fret board produced notes that wailed and moaned as if they were in great pain.

Amba's hands went up to her ears to block out the disconnected jerky notes jumping out of the king's *veena*. There was no way those notes could produce a melodious *raga*.

It was obvious the king was disturbed; deeply disturbed. Amba clenched her sweaty palms. She had to find a way to help him. No person, no situation should get under his skin to cause such discordance in his music. Was he planning another useless battle? Who would it be this time?

Amba was not ready to part with him so soon after the last expedition, which had been a vain attempt to cement deep cracks in the waning Vijayanagar empire. King Raghu Nayaka's second queen, Tara, was from that kingdom and the Nayakas of Tanjore, since the time of his grandfather, had owed allegiance to the Vijayanagar kingdom.

The king had not visited Amba's quarters the last couple of nights, but that was not unusual. He was a king with a palace full of adoring courtesans and queens waiting to please him, and he had made it a point to keep them all happy. Amba's relationship with King Raghu was not merely physical; it was built on a foundation of shared love of music.

Another jarring note from the king's *veena* drew her back to the unsettling present. She took a deep breath, puffed her cheeks and blew out her breath. The king's music should not wail. She would help him deal with this pain, no matter who or what had caused it.

A few nights ago, the king had expressed his growing anxiety about Thimma. He had paired up with Portuguese mercenaries to instigate rebellions in neighbouring regions ruled by weak kings or princelings.

The king's eyebrows had knitted with anxiety. 'My spies tell me that Thimma has promised to help the Portuguese establish a trading route passing right through Tanjore.'

Amba had not wished to talk about the altercation she had had with Thimma three years ago. Since then, Amba had kept a close watch over Thimma's movements with her own network of informers. Thimma had attacked local traders of the neighbouring regions as they approached Tanjore, but he had kept a safe distance from the capital. The one time he had instigated the Portuguese to attack Tanjore, the king's foot soldiers had been quick to capture those pale men with big boots. They had tied them to the legs of the elephants and dragged them through the streets of Tanjore.

The king should have squashed them then and there. Amba had never understood why the king spared those soldiers with a warning, instead of throwing them into prison. Now they were back. This time with a larger contingent of armed local mercenaries like Thimma, crawling like cockroaches along the alleyways of Tanjore.

Her task now was to restore the king's composure and get his music back on track. Music alone could restore his balance and help him deal with this new crisis, whatever it was.

Amba tiptoed into the music chamber and stood still, allowing the king to feel her presence. The sounds from his *veena* gradually faded. A painful expression clouded his eyes, and Amba's heart wept. She moved closer and sat down on the silk mat in front of the king.

Amba half-closed her eyes and sang the morning prayer. Their daily morning ritual was to invoke the Sun God Surya to illuminate their minds with his brilliant rays. She chose a morning *raga* with notes that led the music on a more joyous path. The king, as usual, followed along on his *veena*. Today, his lead note merged into her seventh, instead of the eighth note required to complete the musical phrase.

Eyes shut, lips pursed, the curved fingers of his left hand moved along the frets of the *veena* producing a crescendo that he could not control, and she could not bear. What was the king trying to say with these notes?

Once again, Amba brought the notes back to the familiar morning *raga*. She could comfort him only after he regained his composure, only after the melody flowed. Note by note, her voice and his *veena* synthesised into the beautiful *raga* she had planned for that morning. Gradually, the descending notes of the *raga* faded into a deep silence.

The clang of bells on the heavy front door pierced the silence. Queen Kalyani stormed into the music room. Bejewelled from head to toe, her shimmering crimson *sari* was an affront to the gentle morning sun. Amba had not expected to see the queen here at this hour of the morning.

The king greeted his queen with a bright smile. 'Welcome, my queen. What brings you here at the crack of dawn?'

The king's mental agony, so evident in his music, seemed to vanish when the queen appeared. How could he bring out this cheerful smile for her? Amba felt her body shrinking into her sari.

The queen looked like a sculpture of a demoness guarding the gates to heaven with her upturned chin and fiery eyes.

Queen Kalyani had come to remind musician Raghu of his duties as King of Tanjore. Her garrulous voice carried an authority the king could never ignore.

'A messenger came running to my chambers this morning. Two foreigners are waiting outside the palace gates seeking permission to visit Your Majesty in court today.'

Unperturbed, the king replied. 'I will meet them at court if I have time after the routine morning assembly with the council of ministers. We have many urgent matters to discuss. The Sultans from the north pose an immediate threat.'

Queen Kalyani's voice rose an octave higher. 'Your Majesty, these new Portuguese ships carry large bronze cannons. The pearl fishers and spice traders of our kingdom are alarmed.'

The king let out a loud guffaw. 'They don't stand a chance against our elephant battalions. Do you know the Portuguese tried to attack the western regions during my grandfather's time? We drove them away. Not once, but twice.'

'But now with your neighbours turning into your enemies, the foreigners have a huge advantage.' The queen pushed her weight around like a rogue elephant walking into the temple shrine, Toppling copper urns, stamping fruit and coconuts, dispersing priests and devotees.

Yet, King Raghu could never ignore his queen. He placed the *veena* gently on the mat and stretched his hands. With a parting smile in Amba's direction, King Raghu Nayaka followed his queen out of the music hall.

Once again, the queen had ignored Amba's presence.

Amba swallowed her tears and tried to hum the tune they were working on until her music gave way to anger and frustration. If she was to help his music flourish, she must enter the king's world and understand his problems.

A couple of hours later, Amba tiptoed to the second-floor balcony above the Nandi Hall where the king held his court. She sat behind a lattice window, invisible to the king, queen, and council of ministers below.

The king strode majestically along the long silk carpet to the central podium and occupied the ornate gem-studded throne of the Tanjore Nayaka kings. Ladies in waiting showered rose petals while bards sang his praises, comparing King Raghu to God Rama, the mythical king of kings.

Clad in a simple white *dhoti* with a thin gold border, Prime Minister Ayya sat to the king's right. His hair, normally tied in a tuft behind his head, was covered with an orange and gold turban like all the other ministers.

Ayya was responsible for both internal and foreign affairs. He knew everything that happened or was about to happen in and around the kingdom. For Tanjoreans, Ayya was more important than the king. Whenever the king went on one of his expeditions, he left the Prime Minister in charge of the kingdom. People often said that without Ayya the king would be like an elephant without a trunk.

Pandya Varma, commander in chief of the armed forces, who went with the king on his frequent expeditions, sat to the king's left. In contrast to Prime Minister Ayya, the commander in chief was dressed in colourful military regalia. Small daggers and swords were tucked under his green and gold vest.

Officials and ministers with important portfolios like Administration, Treasury, Trade, and Commerce, and a couple whom Amba could not recognise occupied designated seats in the first row. Their secretaries sat right behind them, ready with their palm leaves and writing styluses.

The king cleared his throat, and the day's proceedings began. 'I understand more ships have reached our shores.'

Turning to the Minister for Commerce, the king asked, 'Do you know where these foreign visitors have come from? Are they the same Portuguese whom we had pardoned some years ago?'

The Minister stood up. 'Your Highness, these new visitors look a bit different. They are also pale but taller and bigger than the Portuguese. Their hats and coats carry a different emblem, which indicates they are from another country. They even smile. something we never saw in other foreigners.'

The minister's comment came as a surprise to Amba. Was the minister hinting that these could be nicer people as they smiled more? Would the king trust them?

From behind the lace curtains, Amba could see the king's shoulders tensing and rising up to his ears. A characteristic posture she had noticed when the king was anxious.

The Minister for Trade presented his views. 'If these people are from the new fleet of ships that attacked the Jaffna king, they will be more than mere traders. The other factor we should remember is that sultans from the north are circling like hawks around the coast. They do not want this new lot of traders to loot away the silks and spices of a region they want to possess.'

The debate moved on to the sultans from the north, and then to the Jaffna king who sought military aid to curb the sporadic rebellion from his local chieftains. The discussions lasted for several hours. Finally, the court proceedings came to a formal close with the palace bards singing the praise of King Raghu Nayaka. Following tradition, the king walked out of the court first and others followed.

As Amba was about to leave her secluded alcove above the durbar hall, she noticed the barely perceptible nod of the king and saw Ayya follow him. She hurried down the steps and came around to the long corridor that the king usually took to reach his palace.

The king and Ayya were walking ahead of her. Amba trod softly and stayed several steps behind so they wouldn't sense her presence. She overheard the king requesting that Ayya meet him privately later that evening.

The king said, 'I am concerned about these new foreigners at our doors. Do their ships carry cannons? Have they anything to offer us in trade?'

Amba couldn't hear Ayya's reply. She knew that whenever the king sought Ayya's private counsel, the matter was complex, and he needed the elderly minister's sage advice.

Ayya had served as the Prime Minister for three generations of Nayaka kings. He had groomed King Raghu from his childhood. Amba, too, loved and respected the Prime Minister. She longed for his respect and acknowledgement of her literary accomplishments. She was beholden to Ayya, as he was one of the few people who had recognised her talents when she was a young girl accompanying her mother to temple functions.

Over the years, Ayya was one of the few people whose affection for Amba had not diminished. Even after she changed her status from a temple musician to a courtesan and moved into the king's palace.

Should she approach Ayya and share the incident about the discordance that had crept up in the king's music that morning? Ayya, being a brilliant musician himself, would understand what she meant.

But then again, perhaps she should use her own means to find out more about these new foreigners. A few days ago, her maid Kamala, who had not turned up that morning, had casually mentioned that her husband was paid handsomely for unloading the ship that had docked in the nearby port of Nagore.

Amba strode purposefully towards the king's chambers.

CHAPTER 9

MAYA

Tanjore, 2013

The horizon was a curtain of moving shades of yellow, orange and pink. The morning air was dense and humid with the smell of fish and sea salt. Fishing boats of various sizes were bobbing around the waves, crashing against the walls of the Dansborg Fort. Fishermen anchored their boats and dragged their fishing nets onto the beach as they unloaded their catch of the day. Fisherwomen, their *saris* hitched high above their knees and tightly wound around their hips, emptied the fish into cane baskets.

Preeti and I loaded our backpacks in the boot of the car for the three-hour drive from Tranquebar to Tanjore.

Driver Gopal honked his way through the narrow roads of Tranquebar, steering the car between a bullock cart and a family of four precariously balanced on a scooter. I fell forward and grabbed the front seat when he slammed his brakes to avoid a pothole.

'Gopal, is it going to be like this all the way to Tanjore?'

'No, madam, the roads will be smooth as soon as we leave the town.'

He was right. The main road was lined on both sides with ancient neem and tamarind trees, a cool canopy against the hot sun. Road signs in Tamil preached, 'Plant a tree and save the earth; educate the girl and save the family.'

Closer to Tanjore, ancient tree-lined roads gave way to multi-lane highways. Traffic lanes blurred as trucks, buses, scooters, cars, and cyclists criss-crossed the width of the road. The lane markings meant nothing to drivers.

I chuckled. 'Sydney drivers wouldn't be able to deal with this chaos.'

Preeti asked, 'Do you drive in Sydney?'

'I have a driver's licence, but I rarely drive. I take public transport to work, and Deepak prefers to drive on weekends.'

It was 9am when we checked into the hotel in Tanjore.

Preeti said, 'The library won't open until 10am. Let's visit the Tanjore Big Temple first. When were you last here?'

I said, 'Perhaps when I was eight. There was a family wedding, but I don't remember anything about the temple.'

The tall, conical temple imposed its presence, blocking out the horizon. Squinting against the bright sun, my eye could not scan the full height of the spire. The sprawling courtyards swallowed the crowd of men, women, and children milling around, either to worship or to pass the time. Big blue boards in prominent locations proclaimed the temple was a UNESCO heritage site. Soothing chants of Sanskrit mantras floated out of invisible loudspeakers.

I stood under a shady corner of the thousand-pillared corridor and gaped at the scale of the entire temple precinct. How did they hoist this humongous dome on top of the spire a thousand years ago when neither cement nor steel was available? The multi-tiered central granite dome was covered with intricate carvings of hundreds of mythical figures, large and small.

Preeti brushed her hand against a sculpture of an elephant supporting the base of one of the pillars. 'Awe-inspiring, right? I'm blown away by the magnitude of the place every time I visit this temple.'

A local guide loitering around the long corridor came towards them and prattled facts and figures about the temple, some of which sounded dubious. Preeti rolled her eyes.

I pointed to the central dome and asked the guide. 'Do you know how that huge central dome was hoisted?'

'The Brihadishwara Temple, now called The Big Temple, was built by King Raja Raja Chola in 1010 AD. It took seven years to complete. God Shiva appeared in his dream and chose this specific spot for his temple.'

He took a deep breath and spoke as if he had memorised the answer to this frequently asked question. 'The central dome, the *vimana*, is two hundred and seventeen feet high, weighs eighty tonnes and rests on a square rock platform. Elephants were used to drag the central dome along an inclined plane, whose starting point was six miles away from the base of the temple. Once the dome was hoisted, the inclined road was demolished. That was their secret.'

The guide pointed to the colossal black monolithic rock sculpture of the mythical bull The Nandi, Shiva's gatekeeper. Perched on a tall rock pedestal, the big bull stared down at the visitors with gleaming eyes.

The guide continued. 'This Nandi sculpture was installed five hundred years later, around 1550, by the first Nayaka King of Tanjore.'

I was no longer listening. From where I stood, under the entrance archway, a woman standing next to the Nandi sculpture appeared to be a tiny doll dressed in a red *sari*. The Nandi, the Shiva Lingam inside the temple, the temple spire, the dome: each one was a magnificent edifice to represent the infinite Shiva. What inspired the Tanjore kings to devote their extraordinary resources to mark their presence on earth through larger-than-life monuments?

I strolled away, expecting the guide to leave. But he carried on. 'The original twelfth-century Nandi was much smaller and had developed cracks. Five hundred years later, King Sevvappa Nayaka, the first ruler of the Nayaka dynasty, decided to replace the old one with this new monument. He wanted to build something strong enough to carry the mighty Shiva on his back. This Nandi is nineteen feet long, twelve feet high and eight and half feet wide, carved out of a single monolithic granite stone.'

The monotonous tone changed. 'Five rupees for one and ten rupees for five cards.' The guide fanned out his picture postcards.

I handed him a ten rupee note and selected five cards. One of the cards was a blow-up of a section of the central dome, filled with mythological characters, dancing damsels, and *asuras* with bows and arrows. A figure with an unusual headgear caught my gaze; it could be Persian or Greek, Chinese or European. Did foreigners visit Tanjore at the turn of the tenth century?

I imagined a sculptor perched up high on the scaffolds, chuckling, as he carved the figure of a foreigner who might have been strolling through the temple courtyard.

I said, 'Such intricate carvings were executed in granite, five centuries before the Taj Mahal. Yet this temple has managed to escape the onslaught of tourists.'

Preeti chuckled. 'Lack of marketing has its upside. For locals this is a place of worship, not a monument to be gawked at. It's visitors like us who notice the architecture or beauty.'

Big Temple. An apt name for a vertical sculpture gallery.

We left the temple together to complete our errands. Preeti had to go to her university. I got out of the car at the Tanjore Palace gate.

'Preeti, take your time at the university. I have to get some reference material for Viji Ma from the library, and I might check out the museum. Ping me when you're ready, and I'll come out and meet you.'

The Saraswati Mahal library, the rare books museum, a huge sculpture gallery, a bookshop, and a couple of souvenir shops were all clustered within the ancient sixteenth-century palace complex. Next to the palace stood a dilapidated, once-beautiful, seven-story structure. A rusty board proclaimed: The music palace, Indira Mandira, was built by the Nayaka kings in 1610 AD.

I walked through a huge stone archway carved out of a single monolithic rock. Blades of grass sprouted out of crevices along the curved canopy of the rocky wall. The shady cave-like passageway drew me into a bygone era.

Faded frescoes lined the walls of the wide corridor leading to the Saraswati Mahal Library. Blue and red celestial figures and mythical creatures wandered along the vaulted ceiling. The library was on the ground floor, but a locked gate prevented access to higher levels of the building. Behind the grills of the gate, the curved wall hugging a spiral stone staircase was covered in red, black, and blue graffiti. Defacers declared their love in words and pictures, in Tamil and English, indifferent to the sanctity of a heritage building. This would never happen in Sydney. I couldn't even imagine anyone trying to deface the Sydney Opera House. Australians cared for their heritage buildings and were heavily into conservation, a valiant attempt to salvage the history they destroyed during their violent colonisation.

I walked into the dimly lit library and approached the librarian sitting in the far corner. The fine layer of dust on the furniture and the musty, damp smell irritated my nostrils, causing a sneezing fit.

I wiped my nose and eyes and spoke with a clogged nose. 'I'm sorry.'

The librarian peered up through his thick glasses. 'Yes, madam, what can I do to help you?'

I greeted him in Tamil. '*Vanakkam.*' Then switched to English. 'My name is Maya. My mother, Vijaya Murthy, is a Tamil writer in Chennai. She needs some reference material about the Tanjore Nayaka kings. She couldn't find what she wanted at the Connemara Library in Chennai.'

'Connemara is not a rare manuscripts library like ours.' The librarian's tone held a touch pride. He cleaned his glasses with a dusty handkerchief.

'It's nice to hear that someone wants to write about a forgotten dynasty. The Nayakas got sandwiched between the great Cholas, who built the temples, and the Marathas, who built forts. The Nayakas were knowledge builders. They created this Saraswati Mahal library.'

The librarian's stooped shoulders straightened, and his rheumy eyes sparkled. 'We are recognised as a national treasure by the Government of India. Even overseas historians come to us.'

It took all morning to wade through the library archive, which included paper-based catalogues, digital photographs of ancient manuscripts and a Dewey decimal classification system, to locate the shelves where the books were stored.

Reluctantly, the librarian hoisted himself from his seat. Those crackling knees must be painful. He said, 'Please wait here. I will fetch the books for you.'

At this rate, it was going to take him all morning. I said, 'Sir, I'm happy to come and help.'

His head went from side to side with a vague expression of distrust. 'Visitors are not allowed into the archives.'

Would he have allowed me to help if I had worn a *sari* and spoken more Tamil?

Finally, the librarian returned from the vaults, an assistant in tow, carrying the books I had requested. I browsed through the table of contents. I needed to photocopy about a hundred pages from different books, but I wasn't able to. It was the assistant's job. I wrote the page numbers from the three books on a slip of paper and handed it to the librarian.

Instead of waiting for the job to be completed, I walked to the library museum. Along the walls of a large hall, glass cabinets were filled with books, brown with age. Cabinets with sloping glass tops displayed moth-eaten parchments and palm leaf manuscripts, brittle and ready to crumble.

One particular stack of palm leaves, slightly longer, charred in some corners, and tied together at one end with hessian string, caught my attention. Each leaf was about two inches wide and twelve inches long. Minute Sanskrit letters were meticulously etched along the length of each palm leaf, with eight lines of text per leaf.

I could not peel my eyes away from the intricate calligraphy. I went up to the caretaker and pointed to the manuscript. 'How old is it?'

'It was written between 1600-1640, King Raghu Nayaka's period.'

'The writing is a piece of art. Who's the author of the manuscript?'

With a careless flick of his hand, the librarian replied. 'A woman. We have kept it here to show the type of writing materials used in the 1600s. This is an incomplete manuscript.'

His dismissive tone made it clear that neither the manuscript nor its author was important to him.

But how could I ignore that exquisite hand? Who was she? Was she as beautiful as her writing?

'What was her name?'

'Madam, we are about to close for lunch. Please come back after 2pm.'

I pulled out my iPhone.

'No photographs,' the librarian pointed to a sign board.

'I won't use flash.'

The librarian glared over his thick glasses.

I shrugged and walked back to the reference section to collect the photocopies. The photocopies were not ready.

I messaged Preeti: 'There's a power outage.'

There was an instant reply, 'I am on my way. Let's have lunch.'

As I waited for Preeti, my mind conjured up an image of a beautiful young woman brushing the dust off her stylus, head bent, and eyebrows knitted, etching Sanskrit verses onto palm leaves. Who was she?

Gopal opened the car door. Preeti said, 'Get in. I have another surprise for you. You'll love this place.'

Preeti googled the address to the restaurant, but with no street signs, driver Gopal had to stop at every street corner to get directions from people hanging around. No matter where you live in India, day or night, people hang around on street corners. That vague sense of purposelessness had a relaxed feel. This, too, was something I missed in Sydney.

The Claypot restaurant was tucked away in a quiet suburb of

Tanjore. It was more an old bungalow than a shop front with a flashy sign board. A huge mango tree hugged the wall of the bungalow and sheltered the veranda from the midday sun. A few ripe golden mangoes hung low enough to be plucked with a little jump.

A waft of roasted coriander seeds mingled with incense welcomed us. A young woman dressed in a crisp, cream-coloured cotton *sari* came forward with a '*Namaste*' and introduced herself.

'Welcome to The Claypot. I am Lakshmi, the manager of this restaurant.'

The carved wooden pillars and ceiling murals in the dining hall were miniature replicas of the faded ones at the Tanjore Palace. Colourful cane baskets and wooden toys added to the vibrancy of the place.

'This is a women's cooperative. The chefs and staff are all women, and we support the handicrafts on the showcase.'

I smiled at the signboard and read aloud, 'Our recipes are made in heaven.'

Lakshmi chuckled. 'Would you like to visit our heaven? It is a workshop.'

'Workshop?'

Lakshmi explained, 'We call this a workshop because we design our own cooking appliances. We use modern technology to enhance traditional methods. We innovate constantly. You'll see what I mean.'

We walked through the main hall and entered a wide open-air courtyard. The sunlight streaming in appeared muted. On closer view, the open-air ceiling revealed a fine net between the sky and the open courtyard, allowing light but not dust.

I pointed to the huge mortar and the long wooden pestle on one side of the courtyard. 'I remember my grandmother used that type of mortar and pestle to pound her curry powder.'

With a twinkle in her eyes, Lakshmi walked over to the circuit board in the far corner of the courtyard and flicked a switch. The pestle moved up and down, up and down, an invisible motor moving it with the same rhythm my grandmother had used. In every house, it was a woman's duty to grind dried red chillies, coriander, cumin and pepper into a curry powder.

Lakshmi said, 'My mother maintains that curry powder, made by gently crushing the spices, has a fragrant punch that can never be reproduced by a high-speed electric grinder.'

Preeti pointed to another corner. 'What's a cow doing here?'

'That's a bull, not a cow. The bull is here to show that we have replaced the bull with a motor but use the same traditional slow oil extraction method. We cook our dishes with the coconut oil and sesame oil produced here.'

The top end of a pestle was attached to a horizontal beam that rotated at a slow speed, crushing sesame seeds in the pit of a wide mortar. A small pipe protruding from the bottom of the mortar allowed the oil to flow out into a collection jar.

I said, 'I have a vague memory of visiting my grandfather's village and watching two bulls yoked to the pestle, going round and round in a wide circle, moving it around in the pit of the mortar.'

Lakshmi led the way past the workshop into the kitchen. Her voice carried a hint of pride. 'No glittering stainless steel stoves or gas cooktops in our kitchen. Our clay stoves are fuelled by sawdust, wood chips, and dry grass clippings. Exhaust fans behind the chimneys pump out the smoke. We cook in clay pots fired to their full capacity to make them waterproof.'

Rice, barley, and lentils were gently boiling in clay pots as if they had all the time in the world. On the far side, from another row of pots wafted the aroma of curries, each pot creating its own magic.

At another end of the kitchen, women in crisp cotton *saris* and white chef caps cut, sliced and cleaned vegetables under a spray of running water dripping from pipes fixed above the long sinks. This could be a Michelin-starred restaurant's cleaning system. There was an effortless blending of tradition and technology in every corner of the Claypot kitchen.

Another lady in a crisp cotton *sari* led them to the dining hall. Tender banana leaves, the eco-friendly disposable plates common in South India, were set out on the long wooden table with beautifully carved legs. Four small clay cups, two large clay bowls and a copper tumbler with cold mint-flavoured water formed the place setting around each banana leaf.

'I presume you can eat with your fingers?' she asked. 'For the rare foreigner who is not ready to eat with their fingers, we do have porcelain plates, spoons and forks.

'Sweet dishes come first in the Ayurvedic tradition,' said our hostess and served a sugarcane and ginger drink and a coconut and *jaggery* pudding in tiny clay cups.

Next, she served three varieties of greens, cooked three ways—steamed, sautéed and boiled—and gently spiced with cumin, ginger or fenugreek. Tiny roasted eggplants stuffed with coriander and cumin masala, a potato and tomato curry, and roasted pumpkin in a peanut sauce were served next, adding colour and fragrance. Little claypots filled with black-eyed peas, green lentils, chickpeas, and red and brown lentils were placed in a semi-circle around the banana leaf. The aromatic visual experience reminded me of a well rendered *raga-maalika*, a song rendered in a sequence of harmonised *ragas*.

The traditional *sambhar* and peppery *rasam* were served with a choice of white rice, brown rice, barley, coconut rice, lemon rice, millet or lentil pilaf.

Buttermilk laced with salt and pepper came last. 'To help you digest the food,' said our hostess.

'What a mind-blowing sensory experience,' I said. 'Such dishes never turn up on the menu in any Indian restaurant in Sydney.'

Preeti congratulated Lakshmi. 'It's amazing the way you have adapted technology to bring out the flavours of traditional cooking.'

Lakshmi's simple answer was, 'We have the blessings of God Shiva and his Nandi.'

We came back to the Saraswati Mahal library office and picked up the thick stack of photocopied papers. On an impulse, I said, 'Preeti, before we head to your hostel, I need to see that beautiful manuscript again.'

Preeti grinned. 'You're smitten.'

She pointed to a gift shop tucked away in the far corner of the library complex.

'I'll wait for you over there.'

At the museum, the caretaker's head was buried in *The Hindu*, the daily newspaper every Tamilian consumed throughout the day, starting with the first cup of filter coffee in the morning.

I went up to the glass cabinet that held the beautiful manuscript and squinted through the thick, dusty glass front. At the bottom right-hand corner of the palm leaf were two words etched deeper than the rest of the text. There was a tiny hole at the end of the last word, as if the writer had concluded with a firm stroke. The first part of the signature was illegible, but the second half of the Sanskrit word was clear.

XXXX अंबा

I had studied Sanskrit in high school and again during my advanced music lessons. As many Carnatic musicians composed songs in Sanskrit, we were expected to learn elementary Sanskrit.

However, this was a five-hundred-year-old text, and the words were faint.

I pulled out my notepad from my handbag and copied the last two words: XXXX Amba?

I dropped my pen, causing a thud on the wooden floor. The librarian lowered his newspaper. His forehead creased with annoyance.

'Madam, please move away from the cabinet.'

I lowered my chin and gave him an apologetic smile. 'Sir, what is the name of the author of this manuscript?'

He clicked his tongue with disdain. 'She was a courtesan of King Raghu Nayaka. One of many.'

My further attempts at polite conversation had little effect, and he ducked back into the newspaper. But Amba had firmly lodged herself in my brain.

At the museum shop, Preeti tried on a red and green antique-style bracelet that could have belonged to one of the ancient dancers painted on the wall of the Tanjore palace. I had never been attracted to that type of jewellery before, but I could see its novelty with my new Australian eyes. I bought a couple of bracelets and silk scarves to take back to my Sydney friends.

We drove back to Preeti's university campus, packed up all her belongings, snuggled into a single bed for the night and hit the road to Chennai early the following morning.

The Tanjore Chennai highway was dotted with temple spires, large and small, covered with sculptures and carvings of Hindu mythological figures. I pointed to an old moss-covered temple hiding behind tall palms and tamarind trees. The carvings on the spire had weathered into shades of grey granite.

I said, 'I bet the sculptor had a big story in his head as he carved these figures.'

As we moved on, Preeti turned my head towards the other window.

'We have these too. Old dreams replaced by new, psychedelic art.'

The ancient stone carvings were painted over with garish colours of peacock blue, magenta, orange, and fluorescent green. It was grotesque, a far cry from the ancient sculptor's intent of carving divine creatures.

As we approached Kumbakonam, our paternal grandfather's hometown, Preeti said, 'Let's stop here for a dose of Kumbakonam coffee. No Starbucks in this part of the world.'

The shopfront was a couple of rickety benches facing the main gate of the Kumbakonam Temple, another ancient structure with intricate carvings smothered behind garish oil colours that glistened in the sun.

The aroma of strong coffee floated out of a tall copper drip filter as fresh, hot milk boiled on a gas stove. The barista, possibly a school kid helping his dad in the mornings, took out a gleaming copper tumbler–*dabara* set, the South Indian version of a cup and saucer. He added the thick coffee decoction from the drip filter into the tumbler and topped it up with hot milk. With a wide flourish of his hand, he deftly transferred the steaming coffee from the tumbler to the squarish *dabara* and back from the *dabara* to the tumbler. The little show was over in a matter of seconds, and then he handed me the tumbler of foaming coffee with a brilliant smile.

He said, 'You can't get this coffee anywhere else. We use a special blend of Robusta coffee beans and a tiny amount of chicory, roasted to a specific temperature––our trade secret. That's why we call it the "degree" coffee.'

I said, 'Do you enjoy brewing coffee?'

'Yes, ma'am. I help my dad in the mornings before school starts. I'll join him in the business as soon as I finish school.'

Preeti said, 'I always stop here when I travel from Tanjore to Chennai during college breaks. Don't be fooled by the shabby shopfront. This man exports his coffee to the UK.'

The young boy piped up. 'You can buy our special brand of coffee powder on Amazon, mam.'

Tanjoreans had figured out a way to adapt and reinvent while firmly holding on to their tradition.

CHAPTER 10

AMBA

Tanjore, 1620

Amba squeezed her body into the curved alcove behind the weapons cupboard in the visitor's room outside the king's chamber. The tall teak cupboard holding the king's swords and spears, daggers and gem-studded sheaths was wide enough to shield her crouched body. But the alcove was musty. To avoid getting into a sneezing fit, Amba covered her nose with the tip of her sari and waited.

How she wished the king and Ayya would include her in their private discussions. If she understood the king's world, she could compose the right music to relieve his stress. For now, the only option she had was to be an invisible fly on the wall and listen in to the king's plans and Ayya's sage advice.

Soon she heard the heavy footsteps of the king and a softer

tread––Ayya's. The sound of shuffling chairs jarred her ears. The king invited Ayya to sit first and then occupied his ornate chair. This was different to the protocol in court, where the king sat down first, and then the ministers followed. However, here in the king's private visitors room, Ayya was a mentor, not a minister.

'Welcome, Ayya.' The king's voice conveyed his respect. 'What have you heard about the new ship that has docked in our waters?'

'The ship carries a flag we have not seen before. My informers tell me that the captain's regalia and the sailor's uniforms are entirely different from what we have seen before. This ship is not Portuguese nor Dutch. It is definitely from another country.'

The king's tone was heavy with worry. 'I feel uneasy whenever foreigners approach our shores. I am not able to trust them.'

There was a pause before the king continued. 'Ayya, I can never forget the plight of the Jaffna king who was double-crossed by both the Portuguese and the Dutch. They pretended to be friends and instigated King Changili's brothers rebellion against him. Now, the brothers are all bitter enemies.' The king's voice was hoarse with sadness.

Ayya's voice was reassuringly mellow.

'Raghu Nayaka, I know how much you care for the Jaffna king. Changili has been your friend since you were a little boy. And you have always supported him, when he sought your help.'

'Yes, we sent out elephant battalion to Jaffna when those European traders turned traitors. The foreigners did not expect us there. Our army sent them scuttling back to their ship.' The king's tone reflected his pride.

Ayya said, 'My informers have verified that this new ship does not have arms or ammunition. Instead it is loaded with large cargo containers. They seem like genuine traders.'

The king's tone was shaky, not at all the voice she was used to.

'What should I do? The queen tells me that I should meet them. But I am not keen.'

Ayya's tone was gentle. 'You don't have to meet them privately. Instead, we'll organise a reception at the Nandi Hall for the new visitors. They should know we do not fear foreigners.'

Oh no! Did the cupboard creak? Amba shrank into herself. Had Ayya sensed her presence?

Turning back to the king, Ayya said, 'Raghu Nayaka, wisdom lies in letting them see your magnanimity: the esteem in which your subjects hold you.'

The king sounded hesitant. 'Are you suggesting that we invite our full council of advisors and ministers for the very first meeting?'

'Yes. You should also invite the prominent traders and scholars of our kingdom.'

Ayya's voice was crystal clear and confident. 'Let us invite these new foreigners to talk about the purpose of their visit in a public forum. Let us give them an opportunity to present their credentials in court. Then we will assess if they are genuine traders or soldiers pretending to be traders.'

The king's robe rustled. Perhaps he finally relaxed in his chair. Ayya's reassurance lightened the air in the room. Amba found herself squatting comfortably to listen in. They discussed possible dates for the reception, the local dignitaries to be invited and the many arrangements to be made. Amba's feet went to sleep in her cramped position. Finally, the king let out a loud sigh and stood up.

When Ayya got ready to leave, the king asked in a low voice. 'Shall I invite my three queens?'

'Why not? You'll get their perspective as well.' Ayya's voice sounded as though he was teasing the king. 'And it will save you the trouble of describing the visitors to them later.'

Amba could imagine Ayya's warm smile. How she wished she

had his respect. Hiding and listening was certainly not the way to gain it, particularly if Ayya had sensed her presence behind the cupboard. After they both left, Amba twisted her body out of the alcove, straightened her *sari* and headed to the garden.

Over the last couple of years, her garden had become a tranquil hide-out where she experimented with new *raga*s and compositions.

Amba walked along the narrow path between two rows of plants, humming to the rhythm of rustling leaves. The air was thick with the scent of jasmine and magnolia, as if a giant hand had sprayed their fragrance into the sky. Amba plucked some eight-layered jasmine, rubbed it between her thumb and forefinger, and held it to her nose. The fragrance was subtle, unlike the single petal jasmine she hated as a little girl.

Amba tucked her *sari pallu*, so it wouldn't get entangled with the thorny shrubs. She paused in front of a plant covered with pale pink roses. Some were buds, some were in full bloom and many in between. She plucked the outermost petal of a large rose and crushed it between her fingers. It was soft and silky to the touch, and the subtle fragrance brought a sweet taste to her mouth, something she had never experienced with jasmine and *champas*.

The semi-circular stone bench near the lotus pond was her favourite place to sit and etch the verses of a new song on palm leaves with her sharp, gold stylus.

Amba rotated the thin stylus between her thumb and forefinger, feeling its smooth cylindrical surface. What a pleasure to scribe with this new shimmering stylus! The impressions it created on the writing surface had depth and precision. The king had given it to her after he had seen her fingers go red when she pressed her old stylus hard on the rough palm leaf.

'Amba, your writing instrument is blunt, and your fingers are bruised with the pressure.' He had taken her hand and kissed her fingers.

'Raja Nayaka, I have used this copper stylus for years. I am used to it.'

The following week, the palace goldsmith was at her door with a long, narrow blue velvet case. 'On the king's orders, I have created this golden writing instrument specially for you. It's thinner and sharper than the silver stylus that men use. Being a special gift from the king, I have inscribed the Nayaka emblem at the base.'

Amba wiped the stylus against her *sari*. Even a tiny speck of dust would smudge the letters. Amba placed a coconut frond on her lap, bent her head and etched eight lines of a verse onto a single frond. When a song stretched across several palm leaves, she stitched them together with banana fibres.

Once gardener Muthu's wife, Shanta, was around when one of the leaves snapped under the pressure of Amba's writing instrument.

'Amba Ma, you need thicker palm leaves. I'll find the right ones for you. What size?

'Thank you, Shanta. Each leaf needs to be three fingers wide and two hand-spans long.'

Since then, Shanta had made it her job to supply palm leaves to Amba's precise requirements.

'Shanta, why do you apply neem oil on the palm leaf. Touching the neem makes my tongue bitter,' Amba grumbled.

'The neem will repel insects, and your palm leaf verses will live forever.'

Shanta could not read. Yet she understood the value of written text. Muthu and Shanta's hut, tucked away in a far corner of the garden, was Amba's resting place after hours of writing. Shanta's buttermilk, laced with salt, pepper and ginger, was kept cool in a clay pot and quenched her thirst on many hot afternoons. The garden would never be as beautiful as it was without this lovely couple.

The thick coconut palm grove around their hut had become a resting spot for garden suppliers and traders from near and far. They dropped their goods, stretched their feet, quenched their thirst, and traded stories that were spicier than Shanta's peppery buttermilk.

A Moghul trader from Golconda narrated a story about a street singer who had inspired their Sultan.

'Our Emperor, Qutub Shah, has built a whole city, a replica of paradise, for Baghmati, the street singer he loves more than his queen. Charminar, the grand four pillared mosque in the centre of the city, looks like a palace rather than a mosque The markets around Charminar are colourful and vibrant, similar to the markets around your Big Temple.'

A whole city inspired by a street singer! Could Amba inspire the king in the same way? Would he build a palace for her?

One time, Amba and her helper Raju were weaving a bamboo trellis for the jasmine creepers. Velu, the supplier from Jaffna, his face contorted with panic, charged into the garden. The long wooden handles of his pushcart slipped from his hands. Pots and plants stacked on the cart smashed to pieces as they rolled over.

Amba said, 'Raju, quick! Fetch some water for Velu.'

A gurgling sound came out of Velu's throat as he guzzled the water. Shanta folded an old *sari* into a pillow and tucked it under his head. Velu's dusty shirt was drenched with sweat, and his words were raspy gasps. 'I knew the shortcut to this garden, so I escaped.'

Velu's fear was contagious. Sweat beads trickled down Amba's blouse. She asked, 'Escaped from whom?'

'Thieves. They have turned vicious and are beating up travellers who enter Tanjore from the south.'

'Why?' Amba had never heard of thieves in Tanjore.

Velu mumbled though his eyes were shut. 'Someone's paying them to create chaos in the streets.'

Amba glanced at Muthu and Shanta. 'Why would someone instigate petty thieves to cause trouble in the streets? What is their motive?'

Shanta and Muthu avoided her eyes. Did they know something she didn't? Or were they too scared to speak out?

Velu mumbled, 'Portuguese men are crawling like spiders, weaving their web all over the region. They are using these petty thieves to coerce local traders to rebel against the Tanjore king. Like they did with our Jaffna king.'

Velu mopped his face with the dirty towel that had served as his turban. 'You can never tell with these foreigners. Some go about their business, others wander around armed, spoiling for a fight with the locals.'

Amba was amazed at Velu's insight. South of Tanjore, the Portuguese were plotting and scheming against the Jaffna king. Meanwhile, Dutch traders were trying to grab control from the Portuguese. Europeans were bringing their wars into the region. From the north, Moghul sultans were encroaching southern lands with the help of the Nayaka from Gingee. With the collapsing of the Vijayanagar Empire, alliances were constantly forged and broken. The world was changing rapidly around her. Every day, Amba scribed her thoughts and impressions on her palm leaves.

Did King Raghu know about this growing unrest and the chaos all around? Was that why he could not focus on his music?

One evening, Amba was supervising Raju while he was fertilising the plants with cow dung. 'Raju, your wife Kamala mentioned that the new foreigners paid you well when you unloaded their cargo. What do you know about them?' Amba did not mean to be sharp, but her tone came out that way.

Raju's voice was low whisper. 'The new foreigners are not like the Portuguese, who refuse to pay the agreed number of coins after we have unloaded their cargo. These new traders kept their word and paid us the agreed amount. We unloaded several trunks from the ship.'

Amba stood there, pulling out the leaves that had turned yellow. 'What did you unload?'

'Leather trunks with big brass locks. Some trunks with curved lids had gilt decorations. The captain of the ship asked me to carry them gently; he said they contained fragile objects made of glass.'

Amba said, 'Can you find out the captain's activities? Let me know when he plans to visit the silk market or the Goldsmiths Street behind the temple complex.'

Like Raju, the husbands of her other maids were valuable sources of information about wandering traders, foreigners arriving on their shores, and other news circulating around the streets. The garden had become her information hub.

CHAPTER 11

MAYA
Chennai, 2013

The Tanjore-Chennai highway with the new overpass gave us a smooth ride into Chennai. We reached Preeti's place in Besant Nagar around 3pm. The mild sea breeze was a welcome respite after the long, hot ride.

Old watchman Ramu held the car door open for Preeti with a wide smile. His teeth were stained orange from years of chewing betel leaves.

'Preeti kutti! College finished?' Ramu's head nod synchronised with his sing-song tone.

Preeti chuckled. 'Yes, I have graduated. I am no longer a little girl.'

For Ramu, who had carried Preeti on his shoulders, she was forever a little girl, *kutti*. Preeti would certainly miss the warmth of such familiar faces, when she flew away to the US. After three years in Sydney, I still missed the warmth of familiar faces.

I blew Preeti a goodbye kiss. 'That was a fun trip. Thank you. I'll come by tomorrow and meet your parents. Tell Chithi I can't wait to eat her *vadai*.'

'*Saappaturami*! What a foodie you are!' guffawed Preeti.

When I reached home, Viji Ma was sitting on the balcony, a book in hand and a pot of tea ready by her side. I pulled out the brown paper envelope from my backpack and handed it to her.

'Here's your reference material. The Saraswati Mahal librarian tested my patience. But together, we managed to hunt down all the Tanjore Nayakas for you.'

Viji Ma's voice muffled a choke. 'Thank you.' She wiped away the tears that were threatening to come out as she thumbed through the photocopies. Viji Ma rarely displayed her sensitive emotions. The Nayaka history must be very special to her.

Viji Ma poured the steaming, fragrant tea into two thin gold-rimmed porcelain cups with matching saucers.

'So, what did you think of Tanjore?' Her smile lit up her eyes.

'It was like time travel. I felt transported to a bygone era. Everywhere you turn, you see a temple. The Big Temple spire was like an open-air sculpture gallery. And the humongous Nandi was scary.'

Viji Ma said, 'That Nandi sculpture was installed in the sixteenth century by King Sevvappa, the first king of the Nayaka dynasty. The Nayakas came from Vijayanagar, further north of Tanjore. When the Vijayanagar kingdom collapsed, the Tanjore region was handed over to the Nayaka clan. They renovated the old temples in Tanjore and also added more new temples throughout the region. So now, wherever you turn, you see temples.'

I sipped the delicate Darjeeling tea, brewed to perfection. 'I was fascinated by King Raghu Nayaka. His hand was visible everywhere during the entire trip.'

I flicked through my photo library on my phone and brought up an image of the Danish fort. 'Have you been to Tranquebar? I found out that King Raghu Nayaka signed the first-ever trade agreement with a European nation. Can you believe it was written on a gold foil! It's displayed in the fort museum. And I had never heard about this fort before.'

I thumbed through the photocopied pages from the library. 'When I went to the library for your reference material, I found a beautiful manuscript on palm leaves written by a woman. Possibly Raghu Nayaka's courtesan, the librarian said.'

Viji Ma nodded. 'You are spot on. King Raghu Nayaka was the best of the Nayaka kings. He was a musician and surrounded himself with scholars, both men and women. Some of the women were *devadasis,* temple musicians.'

'Where did the *devadasis* come from? Did they belong to a specific community or caste?'

'It's an ancient tradition. We'll talk about it later.' Viji Ma picked up the photocopies and headed to her study.

Viji Ma was on the balcony with her morning coffee and *The Hindu,* a century-old newspaper created by freedom fighters to protest the policies of the British Raj.

I stretched out on the cane chair with my *masala chai.*

'I googled *devadasis.* Wikipedia says they were women who dedicated their lives to God and temple.'

Viji Ma said. 'That's right. Many of them were highly skilled dancers, musicians, and composers.'

'What about the men? Were there no "*devadasas*"?' My fingers drew quotes in the air. 'Why don't we hear of men who devoted their lives to God and temple?'

Viji Ma's lips curled into a crooked smile. 'They are called priests. You see them in all the temples today. Women didn't have that privilege, yet needed the protection offered by temples.'

'Protection from whom?'

Viji Ma lowered her chin and looked over her specs in mock disbelief.

My tone was tentative. 'Abusive men?'

'Exactly!' Viji Ma's vehement thump rattled the coffee mug. 'Women needed a safe place where they could practice their chosen art form without being forced into marriage or controlled by abusive men. Those ancient *devadasis* had full control of their life and sexuality.'

'Did they really? All those years ago?' I couldn't mask my scepticism. It was hard enough today for me to take control of my life.

Viji Ma said, 'In the old days, intelligent and independent women chose to become *devadasis* if they didn't want to follow a traditional married life. They were free souls.'

'It sounds dubious to me,' I said, unable to mask my cynicism. 'Why was the system abolished then?'

Viji Ma closed the newspaper firmly and squared her shoulders. '*Devadasi* women were not afraid to express emotions that depicted erotic love towards God. This externalisation of love was not palatable to conservative men who lacked the sensitivity to understand emotional expressions. If they did, society considered those men weak and spineless.'

After a few more sips of coffee, Viji Ma continued. '*Devadasis* played another important social role. They took abandoned orphans and abused girls under their wing and offered them a life of learning and devotion. The system deteriorated gradually as royal patrons disappeared from the scene.'

To me, it didn't stack up. 'Why were the *devadasis* looked down upon? Did they have a sexual relationship with their patrons?'

Viji Ma's voice was tinged with annoyance. 'Maya, you studied in a Catholic school where many of your teachers were nuns. Did you question their motives? You loved the nuns and learnt a lot from them. Why is it difficult for you to accept Hindu women who dedicate their lives to God and temple?'

'If it was such a great system, why was it abolished?'

Viji Ma snapped. 'It was the British. They could not understand the *devadasi*'s role. It was a rare social system that was not based on caste. Even princesses became *devadasis* if they chose a life of celibacy.'

British India was not a topic I wanted to get into. Viji Ma's father, a schoolteacher, had walked with Gandhi on his salt march. I steered the conversation back to the *devadasis*.

Loved, respected, envied, and hated? A *devadasi*'s life could not have been simple.

Viji Ma said, 'Do you remember your old *veena* teacher, Ramaswamy? His teacher, a famous *veena* player, was a *devadasi*. She always played the first song during temple festivals.'

The story rang a distant bell. I mumbled. 'Marriage has dulled my memory.'

'Marriage is not a bed of roses,' Viji Ma said. 'It's a lot of give and take.'

My eyes welled up unexpectedly. 'Marriage is nothing but give, give, give. There's nothing to take. Your generation will never understand.'

I stormed out of the room and texted Preeti. 'Free for a jog?'

'Sure. See you in thirty minutes. Near Gandhi.'

I stood under the shadow of Gandhi's statue waiting for Preeti. Gandhi's bird-shit-dotted bronze statue served as the standard meeting point at the Marina. The foreshore walkway swarmed with objects and people in random motion. Hawkers on foot, vendors on bicycles, an auto driver using his engine as a sugar cane crusher—there was something for everyone. Steamed peanuts, chickpea and raw mango salad, freshly squeezed bitter gourd juice for the diabetics, aloe vera juice for the adventurous and sugar cane juice with lemon for the sweet-toothed. A Chennai jogger could never resist the street food on the beach.

Preeti ducked out of an auto and waved. 'I thought you would sleep in late this morning, after yesterday's long drive.'

'I got into an argument with Viji Ma first thing in the morning.'

'What about?'

I bent down and picked up a large conch shell that had washed in with the tide.

'We got talking about *devadasis* and how they avoided marriage. I said marriage was society's construct to entice unsuspecting women into submission. Viji Ma said marriage was all about give and take. I think it's nothing but give, give, give.'

I removed my shoes and sprinted ahead. The moist sand cooled my feet but not my head.

Preeti caught up. 'What's bugging you? Is Deepak not treating you well?'

'I thought he loved everything about me. But he hates my music. He wants to turn me into a money-making machine.'

'Does he know you are unhappy?'

'I don't know. Ever since we moved out of his parents' home, our conversations are stunted. All he dreams about is buying a big house.'

'Do you share the dream?'

'I don't know what my dream is any more.' I dug my feet into the sand and kicked some shells that had washed in with the waves.

Preeti caught hold of my shoulders and turned me around. 'Deepak realises you are pliable and has got you wrapped round his little finger. You were naive to think marrying to a handsome guy was enough to make you happy.'

'Don't you pile on me. Deepak's a good guy. It's just that he doesn't like music, and I can't live without music. I don't want to be what he wants me to be––a data analyst forever. I want to be a musician. I don't know how to get there.'

'If music is that important to you, make it clear to him.'

'Easier said than done,' I muttered.

The sun was high, and my T-shirt was sweaty and sticky. 'Let's get some coconut water.'

The coconut seller's bicycle was loaded with clusters of green coconuts, precariously balanced on both sides of the rider's seat.

Preeti grinned. 'Bet you can't get coconut water in Sydney.'

'We get it in cartons. They don't have the same taste or smell. Some Asian stores do carry green coconuts, though.'

I guzzled the coconut water and threw the shell into a sack for pickup by a recycling business.

Preeti said, 'Let's go to Woodlands for breakfast; it's air-conditioned. You'll be able to think better with a cool head and a full belly.'

Tiny *idlis*, crisp *masala dosa*, two crunchy lentil *vadas*, and three different chutneys were food for my soul. Strong filter coffee concluded the divine breakfast and recentered my chaotic mind.

Preeti asked, 'Do you have any Indian friends in Sydney?'

'They are Deepak's friends. All they talk about is cricket and the housing market in Sydney.'

The garlanded Ganesha behind the cashier's desk reminded me of the Sydney Helensburgh temple during the Ganesha festival.

'I once went with Deepak and his parents to a temple in Sydney. His folks and their friends all speak Gujarati, which I don't understand. But I heard many people speaking Tamil at the temple.'

I moved the sticky strands of hair from my eyes and tied my hair with a scrunchie. 'Tamil families might have kids who want to learn Carnatic music.'

Preeti grinned. 'The *idlis* have opened your mind.'

I pointed to the counter. 'It's that Ganesha. He's doing his job, removing obstacles in my mind. Let's go to Higginbotham's this evening. I'll buy some beginner Carnatic music books to teach kids. Maybe a basic text on the theory of Western music for me, too.'

Higginbotham's, the iconic red and yellow stucco bookshop on Mount Road, is one landmark that has remained the same in the ever-changing Chennai landscape. For me, the ancient building was like Aladdin's cave, full of hidden treasure. Growing up, it was a family ritual to visit the bookshop on my birthday. Viji Ma went after Tamil classics, and my father browsed through the ancient editions of Socrates, Plato, Victor Hugo and Emerson. I spent my time amongst the shelves that had children's books and comics in English and several Indian languages. Even Deepak had been impressed with the entire floor of technology books. He had bought books on security and encryption with the gift voucher we received at the wedding.

Preeti wanted to buy a new book that had hit the *New York Times* best-seller charts. She described it excitedly, 'It's a novel that combines Indian mythology with fantasy, where gods fly to Mars, villains to Venus and demons inhabit underwater submarines.'

I left her in the fantasy wing as I wandered into the music section and picked up some beginner Carnatic music books. They would come in handy to teach Indian classical music to kids in Sydney. I wandered into the Western music section and was instantly captivated by a book that talked of mathematical sequences, graphic art, and music. It used examples of Goedel, Escher and Bach. The blurb at the back of the book challenged my brain. I had compartmentalised my interests in maths and Carnatic music into air-tight compartments that could not share their magic. This book linked music, maths, and art in ways I could never have imagined. I added the book to my cane shopping basket and wandered into the history section.

My eyes fell on the *Chronicles of a Portuguese Merchant* by Domingos Paes, who visited Vijayanagar and Tanjore in 1520. The book would be a good resource for Viji Ma. I also picked up a Tamil book on *devadasis*.

Preeti let out a loud whistle when she saw the books in my basket. 'The road trip has clicked open a hidden part of your brain?'

'The catalyst is that woman, Amba, the author of that palm leaf manuscript at the Tanjore Library Museum. Viji Ma's guess is that she could have been a *devadasi* or a courtesan.'

Preeti said, 'Maybe she was a courtesan who had a cushy life with lots of time to write.'

I said, '*Devadasi* or courtesan, she had to be a scholar to write in Sanskrit on those flimsy palm leaves. They were such narrow strips, barely two inches wide. How many palm leaves would she have used for her manuscript?'

I tried to picture a two-inch width strip with my thumb and forefinger.

'Can you imagine the skill and concentration needed to etch her thoughts into words on those surfaces? It's brittle now, but it must have been softer when she wrote on it.'

I rambled on as we got into an Uber. 'I pestered the librarian to give me more details about the manuscript. An incomplete biography of King Raghu Nayaka, he said.'

'You are besotted with that woman,' Preeti said. 'If you are really keen, I can hook you up with my classmate's father, Professor Krishnamurthy. He's a Sanskrit professor at Tanjore University. His constant rue is that young Indians lack a sense of their history. I am sure he'd be delighted to talk to you.'

After I exchanged a few emails with Professor Krishnamurthy, my iPad was full of articles about King Raghu Nayaka and women scholars of that period.

Whether Amba was a *devadasi* or a courtesan with a cushy life, she had created a beautiful piece of work that had outlived her for centuries. Was she respected in her society?

I had my reading cut out for the flight back to Sydney.

CHAPTER 12

AMBA
Tanjore, 1620

Amba draped a pale, yellow silk *sari* around her body. She twirled around to feel the smooth silk caress her waist, pleating and adjusting the green and gold embroidered end of the *sari* on her left shoulder. She clipped on the new pair of emerald earrings the king had given her recently and admired herself in front of the polished bronze tray propped up on the ornate wooden stand. She liked the way the earrings dangled behind the loose tendrils that escaped from her long, plaited hair. A thin gold chain with a diamond and emerald pendant completed her attire.

She had been careful to pick a time for her outing. Siesta time at the palace. She slipped through the side gate of the courtesans' palace and climbed into the waiting palanquin.

'Let's go to the jewellers.'

Four men, two in front and two at the back, deftly lifted the palanquin off the ground. With a swift tug, she closed the brown silk curtains on either side, blocking out the glare of the afternoon sun and the gaze of random strangers.

With years of practice carrying palace women around, the bearers' synchronised move was rhythmic, like a gentle swing.

As they set down the palanquin outside the jeweller's shop, the goldsmith was at the doorstep to greet her. 'Welcome, Amba Ma. I knew it was you from the tinkle of your anklets.'

'*Vanakkam*, Chinna.'

Goldsmith Chinna led her to the inner chamber, where he entertained special guests.

A dazzling array of jewellery was organised in small display units. Gold bangles with delicate etchings sparkled on a maroon silk base.

Amba asked, 'Do you make bangles embedded with pearls and rubies?'

'The bangles in that cabinet are not studded with gems, but we can embed pearls and rubies.'

He took out a pair of bangles and showed her the shallow grooves along the circumference.

'We have new rice pearls that arrived from Jaffna last week. They are flat and will be ideal to fit into these grooves. But rubies...' He stopped midway and stroked his jaw.

'Have you not received rubies from up north?' asked Amba.

Chinna's mouth drooped and his head went from side to side. 'We had a regular supply from the Moghul traders, but now the Portuguese pay them higher prices. Much more than what we have been paying, and now, suddenly, we have no good rubies.'

'Don't you have other suppliers? Are there no other traders around?'

Chinna scratched his ear. 'The new ship docked in our port has gemstones for trade.'

'I thought foreigners come here to buy our gemstones. What type of gems do these people have?'

'They call them garnets. They are red like rubies but not luminous.'

This was her chance to know more about the ship that disturbed the king.

'Has anyone from that ship been here to show you these garnets?' Amba made her voice sound casual.

'A messenger came here yesterday. He said the captain wants to visit after closing time to show me.' The moment the words came out, Chinna bit his tongue.

Amba realised it was not wise to prod him further. She pointed to a strand of pink pearls. 'Can I hold them? I want to see if these will work with my pink and silver *sari*.'

Chinna handled the strand of pearls with the same reverence as a temple priest who offered flowers to the deity.

'Please try them on.' He added after a pause, 'If you wish, you can take them with you and see if they match the *sari*.'

'That's kind of you. I have a few more errands. I don't want to go all around the market with these beautiful pearls in my palanquin.'

'I can send it over to you at the palace.' Chinna didn't want to lose a customer from the palace.

'Can you? But wait, I will be passing this way again after my errands. I will stop by to save you the trouble of sending them to the palace.'

A couple of hours later, Amba was back at the jewellers. Chinna placed the pearls in a blue velvet-lined box, and a happy smile spread over his face. He closed the lid with great care and was about to give it to her when she heard the crunch of heavy footsteps.

A tall foreigner was at the doorstep. He removed his hat and ducked his head low as he came through the narrow doorway. She couldn't suppress the spontaneous giggle. His pale face was flushed, matching his bright red coat. In this warm, humid weather, he wore a thick coat and heavy boots. His forehead was dotted with drops of sweat. The coat fabric appeared coarse, but the gold embroidery on the high collar was intricate.

The visitor shuffled his legs, his boots scratching the stone floor. He then brought his hands together with an awkward smile. '*Namaste.*'

She returned the gesture.

He hesitantly spoke in Tamil. '*En peyar Ove.* My name is Ove Gjedde. I am from Denmark.' The words had a strange intonation and were hard to understand.

With a smile, Amba greeted him in Portuguese. '*Ola.*'

'Ah, you speak Portuguese!' exclaimed Ove.

'Um, *pouco.*' She gestured with her thumb and forefinger a little. 'Do you speak Portuguese in your country?'

'No, we speak Danish, but I understand Portuguese.'

Ove's smile lit up his eyes, and his pupils turned into two blue sapphires. Amba caught her breath. Her fingers curled in and out as she tried to hide her sweaty palms in the folds of her *sari*. Strange emotions clouded her thoughts. She lowered her eyes.

'It's getting late. It's time for me to head back to the palace.' Amba took the jewel case from Chinna and thanked him. With a slight nod at Ove, she disappeared into her waiting palanquin.

The music session was mellow and soothing that morning. The king's improvisations were haunting, yet peaceful.

The king set down his *veena* and embraced her with his large arms. Amba melted into his soft robe, her head resting on his chest. Two heartbeats merged into a single rhythm. Fast at first and gradually slowing down with each breath. The king released her from his embrace. Amba placed the king's *veena* on its stand and covered it with a silk shawl.

'Your Majesty, word is out on the streets that you plan to hold a special welcome ceremony for the new foreigners.'

'Is there anything that escapes you, my darling?' The king's shoulders shook with mirth. 'Who is your source?'

'My maid's husband has been unloading goods from their ship.'

'Then you probably know more about these foreigners than I do.'

They climbed down the spiral staircase and then he addressed her question. 'Yes, we have decided to host a reception for the new visitors at our Nandi Hall.'

Her voice rose with excitement. 'The Nandi Hall can be turned into God Indra's palace on earth. That will show the foreigners who we are.'

The king threw his head back and laughed. 'If you know how God Indra's palace in heaven looks, you should oversee the decorations of the Nandi Hall.'

'With pleasure, Your Majesty. I have a good image of heaven in my mind,' laughed Amba. 'Second Queen Tara has asked me to help her select the jewellery for the event. She wants to wear what a heavenly nymph would wear.'

'I don't have to go to heaven; my nymph is here.' He gave her a little kiss on her forehead.

'And you, my darling, what are you going to wear?'

'You will see,' she smiled.

The kiss turned into a passionate hug. 'What will I do without you, my darling Amba? You are beautiful and intelligent, and no one in the palace has the natural ability you have with music and languages.'

A sudden frown turned up between his eyebrows. *What is he thinking?*

The king said, 'I want you to take a seat on the dais. From where you are able to hear as well as see the visitors.'

The king never invited his courtesans to a formal reception; he had too many of them. Certainly not when his queens were present. He kept his women apart, but she was an exception. The king valued her views.

During their next music session, Amba composed a song on Nataraja, the dancing Shiva, using both Sanskrit and Tamil words in the same stanza.

The king tried to play that stanza on his *veena*, but he could not frame the lyrical segments within the standard rhythmic *tala* of eight or six beats. The standard even-numbered *talas* didn't work for this particular bilingual composition. After several attempts, they decided that this composition needed a different approach. They decided to create a new *tala* with an odd number of beats.

The king said, 'We need to spend a few more sessions to perfect this new *tala*. But this morning, I have another important agenda. I have to meet Ayya.'

As they walked back towards the palace, the king said, 'I have invited Ayya for breakfast this morning to discuss the Danish visit. Would you like to come along to discuss the arrangements?'

Amba had never imagined that her chance to voice her thoughts with the renowned Ayya would arrive so suddenly. She felt the same flutter of excitement as she did when the king had showered her with rose petals that first night they had come together.

She felt a deep sense of gratitude. 'With pleasure, your Majesty.'

Ayya arrived just as they reached the king's visiting chamber. Today, she didn't have to hide behind that musty weapons cupboard. This was her chance to gain Ayya's respect, which was even more important than the king's.

Breakfast that morning, was a platter of fruit and warm milk laced with saffron and cardamom. A *Brahmin* attendant, wearing a sacred thread hanging across his left shoulder, his long hair twisted into the traditional knot at the back of his head, brought in a large silver tray with red and yellow bananas, purple and green grapes, gleaming red pearls of pomegranates and mangoes cut into little golden bowls. Being a *Brahmin*, Ayya always ate food cooked and served by a *Brahmin*.

The king waited for Ayya to have a piece of fruit. 'Ayya, you know my concern about foreigners who turn up on our doorstep uninvited. I don't ever want to get into a situation like King Changili of Jaffna. The Portuguese and the Dutch have made his life miserable. Now they have riots everywhere in Jaffna.'

Amba felt sorry for the Jaffna king. He was like a tiny mouse caught in the claws of two quarrelsome cats.

Ayya lifted the silver tumbler and drank the warm milk without the rim touching his lips. His eyes were focused on his hands as he placed the tumbler on the side stool, slow and deliberate, as if shaping his thoughts with every tiny movement.

'Your Majesty, the Danish have reached our port after a bitter experience in Ceylon. They approached Jaffna with five ships. The Portuguese shot down three, and the Dutch chased the remaining two ships away from the region.'

The king leaned forward. 'What's on your mind, Ayya?'

Ayya continued. 'The Danish set sail from Ceylon with two remaining cargo ships. One was gobbled up by storms, and they finally landed in our port Nagore with just one cargo ship. At the moment, the Danish are like elephants without trunks. It is up to us to steer them in the direction we choose.'

The king's eyes pleaded. 'Ayya, why don't you meet the captain of the ship and ascertain if he is worthy of our friendship.' The king was trying to avoid meeting the captain.

The captain had been polite when Amba met him briefly at the jeweller's.

Amba cleared her throat.

'Yes, Amba.' Ayya could sense that she was bursting to speak.

'Ayya, before we invite the captain to the palace, do you think we should find out if he is a representative of the King of Denmark or a merchant on his own?'

Turning towards the king, she said, 'Raja Nayaka, would you feel more comfortable if we first assess his status and position? If he is a representative of the King of Denmark and not a private trader, you may choose to meet him and perhaps use him to establish a relationship between the King of Tanjore and the King of Denmark.'

Ayya's face was covered in smiles. 'That is a great suggestion, Amba.'

The next moment, Ayya's face drew into deep, symmetrical lines that ran from the bridge of his nose to the edge of his mouth. The determined expression was a typical characteristic of the wise counsellor.

'Your Highness, we will establish the principles of engagement from the very first meeting. All meetings will be recorded as a discussion between two kings and not with a merchant. The Danish captain must serve as the representative of the King of Denmark.'

The king's shoulders drew back from the hunched position. Amba relaxed with a deep sigh. They had listened to her suggestions.

CHAPTER 13

MAYA

Chennai, 2013

I brewed a large pot of spicy *chai* and piled a plate with crisp, savoury *murukkus* I had bought at Krishna Snacks and Viji Ma's favourite, Australian Tim Tams. As always Viji Ma sat on the balcony in her favourite cane chair; feet stretched out on a footstool, immersed in *Kalki*, the Tamil weekly. The evening sun was giving way to the hesitant sea breeze.

I placed the tray on the side stool and grabbed a crunchy *murukku*. Viji Ma said, 'Maya, you left Chennai three years ago, but Chennai has not left you.'

'How can the city of my childhood leave me?' I held up a Tim Tam. 'I have the best of both worlds, Australian Tim Tams and *Madras Murukku*.'

Viji MA said, 'I hope you have more than Tim Tams in your new world. I got worried about the way you carried on about marriage being a trap. Is marriage the problem, or is something else holding you back? I hope Deepak is caring and loving?'

How could I tell Viji Ma that Deepak was a wonderful lover but not a caring husband because he hated my music. I escaped into the bedroom and fetched the book I had bought for Viji Ma at Higgin-botham's.

'I thought you might like this book. *Chronicles of a Portuguese Merchant* who visited Vijayanagar and Tanjore in 1520.'

Viji Ma browsed through the pages. 'Maya, looks like the history bug has caught you too. The dairy of a European merchant is an interesting find. It might offer a new angle to my essay.'

I said, 'The Tanjore Nayakas have aroused my curiosity. Did the magazine ask you to write about the Tanjore kings?

'No. All they wanted was a feature about forgotten history of south India. I chose the Nayaka period because of their significant contribution to music and art. Most importantly, the Nayakas restored the ancient Tanjore temples built by the Chola kings, who dominated the southern region in the tenth and eleventh centuries. Tamilians know about the Cholas from the brilliant novels of Tamil writer Kalki. But Nayakas have remained hidden.'

Viji Ma broke a small piece of Tim Tam, which crumbled on the plate and spilled over the floor. A couple of crumbs were enough for the tiny brown ants to crawl out of their humid holes. I rushed to the kitchen and brought out a dustpan.

Viji Ma said. 'The maid will clean it up; you don't have to do it.'

'Viji Ma, I have gotten out of the habit of waiting for maids. We don't have that luxury in Sydney.'

I emptied the crumbs in the trash and came back. 'Did the Nayakas descend from the Cholas?'

'No. The Nayakas were not from a royal clan. They held influential positions in the Vijayanagar Kingdom, which ruled all of South India from the thirteenth to the fifteenth century after the Cholas.'

Viji Ma's gaze turned to the distant palm trees swaying in the breeze. She continued after a long pause.

'After a century of dominance, the Vijayanagar empire imploded because there were too many claimants to the throne. The region got partitioned into smaller feudatories and handed over to the militant Nayaka clan. Tanjore was one such small kingdom. There were other similar kingdoms like Madurai and Gingee. Once they became kings, they too quarrelled. They were friends or foes with their neighbouring king depending on which prince married which princess.'

I burst out laughing. 'You are writing your article as you speak. We should be recording this.'

Viji Ma's eyes took on a softer expression. 'I think the Tanjore Nayakas were the wisest. When the neighbouring king of Gingee flirted with the Portuguese and procured their weapons, Raghu Nayaka of Tanjore married the Gingee Nayaka's daughter, Princess Kalyani.'

I broke into a loud guffaw. 'Checkmate! King Raghu is quite a character. Married the plotting king's daughter, avoided the Portuguese, wooed the Danish. This is world history, Indian style.'

The doorbell chimed with an old Bollywood tune. Unlike in Sydney, where our front door remained silent for weeks, doorbells chimed continuously in Chennai. Whether it was to the maid visiting twice a day, the ironing-cart lady, the flower girl, the fruit vendor, the bill collector, a donation solicitor, an old friend or a second cousin one could spend all day opening and closing the front door.

I held the door open for Preeti. 'Come in.'

Viji Ma offered her the plate of Tim Tams. 'Your cousin has come back fully charged from the road trip. We were talking about the Tanjore Nayakas.'

Preeti said, 'Did Maya find the right references for you? She got side-tracked by an old palm leaf manuscript written by a woman.'

I said, 'I have to find out who the writer was.'

Viji Ma said, 'I am fascinated by another scholar, Govinda Ayya. Prime Minister and mentor for three generations of Nayakas. He was a great musician and *veena* player. Govinda Ayya's sons were scholars, too. His son Venkata was a musicologist.'

Preeti chuckled. 'Can you imagine the conversations in their family? Bet they argued over music.'

Viji Ma joined the laughter. 'It doesn't stop with the men. Ayya's wife, Nagamma, was also a musician and composer.'

A mischievous gleam lit up Viji Ma's eyes. 'Now that you girls are into Tanjore history, I have a surprise for you both.'

Preeti's eyes grew wide. 'What is it?'

'Preeti, your father, Vishwa, called me yesterday when you girls were out. We got talking about Tanjore. Your father has traced his ancestry to a great scholar, Narayana Dikshita.'

Preeti shrugged. 'Tracing his ancestors has become my father's hobby after retirement.'

I poured another round of *chai*. Viji Ma's beaming smile covered her entire face. 'The plot thickens. That scholar, Narayana Dikshita, was Nagamma's father.'

My teacup rattled on its saucer. 'Viji Ma, that's huge. That means Preeti and I are related to Nagamma, a great scholar. People in Australia go to great lengths to trace their ancestry, and here you are, casually tracing our lineage back over five hundred years. Are there any documents to prove this?'

'Ask Preeti's dad.'

Preeti rolled her eyes. 'These days dad's constantly on the phone talking to long lost cousins, populating the family tree.'

I said, 'Imagine for a moment. If that palm leaf author Amba is related to Nagamma, then I am related to Amba.'

Viji Ma said, 'I thought you said Amba was a courtesan.'

'And you, Viji Ma, said courtesans could be *devadasis* who came from good families. What if Amba was Nagamma's niece, and she decided to become a *devadasi*, who later became a courtesan? Would Amba be viewed as a black sheep of the family or as a scholar?'

Viji Ma chuckled. 'Vishwa will drive you out of his house if you construct a wild story that links him to a courtesan.'

Preeti threw her hands up. 'I am staying out of this. I had enough battles when I applied for an overseas PhD without my dad's permission.'

Preeti's head bobbed up and down, mimicking her father's voice. 'Maya, put some sense into your cousin. Why can't she be an obedient daughter like you and marry a nice Indian boy?'

All three of us roared at the realistic imitation.

Back in her normal voice, Preeti said, 'Maya, my mother wants you to come over. She's made special sweets for you.'

Bright *rangoli* designs on the veranda welcomed me as I entered Preeti's house. Colourful floor stickers had replaced the traditional hand drawn *mandala* designs at the entrance of houses. Tiny clay oil lamps were lit and placed on either side of the front door. Preeti's mother, Indu Chithi, opened the door. Preeti too emerged from the house right behind her mother.

'*Vanakkam*, Chithi.' I pointed to the clay lamps. 'Are these for any special festival?'

'It's *Karthigai*. The night of the full moon in December when Shiva appeared in the form of a flame to illuminate the mind of his devotees.'

'I remember now. Grandma used to make puffed rice balls with jaggery for this festival.'

Indu Chithi's eyes conveyed her love. 'Come in. You are glowing. Marriage suits you.'

Preeti winked at me from behind her mother's back. 'Chithi, you talk of marriage as if it's a dress.'

'*Podi*, naughty girl.' Chithi tapped my cheek. 'I have made puffed rice balls for you. Preeti doesn't care for traditional jaggery sweets.'

As soon as Chithi brought out the sweets and some *murukkus*, Uncle Vishwa joined us. 'Hello, Maya. How's Sydney treating you? How are your husband's family? You are a lucky girl. They came, they saw and snapped you up.'

I felt like a *laddu* to be gobbled. Did that make me lucky? My eyebrows gathered into a frown.

Preeti said, 'Dad, Maya says Australians are big into tracing their ancestry.'

Vishwa said, 'I happened to read the biography of a fifteenth-century Sanskrit scholar, Neelakanta Dikshita. The appendix of the book had a family tree, and I found my grandfather at the bottom of that family hierarchy. All I had to do was go up that link and track my great-grandfather's grandfather. He was Neelakanta's brother.'

I said, 'Uncle, what about the women? Are you able to track your great-grandmother's parents?'

'It should be possible if I talk to my maternal relatives,' he said. 'Family trees are usually patriarchal. The tree becomes too unwieldy if all the daughters and their children are included.'

Preeti said, 'Then you should construct a separate matriarchal family tree.'

Vishwa glared. 'Preeti, you are forever asserting your feminist views while you disregard your duties as a daughter.'

Preeti snorted. 'Dad, Maya is not here to listen to your lecture on women's duties over their rights. She wants to see the family tree.'

Uncle Vishwa lifted his heavy body with a groan. 'Maya, your father was the athletic one. He defeated me in every game at school despite being two years younger than me. All this stuff about fitness and longevity. Hogwash.'

No one in the family could get over my father's sudden death after his morning walk. He collapsed when he bent to remove his joggers as I was getting ready for college. I rushed to him with a glass of water. I took the glass to his lips. He moved the tendrils on my forehead away from my eyes, and then his eyes closed. Viji Ma called the emergency number, but it was too late by the time the ambulance arrived.

The aroma of filter coffee broke my reverie. Indu walked in with a tray that held matching mugs of coffee for Preeti and me and *dabara* tumblers, for the olds. Uncle Vishwa lifted the narrow tumbler, poured the hot coffee into the broader *dabara*, and transferred it back to the tumbler in a long, narrow stream, releasing the aroma of the freshly brewed coffee.

I had never been a fan of the metal *dabara* tumbler. It burned your lips if you were not careful. The mug was comfortable, but it did nothing to enhance the coffee's flavour. Tradition. We mock and reject it when we have it, but we pine for it when it disappears.

Uncle Vishwa finished his coffee with a noisy slurp and placed the tumbler back in the *dabara*.

'Do you want to see the family tree or hear the story?'

'Both,' I said.

'Let's go to the study. We need a large table to spread it out.'

Vishwa carefully unfolded six A3 sheets, sellotaped together. Two people per row, three levels deep.

'Neelakanta Diksita's grandfather, Appayya, was a great scholar who lived from 1520 to 1593. There's plenty of documented evidence about Appayya's life and scholarly works. Our family has a direct link to Appayya's younger brother, Narayana Dikshita. Narayana's daughter, Nagamma, was married to the great scholar Govinda Ayya of Tanjore fame. He was the Prime Minister for three generations of Nayaka kings. His son was Venkata Makhi, the famous musicologist. I have not yet extended that part of the tree.'

I zigzagged my finger from Narayana Dikshita down to Vishwa and my father, Raja. Our great-great-great grandfather's sister was Nagamma.

Preeti grinned. 'Dad, you have highlighted all the male scholars in the family tree. What about the black sheep in such a large family? I am sure there would be an equal number.'

Vishwa glared at Preeti and didn't bother answering.

My finger rested on Nagamma's circle. She was my grand-grand-grand aunt, and Venkata Makhi was a grand cousin of sorts.

Viji Ma's sage advice rang in my ears. Don't air your views about Amba's relationship with Nagamma.

'Uncle Vishwa, you should highlight Nagamma, along with her husband and sons. Viji Ma says Nagamma was a prolific composer.'

Chithi patted my head. She said, 'At least one person in this generation carries those strong musical genes.'

My face grew hot with shame. Was I worthy of those genes? I had accomplished nothing.

Preeti said, 'I am tone deaf. It's Maya we have to rely on. She won every music prize in school and college.'

What was the point of all those prizes? I felt a deep pressure in my chest, as though the musical genes had stuck in my throat, unable to express themselves.

I felt burdened when I took leave.

Indu Chithi asked, 'When are you heading back to Sydney?'

'I leave next week. I need to get back to work.'

'Preeti too will be gone next month.'

Preeti said, 'Amma, you'll see me on FaceTime every week. Don't wait for Dad to hook you up to his computer. Call me on your mobile phone; I'll set you up before I go.'

Indu's eyes turned moist. 'What will I do without you girls?'

I touched Indu and Vishwa feet and received their blessings.

Before leaving, I said, 'Preeti, Let's go to Chennai Handicrafts; I have one final round of shopping before I head back to Sydney. I want to get a Tanjore painting of Goddess Saraswati and a pair of hanging brass lamps.'

CHAPTER 14

AMBA

Tanjore, 1622

Amba pointed to the lamps along the walls of the Nandi Hall and asked the brass smith, 'Is it possible to forge those individual hanging brass lamps into a cluster of lamps to hang from a chandelier?'

'Yes, My Lady. I can weld brass chains along the rim of a metal disc, and the lamps can hang from the chains. How many lamps would you like in each cluster?'

The brass lamps were few and far apart, and the hall needed additional lighting to highlight the delicate sculptures on the wooden pillars. Three generations of Tanjore artists and sculptors had poured their emotions into their work for the Nayaka kings, and Nandi Hall was the pinnacle of their emotional outburst.

'Attach six lamps to chains of different lengths; three short and three long. Make sure the brass hooks attached to each chain are in the shape of Nandi.'

She pointed to the brass lamps with red and green gems. 'Find gems of the same colour but larger in size and embed them in the centre of the bronze disc in the form of a lotus.'

The brass smith nodded with a big smile. He caught on and repeated her instructions in an excited voice. 'Each chandelier will have six hanging lamps, three with short chains and three with long chains, suspended from Nandi-shaped hooks which will be attached to the rim of a gem-studded bronze disc.'

'That's right.' Amba counted the number of pillars. 'We need twelve chandeliers, one in every alcove, to highlight the sculptures on the wooden pillars on either side.'

At the other end of the hall, a carpenter was waiting for instructions. Amba said, 'The wooden pillars are dull with mould. Apply teak oil and polish them till they gleam. Every dancer and drummer carved on the pillar should spring to life when the lamps are lit.'

Amba touched the breast of a curvaceous figure and chuckled. Wouldn't it be funny if this figure came to life at my touch? Like that mythical woman, Ahalya, who came out of a curse and turned into a beautiful woman when God Rama touched her statue.

A new energy surged through her veins. She called the artist. Pointing to the murals up on the ceiling, she said, 'The colours on those paintings have faded. Please create vivid blue and red pigments and touch up those faded parts.'

Gardener Muthu was waiting outside. 'Muthu, I would like the entrance archway to be decorated like a traditional Tanjore home on festive days. Can you get some people to help you with this decoration?'

Muthu removed his turban and sat down on his heels, ready for a long chat. 'I shall place two large clay pots of banana plants on either side of the entrance gate, as we do for weddings. And then...'

Amba was in a tearing hurry. 'Yes. Make sure the two banana plants are the same height with bunches of raw bananas.'

A vision of the dazzling archway appeared in her mind's eye. Garlands of mango leaves, garlands of marigolds and magnolias along both sides of the walkway; visitors mesmerised by the perfumed pathway as they approach the palace.

Pointing to the carvings on the front door, she continued, 'Muthu, arrange the flowers and leaves to mimic the carved flowers and leaves around those mythological figures on the great front door.'

Turning to Kamala, her maid and chief helper, Amba said, 'Place wide silver bowls of floating rose petals and jasmine in perfumed water under each pillar.'

By the end of the month, the Nandi Hall had turned into her palace of dreams. If God Indra came down from heaven, he would be envious. Would the Danish Captain be impressed? Would the beauty of this hall light up his sparkling blue eyes?

Prime Minister Ayya helped determine the seating arrangements and the protocols to be followed. His chamber was at the end of the Ministers' building, surrounded by shady oaks and banyan trees. A common corridor ran around the building. Amba paused by the moist vetiver screen outside Ayya's chambers and inhaled the delicate perfume of the rough reeds.

Ayya used a stylus dipped in soot and created a pattern of dots on a white cotton sheet. Each dot represented a person. The large central dot represented the king.

'As per standard protocol, the Commander-in-chief General Pandya Varma, being the defender of the throne, will sit next to the king on his right. Being the Prime Minister, I will sit next to the commander. The queen will be next to the king on his left and then the ministers.' Ayya placed five dots in a semi-circular form, to represent other ministers.

And then Ayya placed a dot next to his position on the map. 'Amba, you may sit next to me, to my right at this meeting. I need help to understand the foreigner's Tamil accent. I hear Captain Ove is bringing his own interpreter, a Danish man who has learnt to speak Tamil.'

Amba felt a tremor of gratitude course through her veins. Her dreams had never stretched to sitting next to Prime Minister Ayya in court. She bent down and touched Ayya's feet. Tears of gratitude choked her throat.

Ayya's gentle hand patted her head. 'Child, there's no need to get emotional. No one else from the royal household understands foreign languages.'

He added after a chuckle. 'Make sure Queen Kalyani's chair is placed right next to the king's throne on his left. The other two queens can sit behind the king. Place their chairs so they are able to see and hear the foreigners.'

Once the protocols were set, the king cast off his apprehensions and agreed to welcome the visitor with his customary warmth and generosity. He decided to send his own horses to bring Captain Ove Gjedde from the port city of Nagore, a privilege rarely granted to foreigners.

Amba spent a whole week planning her clothes and jewellery and settled on a sky-blue silk *sari* with silver sequins. She didn't want to out-dress Queen Kalyani, who never wanted Amba to be present at court meetings. *But that's her problem, not mine*, thought Amba.

Today, Amba was here, not as a courtesan but as a political adviser. Her hand caressed the new pearls she had picked up from the jewellers the day she had met Captain Ove.

Amba waited in the wings for the visitors to arrive. Nandi Hall dazzled like a bride dressed to welcome the groom's party. Floral arrangements, brass-lamp chandeliers, scented bowls of rose water, sandalwood incense, and twinkling lamps drew attention to the carved pillars. Every pillar competed with its neighbour to draw the visitor's attention. They beckoned to the attendees: "Come, sir, hear my story."

The scholars took their seats in the first row. Chins up, heads and necks erect, their plain white *dhoti* was their recourse to proclaim their pure intellect and enhanced status in Tanjore society. Thick-neck Venkata, who years ago had refused to recognise her music and literary talents, sat prominently amidst the scholars.

The five businessmen Ayya had chosen sat across from the scholars. The merchants' colourful turbans, woven with gold and silver threads, made no apologies for their wealth-induced influence.

Ove and his two companions were offered the traditional welcome by the palace maids. They sprinkled rose water around them, offered sweets and flowers and led them to their designated seats. Amba had selected a tall, straight-backed chair with red velvet cushions and gleaming rosewood armrests to accommodate Ove's tall frame. His companions occupied smaller chairs on either side of him.

Once the guests were seated, Commander-in-Chief Pandya Varma, Prime Minister Ayya and Amba walked to their positions on the dais. The titillating hoot of the conch proclaimed the king's arrival. For Tanjoreans, the king was a representative of God, and, therefore, his arrival followed the pattern of the temple ritual, where God was welcomed with traditional music, played on the *nadaswaram*. Two drummers walked on either side of the reed player, their *tavils* slung across one shoulder and resting on their huge bellies.

The conch sounded again, and everyone stood up. Four young

women showered the king with rose petals and sprinkled sandalwood-scented water as he approached. Taking his cue from others, Ove stood to welcome the king.

The king's gait was laboured, as he struggled to balance the weight of his gold robe trailing behind him. Queen Kalyani, his principal queen, and two more queens, daughters of defeated kings and sacrificial pawns in the game of war, followed the king. Their dazzling clothes and jewels did nothing to illuminate their dull eyes.

I will never become a political pawn like those queens, thought Amba. She would rather be a mover of pawns. From her vantage point, Amba sensed the mutual disrespect the scholars and merchants had for each other, exchanged through silent expressions more powerful than words.

Ayya, guru to three generations of Tanjore Nayakas, cleared his throat and people snapped to attention. While others depended on external embellishments to assert their status, Ayya's brilliance illuminated the thin gold border of his white turban. His mere presence made people bow with respect. Would she ever get that kind of respect?

Ayya's sonorous voice rang out. 'King Raghu Nayaka of Tanjore is delighted to welcome the representative of the King of Denmark. Our scriptures stipulate that every visitor should be treated like God. Our gods are many, and so too are our visitors. Ancient visitors from distant lands have written glorious accounts of Tanjore.'

Ayya's words carried the weight of his conviction. 'Tanjore is blessed with peace and prosperity. We honour our tradition and follow well-established principles of governance based on knowledge, truth and righteous behaviour, tempered with restraint. Our warmth and hospitality should never be misconstrued as guilelessness.'

With a warm smile that spread all over his face, Ayya said, 'Kindly convey our warm friendship to King Christian of Denmark.'

It was Commander-in-Chief Pandya Varma's turn. His fine military regalia proclaimed his position and status. 'In Tanjore, we plan for peace, not war.' The commander's voice was loud and clear. 'Peace leads to prosperity. War results in poverty. We are aware that not all wars are fought on the battlefield; some are covert and silent, propelled by greed and deceit.'

Captain Ove Gjedde's shoulders straightened. His eyes stayed intently focused as the commander as he continued. 'We train our soldiers to be heroes. We also teach them the benefits of restraint. While many see the sword as a symbol of power, we, in Tanjore, see it as a symbol of wisdom to protect *dharma* and ethics. Our ethical codes enable people to live in peace and prosperity in this beautiful land of temples.'

The commander-in-chief took out his sword and pointed to its hilt. 'The carvings and decorations you see on the hilt represent auspicious forces. They animate power in the inanimate blade and protect the swordsman when he uses it for a just cause. Every soldier is trained to induce the sacred power into his weapons before their use in battles. We select our weapons of war with care and consideration. Every weapon is selected for a specific purpose to deal with the situation at hand.'

The commander-in-chief bowed to the king and sat down.

The king took over. 'We open our doors to traders who come in peace, with no other ulterior motive. My grandfather welcomed the Portuguese when they first arrived, but soon their interests expanded into territorial power which we had to curb. That is not acceptable to us.'

The king leaned forward like an angry cat, ready to pounce. 'We know that European kingdoms fight frequent battles to expand their territories and assert their power. We do not want your battles to be fought on our shores. Portuguese ships come equipped with arms and ammunition. They turn gun powder into gun power, a single weapon used without restraint. This behaviour is not in our code of ethics.'

The king took a deep breath and addressed Ove directly. 'When you approached Ceylon, the Portuguese shot down three ships out of your fleet of five, and the Dutch chased your remaining ships away from that region. The ambitions of the Dutch and the Portuguese have gone beyond trading into annexation. More recently, into the religious conversion of people with limited means who cower under gun power. We seek neither war nor religion. You will be treated as our guest of honour as long as you do not bring your wars to our region.'

Ove's pale face turned red. Beads of sweat gleamed on his forehead. He took out a white handkerchief and mopped his face and neck. Amba wondered if the king's words had alarmed Ove.

He made a deep bow. His tone was gentle as he addressed the king. 'Your Royal Highness, the King of Denmark holds you in high regard. He has heard about your prosperous kingdom and the respect you command in the entire region.'

Ove unwound a parchment scroll and read out the Danish king's message. 'Dear Raja of Tanjore, we have heard about your prosperous and peaceful kingdom from many who have visited Tanjore. Your patronage of arts and music is well known to the European kings. We admire your achievements on the battlefield and in the concert hall. We wish to have a warm and friendly relationship with your kingdom. I have sent my emissary, Captain Ove Gjedde, to your kingdom to forge a peaceful trading partnership, which will help both our kingdoms to prosper. We assure you that we have no territorial interests.'

Ove's shoulders stooped as if he carried the heavy burden of that encounter. 'Yes, our ships were destroyed by the Portuguese when we approached Ceylon. We understand why you are not able to trust the Portuguese. Our king does not wish to fight battles in a foreign land where we have no control. We hope you are able to trust us and grant exclusive trading rights, as exclusivity will allow us to guard the region against the Portuguese, the Dutch, and other ships that roam your waters.'

The king's torso grew tall, and his face froze like a rock sculpture with piercing eyes.

He roared, 'Years ago, when the first Portuguese ship landed here, my grandfather, King Sevappa Nayaka, welcomed them with open arms and granted them the privileges they sought. He allowed them to trade freely. Gave them the same exclusive rights you have come to request. But what did they do? The Portuguese turned local rebels into armed mercenaries. They paid them to instigate riots in areas where our most vulnerable people lived. That's when my father, King Achuta Nayaka, stopped their exclusive trading rights. Now they hover around Ceylon like hyenas waiting to pounce on ships that threaten their presence. The Tanjore kings have managed these shores for centuries. We do not need your help to guard our shores.'

Ove would have been reduced to ashes if the king had a third eye like God Shiva.

The king said, 'You have now landed at our doorstep with the last remaining ship. Do not misunderstand your position, Captain Ove. You have come seeking our help.'

Coughs and grunts were suspended in mid-air, too scared to emerge.

The king caught himself and took a deep breath. 'Prime Minister Ayya will guide your discussions with our scholars and businessmen assembled here. Listen to their thoughts and views. That will help you recommend the right trading strategy to your king.'

Ove acknowledged the king's words with a deep bow. There was a collective sigh of relief when the king sank back in his chair, anger abated. Amba caught his eye and smiled.

With a nod and a smile that included Amba, the king pointed to the adjacent hall. 'An empty stomach can't feed your thoughts. Enjoy the refreshments before you start the discussions.'

The king rose to the synchronised sounds of the conch and *nadaswaram* and strode out of the hall. The queens followed close on his heels.

Pandya Varma led Captain Ove to the dining hall, and Amba walked alongside Ayya. The scholars and the businessmen followed.

Amba had spent a whole day with the palace chefs to plan two sets of menus to cater to the food preferences of the *Brahmins* and the merchants. The two groups worked together but rarely ate together. The *Brahmins* preferred vegetables lightly steamed or boiled and never ate food cooked outside their own homes. The businessmen relished rich foods and ate heartily.

Two long tables were set on either side of the hall – one for the *Brahmin* scholars and the other for the businessmen. Fresh green banana leaves cut from the narrow end served as triangular plates and were laid out on both tables. *Brahmin* cooks from the palace kitchen served the scholars.

Ove was allocated a seat at the merchants' table, as their menu offered a wider choice. Amba hoped Ove and his friends would enjoy the culinary experience of Tanjore.

Amba sat next to Ove and explained the ingredients in every dish and how they were cooked. *Payasam*, the rice porridge, was cooked in coconut milk sweetened with thick jaggery syrup. Steamed rice *idlis* and fried lentil *vadas* were served with coconut chutney. Dumplings stuffed with coconut and *jaggery* were also served. Amba demonstrated how to use your fingers to create tiny bites of the *idli* and dip it in the chutney before eating it. The visitors struggled to eat with their fingers; the crumbs slipping through their fingers. Eventually they relaxed and ate in the comforting silence of good food.

Ove smiled, stretching his thumb and forefinger to mimic her humble gesture.

'Your Portuguese is fluent, not *"un pauco"*.'

Amba felt her cheeks glow with the memory of that encounter. 'Ah, you recognise me from the jeweller's store?'

'How could I forget a beautiful lady like you? I did not realise you were a member of the Council of Ministers. It is rare to see a woman achieve your status in our country.'

For all their talk of light meals, the *Brahmins'* belches were loud and clear – signalling the end of the meal.

I hope the discussions and debates show our collective wisdom and do not expose our cracks, thought Amba as they walked back to the Nandi Hall. The scholars' egos knew no bounds. The merchants believed they had all the answers to the king's questions. They could never understand why the king approached the scholars, who could debate endlessly without offering solutions.

For all their inflated egos, no member of either group could converse in Portuguese. No wonder the king relied on her to interpret the intent behind the foreigners' words.

Back in the hall, once everyone was seated, the senior scholar, Narayana Dikshita, outlined the code of ethics and rule of law followed in Tanjore.

'Every rule of law has a purpose. People obey when they understand the advantage it offers to every citizen who upholds the law. Our laws are designed to protect everyone in our kingdom.'

It was idealistic theory. *Not true*, thought Amba. Customs and traditions bent the law when it came to *Brahmins* and their privileges.

Although the court interpreter translated the Tamil words into

Portuguese for the visitors, Amba made sure that Ove understood the meaning of the words and kept her thoughts securely locked in her head. At times when Narayana Dikshita launched into a monologue of jumbled words, she paused and let the verbal onslaught subside.

Ayya moved the conversation to the next person. No one could read her thoughts the way Ayya did.

Merchant Ranganna spoke next. 'We collect tax from producers of goods after they pay wages to their labourers. Taxes are like fruit. We collect them when they are ripe and ready. Collecting tax from hungry stomachs will lead to rebellion.'

Ranganna smiled at the interpreter as he continued. 'Tax collected in our kingdom does not hide in the coffers of the king. This beautiful palace, with its carved pillars, is built from the tax collected. Architects, builders, artists and sculptors swarm to Tanjore, as it offers an environment where they can express their creativity and live with pride and dignity. I hope you understand why Tanjore is the envy of everyone who visits us.'

The next merchant raised trade-related questions.

How were the Danish planning to conduct trade with Tanjore? What were they planning to bring to Tanjore, and what did they want to export? Did they plan to hire local labour? What currency would he use? Would it be local Tanjore currency, or did they want to use Portuguese currency or mint their own silver?

Ove's reply was courteous. 'Sir, you have raised many important issues that need careful planning. Please allow me some time. I would like to understand the culture, customs and lifestyles of the local people first. I see no value in pushing goods that are of little use to the locals.'

After the meeting concluded, Amba walked with Ove to his carriage.

Amba said, 'I would like to know more about your country, culture and the flowers that grow in your country. I am passionate about growing new varieties of flowers. You are welcome to my garden; maybe you can tell me if Danish flowers can grow here. We might import flowers from Denmark in exchange for our perfumes,' she said with a mischievous grin on her face.

Ove's smile reached his eyes. 'It would be my privilege to explain our life and culture to you.'

A few weeks later, when Amba came to the lotus pond with her palm leaves and stylus, a colourful bouquet of exotic flowers rested on the marble bench next to the pond. The transparent blue-green vase cast tiny rainbow strips on the white stone bench. She lifted the vase and inhaled the gentle perfume of the purple, yellow and pink flowers. The silky-smooth petals caressed her cheeks without making her nostrils itch. The inverted bell-shaped flowers had a compelling presence; they didn't rely on their scent to draw attention to their beauty.

A silk ribbon tied around the flowers held a tiny parchment neatly tucked into the stem of the unusual purple flower. Amba's heart raced as she unfurled the parchment. Disappointment clouded her face. She couldn't read the foreign words. There was no point in being able to translate the spoken word without the ability to read the language. She must ask the king to find her a foreign language tutor. Better still, she would get Ove to teach her to read and write both Portuguese and Danish.

She turned around at the unusual sound of boots against gravel.

A naughty smile danced on Ove's lips. 'Your gardener, Muthu, told me where to find you. What a beautiful, fragrant garden you have here,' said Ove, as he lifted his head up and inhaled the scent of jasmine.

His compliments left a woozy feeling in her chest. 'Thank you. Gardner Muthu helped me create this jasmine canopy. It took us two years to get it in shape and create a shady walkway to the lotus pond.'

Pointing to the bouquet, she said, 'These flowers are beautiful. Where are they from? What are they called?'

'They are tulips. They grow from bulbs. A Dutch missionary took tulip bulbs from Holland to Ceylon. Now their monastery in Colombo has a garden full of tulips.'

'We use seeds, seedlings and cuttings to propagate flowers,' Amba said. 'I have never heard about transporting bulbs across the seas. What a great idea! If these flowers are available in Ceylon, I'll get my supplier from Colombo to bring me some tulip bulbs.'

Ove's voice had a note of caution. 'Yes, bulbs are easy to transport. But tulips require a cold period before the flowers bloom. I am not sure if they can survive in Tanjore, as it is hot all year around.'

'How do they manage in Ceylon? It's hot there too. The Dutch Padre might know some tricks,' said Amba. 'Let's walk around the garden, and you can tell me about Denmark and what made you come on this long journey.'

'I can't talk about Denmark or my voyage without talking about our king.' Ove asked with a smile, 'May I call you by your name? Or should I say *rani*?'

Amba laughed. 'You may call me Amba. And what should I call you? Captain Ove Gjedde?'

'Call me by my name, Ove.'

They walked through a section of the garden and settled on a stone bench under a shady banyan tree. Amba clapped her hands, and her garden helper, Raju, came running with a bowl of red and yellow bananas.

Ove turned the red bananas around. 'I've never seen red bananas before.'

'We have ten different types of bananas here. I'll take you to our banana plantation another time. Let's go to Denmark now,' Amba said with a smile.

'Denmark is surrounded by the northern seas and gets cold in winter. That's' why we wear these thick boots. I can't walk without them, even in a hot place like Tanjore.'

Ove's boots came up to his ankles. Amba said, 'I would never be able to walk straight with something so heavy on my feet.'

Ove chuckled. 'You'd change your mind if you visited cold Denmark.

Amba said, 'I don't see that happening. Please paint me a picture of Denmark.'

Ove said, 'Our King Christian IV has been ruling Denmark and Norway for forty years. He became the king when he was nineteen, but he was ambitious and had the energy and vision to make Denmark the most modern country in Europe. He became popular, and Denmark became wealthy. Like your King Raghu, he too loves architecture. We have many beautiful palaces and forts in Demark.'

Amba exclaimed, 'Forty years, and nobody overthrew him? Why do you add a number after his name? Do all your kings have the same name, and you add numbers to differentiate them?'

Ove threw his head back and laughed. 'I never thought of it that way. Don't you folks repeat the names of kings in Tanjore?'

'Everyone in Tanjore, including kings and queens, has the name of some god or goddess. We have hundreds of them. We don't attach numbers to the names of kings. We attach the names of their ances-try––like Nayaka.'

A thoughtful expression clouded his eyes. 'Over the last few years Denmark's wealth has dwindled in wasted wars.' Ove's sigh was loud and sad. 'King Christian's fame and fortune have become his enemies.'

'That's the problem with most kings, isn't it?' Amba said as they walked along. 'The moment the country is stable, and people are happy, the kings start getting itchy feet and long for the neighbour's kingdom.'

The distant dome of the Big Shiva Temple was visible from this section of the garden.

Pointing to the temple, Ove asked, 'That's a huge ornate cupola on the temple. I have never seen such intricate carvings. Did King Raghu's ancestors build that temple?'

'No. The temple was built by a famous Chola King, Raja Raja Chola, about five hundred years ago. But the huge Nandi--the mythical bull sculpture outside the temple--was installed by the current king's grandfather. The Nandi has become the national emblem of the Nayakas. You would have seen flags and banners all around Tanjore carrying the image of the bull.'

'We don't have a monument like this in Denmark. Although, the walls around the temple remind me of the walls around our Kronberg fort.'

Amba shielded her eyes against the sharp rays of the evening sun. 'Did your current king build that fort? Is it a palace, or is it for military purposes?'

'The Kronberg fort was built two hundred years ago by the king's ancestors. Our current king was clever enough to use the location of the fort to stop the ships that crossed the Oresund Strait and collect levies from all ships that cross our border to enter the Baltic Sea. Though it has made our kingdom wealthy, it has also earned us many enemies.'

Did King Raghu collect levies from the Portuguese and other foreign ships that came to our shores? She would ask Ayya.

'Indeed, fame and fortune attract both enemies and friends. Who are Denmark's friends? Surely not the Portuguese?' Amba asked with a grin.

'Not the Portuguese, but the Dutch are,' said Ove. 'A couple of smooth-talking Dutch merchants, who are brothers, visited Denmark and influenced our king to fund this voyage. They had returned from Ceylon and the East Indies loaded with gold, silks and spices. They convinced our king that there was plenty of wealth to be made in the Southern Peninsula and guided us in return for a share of the profits.'

'What happened when you reached Ceylon? How come the Dutch friends were not there to protect you from the Portuguese assault?' asked Amba.

'That's a long story.' Ove resumed after a few minutes. 'The Dutch were friendly with the King of Kandy in Ceylon and therefore had control over the seas around the southern part of Ceylon. As we approached the south-eastern peninsula, we were buffeted by huge storms and reached the northern part of Ceylon, around Jaffna, completely unaware that the Portuguese were in control in that part of Ceylon.'

Her knowledge of Ceylon was based on information trickling in from Jaffna labourers and seed suppliers. Occasionally, King Raghu would refer to his childhood friend, King Changili of Jaffna, who was thrown out of his own kingdom by the Portuguese.

Amba's mind was in turmoil. Her hand twisted the corner of her as they walked in silence. Storms created by nature subside, but storms created by human greed have no end.

Amba's sigh was louder than she intended. 'The Portuguese and the Dutch are both trying to control different parts of Ceylon. What do the Danish want? Trade or war?' asked Amba.

Ove's smile turned into a frown, and Amba bit her lip. Such talk was not the way to develop a new friendship. Amba guided Ove towards the coconut grove. 'It's getting hot. Let's get some water.'

Muthu must have seen them from a distance. He came running to greet them. 'Amba Ma, would you and your visitor like some fresh coconut water?' He had his sickle and harness ready.

Muthu deftly tied a jute rope around his hips and used the free end to circumnavigate the coconut tree trunk. He looped the rope back to his waist, tightened it with a knot, and tucked in his sickle. With the speed of a squirrel, he reached the coconut cluster at the top of the tree and firmly lodged his spidery feet on the trunk. He released both his hands as he removed the sickle from his rope belt.

Amba took Ove's elbow and nudged him out of away. 'Move over; we don't want the coconut to fall on our heads.'

Ove's mouth flew open. 'He climbed the tree in the blink of an eye!'

Muthu yelled from up the tree. 'Amba Ma, I know you like a tender coconut with lots of water. And for your foreign friend, I'll find one that has a bit of soft flesh.'

Before she could answer, a large green coconut came down with a thud a few steps away from where they stood.

Muthu called down from his perch. 'That's for you. And this slightly smaller one is for your friend. This pulp will be sweet.'

One look at a coconut, and Muthu knew its taste. With the rope harness around his waist, he took a few long strides down the trunk. He removed the harness and picked up a green coconut. Using the curved end of his sickle, he shaved the stem end, pierced a small hole and handed it to Ove.

Ove's blue eyes gleamed as he turned the green coconut around, which looked small in his large hands. He took the coconut to his lips and slurped it all in one gulp. Muthu took the empty shell from him and, with a couple of deft chops, slit the coconut right in the middle.

He cut out a flat piece from the outer fibre for Ove to scoop out the soft pulp.

Amba took her time with her drink. 'Tell me more about the Kronberg fort and how it helps to monitor the ships passing through the seas around Denmark. How big is that fort? How many years did it take to build?'

Ove waited for Amba to finish her drink, thanked Muthu with a *namaste* and gently steered Amba back towards the lotus pond.

As they reached the pond, Ove asked, 'Do you like the idea of a fort?' Then that's what we should do. Build a fort! Both our kings love grand structures.'

He added in a softer voice, 'I was an architect in Denmark before I set out on this voyage.'

His blue eyes were brilliant, and his enthusiasm was contagious. He had given voice to her thoughts, and her thoughts had shaped a fort standing on the waves. A Ganesha temple stood right next to the fort, guarding it against all obstacles.

'What a wonderful idea,' Amba exclaimed. 'King Raghu once mentioned that his grandfather believed that sculptures, temples, palaces and forts had much longer lives than humans and would remain to tell the story of the kings who built them.'

Ove said, 'The fort might remember Ove and Amba as people with a big vision.' Ove's smile was beautiful to watch.

Amba hastily averted her eyes. 'How long will it take to build a fort?'

'Assuming we have access to undisputed land and labour, it will take two to three years,' he said.

'The fort should be used as a vantage point for trade and not war.' Her voice turned sharp. 'Can you convince your king about that?'

Ove fell silent.

Amba said, 'If we want to translate this dream into reality, we must convince Prime Minister Ayya about the long-term benefits of this fort. If Ayya is convinced, the king will allot the land. Then you should convince your king about the benefits of building a fort here.'

'Yes,' answered Ove, 'this fort can be an architectural seal of a historic trading partnership between King Raghu and King Christian IV.' After a pause, he said, 'A symbol of deep friendship.'

This time when he held her gaze Amba had no wish to turn away.

CHAPTER 15

MAYA
2013

I stuck my nose to the aircraft window until the Indian Ocean hugging Chennai turned into a distant blip. I settled into my seat and connected my new headphones to the world music channel on the tiny monitor in front of me.

My eyes clouded when I thought about the scene at the airport.

'Here's your escape from sport sounds,' Preeti said as she presented me with a noise-cancelling headset.

Viji Ma planted a gentle kiss on my forehead. 'Be happy,' she said, more in prayer than instruction.

Happiness in marriage was like my name: Maya—an illusion, a social construct sanctified by society. My music teacher once said the Sanskrit word Maya had another connotation: invisible *shakti*, inner strength, potential energy coiled up to propel action. I had to discover that source of my inner strength; it had to come from within. Deepak was not that source.

The sound of a deep wind instrument floated through my head-phones; it was the didgeridoo. Gusts of air coaxed a distant orchestra to follow its lead. Strangely, the music reminded me of Krishna's flute cajoling the *gopis* to dance to his tune.

The ethereal music up in the sky was effortlessly spanning cultures and continents; the ancient and modern. But me? I had confined my music to the world I had left behind.

I pressed my headphones closer over my ears. I had heard the didgeridoo once when Deepak and I were strolling along the wharf at Circular Quay during my first month in Sydney when I still had my tourist hat on. Apart from that, I had barely listened to Australian sounds other than those noisy cockatoos outside our home. The music stirred a deep emotion I had never experienced before.

I read the title of the song on the tiny screen glued to the seat in front of me: William Barton, 'Earth Cry', with Queensland Symphony orchestra.

Waves of melody and harmony caressed my bruised heart. I closed my eyes.

The steward came in with tea and a chocolate brownie, my favourite Australian snack. Being a foodie, pasta, nachos, and noodles had made their way into my kitchen. Sometimes, I followed a recipe to the end, but often, I threw in other flavours and created fusion food. Deepak loved my culinary creations. Food had become my medium to reach his heart.

Having yoked my happiness to Deepak's approval somewhere along the way, I had lost the capacity to open my ears, something I did effortlessly when I was in Chennai, in my comfort zone. I had to train my ears to listen to new sounds, the way I had trained my taste buds. This was the way to bridge my two worlds and not feel dejected by Deepak's rejection of my music. The language of music was universal, not constrained by culture or genre. Suddenly I felt light as if a bird had escaped from the cage of my heart.

I opened my iPad and browsed the two files the Tanjore professor had sent me; a newspaper article on 'King Raghu Nayaka and his Music', published by Madras University Press, and a journal paper on 'Indo-Danish Trade Pact of 1620', published by the Department of Cross-Cultural Studies at the University of Copenhagen.

I landed in Sydney, brimming with a new energy injected by Amba's story and Barton's music.

The moment Deepak saw me at the arrival gate, he rushed forward and folded me into his arms. His body turned taut with desire. He had missed me! I allowed my head to rest on his chest, filling my lungs with his aftershave-infused scent. We kissed deeply and passionately.

I took the next day off from work to get over the jet lag. For dinner, I cooked a rice and yellow lentil *pongal,* spiced with cumin and pepper, smoked eggplant and tomato chutney that Deepak loved, and *raita* with grated carrot. I set out the new placemats and matching cotton serviettes I had bought at the handicraft emporium in Chennai. I brought out the silver plates and matching tumblers, the family heirloom that Viji Ma had given me. The fragrant candles on the sideboard added the ambience I was after.

Deepak walked in, and his eyes scanned the room. 'Like me, the house missed you. Your presence has brought the sparkle back.'

I reached up and touched his stubble. 'I missed you too, especially in Tranquebar, where different worlds came together. Did you see the picture of that fort?'

'A picture postcard, right out of Denmark.' And then he laughed. 'You are not going to believe this. I, too, have a slice of

Denmark here in Sydney. We have a Danish software vendor, trying to sell us a new cyber security software.'

Deepak had a wash, and we sat down for dinner. He said, 'It smells like Chennai. What have you cooked?'

'*Pongal* and eggplant chutney. Viji Ma gave me these silver plates. They belonged to my grandfather, and I thought I would cook a special Tamil dish to honour him.'

It was a leisurely dinner that night. When Deepak reached for the TV remote, he paused. 'Do you want to watch anything on Netflix?'

'No, you go ahead.' I held up my new headphones. 'I'll listen to some music while I clean up. I found some amazing new music.'

'No worries.'

He surfed a few sports channels, but not for long. Then he came back to the kitchen, hugged my waist, and kissed the back of my neck, and that was the end of cleaning for the day.

The aroma of spices wafting out of the Indian store on Harris Street made me feel I was back in Chennai. I walked through the narrow aisles, stacked my basket with green and yellow lentils, *paneer*, frozen *chapatis*, cumin, coriander, a packet of *garam masala* and arrived at the checkout area. Photos of well-known Carnatic musicians smiled from the cover page of the Indian tabloid stacked on the counter. Tickets were on sale for the three-day Sydney Carnatic Music Festival to be held at Parramatta Riverside Theatre. The program was like a miniature version of the Chennai Music Festival. Four concerts per day during the Queen's Birthday long weekend. Pure heaven.

Despite being a frequent visitor to this Indian grocery store, I had never noticed this magazine before. *Goes to show what a muted mind can do. Blind you.*

That evening, after dinner, Deepak was sitting next to me on the couch, surfing through Netflix. I flicked through the pages of the Indian magazine I had picked up.

'I never knew there were so many Indian events happening in Sydney,' I said.

Deepak clicked his tongue. 'I don't read these local rags.'

'There's a Carnatic festival during the long weekend in June at the Riverside Theatre. I want to go; they have music and dance concerts by accomplished artists visiting from Chennai. It'll be a fun three days, there'll be good food too. Do you want to come along?'

'I thought you would have had your fill of music in Chennai.'

My throat tightened. *Maya. Stand up.*

'Are you able to stop watching sports after you have watched one game? Music is no different. I can never have enough.'

'I'd go with you if you went to an Australian music concert,' Deepak said.

'That will happen soon. I'm happy to go as long as the music is melodic and not a cacophony of overproduced sounds. I listened to this amazing didgeridoo concert with the Queensland Symphony on the flight home. That's the type of music I want to listen to.'

'Discerning, are we?'

'I'm a trained musician, remember?'

The afternoon sun cast a warm glow over the deck. Deepak had gone out for a barbecue with his workmates. A free Saturday to stretch out and dig into Tanjore history. The professor had sent me a PhD thesis on 'Women Scholars in the Tanjore Kingdom'. Not surprisingly, it was the work of another woman scholar from Hyderabad.

I browsed through the abstract. The author mentioned that

Sanskrit anthologies had compiled short works by female poets, but full-length texts by women were rare. The few remaining were written by princesses or courtesans. The largest full-length Sanskrit work that had survived was by a female scholar named Ramabhadra Amba and a translated work by poet Madhura Vani. Both Amba and Vani had lived in Tanjore during King Raghu Nayaka's time.

My phone rang out the '*Kalyani*' *raga* played on the *veena*. When I was in Chennai, I had downloaded a whole set of ringtones based on Carnatic *ragas* and set different *ragas* for different people in my contacts.

That was Viji Ma. 'How are you? How's Deepak?'

'Deepak's fine. I'm fine; I needed that break. Let me call you on Facetime.'

Viji Ma's wide smile covered the screen. 'That's good to hear. I was a bit worried when you were here.'

'That's why I called you on Facetime; you can see my smile. How's your Nayaka article coming along? Are they telling you their story, or are you telling theirs?'

Viji Ma's laughter sounded like tiny bells tinkling during an *aarti*.

'That's a clever question. I know what I want to write, but I don't know what the Tanjore Nayaka's want me to write about them.'

I said, 'What about their patronage of music and arts?' Amba and Vani seemed to be nudging me. 'What's the one thing that is unique about the Tanjore Nayakas that made them different from the Nayakas of other regions, like Madurai and Gingee?'

'The Tanjore Nayakas rule was like a smooth relay race. Even when the first Nayaka King Sevvappa was alive, he passed on the baton to his son Achuta. Then Achuta passed the reins to his son,

Raghu Nayaka. There was a brief period when three generations of Nayakas were alive, when Raghu Nayaka was crowned as the king. Theirs was a rare dynasty where wisdom and power were handed over by the ruling king to the next in line. It was a proactive transition.'

I said, 'That's unique. Did they have one son each? Was there no competition among the heirs? How did that happen?'

Viji Ma pursed her lips, a habit she had when forced to think. 'I think it was due to their brilliant minister. Remember we talked about Govinda Ayya? He had a long life and served as Prime Minister for three generations of Nayakas.'

'Who would you rate as the best among the Tanjore Nayakas?'

Viji Ma grinned. 'I know where you are leading. Your guess is right. It was Raghu, the third Nayaka king. His period is considered the golden age of Tanjore.'

I waved my iPad.

'Tanjore's history is scattered across the strangest surfaces. Stone inscriptions, gold foil, palm leaves, and now this iPad.'

Viji Ma said, '*Sabhash*. At this rate, you will know more about the Nayakas than me. You can help me with my article.'

'Viji Ma, what you write will be perfect for Tamil readers. I might write some blogs for fun if this Amba character has interesting stories to tell. We'll talk about it again, but I have to go now. I cook for the entire week on Saturdays.'

'What are you going to cook?'

'I'll make a couple of vegetable curries and a whole green lentil *dal*. Do you have a quick recipe for a veggie *korma*?'

Viji Ma said, 'First, steam whatever vegetables you have. Then grind fresh coconut, green chillies, ginger, cumin, and aniseed into a paste and add it to the steamed vegetables. Don't forget to add salt.'

'Grinding fresh coconut is too much work. What about coconut milk instead?'

Viji Ma lowered her glasses on her nose.

'I'll tell you how it comes out with coconut milk.' I grinned mischievously and blew her a kiss. 'Talk later.'

CHAPTER 16

AMBA

Tanjore, 1623

The fragrance of sandalwood incense greeted Amba as she set her right foot forward and entered Ayya's porch. This was an auspicious moment for her. It was a privilege to be invited into the home of Prime Minister Ayya and his wife Nagamma. Peaceful vibrations of Ayya's morning *puja* permeated the air.

Last time when she met her mother, Amba had casually remarked that she was planning to visit Ayya. Paru Ma was beside herself with excitement.

'Amba, an invitation to Ayya's house is a rare honour. Everyone knows Ayya is a great musician and a scholar. But did you know his wife Nagamma is also as good a scholar as Ayya? She has composed several songs in Sanskrit, Telugu and Tamil. Nagamma's father was a great scholar, and he trained his daughter to be one too. We don't hear about scholars like her. Thank God, Ayya treats her like the precious gem she is.'

It was obvious Paru Ma admired Nagamma, but did she envy her as well?

Amba had expected Ayya's house to be like her guru's house in the *Brahmin* quarter, but this was a huge mansion with ornate teak doors and pillars. As she stepped onto the front veranda, Amba could see layers of pillars and doors, each living area leading to another, and halls within halls. *This was like the temple courtyard, big enough to play hide-and-seek*, thought Amba.

A young girl welcomed Amba and led her to the central hall. Three gem-studded paintings of Parvati, the Goddess of Energy, Saraswati, the Goddess of Knowledge, and Lakshmi, the Goddess of Prosperity, occupied an entire wall.

As Ayya entered the hall, Amba touched his feet and received his blessings.

She pointed to the wall. 'I am surprised their male counterparts with their assertive influence are not accompanying the female goddesses.'

Ayya's eyes twinkled. 'Males by themselves are inert; it's the female energy that moves the world.'

Ayya's grin turned into a broad smile when his wife emerged. 'Nagamma knows how and when to channel that energy.'

Their love was beautiful to watch. *I would never have thought that Ayya was romantic.* Amba bowed, touched Nagamma's feet, and handed her a large tray of bananas, coconuts and flowers from her garden.

Nagamma led her to the breakfast hall. In traditional homes, men were served first, and the women ate later. But here, Nagamma insisted that Amba sit with Ayya and have her breakfast.

Nagamma laid out fresh green banana leaf on which she first served smooth, silky *appams* made with coconut milk. The next dish was steaming rice dumplings, soft like the petals of jasmine, with coconut chutney and, finally, hot and crisp lentil *vadas*. Amba's heart melted under the warmth of Nagamma's love as she served the dishes one by one. *Nagamma must love cooking and the people she cooks for*, thought Amba.

'We have four sons and no daughter,' Nagamma said, serving one more *vada* on Amba's banana leaf.

Ayya spoke to his wife, eyes tender with love. 'Nagamma, did Venkata tell you that our king has been playing Amba's multi-lingual compositions during the morning prayers? Amba's new way of weaving Tamil and Sanskrit words into a composition has challenged King Raghu. He says his *veena* is inadequate to capture the hidden emotions and wants to modify the *veena*, adding a few more frets to capture the nuances in her ragas.'

The hostess turned to her abashed guest and said, 'Now that you are not singing at the temple, we don't get to hear your new music anymore.'

Amba said, 'This house is a temple, a temple of knowledge. I will sing for you another day.'

Ayya came to her rescue. 'I have invited Amba to our house to talk about some confidential court matters. The palace walls have too many ears and eyes.'

Acknowledging her husband's wishes, Nagamma shared a knowing smile with Amba before she left their company to continue about her day.

Ayya led her to the music room. Two *veenas*, a *tanpura*—the long drone that set the pitch—and bundles of palm leaf documents were arranged on shelves all along the wall. As soon as they settled on cushioned seats, Ayya did not waste any time.

'I hear you have been meeting the Danish captain. What have you learnt about him?'

Amba said, 'Captain Ove has been respectful and polite. I wanted to assess if the Danish could be good friends, unlike the plotting Portuguese.'

'Amba, you might find that Captain Ove is a good man, but that does not mean that the Danish king will have no territorial interest.'

'Ayya, I confess I do not have your wisdom. I want to make sure that their motive is trade and not war. Captain Ove mentioned that, like our king, their king too was fond of constructing grand palaces and forts...' Her voice faded as she held her thoughts.

'Yes?' Ayya dragged her thoughts out.

She was hesitant at first, but soon her voice rose with excitement.

'Captain Ove mentioned that the Danish king's ancestors had built a fort, and now they use the structure to monitor ships that cross their waters and collect levies for their passage. We don't monitor our ports. If we get them to build a fort right near the sea, we can collect levies from all the foreign ships that come to our region. At the moment, we don't hear about the foreign ships before they dock in our ports.'

'Um,' Ayya's voice was thoughtful. 'We turn their attention towards building a fort rather than building an army. We'll have to think about this.'

Ayya was a busy person, and Amba did not want to overstay her welcome.

As she was about to leave, Ayya said, 'Let the king feel the full force of your new compositions.' He added with a grin, 'Let him fret over the missing frets.'

Amba skipped down the steps into the waiting palanquin.

Six full moons later, Amba met the king in their usual chamber at the music palace. She had composed a new lyrical piece in Sanskrit that compared King Raghu to God Krishna and his women.

It was one Krishna who danced around,

His magic flute spread love around.

When King Raghu rode around

Women swooned all around.

A single glance is all it took

For him to sprinkle charm around.

She had based it on a traditional *raga* but had added a variation by raising the seventh note by half to highlight the king's courage.

The king was pleased with the lyrics and the melody, but his calloused fingers could not render this variation using the available frets in his veena.

'I wish I had a few more frets on the *veena* to capture those tiny nuances,' the king complained.

The king's personal *veena* had sixteen frets on the long fingerboard and could play two octaves, but the half-note was a challenge.

'If you added a few more frets, you could capture the highs and lows of the main notes,' suggested Amba.

'That's a brilliant idea, my darling Amba. Eight more frets would capture all the combinations we want. I'll talk to my *veena* maker.'

As he played the song, the king added two additional notes of a victory march to the composition, which allowed him to glide through the new variation she had introduced.

Together, they came up with a new name for the *raga*: '*Jayanta Sena* – Victorious Army'.

King Raghu had returned victorious after another skirmish with the Bijapur Sultans. They were trying to wrench power from the dying Vijayanagar Empire, who had sought his help. King Raghu could never refuse a plea for help from Vijayanagar; his grandmother belonged to the Vijayanagar royal family.

The victory was narrow. Hundreds of soldiers were killed on both sides, and the king knew it was a wasted effort to save the Vijayanagar empire.

The king's face sagged with sadness. 'The current Vijayanagar king has neither wit nor wisdom, and none of the valour of his grandfather, Emperor Krishnadeva Raya. It's a matter of time before the hungry sultans gobble up his kingdom.'

The king placed the *veena* on the silk mat, entwined the fingers of both hands and stretched out his elbows. His shoulders sagged, and his eyes lacked their usual lustre. Amba took the king's fingers in both her hands and massaged them one by one.

The king's voice was weary. 'The Gingee Nayaka have teamed up with the foreigners. They have learnt nothing from the events in Ceylon. Those kings lost their territories due to their short-sighted alliance with the Portuguese.'

The king's shoulder joints crackled as he stretched his hands over his head. He said, 'The Gingee soldiers, who fought alongside the sultans, had Portuguese weapons. Our soldiers are not trained to deal with foreign artillery. Fortunately, their soldiers could not stand up to our elephant battalion. That worked to our advantage, but we had too many casualties.'

The king's eyes were bleak with the weariness of war. His voice was barely audible. 'Our traditional weapons are no longer adequate.'

Amba asked, 'How did the Gingee Nayaka get Portuguese weapons?'

'Our informers tell us that gangster Thimma, who roams around with Portuguese soldiers, is now the right-hand man of the Governor of Gingee. Thimma has convinced the governor to employ Portuguese soldiers to train the locals in using muskets and firearms.

Now they have plenty of those weapons as their craftsmen have copied the firearm blueprints.'

Amba broke into a sweat. She clenched her fists to stop the tremor threatening to engulf her whole body. But for Selvi appearing out of nowhere, Amba would have been raped by a Portuguese soldier. Had the king heard about her escapade with Thimma, he may never have invited her into his life.

Amba lowered her eyes and massaged the king's hands. He leaned forward and planted a kiss on her forehead, his eyes tender with love.

How could she not confide in him? She stroked his face and spoke in a soft voice.

'I have a story to tell you, but not now when you are exhausted.'

Amba picked up a *Champa* flower from the ground and tucked it behind her ear as she walked to the lotus pond. The slanting rays of the evening sun formed a halo around the yellow *Champa* flowers, which were in full bloom. This was the season when the lime-green leaves of the tree hid behind the flowers. She stood there for a moment, filling her nostrils with the cool, fragrant breeze.

'*Ola*, Amba. If I were an artist, I will paint your profile with your chin up reaching for the sky. What perfume is that?'

She turned around at the familiar voice. 'It's from the *Champa*.' She tilted her head and showed Captain Ove the yellow flower lodged in her hair. 'Local perfumers extract the fragrant oil at this time of year. Have you walked along the narrow streets around the temple? You will see perfume vendors selling tiny silver vials of *Champa* oil.'

Ove picked up a flower from the ground and crushed it between his fingers.

'I'll buy perfume oils when I go back to Denmark.'

'As a present for your sweetheart?' Amba asked with a smile.

'Will I be here, so far from home, if I had someone pining for me?' Ove flicked a little pebble with his shoe.

They walked in silence under the jasmine canopy until they reached a spot in the garden where the temple dome loomed large, covering the horizon.

'Have you thought about the fort?' asked Amba, raising her chin to meet his eyes. Ove's hand gently flicked a tiny insect that hovered around her left ear. A tremor ran through her body at the feathery touch of his hand brushing over her cheek. Did anyone notice them together? Amba had given strict instructions to gardener Muthu not to let anyone enter her garden when Ove was around.

'I have thought of nothing else,' answered Ove.

'What do you mean?' She felt her cheeks turning hot. Her left palm crushed the free end of the *sari*.

'I mean the fort,' he said with a naughty smile. 'We need to be clear about the purpose of the fort. Prime Minister Ayya has asked me to meet him next week. Perhaps he has some ideas.'

'Ayya will be open to the construction of a fort if it is going to help with trade. The fort might be used as a warehouse for loading and unloading cargo from ships.'

They continued along a dirt path and reached the mango grove.

Amba said, 'It should have a lighthouse, like the Danish fort you talked about. To spot ships crossing the waters, but not as a garrison for artillery.'

Ove picked up a twig, went down on one knee and rapidly sketched an outline of a sprawling building on the mud. With just a few strokes, he sketched a tall lighthouse in one corner and a three-dimensional outline of a two-storey structure by piling up dirt and leaves around the corners.

Kneeling on one knee, he asked, 'What do you think?'

Amba bent down, her head close to his and moved a few stones to extend the central courtyard. His face smelt of a strange spice she could not place. She could see the reflection of her face in his blue eyes as they talked and sketched.

Finally, Ove dusted his hands and stood up. He took her hand and hoisted her into a standing position. Palms interlocked, they stood together staring down at the sketch, acutely aware of each other's touch. Her skin tingled with pleasure under his warm hand. For a moment, she forgot where she was. Reluctantly, she extricated her hand, shaking her head at the futility of the emotion.

Amba scrubbed her body with sandalwood paste and immersed herself into the rose-water bath her maid Kamala, had set up. Amba could never tell if Kamala kept track of the king's schedule with his women, or if the ubiquitous maids network knew where the king would stop for the night. The silk bedspread was sprinkled with rose petals and velvet cushions and bolsters were laid out along the low square bed. Kamala had placed wide shallow bowls of water sprinkled with rose petals at the foot of the frame. An ivory-carved tray held a bowl of grapes and a silver jug of warm saffron milk.

Amba moved the baskets of magnolia barks and sandalwood shavings from her writing room to the carved pillars of the arched doorway. The woody aroma atop the entrance would help the king relax as soon as he stepped inside. There was no place in her life to entertain those *Champa*-infused thoughts. Best to leave that experience behind in the garden, where it belonged.

Amba covered her breasts with layers of pearls and fastened a broad filigree gold belt around her waist. The transparent yellow robe covered her body without hiding the curves of her hips and breasts. The king would remove her jewellery, piece by piece, during the course of the night.

She swallowed the castor seed kernels and myrrh from the little silk pouch she kept under her bed. Her mother Paru Ma had hidden the pouch in the folds of a *sari* and given it to Amba when she moved to the palace. 'Myrrh and castor seeds, pleasure without the burden,' Paru Ma had whispered.

Amba had not understood then, but now she did. A courtesan's child had no place in the conservative Tanjore society.

Amba felt as light as a leaf floating in the breeze when the king walked in. His bodyguard politely stepped back and closed the door behind him. The king's shoulders visibly relaxed as he breathed a loud sigh of relief, blowing out air from his puffed cheeks. Amba took his hands and led him to the bed.

Neither of them needed words as their bodies entwined.

Finally, the king rested his back against the cushions and stretched out his legs. Amba massaged his feet gently at first, and then more firmly, until he groaned with pleasure.

Amba said, 'I heard women threw themselves over you during your victory march after the Vijayanagar battle.'

The king's belly went up and down as he laughed. 'They were hanging from the balconies of the main street, showering flowers on us and singing victory songs. One woman threw her perfumed silk scarf, and it landed on my face. I threw her a string of pearls in return.'

'Your procession with your troops must have given the women the confidence to show themselves. Women rarely step outside their homes these days.'

Amba waited for her words to sink in. No response. She tried again.

'Raja Nayaka, women have stopped going out in the evenings to buy their trinkets at the night markets.' She repeated. 'The night markets close early these days, because women don't dare to come out.'

A deep frown appeared between his eyebrows. 'Are you telling me that women don't feel safe to come out? In Tanjore?'

The king's tone was sharp. Was he annoyed with her or the situation in his kingdom?

'Yes,' Amba said. After a pause she said, 'I too had a narrow escape once.'

Thimma's evil grin and the foul Portuguese soldier's breath gagged her even now. Her hand reached up to the scar behind her ears.

The king's back straightened as if a spring attached to his head hoisted him up. His nostrils flared like a pair of bellows puffing out smoke.

Amba wished she could put her words back in her mouth. What had she done?

Amba caressed the king's arm in an effort to relax him. In a soothing voice, she said, 'Raja Nayaka, this was long before I came into your life.'

Amba leaned against the king, planted a kiss on his hairy chest, and rested her head on his battle-scarred chest. Now that she had let out her secret, she narrated the nasty incident.

'When I used to sing at the Big Temple, a stranger invited me to sing at the Gingee Temple. I accepted his invitation, unaware of his real identity.'

The bitter bile in her mouth made her voice hoarse. 'That stranger was Thimma. He tried to abduct me, and I escaped in the nick of time.'

They stayed silent for a long time. When he finally spoke, the king's voice sounded heavy.

'Thimma once saved Queen Kalyani's father, the Nayaka of Gingee, from the sword of the Bahmani Sultan. So, Kalyani feels indebted to Thimma. That's the reason I have turned a blind eye to Thimma's antics.'

The king's body sank into her outstretched arm. His snores came out loud and soft, rhythmic and peaceful; nothing like the storm raging in Amba's mind.

He calls them Thimma's antics! Clearly, the king has washed his hands off this problem. Is it right to leave Tanjore women at the mercy of Thimma?

The shrill sound of the reed pipe shook her awake. The *nadaswaram* players were at the door, following an ancient tradition to wake the king at the same time the temple priests woke up God Vishnu, the preserver of life.

No point in being a preserver of lives like Thimma's. Tanjore needed a dynamic Shiva to destroy evil Thimma.

As he did on most days, the king had his ritualistic oil bath in the women's courtyard. Amba and a few other courtesans massaged his body with sandalwood oil, bathed him in rose-water, and applied sandalwood paste to cool his body. The second and third queens dressed him in silk robes, then covered his broad chest and arms with gold jewellery and bracelets embedded with pearls and rubies. Finally, Queen Kalyani, the first queen, handed him the royal sword. The king muttered a brief prayer before accepting the sword, to seek the blessings of Shakti, the Goddess of Strength and Power.

Back in her apartment, Amba draped a parrot-green *sari* with a thin gold border over herself in haste. She reached the music palace, Indira Mandira, and was ready with her composition by the time the king arrived.

Music was their language of love, she with her songs and he with his strings. Neither wanted to stop, but the king had his schedule. Ayya could not be kept waiting.

As they walked back to the palace holding hands, the dome of the big temple reminded her of Ove's sketch of the fort.

'Raja Nayaka, I have been working on my Portuguese vocabulary with the new Danish visitor. He likes to visit my garden. He says it reminds him of his own garden in Denmark. Captain Ove was an architect before he came on this voyage.'

The king asked, 'Has he seen our Big Temple? Do they have anything like this in their country?'

'They have tall churches, but nothing like our Big Temple sculptures. He talked about a big fort with a lighthouse built a hundred years ago. They use the lighthouse to monitor the movement of ships and collect taxes when they cross their waters.'

'Darling Amba, I had no idea your mind was wandering beyond music and into art, architecture and taxes.' He pecked a little kiss on her head. 'Ayya has some thoughts on establishing a trading post for the Danish. Come, join us for this meeting.'

'It's my honour, Raja Nayaka.'

CHAPTER 17

MAYA
Sydney, 2013

As I walked along the promenade in Homebush Bay, the lush dwarf palms in pine planter boxes reminded me of Amba's palm leaves scripts. I paused the music playing on my iPhone and called Professor Krishnamurthy.

'Professor, thank you for those articles about the Tanjore Nayakas.'

'Maya, my family has been connected with the Tanjore Saraswati Mahal library for generations.'

Professor Krishnamurthy was in a great mood to talk. 'My grand uncle, Professor Ayyangar, was a frequent visitor to the library in the 1900s. He discovered some palm leaf manuscripts tied up in a gunny bag, dumped in a corner storeroom of the ancient library.'

He cleared his throat, and his voice rose with excitement. 'Those palm leaf manuscripts wasn't even listed in the English catalogue of the library created in 1870.'

'How old were those manuscripts? Were they in good condition?'

'We restored some of them. But many had moth holes.' He continued with a chuckle. 'Your friend's manuscript was in that gunny bag along with others.'

I burst out laughing. 'So Amba's my friend, is she? Then, I need to get to know her better. What was her manuscript about?'

'Her Sanskrit manuscript was intact. My uncle Ayyangar and another colleague from Madras University translated that work to English.'

There was a long pause. I raised the volume on my phone.

'Professor! Was she a scholar, a musician, or even a queen? What did she write about?'

His answer was roundabout, typical of an academic. 'Her manuscript was a biography of King Raghu Nayaka. She must have known him intimately, even at the physical level.'

A discrete cough broke the awkward silence. I imagined the Professor's face turning red with embarrassment. He said, 'Hers was a rare contemporary biography. The translators found a long colophon at the end of her work. Ramabhadra Amba was a recipient of several distinguished titles. She was someone who could write a hundred verses a day, in eight languages. She was given the title Empress Among Poets.'

The Professor's voice carried a deep conviction. 'Historians have verified and validated the historical events described in great detail in Amba's biography of King Raghu Nayaka.'

'Professor, is there a way for me to read the translation of her manuscript?'

'Maya, I wish you were my student. Most of my students come

here to earn their degrees, solely to get a job. They lack your passion. Let me talk to the Sanskrit Pundit at the Saraswati Mahal Library; they must have the original English translation.'

A few days later, Professor K sent me the English translation of *Raghunathabhyudayam–The Life and Times of King Raghu Nayaka*. It was an epic Sanskrit poem that described King Raghu Nayaka's heroic military exploits, his personal habits and erotic scenarios with courtesans. Tale after tale, tales within a tale, the events of King Raghu Nayaka's life unfolded, narrated like stories in epics like *Ramayana* and *Mahabharata*.

Nine hundred verses were distributed across twelve cantos, starting with the history of Tanjore and King Raghu's ancestors. How many years did it take Amba to write on those narrow palm leaves, making sure that each verse fitted neatly onto one leaf?

To understand and unravel the work of Amba, I had to anchor my roots to my ancestry and understand the family's connection to Tanjore. Deepak's approach of blending into Australian society by discarding his roots might work for him. But for me, it was a mere mirage. There was no way I could follow Deepak into a lifeless bubble that tore me away from my story, my language, and my music.

Night after night, as I continued reading Amba's work, a cocktail of emotions washed through my mind: joy, admiration, awe. My music was anchored to Tanjore, to Amba's time and location. However remote Tanjore might be from Sydney, Amba and I were bound by the same *ragas* of Carnatic music.

The perfect prosody of Amba's Sanskrit verses rolled off the tongue in rhythmic phrases. For the first time, I realised the value of my Sanskrit language training. It equipped me with skills to disambiguate morphemes of compound words. Corresponding English words lacked the lyrical beauty of the original text. Thankfully, they still wove a colourful tapestry of historical characters, places and events that occurred during King Raghu Nayaka's rule.

Amba drew me into a world of palaces purpose-built for music and dance, scholars engaged in debates, and foreigners gaping at shimmering silks. Glittering gems flaunted by the royals and rich merchants of Tanjore sparkled in my mind. The precinct—*Agraharam*—echoed with the chanting of scared mantras. Songs and *ragas* played to the rhythm of drums *Gurukul* boys in their teachers' homes learnt art and music and debated philosophy and politics.

Every evening, I rushed back from work, gobbled my dinner and raced to my iPad. Deepak left me alone during this time, watching sport or working on his computer. I dropped into bed long after Deepak, exhausted or exhilarated. At times, I kissed Deepak awake until we made love.

In one section, Amba described King Raghu Nayaka as a male beauty like the God of Love, Manmatha, who was forever surrounded by beautiful women, making love to every one of them in a single night. If this was an established norm of that time, Tanjore would have been the city of erotic delights. Was Amba one of these lovelorn women, or was she a scholar left to pursue her work? What was her daily life like? Did the king keep his royal wives away from this all-night orgy?

If I believed Amba's manuscript, King Raghu Nayaka's life was exotic, erotic, sometimes violent but always artistic. The musical contributions of the king, his standardisation of the *veena* with twenty-four frets, and his creation of a new *raga, 'Jayanata sena'*, after his victory in a battle, were all documented in Carnatic music literature thanks to Amba.

The middle section of the biography dealt with supporting the Vijayanagar Kingdom as they fought wars with Europeans, who came in the name of trade but had territorial motives, or battles with sultans from the north. In addition, skirmishes with neighbours like the Gingee Nayaka and their allies was a constant threat. Because they were neighbours, their soldiers mingled with the locals, roaming the streets with Portuguese weapons, looting, and sticking the heads of murdered men on stakes.

I was fascinated by the section about Tarangambadi, leased to the King of Denmark, and a casual mention that the deed between King Raghu Nayaka of Tanjore and King Christian IV of Denmark was drawn up on a gold foil.

With such a hectic life, how did the king find time for music? I wondered what Amba had to say about that.

In later sections, the biography turned into an adoration as Amba wrote lyrical verses that compared King Raghu to the mythological King Rama, who destroyed his enemies and built a bridge across the ocean between India and Nepal. King Raghu helped the king of Nepala fight against the Portuguese. *Where was Nepala?*

It was no surprise that some scholars dubbed Amba's work a hagiography. They criticised her for elevating the king to the stature of mythological King Rama, who is still worshipped as a god.

The June long weekend was upon us. It was time for the three-day Sydney Carnatic Music Festival at Parramatta Riverside Theatre. The auditorium foyer was transformed into the Chennai Music Academy. Hundreds of Indian men and women in colourful *kurtas* and shiny silks smiled, laughed and greeted one another. The fragrance of sandalwood incense drew me to the service desk covered with a red silk *sari*. A bronze idol of Krishna at one end of the table served as a weight to hold the *sari* in place. The tickets sold out quickly, but luckily, I had booked my tickets online a month ago for all three days. With four concerts per day, I was in for a treat. I collected my tickets and scanned the foyer for a familiar face. There were around seven hundred people there, and yet I felt like an outsider among this confident bunch of people.

I wish Deepak had come. He probably knew some people here and may have been at school with a few. Deepak's mom, Neetu, had introduced me to her Indian friends. But like her, they all spoke Gujarati, which had nothing in common with my native tongue, Tamil. My facial muscles ached with the fake smile I had plastered on. There was a cacophony of Tamil, English and a unique mixture of the two, which many referred to as Thanglish. Yet I couldn't see a single familiar face.

'Hello, you look lost. I'm Meena, a volunteer. Is this your first time at the festival?' With silver strands of grey hair, stylishly cut, and draped in a maroon silk *sari* edged with a thin gold border, Meena was a picture of elegance. The shimmering string of pearls around her neck and matching dangling earrings lent a warm glow to her face.

That's how I would like to grow old, full of grace and confidence.

I said, 'Yes. I'm Maya, and I'm kind of new to Sydney. I used to live in Chennai before I got married and came here. Perchance, I stumbled upon the *Indian Link* paper at the grocery store. The cover page had photos of Carnatic musicians who were singing at this festival. So here I am.'

A couple of men walked past, complaining about the quality of coffee in Tamil. '*Nanna illai.*' Not at all good.

I burst out laughing. 'This is like being in Chennai. If you are a true Tamilian, you have to complain about the coffee.' Adjusting my *sari* pleats, I asked, 'How long have you lived in Sydney, Meena Aunty?'

'Do I look that old?' Meena raised her eyebrows in mock horror.

'No, no. It's my way of showing respect.'

'I could be your mother's age, I suppose. Here in Sydney, we call each other by our first name. That's the work culture; makes you ageless.'

Meena led me to a group of women in silk *saris* and *kurtas*.

'Hi folks, meet Maya. She's new around here.'

'Welcome, Maya. I'm Radha, and this is Shanti. We run the Sydney Music Circle for Carnatic music lovers.' I felt my shoulders relax under Radha's homely tone. She too was around my mother's age.

Shanti was younger than Meena and Radha, perhaps in her forties. She wore trendy black palazzo pants and a flowing *kurta*, which were all the rage in India. Her heavily mascaraed eyelashes blinked rapidly when she spoke.

'We have a managing committee that rotates every couple of years. We organise free concerts by local artists on the last Sunday of every month at the Ermington Community Centre. Overseas artists visit once a year, which is when we organise on a grand scale for three days at this venue.'

My sluggish soul felt a new shot of energy. 'It's wonderful to know there's a group in Sydney that's passionate about Carnatic music. I'm thrilled to meet you all. Relieved, really.' I let out a deep sigh.

'That's effusive. Are you a musician?' asked Meena.

'Do you sing or play an instrument?' asked Radha. 'We are forever on the lookout for new local talent to perform in our monthly concerts.' Radha's way of slanting her head when she spoke reminded me of Viji Ma.

I said, 'I sing and play the *veena*, but I'm a bit rusty. I've not been practising regularly since I came to Sydney.'

'Don't worry,' smiled Radha, 'we'll make you practice.'

Most people in the foyer were in their fifties and sixties. Perhaps they had migrated before the turn of the century like Deepak's parents.

I asked, 'Has your music circle been around for a long time?'

Meena said, 'Early migrants who missed their Carnatic music created this association in the eighties. I was new then and felt as lost as you must feel now, Maya.'

Shanti exclaimed, 'Meena, I can't imagine you ever feeling lost.' Turning to me, she said, 'Maya, don't let Meena fool you. She's a highly regarded scientist.'

Meena's eyes danced as she spoke. 'Believe me. I was totally out of place when we first migrated in 1989. I attended my first job inter-view wearing a *sari*, and, of course, I didn't get that job.'

My mouth flew open. 'What then?'

Meena said, 'A friendly female recruiter later told me that they rejected me because of my *sari* and not my skills and knowledge. That got me thinking. I went to GBs, bought myself a donkey grey skirt and jacket and got the next job.'

Shanti laughed. 'Donkey grey?'

'Yes, if you didn't like black, your choices were limited to what I call donkey colours: dull grey, dirty brown, dishwater green. I hated those colours.' Meena gave a mock shiver. 'I made up by wearing bright floral shirts. Colour was what I missed most when I was a new migrant.'

'Music is what I miss most,' I blurted out. 'My years of training and practice have fallen by the wayside since I came to Sydney.'

Meena and Radha exchanged glances.

Meena said, 'Maya, Radha too is a musician. Had she lived there, she would have been a hot favourite at the Chennai Music Festival.'

'Meena exaggerates.' Radha's smile was wistful, her eyes wandering to a long-lost past. With a shake of her head, she was back in the present, calm and composed.

Did she sacrifice her music too? Would I become another Radha in thirty years?

Radha said, 'You must find a way to fit your music practice into your daily routine, even if it's 30 minutes a day.' Her voice was low but had an edge to it. 'Don't let anyone take your music away from you. It's a gift to be cherished, not wasted.'

I sensed a musician's pain in her voice, and my eyes grew moist.

Radha said, 'With your formal training and years of practice, you'll get back on track. We have a couple of violinists and *mridangam* players who are eager to accompany new artists. They need a fresh challenge from newcomers like you. We would like to invite you for a two-hour performance.' After a pause, she added, 'Will three months be enough time for you to prepare?'

Radha and I hurriedly exchanged phone numbers as the theatre bell rang.

I didn't need to be persuaded to perform a vocal concert in Sydney. I'd have three months to practice. I could dazzle the Sydney Indians if I accompanied myself on the *veena*, but the strings had to be replaced. I didn't want to sound like a novice *veena* player, so I settled on a vocal concert.

Radha had said, 'We can't have three-hour concerts like Chennai. Two hours is adequate for our crowd here; they have too much going on during weekends.'

Every morning, I jumped out of bed at 5am without an alarm. I practised for about an hour, showered and rushed to work, got back home by six, ate dinner by seven, and practised again until 9pm.

Deepak embraced me passionately one night. 'Maya, you have changed ever since you found your music buddies. Your eyes sparkle, and you're passionate again. This is the Maya I fell in love with.'

I kissed him back. 'Maya minus music is meaningless for both of us.'

For the concert, I selected a set of songs and *ragas* that alternated between fast-paced rhythms and mellow melodies that evoked a sense of peace. I chose *raga 'Thodi'* as the centrepiece of the concert. That was the *raga* that had helped me win that award in Chennai. Maybe life was throwing me another opportunity.

Deepak drove me to the Ermington Community Centre for the concert. I placed the *tanpura* horizontally on the back seat of our Mazda and fastened it with seat belts. Meena and Radha were at the door to greet me, and I introduced them to Deepak.

'Deepak, meet Meena, a scientist at CSIRO. Radha is a musician.'

Meena said, 'Welcome to our music circle, Deepak. Maya mentioned you were a techie. There are plenty of them around here. Come, let me introduce you.' Meena led Deepak towards a bunch of young men in jeans and *kurtas*, laughing and talking in a mixture of accents.

Radha took my *tanpura* from me. 'Let's go backstage. The accompanists are eager to meet you.'

The accompanists, violinist Raghu and *mridangam* player Shankar were in their twenties, like me.

With a lop-sided grin, Raghu said, 'I'm a trained lawyer but a wannabe violinist.'

'I'm an accountant beating my own drum,' said Shankar. 'I wasn't born in Australia like Raghu. I'm a student at Western Sydney University.'

I burst out laughing. 'I'm a musician turned data analyst, training to be a wife.'

There were over a hundred people in the hall. Because it was a free concert, people had come with their kids, making it more of a social event than a concert. But as soon as Radha walked up to the microphone and cleared her throat, everyone took their seats, and the hall grew quiet.

'Ladies and gentlemen, I'm delighted to present Maya, who has been hiding from us for over three years. When I met her three months ago at the Riverside Theatre, she said she loved music but was out of touch, and I thought she, too, was a hobby musician like most of us. But when I talked to my cousin in Chennai, I came to know that Maya was a rising star in Carnatic music. We Sydneysiders are lucky to have her here.'

With an embarrassed smile, I folded my hands in a *namaste*. I hadn't expected anybody here to know my past. My eyes flew to Deepak. He was grinning, enjoying my discomfiture.

I started with a fast-paced *varnam* in *raga 'Bhairavi'*, set to a complex rhythm of fourteen beats. The accompanists matched the rhythm and pace I set for the first piece, and we clicked instantly. The next two pieces I chose were by well-known composers, Thyagaraja and Dikshita.

The centrepiece of the concert was *raga 'Thodi'*, which I followed with a Tamil song about the God Shiva, the power of his third eye, and his capacity to burn evil thoughts. During the improvisation segment, Raghu and Shankar were spontaneous and enthusiastic, but they were not professionals yet.

We concluded the concert with a finale, an elaborate rhythmic pattern of a ten-beat *tala*. My heart was beating to the rhythm of the music as I folded my hands into a *namaste*.

The audience rose from their seats and gave us a standing ovation. I hadn't expected such enthusiastic applause. The moment I stepped down from the podium, Radha led me around the hall, proudly introducing me as the new star of the Sydney Carnatic Music Circle. A couple of young mothers asked me if I could teach

Carnatic music to their kids on weekends. I responded with a guarded smile, unsure of what it involved.

Volunteers served coffee and biscuits in the far corner of the hall. Handing me a cup of coffee, Radha said, 'Maya, we don't have accomplished Carnatic musicians like you in Sydney. Our community would benefit if you offered music lessons to those who seek to learn. Trust me, I find it deeply rewarding. I have more students than I can handle. This is our way of sharing our culture.'

Radha had given me a reason to keep my music alive for both me and the community. As we drove back home, I realised I could be more than a money-making machine.

CHAPTER 18

AMBA

Tanjore, 1624

The fragrance of jasmine and sandalwood greeted Amba when she entered the meeting room alongside the king. Paintings of two generations of Nayaka kings and queens and a large painting of the great Chola king, the visionary who built the Big Shiva Temple, covered the walls of the room. In a far corner, a silver lamp was burning in front of God Rama's bronze sculpture.

Ayya arrived within minutes after us, and the king bent down and touched Ayya's feet.

'May you live a hundred years,' blessed Ayya, his wide smile loaded with love.

It was beautiful to watch their shared affection. The king's enormous respect for Ayya was obvious in the way he bent his head and listened to every word Ayya had to say.

The king said, 'It's Ayya's birthday today. My father and grandfather before him never forgot his birthday. For grandfather Sevappa, Ayya was father, mother, mentor, guru, everything. Tanjore is Ayya's gift to the Nayakas.'

Amba took the cue and touched Ayya's feet and sought his blessings.

'May you shine with brilliance.' Ayya touched Amba's head with affection, and she acknowledged the gesture with folded hands.

She couldn't have asked for a better blessing.

The king showed Ayya towards one of the new chairs, and he took the other. He had recently received two new teak chairs with beautifully carved ivory armrests, a gift from the King of Jaffna. Amba picked up a soft cushion from the pile in the corner, placed it on a low stool, and carried it across to where they were seated. A palace attendant arrived with Ayya's breakfast—fruit and milk. The flavour of jackfruit and coconut milk made her mouth water.

After Ayya had eaten his fruit, the king asked him, 'How do we ensure that the new Danish guests focus on trade and trade alone?'

Ayya said, 'They won't interfere with the Portuguese after their last experience in Ceylon.'

The king's face creased with worry. 'We also have to keep them away from the scheming Sultans in the north. They are creeping in like cockroaches, through every nook and corner, by land and water.'

A shudder ran through Amba's body at the king's description.

Ayya said, 'We need to establish a separate trading post with a warehouse for them near the sea and ensure that our tax collectors are present every time they load a cargo ship.'

The king tapped his fingers on his thighs, a habit when he was thinking. 'What goes in and out of the warehouse must be monitored by our men.'

Ayya was quick to notice her fidgeting. 'Yes, Amba.'

'Ayya, Captain Ove mentioned in passing that he was an architect and that the Danish king loved designing new buildings. If we keep them engaged in a construction activity, it will keep them away from meddling with the affairs of the kingdom. So....' She did not complete her thoughts.

Ayya smiled. 'Go on, Amba, I can see more thoughts churning in your head. Let's see if they are practical.'

'The captain also mentioned that they have a huge fort with a lighthouse built over a hundred years ago. If we ask them to build a similar structure including the lighthouse, we can monitor the ships and collect revenue from them as they enter our region.'

Narrow frown lines appeared on the king's brows. He said, 'What if the fort becomes a storehouse for arms and ammunition? How can we prevent that from happening?'

Amba remained silent. She didn't have the king's foresight.

Ayya's tone was confident. 'Raja Nayaka, we'll deal with that possibility at the appropriate time. We'll make sure our men are stationed within the fort once it is built. In the meantime, for the next couple of years, they'll be busy with the building activity and have no time to wander around.'

'What's the best location for a fort like this?' asked the king.

Ayya spread out a wide parchment map of the region, marked with symbols of trees and ships and ragged lines separating land and sea. The names of a few places were scratched in Tamil. He traced his forefinger along the coast.

'The coast up north is ragged and not monitored. Portuguese ships frequently wander around the area, provoking the fishermen of the region. A lighthouse on the coast of Tarangambadi can help to detect ships that stray into our region.'

The king nodded. 'Let us allot the land, free of charge, and allow the Danish to build a fort near Tarangambadi. I want to formalise this arrangement with a signed agreement from King Christian of Denmark.'

Amba cleared her throat.

The king nodded. 'Yes, Amba.'

'If our masons are involved in the construction, they could learn some new techniques about Danish design and construction material.' She glanced at Ayya to see if he agreed.

'That can be done,' said Ayya. 'We shall stipulate that they use local labour, which will be to their advantage. They too will learn from our expert stone masons and sculptors. Of course, they have to pay for labour.'

The king's voice reflected his enthusiasm. 'How will they pay? Our coins or their coins?'

'Let us bring this up with Captain Ove,' said Ayya. 'He may have some ideas.'

The discussions moved on to taxes, rules of trade and coinage. Amba's mind wandered to a sprawling fort and waves splashing against its beautiful sandstone walls.

Once the terms of engagement between Tanjore and Denmark were agreed upon, Ayya wanted the formal trade pact written in both Tamil and Portuguese, the two languages most traders could read. Amba and Ove were to write the text, Amba in Tamil and Ove in Portuguese. The meeting was scheduled to take place at the Foreign Visitor's room in the palace.

On the scheduled day, Amba came with her golden stylus and a new set of long and wide palm leaves. Ove and his interpreter came in with a long roll of parchment from Denmark.

But King Raghu had other plans. He clapped his hands, and the palace goldsmith appeared with two footmen holding a long gold foil. With great care, they laid the thin film across the rosewood table in the centre of the room.

The king said, 'Our deed will be written on a surface that will not erode with time. It will live long after us as a testament to our friendship.'

Amba brushed her hand against the gleaming surface. She had never written on such a soft and slippery surface. If she made an error on a palm leaf, she discarded it and picked up a new leaf. There was no scope for error on this gold surface. She rubbed her sweaty palms against her *sari* and steadied her hands. This was no time to reveal her anxiety.

Ayya waited for her to take her seat at the table and dictated the Tamil text word by word. Amba pressed her stylus hard against the gold foil, making sure the lines were straight. As she approached the edge of the scroll, the thin foil furled and coiled, smudging the words at the end of the first line. She became more cautious after that. She placed small brass ornaments along the edges of the foil so that the surface remained flat.

Ove's interpreter translated Ayya's words into Portuguese. Ove wrote effortlessly on his parchment. His translator would later scribe the text on the same gold foil in Portuguese.

The king sat listening to every word with his hands resting on his chin, an occasional frown creasing his forehead.

Amba read out the text.

'Treaty between Raghunatha Nayaka and Christian IV.

We shall always and for all eternity observe and maintain peace and irrevocable alliance with His Majesty the King of Denmark and his subjects.

The village of Tarangambadi shall remain the property of the King of Denmark for the next two years, after which we shall collect duties and other incomes imposed on merchandise unless contracted otherwise.

The King of Denmark and his subjects or companies shall be permitted to build a fortress in Tarangambadi according to their wishes, and we shall supply them with as much lime and stone as they require.

After the said two years have elapsed, the Danes shall never freight goods or merchandise in their ships for other people, in order that we not be defrauded of duties on merchandise being landed on Tarangambadi.'

'Signed in our royal city, Tanjavur, on the 19th day of November in the year 1620.'

Amba couldn't suppress a giggle at the irony of the situation. Neither of the two kings could read the text of the agreement they signed; King Christian could not read Portuguese, and King Raghu could not read Tamil. The kings would sign the treaty in the languages they knew--Danish and Telugu.

After signing in Telugu, King Raghu dictated an addendum.

"Danes and Portuguese shall not inflict harm on one another within these territories."

Ove fidgeted with his writing instrument, and his voice held a tremor when he spoke. 'Your Royal Highness, the Portuguese are butchers. They killed our people and sank our ships when we approached Jaffna.'

'That happened in Ceylon, not on our shores,' the King retorted.

Ove's troubled expression was worrisome.

We have worked hard to make this happen. No skirmishes, please, thought Amba. She spoke in a gentle voice. 'Captain Ove, the king has offered you a safe haven in Tanjore and a place to build your fort. You will be able to conduct your trade without interference from the Portuguese.'

Two full moons later, Amba and Ove travelled on a Danish boat to Taranagambadi. Ove referred to the village as Tranquebar, which rolled off his tongue with more ease. Amba tucked the loose end of her *sari* into her waist, took Ove's outstretched hand and stepped out of the boat onto the sandy shores of Tranquebar. Waves swished and roared as they smashed against the rocky shore, generating sounds impossible for a human voice to reproduce. No wonder the place was called the town of singing waves.

She lifted her *sari* above her ankles, let the ripples tickle her toes and inhaled the salty spray. She wrinkled her nose. 'Disgusting.'

'Dead fish,' said Ove, pointing to fishing nets in the distance. 'This is a fishing village.'

Seagulls squawked and squealed as they flew in and out. Their calls merged with the sounds of wind and waves, and the sky and the ocean merged into one continuous blue space. Amba hummed a low, throaty note to resonate with the waves. Tiny pools of water in crevices on the surface of a large grey-green rock looked like green velvet pouches holding sparkling diamonds. A tingling sensation ran up her neck when she dipped her fingers in a tiny rocky pool.

Further along the sandy shore, a small temple stood hugging the waves as though it had sprung out of the sea. Amba stood transfixed, taking it all in.

Ove walked up and down the beach. Every now and then, he sat down and wrote notes on his paper. Amba had never seen the type of paper or writing instruments he used. Ove's hand glided over the surface of the paper; it was nothing like her laborious etching.

Writing paper! That's what we should import from Denmark, thought Amba.

Walking beside Ove, her feet waded through moist sand. When their hands intertwined, she felt a deep sense of companionship rarely experienced with anyone in the palace. She let go of Ove's hand when a fisherman limped towards them; he looked familiar. As he drew closer, the fisherman bent his head low to show his respect.

'*Namaste*, Amba Ma. You may not know this humble servant. I come to the garden to help Muthu.'

There was something shifty about his eyes.

Amba asked, 'What's your name?'

'Selva. I collect shells for my wife. She makes necklaces and bracelets and sells them in the temple market.'

Selva's crooked smile sent shivers up her spine.

CHAPTER 19

MAYA
Sydney, 2014

I was checking out the photo frames at IKEA at the Rhodes shopping centre on a Thursday evening when a familiar voice called out.

'Hello, Maya.'

I spun around. 'Meena!'

She was elegant, dressed in a navy-blue *kurta* and a floral silk scarf; Meena was a picture-perfect model for IKEA's colourful furniture. Her hug was warm and spontaneous. 'How's your music going? Radha mentioned you teach quite a few students now.'

'I owe it to you and Radha; you two rescued me from my quandary.'

Meena chuckled. 'You were lost when we first met you at Riverside Theatre. But when you sang at the Sydney Music Circle, a different persona emerged. You are seriously talented, Maya, and don't you forget that.'

'Thank you. It means a lot coming from you. Do you care for a coffee?

Meena wrinkled her nose, 'Not at IKEA. Let's go down to the shopping centre. I like the Italian coffee place on the ground floor; their biscotti are good, too.'

We found a corner table overlooking Homebush Bay. The sky was an evolving panorama of shades of orange and purple. The colours were reflected in the shady mangroves hugging the walkway along the bay. Meena's calm expression enhanced the serene background; everything about her exuded confidence as if the world rose to her bidding while I stumbled through life, not knowing where to focus. It felt like I was constantly glancing over my shoulder to see if Deepak approved of my actions as I juggled work and music and now Amba, my muse.

'Meena, how did you manage such a brilliant career as a scientist? Was your husband supportive?'

Meena's beautiful smile had a shadow of sadness.

'I'm sorry.' I bit my tongue. The words were out now; I couldn't pull them back. Radha had mentioned that Meena's husband Raj had passed away after a long struggle with cancer.

'My husband Raj was a good man. He became supportive *after* we came to Australia. That was thirty years ago, but it didn't start out that way. He didn't want to ruffle any feathers, particularly his mother's. When I went to work against his parents' wishes, he was stressed. That was fifty years ago, when most women sat at home, cooked, and bred children.'

'But eventually you managed to convince Raj, right?'

Meena took a tiny bite of her almond biscotti and gazed into my eyes. 'Maya, I can hear your thoughts. What's bugging you?'

I leaned back in my chair. Would Meena understand? She was about Viji Ma's age. Would her thoughts match her chic hairstyle?

'If I talk about marriage and what it implies, my mother shushes me. Says it's all about give and take.'

'It *is* give and take, but it depends on what you give and what you get in return.'

I twirled the spoon around the froth of my cappuccino.

'If you were pushed into working in an area that didn't interest you, would you have accepted?'

Meena took a deep breath and paused before answering.

'Today, no. When I was young, I was not as strong as I am now. My views and voice have changed with age and experience.'

I said, 'I wish I had your strength and resilience. Deepak loves me, but....' I lowered my eyes, but there was no hiding from Meena. Thoughts I had pushed away gushed out.

'Deepak's convinced my music is worthless here in Sydney. For me, life is meaningless without music, and my tech job doesn't excite me.'

Meena persisted. 'What does excite you?'

'Music, arts, history. None of which can generate income, as Deepak puts it.'

Meena's wise eyes opened wide. 'Embrace your life here in Australia and follow your heart.' She emphasised the 'and'.

'In time, you can prove his assumptions wrong. You'll be surprised.'

Meena put down her coffee cup and took my hands into her own. 'Maya, explore the music and history of this country. It's not two hundred years old; it's over sixty thousand years.'

I said, 'Growing up in India, Australian history was about convicts shipped out of England and the white Australia policy. The geography was about cattle, sheep, and mining.'

The moment I uttered those words, I felt ashamed. My education had nothing to do with the ancient people of this land or how multicultural Sydney is. You couldn't deny how all corners of the world met when rosemary, soya sauce, and garam masala wafted in the same breeze as you walked along the Parramatta River. My thoughts flew back to the sounds of the didgeridoo.

I said, 'I heard a didgeridoo player, William Barton, performing alongside a symphony orchestra. The way the didgeridoo evoked sounds from the soul made me realise the deep connection music has with the ancient people of this land. I have so much to learn.'

Meena asked, 'Which part of world history are you interested in?'

I licked the crumbs of biscotti sticking to my lips. 'I'm drawn to the history of Tanjore, where my ancestors come from. When I visited last December, I stumbled on this ancient Sanskrit manuscript written on wads of palm leaves––by a woman. I want to find out how she overcame the challenges of a male-dominated *Brahmin* society in the 1600s and produced that literary work.'

'Have you visited the State Library on Macquarie Street? I'm sure you'll find journals written by Europeans who visited Tanjore during that period.'

The thought of exploring European documents had never occurred to me. No wonder Meena was a hotshot scientist.

'I'm in touch with a professor from Tanjore University who sends me historical references from Tamil and Sanskrit sources. I will follow up with the State Library, though.'

Meena said, 'I haven't been to Tanjore in a long time, but I visit Chennai every few years. Last time, I visited a couple of forts near Chennai. Most of them are in ruins.'

'Talking of forts, here's a trivia question. Apart from the British, who were the other Europeans who travelled to India in the 1600s?'

Meena counted with her fingers. 'Portuguese, Dutch, French,

British, maybe Italian missionaries? I don't think the Spanish came to India; they went to the Americas. I can't think of anyone else.'

I broke into a wide grin. 'Meena, you missed an important history lesson in school, like the rest of us.'

Meena looked surprised. 'Who have I missed?'

'The Danish. The Tanjore King, Raghu Nayaka, allocated the seaside town of Tranquebar to the Danish traders so they could build a fort and a warehouse. My cousin Preeti and I visited this huge Danish fort in Tranquebar where I saw Indo-Danish history written on a gold foil.'

Meena's eyes went wide, and she broke into Tamil. '*Nijamma?*' Then, quickly switched back to English. 'Really? I knew Tranquebar and the surrounding coastal towns of Tamil Nadu were affected by the tsunami of 2005. We raised some funds here in Sydney for the fishing community in the region, but I had no clue about the Danish connection.'

'The Dansborg Fort in Tranquebar is intact, in spite of the tsunami. That's when the Friends of India: Danish Society was formed. Now the town is swarming with Danish visitors and research students.'

'Maya, I sense your passion. Your eyes sparkle and your voice sings when you talk about Tanjore's history.'

Meena swiped her fingers over her phone.

'My friend Carl volunteers at the State Library; I have forwarded his contact details to you. Get a reader's ticket and pursue your passion. It'll work, trust me.'

Would it? Did Deepak have the resilience to support me if I followed my passion? Or would he grumble about how I could earn more money if I focused on my career?

That evening I was too tired to cook and ordered a pizza and garlic bread. As I was tossing up a green salad with rosemary oil and apple cider vinegar, Deepak said, 'Remember my colleague, Gita? Her husband, Dave, is a professional cello player. When I mentioned you were a musician, Gita got all excited and highlighted a bunch of programs where Dave is playing.'

Deepak handed me a glossy brochure of the Australian Chamber Orchestra.

'Pick a concert you fancy, and I'll buy the tickets. You'll get to hear music from this part of the world.'

Deepak rarely missed an opportunity to point out that I was ignorant about 'this' part of the world, a world where he grew up, and I was groping my way around.

I said, 'I have no problem listening to music from any part of the world; it's you who seems to have a problem with Indian music.'

After dinner, Deepak turned to his TV and I to my iPad. I plugged my noise-cancelling headphones in and picked a random song from a string quartet album I had downloaded. A melody on the cello tugged at my heartstrings. I listened to it again and again; I couldn't stop listening to that haunting melody. Finally, I paused the music and hummed the notes. How I wished it would fit into a *raga, any raga*. I knew hundreds, but this didn't fit any of them. The melody and the chords were tightly bound yet progressed independently of each other. This was entirely different from the classical music I was used to.

I scrolled through the album. The song was '*Arioso*' by Bach.

My fingers moved along the imaginary frets of my *veena*, tracing the melody one note at a time. '*Arioso*' sounded like a *raga-maalika* – a garland of melodies, seamlessly creating an entirely new shape and structure to the song. Some chords fitted into a pentatonic *raga* that had five notes. Bach's music was elemental, a universal language not constrained by geography or culture.

I learned Carnatic music by training my ear to listen to *ragas*. To understand Bach's music, I had to learn to read Western classical music.

A few days later, I removed the dust cover from my *veena*, tuned the four strings stretched along the fretboard, and traced the melody of '*Arioso*'. As I was playing, Deepak walked in through the door.

He said, 'This doesn't sound like your usual traditional music. What is it?'

I set down my *veena*. 'I was experimenting with Bach.'

'I thought you had given up playing the *veena*.'

'There's only so much I can do in a day; I'm too tired to practice.'

Deepak said, 'But you have time to read about that Tanjore woman.'

I grinned. 'I'm not sure whether I have found her, or she found me. At least I don't hum when I'm reading about her. You won't have to mute me to watch your sport.'

'What?' Deepak's mouth flew open as if he had no clue of what I was talking about.

'Remember you pointed the TV remote at me and asked me to mute and stop humming.'

'That was a joke. You should have snatched the remote from me and muted me back.'

I said, 'Aggression is not my style.'

Deepak shrugged his shoulders. 'I can't fathom what's going on in your head if you go quiet and sullen. I'd much rather you stand up to me when you disagree.'

Then his tone softened. 'I came home early today so we could go out to dinner and celebrate.'

'What's the occasion?'

'Our bank has asked me to go to Denmark to attend a software workshop and present my ideas to modify the vendor's software. I have been in touch with them for several months, suggesting changes to their security protocols. Finally, they have agreed. It's a big career win.'

'That's wonderful. I'm happy for you.' I gave him a big hug. Deepak pulled me to him and kissed every part of my face.

I murmured, 'You don't want to miss your dinner.'

I wore a cream raw-silk *kurta* over black pants and my double strand of pearls, which I had not worn since our honeymoon. I also splashed on the new herbal perfume that was all the rage in Chennai during my last visit.

The modern Australian restaurant in North Sydney offered a sweeping view of the opera house crawling out of the waves, the way it was designed to be.

The sauvignon blanc was smooth and slightly sweet. I closed my eyes, savouring the moment. My hand fell on Deepak's thigh. 'When do you have to go to Denmark?'

'In a couple of months, sometime in April.'

I took a bite of the polenta chip dipped in mint and yoghurt. It tasted like semolina *pakoras*, but without chillies. Fried to perfection, it was crunchy outside and melted in my mouth with every bite.

'Can I come along? I'd love to visit the Copenhagen Museum.'

'I'm going for a week. There won't be any time for sightseeing.'

'I'll go sightseeing while you work.' I grinned. 'Remember the Tranquebar fort I visited? The original gold foil of the Tanjore – Denmark trade agreement is displayed in the Copenhagen Museum. If you manage to get a weekend, we can take a river cruise. I'll work out a schedule.'

I tossed my head to move the bangs away from my eyes. Deepak twirled his fingers around the tendrils that fell over my forehead. 'I love the way your hair and eyes dance when you are excited. But...,' Deepak grew quiet.

'I know you are worried about the deposit for the house. I'll shop around for cheap economy fares. I have additional savings from my weekend music tuitions.'

I had eight Carnatic music students, boys and girls between the ages of eight and thirteen. Four on Saturday and four on Sunday between 2-4pm at the community hall in Ermington. I had chosen the afternoon time slots when Deepak was busy watching sports and would not miss me.

The mains arrived: saffron and mace-infused ravioli, a unique Indo-Italian flavour.

Towards the end of dinner, Deepak said, 'Music and now history. The house will have to wait if it all means so much to you.'

CHAPTER 20

AMBA
Tanjore, 1625

Amba brushed the dirt away and perched on the smooth surface of the tree stump in the garden. Muthu plucked out the yellow leaves, one by one, from the new orchids that had arrived from Jaffna. The new shady area was covered with coconut fibre to grow new varieties of flowers that required filtered light and a reprieve from the Tanjore heat.

'Muthu, do you have any new helpers in the garden?' asked Amba.

Muthu scratched his chin, removed his turban and squatted on his heels, ready for a leisurely chat. 'Three people come every day. Occasionally, I get extra help.'

His smile revealed his betel-stained teeth. 'Don't worry, Amba

Ma. I have not forgotten your instructions. Everyone who works here gets paid their due silver. They bless you every day.'

'That's good. Who are the extra helpers? What are their names?'

'Selva comes every week. He works here for two days. For the rest of the week he goes to collect shells. His wife makes trinkets and sells them in the markets. He says the money he gets for his garden work is not enough to feed his four children. He is good at weaving these coconut fibres,' Muthu said, waving his hand around.

'Does Selva have a slight limp?' asked Amba.

'Yes.' Muthu crunched his eyebrows. 'Why do you ask?'

'I saw him on the seashore in Tranquebar. What do you know about him?'

'His wife's sister works in Queen Kalyani's palace.'

Amba winced. 'Get rid of him. I don't want him in the garden.'

Muthu unrolled his turban and mopped his sweaty face. Perhaps he is not happy with my decision, thought Amba. She dusted her *sari* and hopped off the tree stump.

'Let's go to your cottage. I am thirsty for Shanta's buttermilk.'

With a cheerful smile, Shanta handed Amba a cup of buttermilk laced with salt, pepper and cumin. Amba held the cool earthen cup against her warm forehead and closed her eyes. None of the women in the palace, queens, courtesans, or maids, had an open smile like Shanta. Amba would rather spend more time in this cool cottage with this loving couple. Muthu and Shanta, simple folks who couldn't read and write, were generous in sharing their love. They reminded Amba of Guru and his wife Mami who had cared for her whilst sharing their knowledge.

Instead of using that knowledge, in her effort to please the king, Amba was spending more time solving his court problems than writing poetry and music. How could she call herself a scholar if she did not write?

Shanta sat next to Amba and gently brushed an unruly tendril from Amba's forehead.

'My little Amba, you were so eager to start your own garden. Watch the flowers grow and write your poetry. Now the garden is full of beautiful flowers from all over the world. We rarely see you these days at the lotus pond with your palm leaves.'

Amba's shoulders sagged. Her voice was feeble, as if it came from a deep well within. 'I miss those days. Do you have new palm leaves for me?'

'I have stacks of leaves ready for your use. I have found a new sap to soften the leaves, so you don't have to press hard when you write.'

Shanta massaged her fingers and didn't stop even when a tear trickled down from Amba's eyes onto her hand.

Amba paced up and down her bedroom. Her fingers twisted the end of her *sari* into tiny knots. She felt like a tigress trapped in a golden cage. The king hadn't shared her bed for many moons and the morning music sessions had stopped too.

The king's courtesans were increasing by the day. Every time he went on an expedition, he returned with a couple of women riding behind him on his elephant. Amba had lost count.

Seeing Amba moping around, her maid Kamala came up with a plan.

'Amba Ma, the king will be in the courtesan's palace for his ritualistic oil bath tomorrow. I'll create a special salve of mint and rosewater to cool his body.'

The king sat on a low wooden platform, naked except for a red silk cloth covering his private parts. He was surrounded by women and didn't notice her. Amba waited for her turn at the large open courtyard of the courtesans' palace and approached the king with a silver tray of rose petals and the bowl of the mint salve.

As if on cue, Queen Kalyani stomped in, her anklets jangling discordant notes. 'Don't pollute the king with your hands. Hands that have touched a foreigner!'

The queen spat out her words. 'Do you think we don't know about your dalliance with that Danish captain? The whole palace is laughing at you.'

Amba froze. Her stomach crunched into painful knots. Queen Kalyani's eyes spewed red-hot venom.

If the queen had the power of the third eye like God Shiva had to destroy her enemies, I would be reduced to a heap of ashes, thought Amba. I wish I could smash her head with this silver tray.

What a stupid woman! Didn't the queen realise the king was in danger due to her allegiance with Thimma? Did she really care about the king, or was she waiting for her son to take over the throne?

Amba shoved the tears that threatened to come out right back into her eyes. She would not allow Queen Kalyani to have the pleasure of seeing her cry.

The king sat like a dumb statue; his eyes focused on the ground. He was a coward in front of his queen. Amba thumped the tray down in front of the king and glared at him, willing him to raise his head. She used every ounce of energy to control her voice, which was clear and firm.

'Your life is in danger. Please talk to General Pandya Varma today.'

The king was startled; his eyes betrayed his fear when he caught her eyes.

Amba stomped out, fingers curling in and out of clenched fists. *Why was it so difficult for people to face the truth?* Why was the king unwilling to acknowledge the turmoil happening around him?

Amba had become a wriggling fish caught in their political net, hated by the queen and unable to protect the king from his enemies roaming the streets of Tanjore.

How did she end up in such a spot? All Amba had ever wanted was for the king to be happy. She had been naive and had assumed her musical bond with the king would never snap.

Where was her music now? Her verses were nothing but political rantings, not the output of a scholar. She missed the thrill of extempore composition, standing in front of her goddess, being one with her music. True, she had abandoned the temple, but she needed her goddess now more than ever. Amba lit an incense stick in front of her shrine and sat down to meditate on the Goddess of Knowledge, Saraswati.

In the months that followed, Amba rarely met Ove. He was in Tranquebar, working on the design of the fort with a recently arrived Danish architect.

One evening, after tending to her new bulbs, Amba walked to Muthu's hut. The tall, unmistakable silhouette chatting with Muthu sent a tingle down her neck. Ove and Muthu had become good friends, and they had their own language of communication, a strange mixture of Tamil and Portuguese. Ove was holding a large, tender coconut and lifted it to his mouth. Amba approached silently from behind, but Muthu was facing Ove, and his eyes grew wide as Amba approached. Ove turned around, spilling the coconut water all over his pants, and Amba burst out laughing at his shocked expression. The coconut shell tilted further, spilling the remaining water all over his clothes.

'Sorry, I didn't mean to startle you,' Amba couldn't stop laughing.

'I miss your gaiety,' said Ove, switching to Portuguese. Oblivious of his wet clothes, his hand reached out and moved the curly tendrils that had covered the corner of her eye. Such tenderness had disappeared from her world ever since the queen took control of the king.

'How's the fort coming along?'

'The architect has modified his original design to follow the topology of the rocky shore at Tranquebar. True to his word, King Raghu has been generous with labour and building materials.'

Ove gestured for them to take a stroll. As they walked towards the lotus pond, Ove muttered under his breath in Portuguese.

'The Portuguese are playing a double game here in Tanjore.'

'What do you mean?' Amba's feet halted.

Ove's blue eyes turned grey. 'The Portuguese have convinced King Raghu that they are his allies, but they are not. They are training rebels to plot against the king.'

'Who are these rebels? Who is their leader?' asked Amba.

Ove's voice was low. 'A crook named Thimma; his soldiers are armed up to the hilt with Portuguese bayonets.'

Amba's hand went up to her cheeks, the scar behind her ear was still itchy.

Amba said, 'If you are sure about Thimma's plot, please inform General Pandya Varma. He is responsible for the king's safety.'

Ove spread his hands. 'It is not my place to interfere in the king's affairs.'

'Well, then I shall,' said Amba in a determined voice. She had warned the king, but he had not given it another thought. Perhaps he assumed the queen's allegiance to Thimma would stop his kingdom from being usurped by the Portuguese. Was his love for the queen turning him into a coward, wondered Amba.

'Let's head back.'

When they reached the garden hut, Amba said, 'Muthu, ask Raju to be here tomorrow morning.'

Back in her chambers, Amba pulled out a palm leaf from her teak chest, which doubled as her writing surface.

Respected General Pandya Varma,
    Greetings.
    I write this letter with a sense of dread and despair. I hear alarming news about threats to our king and state.
    It is my firm conviction that you alone can squash the rebels lurking around our kingdom like hungry jackals.
    Please send a return reply with a place and time for a confidential meeting.
    With respects,
    Amba

Raju was waiting in the garden as she had instructed. He was the only person who followed her instructions and understood the importance of not gossiping with palace servants.

'Raju, take this note to General Pandya Varma right now. It's Tuesday, and he will be in his office. Wait until he gives you a reply and come straight back.'

Amba paced up and down the garden path, circling Muthu's hut anxiously. Had she been hasty in sending that letter? What if Raju got intercepted by the queen?

Amba went into the kitchen. 'Shanta, please give me a glass of your special buttermilk. I am exhausted.'

Muthu walked in from the backyard with a long, thin ash gourd. With the tiniest twist of her wrist, Shanta snapped the gourd into two, releasing the sweet smell which enveloped the whole kitchen.

Shanta said, 'Amba Ma, stay and have lunch with us. This gourd will cook in no time. I'll sprinkle some fresh coconut on top, the way you like.'

'Shanta, how can I say no to your cooking? It's loaded with flavour. The palace food tastes nothing like yours. I'll wait here a bit longer until Raju gets back.'

Amba couldn't keep Muthu and Shanta waiting any longer and returned to the hut.

Shanta spread out the narrow end of the banana leaf, sprinkled a few drops of water and brushed them with her fingertips till the leaf glistened. She served rice with the tender gourd sprinkled with coconut. Amba loved Shanta's cooking. Now, she was too distracted to feel the taste. Raju had not yet returned. Morsels of rice slipped through Amba's fingers, not even making it to her mouth. 'Where is Raju?'

'Amba Ma, don't worry; he'll be here soon. Here, drink some water.' Shanta handed her a cup of cold water.

Amba cradled the cup in her hands and came out of the hut. She paced up and down, craning her neck at the rustle of every leaf. What happened to Raju? It would be foolish to send another messenger. She should have gone herself to see General Varma. Perhaps she should never have written the letter in the first place. The whirlwind of thoughts made her dizzy, and she sat on the stone bench outside the garden hut.

Raju burst in and collapsed at her feet. His mouth opened and closed like a fish gasping for air. Tears streamed down his hollow cheeks, his turban slipped from his head, and his body went limp.

Shanta and Muthu rushed out of the hut at the sound of the commotion. Amba sprinkled the water from her cup onto Raju's face. Muthu sat next to him and wiped his wet forehead while Shanta fanned him with the corner of her *sari*.

Reeking of sweat and tears, Raju slowly opened his eyes and

propped himself against a stone bench. His words came out in spurts, sobs and hiccups.

'I was hurrying back. When I came to the corner of the main street, I heard a woman scream. Hooded horsemen galloped through the street and rammed into people. They toppled the carts of vendors; vegetables rolled everywhere.'

Raju continued with grunts and groans. 'The horsemen dumped heavy sacks on the road right where I stood. They rode away before I could see their faces, but I think some of them were white men.'

Raju's tears drenched his muddy shirt. 'The sacks contained dismembered bodies of men.'

Amba's body froze. She felt the same anger as she did when Thimma and that Portuguese man had tried to molest her all those years ago. She felt like a trapped tiger unable to protect her cubs against predators.

Amba gritted her teeth. 'Traitor Thimma owns the streets of Tanjore.'

Raju pulled out a crunched palm leaf tucked under his waist and gave it to Amba.

The crumpled note from the General was cryptic; only a time and location were hurriedly etched onto the leaf.

The following day, Amba dressed in a plain brown *sari*, tied her hair into a tight bun, removed her anklets, and left a single bangle on each hand. A brisk walk from the courtesan's palace brought her to the southwestern corner of the Big Temple, where a palanquin was waiting for her. The bells rang for the evening *Aarti*.

Amba ducked in and closed the curtains on both sides. The palanquin bearers moved swiftly as if they were on wheels.

The ride was longer than Amba had anticipated. She was not sure how the general would react to her concerns. She had to be cautious and keep her emotions under check.

It was clear the king would never displease Queen Kalyani, the daughter of a powerful king. A king who had caused the slow demise of the great Vijayanagar Empire, which once controlled the entire southern peninsula.

In the past, the Tanjore Nayakas had avoided skirmishes with neighbouring kingdoms, a strategy that made Tanjore prosperous and peaceful. She had heard King Raghu's marriage to Kalyani was a political arrangement to ensure that Tanjore would not come under attack. But now King Raghu's life was in danger. Amba did not want the king to dig his own grave.

One of the palanquin bearers cleared his throat and set down the palanquin. Amba waited a couple of moments, parted the curtains and stepped out.

There was something familiar about the narrow street and dingy doorway. The fleeting image of a hand dragging her to safety flashed through her mind, and then it hit her. This was the same place where that woman Selvi had rescued her from Thimma all those years ago. Amba adjusted her eyes to the dim lights, and the tall figure of General Pandya Varma framed the doorway.

He closed the front door and led her into a larger room lit with hanging lanterns

'*Vanakkam*, Amba. I hope you had a smooth ride, with no incidents this time,' he grinned.

Amba's heartbeats pounded in her ears. The General knew about her altercation with Thimma!

'Selvi is our friend.' The General's tone was sober. 'She allows me to use her house for covert meetings, when she is away.'

Amba's voice came out louder than she intended. 'You must have heard about the commotion on the main street yesterday. I believe both locals and Portuguese are involved in instigating riots around Tanjore.'

'Amba, we know how to deal with the Portuguese.' His voice was slow and deliberate in an attempt to calm her. 'King Raghu's father allowed them to trade in our region, though there was no formal agreement. There was a time when they tried to control our Nagore port. We thrashed them, and they withdrew.'

He continued after a pause. 'The Portuguese keep a low profile in Tanjore. Their attention is on Ceylonese kingdoms; they are dismantling them one by one.'

Amba hissed. 'They will do the same thing in Tanjore. They are training local mercenaries.'

The General squared his shoulders. 'Yes. I realise you are talking about Thimma.'

Amba struggled to keep her voice under check. 'King Raghu will not deal with Thimma because Queen Kalyani will not let him.'

The General's eyes were like sharp needles and his tone was firm. 'Amba, stay out of this. Leave it to the experts.'

CHAPTER 21

MAYA
Sydney, 2014

The New South Wales State Library on Macquarie Street was a short walk from my client's office. After a gruelling meeting, the library was the perfect place to take my mind to another place and time.

I had arranged to meet Carl, the librarian Meena had introduced me to. I was early and didn't expect to be greeted when I approached the information desk.

'Hello, Maya.' The tall, grey-bearded man stretched out his hand, a wide smile breaking out of his bushy beard.

'Carl?' My voice was tentative.

'That I am.' He bowed in a comic way. 'We are both early. There's time for a quick bite. Lunch?'

'Sure.'

We headed to the library café adjacent to the entrance foyer. Carl bought a sandwich, and I picked up a Greek salad. We ordered our coffees and sat down in the courtyard overlooking Sydney Harbour. The spotless blue sky, sparkling waters and boats bobbing in the distant waters reminded me of Tranquebar. I preferred the original Tamil name Tarangambadi—the town of singing waves. My thoughts flew back to the gold foil and the palm leaf manuscript.

'Carl, what's the oldest manuscript in this library?'

'Let's see.' Carl scratched his beard. 'There's a clay tablet that's four thousand years old. And then we have several manuscripts from 1780 onwards. Why do you ask?'

'During my last trip to India, I was amazed at the variety of writing surfaces they used before paper made its presence. Stone inscriptions, silk fabrics, copper sheets, gold foils and palm leaves. I saw this exquisite calligraphy written on a stack of palm leaves at the ancient Saraswati Mahal Library in Tanjore. It's etched in my mind.'

'Do you know which period it was written in?'

'The Tanjore librarian said the palm leaf manuscript was dated somewhere between 1600-1650 CE.'

The froth from the cappuccino stuck to Carl's thick white beard and moved around his chin as he spoke. 'That's the time when all of Europe went to India. What's the manuscript about?'

'It's the biography of King Raghu Nayaka of Tanjore, written in Sanskrit.'

'Where's Tanjore?'

I took a serviette and drew a V-shaped map of southern India.

'Tanjore is in the south-east part of the Indian peninsula, part of the current state of Tamil Nadu.'

A few crumbs of the sandwich became lodged in Carl's beard as he watched me draw. I pointed to his beard and flicked my finger under my chin. Carl broke into a wide grin and gave his beard a rough brush with the back of his hand.

'Do you know anything about the author of the manuscript?'

'Not much, except that she's a woman. I could read only the second part of the Sanskrit signature. There's a long prefix followed by Amba. I have called her Amba. I am amazed that the work of a female scholar from conservative Tanjore has survived to this day.'

I set down my fork. 'I have an English translation of the Sanskrit manuscript from a professor in Tanjore. I want to find out more about the author and get an idea of the events that shaped her life.'

I took a sip of my lukewarm coffee. 'If you had an English translation of a seventeenth-century Sanskrit document, how would you verify the authenticity of the text? I mean, how do I find out if the events written in that document are fact or fiction?'

Carl said, 'As a first step, I would search for historical accounts of other scholars from that period and place. Then, I'd compare their accounts with the events in your manuscript.'

I grinned. 'Not my manuscript, Amba's biography of King Raghu Nayaka.'

Carl passed his hands over his beard. 'You know what would be interesting? Travelogues. I bet there'll be reports and records by Europeans who visited Tanjore during that period.'

'Carl, that's a wonderful idea. How do I find these?'

'I'll help you. It'll be a good excuse for me to brush up on my history. I recently learnt from Ancestry that I'm seventy percent Danish.'

'What?' I broke into a wide smile and swiped through my photo library. I brought up pictures of Dansborg Fort and three girls standing on a rock hugging the wave.

'This is a Danish fort in a little coastal town in South India.

That's where I saw history written on gold. The King of Tanjore leased the town of Tranquebar to the Danes for use as a trading post.'

I zoomed in on the photo. 'That blond-haired girl, Sofia, is from Denmark. She's studying for a PhD at Tanjore University. She says one of her ancestors is buried in Tranquebar.'

Carl rubbed his hands together; his eyes sparkled like bright blue buttons. 'I say, Maya, this is going to be fun. Do you have your State Library card?'

I shook my head. 'No? In that case, fill out the online form and become a member. It'll be easy for me to help you with your research.' He glanced at his watch. 'It's 2pm. Let's get you all organised, and then I'll see what I can find.'

Once I completed the online form, Carl got behind his desk and handed me a NSW State Library card.

The shiny blue card, embossed with a colourful photograph of the library, was my window to Amba's world. A pleasant shiver ran down my spine as I brushed my fingers over the glossy card. Did the Tamil *Brahmins* respect Amba? Did she meet any foreign travellers scouting for spices? Was she a courtesan or a queen? My head was spinning with questions.

Carl tapped a few keys on his computer and gestured for me to come and watch. 'I'll show you how to search the catalogue. You'll be able to access it from home and download any PDFs you want to read. If there's a specific book you are after, place a reservation on it. If we don't have a physical copy, we'll get it from interstate. It'll be held for a week, and you'll need to come to the library and read it. Unfortunately, you can't take the books home; this is only a reference library.'

My thoughts flew to another reference library in another part of the world, where a grumpy librarian asserted his authority. Here, cheerful Carl went out of his way to help me traverse a distant past anchored to my roots.

A few days later, Carl called me. His cheerful voice rang with excitement. 'Maya, remember how I mentioned my Danish ancestry? It turns out my mother's ancestor, a great-great-great aunt, is buried in Tranquebar. They think she died of some tropical disease. She lived there with her husband, who was an officer with the Danish East India Company.'

'Carl, this is unbelievable. I want to know more about your family. I'll come to the library tomorrow. Let's catch up over lunch.'

'What time?'

'Will 12.30 work? I've found this new Indian restaurant, which serves Indian street food, on Pitt Street. It's a ten-minute walk from the library.'

The restaurant was tucked away in a basement on a narrow alley behind Martin Place. They had managed to create a street setting, a refreshing change from the plastered paintings of maharajas and maharanis typical of an Eastern restaurant in a Western country. Walls decorated with strategically placed graffiti gave the impression that you were on a street corner of a crowded Indian village. Part of the pleasure of eating street food in India is to stand around on a street corner with friends and eat out of dried banyan or banana leaf cups and drink from burnt clay bowls; it's an authentic experience completely different to sitting in an air-conditioned restaurant and using a knife and fork to eat a *dosa* or *roti*.

When I walked in, Carl was sitting on a dusty bench under a broken brick wall, glasses perched precariously on the tip of his nose, perusing an old Indian newspaper, *The Times of India*.

Once we were seated, I dug out a red and white cylindrical

container from my handbag and handed it to Carl. 'A piece of Danish history for you.'

Carl unfurled the long glossy poster, a replica of the gold foil signed by King Christian IV of Denmark and King Raghu Nayaka of Tanjore, dated 1620.

'Maya, what a thoughtful gift. Where did you find this?'

'The online Danish Museum in Copenhagen. I managed to download a high-quality digital image of the original gold foil from their digital archives.'

I ran my finger along the first line. 'Some parts are barely legible, and the Tamil words are smudged towards the end. It says the King of Tanjore grants the village of Tranquebar to King Christian IV of Denmark to build a commercial warehouse.'

A young waiter dressed in a white *kurta* and a black embroidered waistcoat brought *Jal jeera,* a welcome drink served in an earthenware cup. It held tamarind water flavoured with roasted cumin, black salt and white pepper. Carl took a big gulp before he closed one eye and choked over the drink.

I handed him a glass of cold water.

'Carl, you have to sip it like fine wine, not swig it like beer. The tamarind is tangy. Let's order something familiar for starters. How about *samosas*?'

'Yup. I've had them before.'

For the mains, I ordered *dosa* for both of us. It came on a large platter with three chutneys on the side: green coriander, red tomato, and white coconut—the same way they had served it at the Tanjore restaurant in Chennai. I tore a tiny piece of the *dosa* with my fingers. Carl tried doing the same, and the *dosa* came out in long shards. I suppressed the urge not to laugh at his clumsy effort as he went back to his knife and fork.

'Maya, I trawled through the digital archives at the library and found a lengthy Danish report––'The First Contact with King Raghoo Nayaka'–– dated 1622. It's addressed to King Christian IV from his envoy. The document describes the journey from Denmark to Ceylon and from there to the Coromandel coast in southern India. The report was recently translated from Danish into English.'

The waiter came back with the dessert menu and handed it to Carl.

'Sir, you must try the Indian ice cream; our mango *kulfi* is the best.' Turning to me, he asked, 'Madam, what would you like?'

I pointed to the menu. 'I'll have that special decoction coffee from south India. Thank you.'

Carl said, 'I, too, will have that special coffee.'

The coffee came in a small stainless-steel tumbler placed in a *dabara*, a stainless-steel bowl.

'Carl, this is the Tamilian version of a cup and saucer. Be careful, the tumbler is very hot.'

Carl gingerly held the rim of the tumbler and inhaled the dark brown brew.

'Strong! Do you drink such strong coffee every day?'

'I don't, but the rest of my family do. My father loved his filter coffee. He came from Kumbakonam, a town whose claim to fame is its unique blend. They call it "degree" coffee. They claim the name comes from the temperature at which they roast the bean.'

I added with a chuckle. 'Or the word *chicory* could have morphed into degree. They add chicory to darken the coffee colour.'

Carl took a sip of coffee from the stainless-steel tumbler. 'Where do you get these special tumbler sets from?'

'You can order them on Amazon. It comes as a set of two with a traditional stainless steel drip filter.'

I poured my coffee from the tumbler into the *dabara* and back into the tumbler slowly until a froth formed on the surface. I said, 'This releases the aroma.'

Carl watched my deliberate movements. He asked, 'Do you have family in India?'

'Yes, my mother lives in Chennai. My father passed away some years ago, but most of his family lives in Chennai as well. My cousin Preeti, who took me to Tranquebar, is from my father's side of the family.'

I had a sip of coffee; it was strong and bitter. I added a teaspoon of sugar.

'Carl, about that Danish report, can you please share that reference with me?'

'Sure. As a library member, you have access to the report. It's a long document, but you can download and read it at leisure. I haven't had time to read the details. From what I gathered, five ships and five hundred men set sail from Denmark in 1618, and King Christian IV funded the voyage.'

I said, 'I read that the Portuguese reached the Coromandel Coast in the early 1500s and tried to gain exclusive control of the seas around Ceylon and the South Indian peninsula. The Dutch and the Danish had to compete with the Portuguese.'

Carl glanced at his watch and asked for the bill.

'Carl, this is my shout. Next time, you can take me to a Danish restaurant if there is one in Sydney.'

That night, after dinner, I opened the Danish report on my new laptop——paid for by my second income. Thanks to my music tuition, Deepak didn't grumble about depleting our home deposit savings.

I skimmed through the first part; it was a daily log of the long voyage of the five ships that set out in 1618. The second part talked about how the reconnaissance ship, *The Oresund*, was shipwrecked by the Portuguese when it approached Ceylon. The Portuguese placed the heads of two crew members from the first ship on poles on the beach as a warning to the rest of the fleet. The Danish captain and a few sailors escaped with one ship before they landed in Nagore, on the southeast coast of India.

It was midnight by the time I showered and got into bed. Deepak was fast asleep, snoring with a constant rhythm. As I snuck into bed, Deepak mumbled in his dream, turned over and pulled me into the crook of his arm, kissed my neck and fell asleep again. I moved the doona and covered Deepak's bare shoulders and snuggled into his arms. When I closed my eyes, heads on poles prancing and dancing to songs I had never heard woke me from my sleep. Careful not to disturb Deepak, I slid out of bed, tiptoed to the kitchen, gulped a glass of cold water and mumbled an old prayer my grandmother had taught me to shake off dreams that wouldn't let go.

It was our fourth wedding anniversary, and I had invited Deepak's parents over for dinner. The tarnished, heirloom bronze bowl from my grandmother took on a new form when I filled it with water, sprinkled a few rose petals on the surface, and lit a floating candle. The orange and yellow raw silk covers from the cottage emporium in Tanjore replaced the old ones. The colours complemented the shades of brown on the new triptych wall hanging I had created with a simple IKEA frame to display my three favourite instruments: the *veena*, the didgeridoo and the cello.

Deepak's dad, Vikram, had had a pacemaker put in a few months back, and this was his first outing after his recovery. I wanted this to be a special evening for the whole family, so I cooked a five-course dinner.

I lit the tea light candles resting on the lotus-shaped holders, and the doorbell rang.

Vikram Uncle handed me a box of Lindt chocolates and gently touched my head with the palm of his right hand, his gesture of offering a blessing.

Neetu Aunty brought a bunch of red roses and her warm hug came from the heart. 'Maya, it's great to see your eyes sparkle again. The transition from Chennai to Sydney was tough on you. We all go through the same pain as we adjust to a new environment after growing up in a culture from another part of the world. I, too, missed my home town, Ahmedabad, when we came to Australia thirty years ago.'

'What did you miss most, Neetu Aunty?'

'Colour. I missed colour. I grew up in Gujarat where even men wore colourful *kurtas* and turbans.'

Deepak piped up. 'Mom, we have way more vibrantly coloured flowers in Australia than in India.'

'Colourful flowers can't replace colourful clothes.' Neetu Aunty smiled. 'We see what we want to see.'

I said, 'And we hear what we want to hear. The sounds of the didgeridoo have finally replaced the screech of the cockatoos that used to bother me when I was new to Sydney.'

Deepak took out the wine glasses, a Hunter Valley shiraz and a chilled bottle of chardonnay from the fridge. His eyes sparkled with mischief.

'Maya has collected a bunch of new friends: Radha the musician, Meena the scientist and Carl the librarian, not to mention the culture-conscious parents of her new music students.'

I brought out a platter of onion *vadas* and a bowl of coconut chutney.

Neetu broke a piece of the *vada* and dipped it in the coconut chutney. 'The chutney is delicious. Did you use fresh coconut?'

I said, 'Fresh, but frozen. A new brand I picked up at the Indian store.'

Deepak handed the wine glasses around.

Vikram made a toast, 'To your happiness. *Kush Raho*, be happy.'

I took a sip of the chardonnay and nodded in Deepak's direction. 'Did Deepak tell you he's going to Denmark for work?'

Neetu said, 'Yes, he did. Would you like to come and stay with us while he is away?'

'I'm planning to go with Deepak. Remember the Danish fort I talked about? I want to see the original gold foil trade agreement at the Copenhagen Museum. Tranquebar showed me a slice of Indo-Danish history most Indians have never heard about.'

Vikram said, 'Why do you need to go? Deepak's going for work.' A frown firmly lodged itself between his eyes.

I wanted to say, *Yes, I'm his wife, and I want to go with him*. But I refrained. I wanted no arguments on this special occasion.

Neetu Aunty clinked her glass, first with Vikram and then with me. She asked, 'Are you in touch with that Danish girl?'

'Sofia, yes. It'll be fun to see her in her home country. I'll check if she plans to be in Denmark when we get there.'

Neetu glanced in my direction. 'The heat and humidity of south India can be tough for someone who comes from a cold country.'

I said, 'Sofia strolls around like a local. She understands Tamil.' I took a sip of wine. 'What's interesting is Sofia and my librarian friend Carl both have ancestors buried in Tranquebar. To think I had never heard about this town a couple of hours drive from Kumbakonam, where I was born.'

Vikram Uncle's frown faded as I brought out the food. I had

spent the whole day preparing the *kofta* curry, lemon rice, spinach *dal*, *raita*, cucumber salad, *pappadum* and *rotis*.

Vikram took a crunchy bite of a *papadum*. He said, 'The Portuguese were the first Europeans to land in India near my hometown. They were also the last to leave.'

I said, 'I thought the Portuguese left before the British.'

'No. They left in 1950, three years after the British,' said Vikram. 'The Portuguese got lucky when they landed on the rich south-western coast of India. From there, they controlled Ceylon, all of south India and western India.'

Vikram's tone got livelier as he talked about his hometown. 'My grandfather had a Portuguese passport. He worked and lived in Diu, near Goa, a Portuguese territory. I have some distant cousins living in Portugal.'

I said, 'I read a travel report of the Danish voyage; the captain says the Portuguese had a superior fleet of ships loaded with artillery. That gave them the power to dominate the entire western coast of India.'

Vikram nodded his head from side to side and Deepak and I exchanged a silent smile. When that signature nod of disapproval made its appearance, we knew we had to stay quiet.

Vikram said, 'The tiny Indian kingdoms were constantly at war with each other. Some of them foolishly sought the foreigners' help to resolve their local skirmishes.'

I said, 'That's exactly what happened in South India, too. The Nayaka of Gingee and his mercenaries took the Portuguese's help to cause riots in Tanjore. But...,' I couldn't suppress my chuckle, 'the Tanjore King averted the problem by marrying the princess of Gingee.'

Vikram's face relaxed into a smile. His eyes sparkled, a rare sight. 'Maya, welcome to the family. You're a history buff, like me.'

Vikram glanced in Deepak's direction. 'Now I have company. Maya won't ask me to shut up when I talk about my ancestors and my home country.'

I grinned at Deepak. Finally, Vikram saw me as part of their family and not as an outsider from Chennai who had charmed his son.

The history bond turned Uncle Vikram into a new avatar, a nicer version of himself I had never imagined.

CHAPTER 22

AMBA

Tanjore, 1625

Amba stepped onto Ayya's porch with a bunch of freshly cut tulips, daisies and orchids from her garden. *Ayya must have a strong reason for this rare invitation. What if he, too, was annoyed with her?* In any case, it would be nice to meet Ayya's wife, Nagamma, whose wisdom hung around her like a delicate shawl. Paru Ma had mentioned that Ayya cherished and treasured her like a precious jewel.

Is there anyone who would think of me as a precious jewel, wondered Amba? Her mother, Paru Ma, had grown cold after Amba refused to sing with her at the temple festival. The king liked her compositions but ignored her.

Nagamma's gentle voice greeted her. '*Ulla va*, Come in. What beautiful flowers! I have never seen them before,' Nagamma exclaimed with pure joy.

Amba bent down and touched Nagamma's feet with respect.

Nagamma blessed, 'May you shine like the jewel that you are!'

Amba's eyes brimmed. She willed the tears to get back in.

'There, there, what's this Amba? Ayya says you are the strongest young woman in Tanjore.' Nagamma lifted Amba's chin.

'Mami, your love is pure and rare,' Amba choked over her words, taking Nagamma's hands and holding them tight.

'Amba, I don't know what's going on, but I can see you are carrying a heavy burden on your shoulders.' Nagamma's hand brushed Amba's cheek and moved away the unruly curls covering her eyes.

At the gentle tinkle of the prayer bell, Nagamma nodded and retreated into the house, and Ayya emerged from his morning *puja*. The only piece of furniture in the inner hall was a broad polished teak swing suspended from the ceiling with shiny brass chains.

Amba touched Ayya's feet, terrified of what he was going to say.

'May you rise and shine, Amba,' Ayya blessed her.

He sat on the swing and pointed to the mat on the floor. 'What have you heard?'

Amba couldn't control the quiver in her voice. 'Captain Ove says that Thimma from Gingee is plotting against our king. The Portuguese are training his men to use their new weapons. Captain Ove believes Thimma's men have infiltrated the Tanjore army. The captain is concerned that the Portuguese might interfere with their building activity.'

Deep frown lines creased Ayya's forehead. He seemed to be thinking aloud. 'King Changili of Jaffna has asked for King Raghu's help to fight the Portuguese one last time. Changili has lost most of his provinces and has a tiny parcel of land left. Raghu will never refuse his childhood friend.'

Amba was quiet for a long moment. She willed her big toe to stop scratching the smooth marble floor. 'Thimma once tried ...'

Ayya raised his hand before she could finish. His eyes were loaded with unspoken words of kindness.

Her voice choked. 'Ove has become a good friend, but the queen has filled the king's ears with untrue stories, and now the king doesn't trust me anymore. I spoke to the general, and he asked me to leave the matter to experts.'

The chains of the swing squeaked to the rhythm of Ayya's movements.

As if on cue, Nagamma walked in with three small bowls of cut fruit and handed one to Amba. The sweet fragrance of mangoes dissolved the heaviness in Amba's chest. Fruit bowl in hand, Nagamma sat next to Ayya, ready for a leisurely chat. The warmth of their relationship soothed Amba's heart.

Nagamma said, 'Did you hear about Venkata's new *raga* framework? He's been pestering me to play the new melodies on the *veena*.'

'I did not know you played the *veena*,' Amba exclaimed. In a lower tone, she added, 'I never learnt to play the *veena*.'

Nagamma said, 'Amba, you are a talented composer, one of our best. Write your songs so musicians can perform your compositions.'

Amba's heart melted under Nagamma's praise.

Ayya said, 'Set some of your songs to the new *ragas* that Venkata has created.'

Had Ayya forgotten Venkata's caustic criticism? She said, 'But Venkata....'

Ayya raised his hand. 'He was young and brash, and so were you, Amba. You have both come a long way, and it is time to show

Tanjore's dominance in Carnatic music. Your lyrical compositions set to Venkata's new *ragas* will be jewels in the crown of Carnatic music.'

Ayya might have his dreams, but would Venkata share the limelight with Amba?

Ayya said, 'We will find a way, so you two get to meet again, this time as collaborators.'

As Amba took her leave, Nagamma said, 'Come over on a Friday and sing one of your compositions on Goddess Saraswati.'

A few weeks later, when Amba entered Ayya's porch, her feet stopped abruptly. The voice was not Ayya's, but it had the same confident tone.

Nagamma must have sensed her arrival. 'Amba, come in. The *champa* fragrance announced your arrival.' Nagamma's smile was like a mother's embrace.

Amba handed her a basket of fresh bananas and fresh flowers from her garden.

'*Namaskaram*,' Amba bowed her head and paid her respects.

Nagamma led her to the central hall. 'Have you met my nephew, Venkata?'

How could arrogant Venkata be gentle Nagamma's nephew, Amba thought.

Venkata got up from the swing, but his eyes refused to meet Amba's gaze. He seemed embarrassed. Did he not want to meet her, wondered Amba.

Amba greeted him with folded hands as she would a stranger.

Nagamma said, 'Venkata, have you heard Amba's compositions? Last week, when she sang a song on Goddess Saraswati, I could visualise the goddess imparting her divine knowledge to Brahma, the creator.'

'I have heard Amba sing,' muttered Venkata, not ready to meet her eyes.

'Recently?' asked Amba, her gaze fixed on him.

Ayya entered at that exact moment, and his imposing presence took over the room.

'*Namaskaram*, Ayya,' Amba bowed with respect.

'Finally, it is good to see you both under one roof.' Ayya had a broad grin on his face as he sat on the swing.

Had Ayya been planning this meeting for some time, wondered Amba.

Venkata stood on one side of the swing, as far away as possible from Amba.

Turning to Venkata, Ayya said, 'You need Amba's compositions to bring out the emotional aspect of your theoretical *ragas*.'

Venkata's frown betrayed his disagreement.

Oblivious to Venkata's expression, Ayya carried on, 'The nuances and frequency variations in the *raga*s will remain as a theory unless the melodic songs convey the emotions and thoughts of a human being. Music without emotion cannot take us to God.'

Amba's cheeks grew warm. Ayya wanted her to realise her true potential instead of wallowing in her own misery. Would Venkata allow her music to come out? What if the king didn't want her to compose music for Venkata's *ragas*? But how could she refuse Ayya?

'I'll try Ayya.' In a hesitant voice she added, 'I need to understand the scales and *swaras* of the new *ragas* so that the lyrics can enhance the melodious elements.'

Venkata said, 'Ayya, has Amba read my treatise on the framework of seventy-two *ragas*?' Venkata addressed Ayya as if Amba was not present in the room.

Nagamma's laughter tinkled like a tiny prayer bell. 'Are you shy,

Venkata? Talk to Amba directly. Tell her about the logic of your new framework.'

Ayya's smile must have irritated him further.

Venkata hesitated a moment and launched into a long lecture. Every main *raga* had a scale of seven notes and every note had at least two tonal variations. The interval between notes gave a *raga* its unique signature. He droned on head held high as if he were addressing a hall full of people.

'Have you named the new *ragas*?' asked Amba.

'Excellent question, Amba.' Ayya glanced at Venkata.

Venkata sounded unsure. 'Some have names. Others are yet to be named.'

'If Amba's compositions can highlight the melodic elements of a *raga*, that could inspire new *raga* names,' said Venkata.

Coming from Venkata, that was a huge acknowledgement.

Ayya got up with a brisk nod. 'I'll see you both at the music palace, Indira Mandira, on *Vijaya Dashami*.'

Vijay Dashami, the final auspicious day of the ten-day festival, was due after three full moons.

Amba turned to Venkata. 'I need to read your treatise. That will help me compose lyrics that capture the essence of each *raga*.'

Contrary to Amba's expectation, Venkata readily agreed. 'I will bring a copy when I come here next week.'

Ayya and Nagamma's faith in her music helped Amba keep her emotions in check instead of constantly worrying about the king's problems. What was she thinking? That her gumption and commitment could solve the kingdom's troubles that had piled up over generations? She was a writer. All she could do was record the events of the last few months on her palm leaves. Getting back to her morning meditation helped her focus on writing and composing.

General Pandya Varma had said, 'We each have to rise to our calling; you do your job, and I'll do mine.' She was annoyed at the time, but now she understood.

Amba placed her stylus carefully on its stand and stared at the words. They were performing a rhythmic dance along the smooth palm leaves. She sprinkled a tiny speck of ash onto the palm leaf and smoothed it with the silk rag beside her. The words sprang to life, black on brown leaves smooth as silk. She must thank Shanta for creating such a soft surface.

Since she was a little girl, prancing around in long skirts, Amba had wanted to be a poet, a composer. Somewhere along the way, she had got sucked into a political vortex. She was glad to find her way back.

A few evenings later, maid Kamala came skipping in with a huge smile, dangling a silk pouch. 'The king asked me to give this to you.'

Amba's hands shook as she pulled the drawstrings and thrust her hand in. The sheen of the smooth pearls caught her breath. The king must be missing their music-making as much as she did.

Amba immersed her body in the rose water tub and scrubbed away the thin layer of sandalwood and rose water paste that Kamala had applied the previous night. Her skin tingled as she rubbed herself dry with a thin cotton towel.

She wrapped the green silk *sari* that the king had given her when he was besotted with her in the early years of their union. She wore the new pearls and tucked a single *Champa* flower behind her ear.

She entered the music room at the blush of dawn, lit the tall brass lamps and placed a sandalwood incense at the shrine of God Rama, whom the king worshipped.

She tuned the king's *veena* and set it out, ready for him to play. She strummed the strings of her *tanpura* and immersed herself in the drone of the hum. The rustle of silk and sure-footed steps broke her reverie.

The king stood there, his eyes brimming with love. She placed the *tanpura* on the carpet and stood up. Before she could utter a word, the king embraced her with a passion she had long forgotten.

'Amba, Amba.' His voice was hoarse, and his breathing turned heavy, yet he had seemed oblivious to her anguish when the queen had insulted her publicly during the bathing ceremony in the courtyard. It was best for her to stay focused on the music.

Amba gently extricated herself and pointed to the *veena*. 'It's tuned and waiting for you.'

The king sat down on the silk carpet and placed the hollow base on his left thigh. He strummed the strings, allowing the sounds to fill the room.

They were back in their world of music.

Amba chanted the king's morning prayer and then sang her new composition, which compared the king's valour to God Rama's. The king followed on his *veena*, and they were immersed in the music.

'Amba, your lyrics are unique. How I missed our morning music!' He added after a long pause, 'I met the general.' His eyes conveyed a myriad of emotions: anguish, regret, love.

'Raja Nayaka, you are a wise king. I know you will do what is right for the kingdom.'

The king held her close with her head resting on his chest. She stayed still until his breath slowed down. The king's life was complicated, and he was not a free man. Gently, Amba lifted herself and held his hands.

Amba said, 'The events of the past months have made me realise that no matter how much I care, I cannot solve the kingdom's problems. I shall stick to what I know best––composing poetry and music.'

Before the king could reply, the bells on the front door rang out in alarm. Queen Kalyani stormed in, cheeks red and eyes spewing hatred like a demoness. All her fine jewellery appeared garish on that angry body.

This is the face of jealousy, thought Amba as she moved away from the king.

The queen spat out her words. 'Has this woman been poisoning your mind again?'

The king meekly waited for the storm to subside. 'My dear queen ...'

Amba caught the king's eye, gave a brief nod and walked out the door, humming the song they had played together. She did not want to watch the queen humiliate the king, nor would she allow the queen to humiliate her.

Amba lit the new oil lamp Ove had gifted her and placed it next to her writing desk. He was in her garden when Amba asked Shanta about the material of the wick she used in her hut. Unlike Shanta's woven wick, Amba's stringy wick burnt out too fast. A few days later, Ove had come to the garden with a huge parcel wrapped in swaths of cotton and hessian.

'This lamp is designed so the wick can burn for several hours. The wide base of glass chimney tapers into a long narrow neck to keep the smoke out.'

Now that she didn't have to get up from her desk every hour to change the waning wick, she could immerse herself in her writing.

Amba opened the top of her slanting desk and took out her stylus and a stack of palm leaves. She scribed a new style of lyrical prose that bards and storytellers in the village square could narrate. The rhythm and metre were simple and easy to memorise. The poem described the beauty of Tanjore.

The chanting of the king's bards sounded in the distance. The king must be on his way to the temple for the evening *puja*. Suddenly, Amba heard those sure-footed steps approaching her door. She glanced at her plain *sari* in panic; she was not dressed for the king.

After their last encounter at the music hall, Amba knew the queen would not let him out of her sight. The poor king couldn't breathe without Queen Kalyani's permission.

But here he was, at Amba's door, his face shining like a bright full moon. 'Did I surprise you?'

Amba was at a loss for words. 'Welcome Raja Nayaka. Please take a seat. I'll get dressed in a few minutes.'

The king led her to the bed. He was gentle, and their union was a flow of intertwined bodies. Fortunately, she kept the little pouch of castor seeds her mother had given under her bed. There was no space for a crawling child in a courtesan's life.

As the king relaxed, he talked about his childhood days when everything seemed possible.

'As a prince, I had the freedom to choose the battles I wanted to fight. My father was a peaceful king and had no interest in expanding the Tanjore Kingdom. I follow his example, and my battles are fought to protect my friends, never for my gain.'

'What's your strategy now, when there is so much unrest within the kingdom?' asked Amba, resting her head on his shoulders.

'I try to please everyone, and now the voice of my conscience has gone to sleep.'

What a sad confession for a king! Amba asked, 'If you were a prince now, what would you do?'

'I would offer asylum to King Changili of Jaffna, my childhood friend. The Portuguese have made his life impossible in Jaffna.'

'What's stopping you?' Amba felt his shoulder grow limp.

'The problem is, Changili is convinced that even if I give him asylum, he will not be safe in Tanjore if Thimma can come and go from our kingdom as he pleases.'

Amba sat up with a jerk. 'What's Changili's connection with Thimma?'

'Thimma recruits rebels, and the Portuguese supply guns and bayonets to these people. Together, they destroyed Jaffna. Changili thinks Tanjore, too, will suffer the same fate if I don't stop Thimma.'

His head resting heavily on her breasts, the king muttered, 'Queen Kalyani is furious with me for welcoming Changili and his sister Chandrika to Tanjore.'

When the king's snores grew loud, Amba let his head rest on two comfortable cushions. The king knew that Thimma had to be killed for Tanjore to stay peaceful, but would he act?

Distorted images plagued Amba's restless mind. Human heads wobbled on stakes. Hands and legs dangled in mid-air from branches of trees. Vultures and hawks circled the air. Amba crouched under a sack of bones. Her screams produced no sound. Amba woke, drenched sweat.

She lay still until the king stirred. The nightmares were her burden not the king's.

Pink rays filtered through the lattice windows, and the fragrance of jasmine and *champa* breezed in. The king stretched his hands above his head and let out a loud yawn. He took her in his arms again, kissed her forehead and moved the unruly curls covering her right eye. 'What were you writing when I walked in last night?'

'A new style of lyrical prose. Have you seen bards narrate *Ramayana* stories in the town square?' asked Amba.

'Yes, I remember watching a dramatic dance when I was a kid. The actors were all male. Even the female roles were performed by men dressed like women,' he laughed.

Amba asked 'Raja, how would you feel if the bards sing your story in the town square like they sing *Ramayana*, our mythology?'

The king stroked his jaw. 'I don't understand.'

'I am writing your story. The story of King Raghu Nayaka as a *kavya*, an epic poem about you, your kingdom, and your valour. The lyrics will allow the street theatre to enact a musical with visual imagery that will touch the hearts of the common people of Tanjore.'

CHAPTER 23

Over dinner one night, Deepak said, 'I want to invite my colleague Gita and her husband Dave for dinner. I need to talk shop with Gita, and you and Dave can talk about music. Is that okay?'

'Wonderful idea,' I said. 'I'd love to get a 101 on Western music from Dave and talk to him about indigenous music. Both Bach and Barton have hypnotised me, and I'd love to understand their music on a deeper level.'

Being Indian, Gita might be fine with normal spice, but I wasn't sure of Dave's tolerance. So, I cooked a simple meal of peas *pulao*, spinach *dal* and *pappadums*. Gita and Dave were perhaps in their thirties. Dave wore an Indian *kurta* over jeans and Gita wore a casual linen dress, which fitted her perfectly. She had an air of confidence, but not a trace of snobbishness. I liked her instantly.

Gita said, 'The spinach *dal* is delicious. Thanks for the light touch with the spice.'

Dave said with a mischievous grin, 'I handle spice better than Gita. Her mother enjoys cooking for me rather than for her.'

After dinner, Gita and Deepak launched into their software architecture discussions and moved away from the dining table.

While I cleared the table, Dave rinsed the plates and stacked the dish washer.

Dave said, 'Gita mentioned you are a musician and play the *veena*. I know it's an ancient instrument, but I haven't seen it played. Can you play a song for me?'

I said, 'I haven't been practicing regularly, but I'm happy to play.'

I brought out my *veena* and strummed the strings; they were out of tune. I settled on the carpet and tightened the knobs attached to the strings.

Dave bent down. 'Do you want me to squat on the floor like you?'

'Not unless you want to. In India, we perform classical music sitting on the floor cross-legged. I'm used to it.'

He counted the strings. 'Seven? Violins and cellos have four, and the guitar has six, but seven is odd. No pun intended,' smiled Dave.

'Like the violin and cello, the *veena* too has four strings on which we play the main melody. The additional three strings, set at a lower level, help to keep the rhythm and the beat.'

I hummed the three basic notes. *Sa-Pa-Sa*, the third being an octave higher than the first note.

'That's C-G-C...,' hummed Dave.

I hooked my left hand over the long fretboard spread across two resonators and plucked the strings with my right forefingers.

Dave's long fingers traced the inlaid work along the rim of the resonator. 'It's a beautiful instrument, a piece of art. Is it handmade?'

'Yes. They use a special type of hollow gourd and wood from the jackfruit tree for the resonators. The craft of *veena* making is retained within a few families in Tanjore, the city that brought the modern *veena* to the world.

'I'll play a simple melody with five notes which form a pentatonic *raga* named "*Mohanam*".'

I played the ascending scale of the raga: sa re ga pa da sa.

Dave hummed then said, 'C D E G A C. The last C, an octave higher than the first.'

I gave a thumbs up. 'Perfect.'

I played an improvisation segment of *raga 'Mohanam'* and followed it with a short composition set to a rhythm of seven beats.

Dave tapped his hands. 'One-two-three, one-two, one-two. That's a fancy rhythm. If I had my cello, I would try replicating the chords of that song. I'm not sure how it'll sound.'

'It'll be unique; I'd love to hear you play the cello. I recently heard a recording of Bach's '*Arioso*' on the cello. I fell in love with the way the melody and chords intertwined so beautifully.'

I traced the notes of '*Arioso*' on the fretboard. 'In a *veena*, I can only play the melody notes. It took me a while to find the right notes. Please don't laugh if this sounds terrible.'

I played Bach's basic melody and added a few notes of improvisation, a habit that was ingrained in my training. I glanced at David, nervous about his response to my digression.

Dave sat up. 'Maya, this is amazing. You are playing without even having the score in front of you.'

'I don't know how to read Western music; I listen to the notes and use my ear to guide me.'

Dave said, 'So, can you play whatever you hear?'

'Yes and no. I can reproduce the melody played on a stringed instrument like the cello or a violin, but I can't play the harmony and chords that you hear on a piano.'

Dave said, 'I wish I had brought my cello. We could have played something together.'

'Looks like you guys had fun,' said Gita, coming out of the study with Deepak. Gita went across to Dave and planted a kiss on his neck. There was so much love in his eyes, as he gently tousled her hair. Deepak turned his head away, as if he was embarrassed by their display of love.

Deepak said, 'Dave, I knew Maya would enjoy meeting you. Maya's pet peeve is that I don't listen to her music.'

Dave said, 'Not to worry, we musicians will find ways to strum together.'

When they were about to leave, Dave said, 'I practice with my string quartet two evenings a week. Maya, come and listen to our practice session. Bring your *veena*, and let's have some fun.'

Later that night, Deepak said, 'I am glad you kept Dave engaged. It gave me enough time to convince Gita about an important module to be included in the architecture that she is designing.'

'Dave was curious about the *veena*, and we had very interesting discussions. He liked my experiment with Bach's music.'

Deepak said, 'You shouldn't feel pressured to play with his quartet. You have enough on your plate.'

My tone was sharp. 'Deepak, That's for me to decide.'

The following week, Dave and I exchanged texts about a convenient date to meet his quartet group. Deepak had mentioned that he would be late on Thursday evening. So, I chose that day to meet Dave's friends, and he offered to pick me up and drive us to Ryde Community Centre were they practiced.

As I got into the car, Dave asked, 'Aren't you bringing the *veena*?'

'Not today, I want to hear you folks play together. I'll bring my instrument when I feel more confident.'

Part of the kids' library at the Ryde Community Centre had been turned into a music room for hire. The walls had paintings of a platypus, snakes and waratah flowers with colourful dots in an indigenous-inspired style, possibly painted by kids. When we walked into the hall, Dave said, 'Everyone, meet Maya, a *veena* player. She plays without the score in front of her.'

I felt my face turn red. What would they think if they found out I couldn't read Western music? My voice got stuck in my throat. 'Nice to meet you all.'

Dave waved his hand around the group. 'Alex, the lead violinist, is from Ireland. Miguel is from Argentina, and he plays both violin and guitar. Eiko, our viola player, is from Japan. I'm the only person in this group born in Australia,' he laughed.

'Dave, I, too, was born here,' said Eiko. She had a soft voice and the longest eyelashes I had ever seen. 'My parents were born in Japan.'

Miguel asked, 'What's a *veena*?'

'It's a string instrument with frets like a guitar. But its bigger and heavier with two hollow resonators supporting the fretboard.'

I flicked through my phone and showed them a photo taken a while ago in Chennai when I had played at a concert at the Ganesha temple. Miguel passed it around to the others.

Alex asked, 'Do you have a regular group you play with?'

'No. We only come together during a concert. Typically, there's the lead musician, a violinist who accompanies them, and a percussionist, who plays a *tabla* or *mridangam* to provide the rhythm and beats for the music.'

Alex asked, 'No rehearsals?'

'No. Indian musicians learn by ear. We first learn the notes and structure of a *raga*. There's plenty of freedom to improvise and explore the nuances of a *raga* around a song.'

I asked, 'Are you practising for a concert?'

Alex said, 'We are playing live music for a ballet. My sister's friend Lenka runs a ballet school, and they are working on a production of *La Bayadere, The Temple Dancer*.'

My eyes swept across all of them. '*The Temple Dancer*? That sounds Indian. Can I listen to the music?'

Dave took out his cello from its case and tuned it. He said, 'This is a small production with school kids. Lenka is raising funds to start dance and music classes for kids on the spectrum. We have six months to practice, but this is only our second session.'

Miguel cackled. 'The original choreography was French, and the music was scored for a Russian ballerina. The story has an Indian temple dancer, a warrior, a *Brahmin*, a *Maharajah* and a princess. Check it out on YouTube; you'll find different productions.'

'Do the songs have words?' I asked.

'Not in this ballet.'

I said, 'I can't imagine an Indian temple dancer dancing without lyrics.'

They propped their music on their stands and positioned themselves comfortably around their instruments. The cello led the way, and the other three followed. By turns, each instrument took a lead, and the rest followed. After a couple of rounds, I caught on and hummed the notes. But I could not visualise how the music and dance worked together without lyrics.

They had a few more practice rounds, and the tune got lodged in my head. As I was riding home with Dave, I was humming the tune. Dave said, 'There you go. You already have the melody. You should be able to play it now.'

'I'll try,' I said as we approached home. I waved him goodbye and let myself in through the door.

CHAPTER 24

AMBA
Tanjore, 1625

Amba sat between Muthu and Shanta on the hessian-covered dirt floor of the street theatre. The large, thatched tent, made of dried coconut fronds, was erected in the centre of the town square, as it was on every full moon night. She covered her nose with a corner of her *sari*, blocking the stench of sweat and stale jasmine as men and women edged closer to the stage.

The street theatre performed dance-dramas on full moon nights, depicting a mythological story of a god or goddess who fought and killed demons who harassed good people on earth. The eternal theme was the victory of good over evil. Gods were the winners, always.

Today, the street theatre was performing Amba's work, a lyrical folk tale in Telugu about King Raghu Nayaka and the battles he won against enemies who threatened to destroy Tanjore and its people.

She had convinced King Raghu that street theatre was the best medium to communicate the greatness of the Tanjore Nayaka dynasty to the common people.

Voices washed over each other as the crowd elbowed their way closer to the raised wooden platform decorated with colourful fabrics and bunting.

General Pandya Varma would not be happy if he knew she was sitting under a tent in the town square. He had warned the palace women not to venture out.

'Violence in the streets has increased. Armed rebels are inciting tenants to fight against landlords for raising their rent. It's best not to go out at night until we put an end to this insurgence,' he had said.

Amba could never understand why the tenants didn't take their appeal to the king when landlords squeezed them. Wasn't it the king's duty to protect his poor subjects?

No matter what the general said, Amba did not want to miss the dramatization of her poem. The street-theatre performers were breathing new life into her lyrics. She had taken precautions to blend in with the peasant women who came to watch the show, heading the general's warning. She wore a coarse cotton *sari*, oiled and knotted her hair into a tight bun at the nape of her neck, removed her gold jewellery and wore a thin silver chain and a pair of glass bangles on each wrist.

The drums rolled as the bards sang a chorus from behind the curtains.

'Among many trees, there is but one wishing tree,
Among many kings, there is but one wise King,
Who, like Rama, is noble and graceful,
And like Krishna, is wise and wonderful.'

The curtains parted, and a tall man in a colourful warrior costume strode onto the wooden platform. His elaborate headdress and layers of padded clothes made him look like the giant sculpture guarding the Big Temple. The wooden stage shuddered under his thundering gait.

Amba craned her neck to watch his expression as he belted out the verse. She had used the same lyrical format that folk musicians used to introduce gods like Rama and Krishna.

The king was amused when she had read out her poem describing him as an incarnation of Rama, who himself was an incarnation of God Vishnu, the creator.

He had roared with laughter at the next verse, in which Amba compared the king and his women to God Krishna and his *gopis,* the besotted women who danced around Krishna when he played his flute.

A chance meeting with Muthu's nephew, Velu, had made Amba realise that she should compose music in Tamil and Telegu. That way, the common people could understand and enjoy it unlike Sanskrit which was the language of scholars.

Velu had casually remarked one day, 'The kings are all the same. They fight with each other, but we, the poor, suffer no matter who wins or loses.'

Amba said, 'But our King Raghu is different; he fights to protect his friends and neighbours against foreign invaders.'

Velu said, 'We know more about Gods Rama and Krishna than our king.'

Amba asked, 'How do you know more about gods?'

'The street theatre,' Velu said. 'You should see their dance-drama about gods Rama and Krishna. They sing and dance every full moon at the town centre. People never miss these shows.'

Amba had watched the story of Krishna when she was a little girl. She had been fascinated by the actor's sonorous voice, the way he transitioned from music to dialogue and back to music, weaving prose and poetry without missing a single beat. Street theatre was as popular with common people as Carnatic music was with scholars. So far, all her writing had been in Sanskrit because she had wanted to impress the scholars of Tanjore.

I am no different from those snooty scholars if simple folks don't understand my writing, thought Amba.

Her epic poem projected King Raghu in a new light ––a king endowed with divine powers like Rama and Krishna.

The musician's voice resonated like the temple bell.

'He is both Rama and Krishna.'

The drums rolled. The crowd roared.

'Like Rama, King Raghu followed his father's wishes,

Like Krishna, he is wise and wonderful.'

There were two distinct rhythms, one for Rama and one for Krishna. Two dancers, one dressed as Rama with a green-painted face and the other as Krishna with a blue face, danced to the rhythm of drums.

'Like Rama, King Raghu listens to his subjects.

Like Krishna, he is surrounded by adoring women.'

Rama carried a bow and arrow while Krishna played his flute. Both dancers mesmerised the audience with their expressive eyes and the fluid movement of their necks, hands and torsos. Their feet tapped a rhythmic pattern: six beats for Rama, sixteen beats for Krishna. They went round and round, reaching a climax at forty-eight beats.

It was a complex rhythm even scholars would struggle with, but the street musicians executed the rhythm to perfection.

The performers transported the audience to a mythological world where King Raghu Nayaka was courageous like Rama and as wise as Krishna. Wide-eyed and open-mouthed, people focused with an intensity Amba had never imagined. Even if written works disappeared, this story would be passed down through generations, much like the oral transmission of the Vedic hymns that priests chanted at temples. Her efforts at composing lyrics that invoked visual imagery had worked. Amba squeezed Shanta's hand every time the crowd roared.

The show concluded as the twinkling stars faded behind the blush of dawn. They exited the tent before the rush of the crowd. Shanta and Muthu waited until Amba entered the side gate of the courtesan's wing before they returned home. Amba tiptoed through the courtyard to her apartment. As she pushed the heavy brass handle of the front door, her feet staggered at the stench of burnt fibres. The foyer was a cloud of smoke. A spurt of coughs choked her throat. Amba rolled her *sari pallu*, covered her nose and mouth, and groped her way through the smoky haze to the front room. The floor was covered in a carpet of ashes. Scraps of charred palm leaves lay scattered everywhere.

Amba ran to her writing room and opened the drawers under her desk. A heap of ash flew into her face; her manuscripts were gone. In their place burnt fibres were everywhere, even in her bedroom. It was the act of a demented soul. Was this the face of jealousy? The terrible stench of destroyed work engulfed her.

Amba blinked as she caught a whiff of mint and camphor. Maid Kamala was mopping her face with a wet towel as sweet sugarcane juice trickled down her throat. A cool hand caressed her forehead, and she realised her head was resting on Shanta's lap. Muthu was sitting on his haunches, rocking back and forth. Amba tried to open her eyes, but her head hurt, so she closed them again. There was a sense of relief; she was with people who cared for her and loved her. She felt her body go limp.

Shanta propped Amba up against a wall and placed a hessian cushion behind her neck.

Amba couldn't recognise the voice coming from her gritty throat. 'How did I get here?'

Muthu removed his turban and wiped the sweat and tears that had settled into the wrinkles of his face.

'After the performance, we waited until you entered the palace gate and then walked home. I was washing my feet and hands when Kamala's husband, Raju, arrived sobbing. I couldn't get a word out of him. All he said was, "Ashes, turned to ashes." Shanta and I panicked and thought something had happened to you.'

Tears streamed down Shanta's eyes. 'I ran to your apartment and found you unconscious on the floor. Kamala sat there sobbing, mopping your face with a wet towel. We decided it was best to get you out of the palace before they burn you to ashes. I got Raju and Muthu to carry you and bring you here.'

Over the next few days, Muthu and Shanta cared for Amba like she was their own daughter. Amba didn't want to open her eyes, didn't want to sit up, didn't want to eat, so Shanta brought a herbalist to get Amba back on her feet. Morning and evening, the herbalist boiled green herbs, burnt brown twigs, ground dark spices and turned them into a slimy decoction. The old woman would not budge until Amba swallowed the bitter brew and inhaled the strong vapours from barks and roots each time. The vapours irritated her nose, brought on a sneezing fit and her tongue lost all taste.

'These hot vapours will drive out the smoke in your head and lungs,' the herbalist said.

A few days later, Paru Ma, came to visit. 'Come home, and I'll look after you until you get well.'

'And then what? You'll send me back to the palace. I am NOT

going back to the palace, ever again.' Amba's eyes welled. She had no energy to argue with her mother.

Amba cupped her hands over the warm bowl and took a sip of Shanta's aromatic *rasam*. The lentil broth spiced with pepper, ginger and tangy tamarind trickled down her throat and shook her sleepy senses. Amba opened her eyes before closing them again; it was too bright.

Shanta propped up the hessian cushions against the cool mud wall for her to lean on. Amba straightened her back and half-opened her eyes. Her heart felt heavy with gratitude. When tears and sobs rocked her body, Amba could not stop. Shanta sat next to her and stroked her back until the sobs became hiccups. Amba rested her head against Shanta's shoulder and stayed there for a long time.

A few days later, maid Kamala came with a large bundle under her arm.

'Amba Ma, I brought a few *saris* and pieces of your favourite jewellery.'

Kamala opened the bundle and stacked the *saris* into a neat pile. The jewellery pouch contained the pearls the king had given her last year, to woo her back after Queen Kalyani's obnoxious behaviour. Amba pushed the pouch aside; she didn't want any reminder of that world.

'Amba Ma, I have cleaned your place for you. The king asked for you. He thought you went away to your mother's place. He asked me to go with his messenger to Paru Ma's house.'

Amba's hands flew to her mouth. 'What did Paru Ma say?'

Kamala's lips twisted into a naughty grin. 'Paru Ma said, "I thought Amba was at the palace".'

Even the tiny smile she had in response to her mother's loyalty hurt Amba's head.

Kamala said, 'Don't worry, Amba Ma. I did not tell anyone in the palace where you were. The king does not know your whereabouts.'

A few days later, Muthu stood around scratching his head.

'What's wrong, Muthu?'

'Captain Ove is in the coconut grove for his coconut water. Would you like to meet him? I have not told him you are here.'

Should she or should she not? Was she well enough to see him? 'Not now. Maybe next week.'

The following week, Ove was at the door with a bunch of tulips - the same flowers he had brought to their first meeting a lifetime ago. He sat down awkwardly on the mud floor and took her hand in his. Amba felt a warm energy seeping through him. She allowed her limp hand to rest there, but she could not bring herself to speak.

Ove came every day after that to hold her hand.

One day Amba asked, 'How long are you going to be here holding my hand? Don't you have work to do?' She was startled at the sound of her voice. It was throaty and gritty.

Shanta's face lit up, and Ove's smile reached his eyes. 'My work will start when you start yours.'

Her words came out in a torrent. 'It's gone. Nothing is left but ashes. It's all gone. I don't care. No one cares,' The sobs took over again.

Ove held her hand, and Shanta brought a cup of cardamom-scented sugarcane juice. The sweet juice gave her a shot of energy.

Amba let out a huge sigh, extracted her hand from his and mopped her brows with the tip of her *sari*.

'Did you hear what happened?' asked Amba.

'Yes, and everyone knows who did it. Queen Kalyani made no bones about it!'

'I never knew jealousy could go that far,' muttered Amba.

Ove took her hand again and gave it a gentle squeeze. 'Amba, don't let jealousy win.'

Shanta moved a few strands of hair that were blocking Amba's eyes. 'Amba Ma, I have new palm leaves for you. Exactly as per your requirements, and Kamala has found your gold stylus.'

Muthu said, 'Yesterday, being a full moon day, the street theatre performed your play again. Raju mentioned there were more people for the second performance than he has ever seen before. Your work is alive and thriving.'

Over the next few weeks, Amba felt her energy creeping back. She stepped out into the garden with Shanta by her side, the first time she had done so in over a month. They walked to the lotus pond from where she could see the temple dome, tall and proud. It was mocking her. "Do you know how many storms and fires I have faced? One fire and you're not able to rise out of the ashes."

She had a persistent dream every night. Goddess Shakti was with Shiva, whispering. 'Wake up, we are here.'

That evening, Amba wrote a Sanskrit song in praise of the invincible Shiva. The god performed his nocturnal dance among the ashes of dead bodies, symbolizing destruction and creation.

Who would understand the intensity of her mental turmoil? Ayya could, but was it fair to burden him with her problems? The king might, but he also might not. The thickness of the veil covering his eyes depended on the person who was around to influence his judgment.

It was the king's duty to protect the women under his roof. He had absconded from his duties. He was allowing his treacherous queen and her accomplice Thimma to take control of Tanjore streets.

Amba took her time to write the note.

'Raju, please take this note to the king, but hide it under your shirt. Don't stop anywhere, and don't talk to anyone. Go around midday, soon after lunch, when the king will go to his chamber to rest. Wait there until he sends you back with a reply. If you can't find the king, don't hang around. Give the note to Ayya; he will be in his chamber.'

The swish of palm leaves, chirps of sparrows and rope rubbing against a clanky wheel enveloped her senses, and the sounds became sharper when her eyes were closed. Amba squinted at the splashes of orange, red, and amber that moved across the little window of the garden hut. A patient blue sky waited in the background.

Amba scrubbed her teeth with a mint-coated neem stick, splashed her face with cool well water and returned to the kitchen. The small lamp at the altar of Goddess Parvati cast long dancing shadows, and the sandalwood incense lent an aura of tranquillity and peace. Shanta's tiny hut had the same divinity as the temple sanctum.

Amba went to the front yard to find Shanta had created a little piece of art at her doorstep. Four large hibiscus flowers marked the corners of the geometric motif, the beautiful *kolam* drawn with rice flour, a decoration common at the doorstep of every house in Tanjore. Busy sparrows pecked the rice flour and smudged the lines of the *kolam* motif as if it were their birthright.

Shanta was in the kitchen. The aroma of coconut oil, curry leaves, and the sizzling sound of batter on a hot girdle drew Amba back into the kitchen.

Shanta extracted a banana leaf from a stack of leaves and then cut it into arm lengths. She sprinkled a few drops of water on it, brushed the surface with her fingers, and placed it in front of the straw mat.

'Amba Ma, do sit down. The *dosas* are hot and crisp, exactly as you like them.'

Amba inhaled the aroma of fresh coconut chutney and tore a piece of the hot *dosa*, which left a light brown stain on banana leaf.

The sensory pleasure of the melting *dosa* and chutney sliding down her throat was like a gentle caress along her neck. Amba licked the last bits of coconut chutney sticking to her fingers. 'Shanta, your chutney is the best I have ever tasted, even better than Paru Ma's.'

'Amba Ma, you should be eating royal food. Instead, you have chosen this humble gardener's meal.'

'Shanta, your food is sprinkled with love. That's why it tastes great. The palace food can never taste like this, not when it's filled with anger, jealousy, hatred and fear. No one trusts anyone in the palace.'

Muthu scratched his head. A frown creased his forehead. 'Amba Ma, there's a messenger from the palace.'

'Muthu, I don't want to meet anyone from the palace. Please send Raju to talk to him.'

Raju came back grinning. 'The king has sent this note.'

Dear Amba,

I have arranged a safe and comfortable house for you where you can write to your heart's content and not be disturbed. I'll send a palanquin tomorrow. The palanquin bearers are trustworthy men. They will take you to your new home.

The emotions expressed in your song on Shiva caused my veena strings to weep. I feel your pain, but the gold bracelets on my wrists are shackles that bind me to the queen and the kingdom.

Keep writing, Tanjore needs to hear your compositions.

May the goddess continue to shower her blessings on you.

RN

CHAPTER 25

MAYA

Sydney, 2014

Over the next few days, I spent several hours watching YouTube videos of the French and American productions of *The Temple Dancer*. Vibrant visuals dominated the senses in both versions, but there were no Indian sounds to match the cliched Indian costumes of the dancers.

I sent a text message to Dave with a sad emoji. 'I can't read Western music notations.'

Dave responded with a smiley. 'No worries. I'll pick you up next week.'

A week later, I sat in the back seat of Dave's car with my *veena* strapped to my adjacent seat belt. Alex, Miguel and Eiko were thrilled to see me arrive with the *veena*. After everyone had their pluck of the veena strings, Alex nodded at the group. 'Let's start.'

Alex was the concert master and conductor as he was the person in touch with the ballet teacher.

'It'll be a summarised version of *La Bayadere,* as it's for kids. It'll be an hour max with six scenes. We need to select the music for those scenes, and if we have time, we'll play a song before the curtain rises.'

Dave said, 'Let's start with the first scene where the *Brahmin* priests and the temple dancers come together and perform the fire ritual.'

Turning to me, he said, 'We'll play first. See how it sounds for a bit, then join in whenever you're comfortable.'

I tuned my *veena* so the main string was set to note C.

I said, 'Go ahead. I'll listen to a few rounds and then follow.'

Once I got a handle on the melody, I hesitantly followed the cello and added four bars based on the same motif. Alex took up his bow, picked up my last note, and moved the music forward then Eiko played her segment on the viola. I added a couple of bars with louder twangs from the three additional strings on my *veena* to invoke the fire chants depicted in the story.

'Bravo!' Miguel's guitar burst into passionate sounds; new, fresh notes, defying genre boundaries.

I clapped my hands. 'That's brilliant. I didn't hear that part in the original score.'

Miguel said, 'I improvised. It's a combination of tango and jazz chords. I got carried away after listening to your strums to depict chanting.'

Eiko held her viola upside down. 'This reminds me of the *shamisen* my father listens to early in the morning.' She launched into Japanese-inspired music, plucking her viola strings instead of using the bow. There was a spontaneous burst of applause from everyone.

Alex said, 'I never knew you could imitate the sound of *shamisen* on the viola.'

Dave said, 'This is an international story. Let's add our improvisations.'

Eiko raised her eyebrows. 'It's one thing to have fun, but are we allowed to change the original score?'

Alex said, 'We'll play the original score first, without any change. Then Maya can play a few chanting chords on the *veena* in the first scene during the fire worship. The *veena* sound will bring in the Indian temple ambience. We'll move on and continue the original score. Towards the end, we'll announce that we have created our own composition inspired by the story of *La Bayadere*. That'll give all of us more freedom in the final section.'

Miguel strummed another tango chord and threw his head backwards. 'This is fun. Let's start with a simple melody. Then let's each improvise around that melody and see where it takes us.'

Alex took up his violin and played a haunting melody on a minor scale. He played it with a slow rhythm, the bow gliding gracefully from one note to the next. Miguel repeated the same melody on his guitar, gradually increasing the pace and effortlessly transposing the melody line to another scale. To me, it sounded like a *raga* with an odd note thrown in. Eiko used a mixture of bow and plucking to repeat the new melody.

Dave nodded in my direction. 'Go on.'

My palms grew sweaty. While I could be spontaneous, this was totally new. I could hear the notes, but it was not a *raga* I could follow.

I said, 'You guys carry on. It's too new for my ears; I need to listen before I can join you.'

After the next round, Dave nodded in my direction again. 'Come on, give us some notes. You don't have to follow us.'

I closed my eyes. Dave's bow produced a single note, first soft and then louder. Although my fingers were hesitant at first, they moved on their own accord. I picked up that note and played the same melody as Alex. I added a couple of tiny variations and allowed the notes to float in the air.

One by one, they all followed, and soon we were lost in our collective music until Alex faded us out, one by one.

'Shoot, I should have recorded that,' exclaimed Alex. He said, 'Let's play this piece at the Manly Music Festival. Maya, why don't you join us? We're already listed on the playbill. Let's come up with a theme and plan the repertoire. We have six months to practice.'

Over the next few months, we produced melodies and harmonies that I could never have conceived by myself. The beauty of our string quintet was that each of us had a solo part and a combined part; no one was a passenger. Playing with this group was a life-changing experience for me. Not one of us could envisage a life without our instruments. With barely a month before the festival, each of us had to practice individually and collectively as much as possible.

Gita came every day after work in her SUV to take me and Dave back home with our large instruments. One night, Dave helped me unbuckle the *veena*, came up to our door, and rang the bell as he did every evening.

Deepak swung the door open, ignored Dave and glared at me. 'You are late. It's well past dinner time.'

Clearly embarrassed, Dave shrugged and nodded in my direction. 'See you tomorrow.' He got into the waiting car, and they drove down the street and out of sight.

Deepak's voice rose, 'Is this going to be your new routine?'

'Yes, until the festival concert.' I didn't recognise my own steely voice. I went into the study, placed the *veena* in its stand and came into the cold, empty kitchen.

'If you were hungry, why didn't you order takeaway?'

Deepak's entire face became a frown. 'I thought you would come home and cook.'

'Really? Do you think I'm a cooking machine?

I glared at him, and my tone took on a stubborn edge. 'I'm not cooking today.'

Why couldn't he order takeaway? Was he incompetent or lazy, or was this his sense of entitlement?

I went into the bathroom, splashed cold water on my face and ordered takeaway from the Chinese place around the corner. The noodles arrived, and we ate in silence. The bitterness in the air rubbed off on the noodles, and my stomach heaved. I ran to the bathroom and threw up.

My music practice with Dave and the crew continued, much to Deepak's dismay. Sensing our strained relationship, Deepak's mother, Neetu, invited us for dinner every weekend. When she tried to bridge our differences, her voice came from a deep well, too weak and too soft for Deepak to hear let alone understand.

CHAPTER 26

AMBA
Tanjore, 1626

Amba wiped the beads of perspiration from her forehead with the corner of her *sari* as she came out of her room into the adjoining veranda. After a warm sticky night, the dawn breeze filtering through the bamboo lattice was a cool respite. The hazy dawn stretched out as the sun was in a hurry to move in.

The silence was deep. She heard no temple bells, no cacophony of the markets, and no shrill reed pipes. The swish of swaying palms and the distant moo of cows were the only sounds that broke the silence. Green paddy fields stretched as far as the eye could see. Far away, high up on the horizon, the golden spire of the Big Temple sparkled like a shiny star.

The fresh smell of grass mingled with the pungent odour of cow dung reminded Amba of her childhood and her early morning walks to Guru and Mami's house all those years ago. Guru had taught her everything she knew—music, languages, poetry and composition. Mami was a treasure house of stories—stories of strong women who never gave up no matter what the circumstances were.

There was the potter's daughter, Molla, who crossed every hurdle set by the men in Emperor Krishna Deva Raya's court and became a great Telugu poet. The men in her town stopped harassing her after the king recognised her talent.

Then, there was that queen from Mangalore, Rani Abbakka. She used her wit and wisdom to lead her tiny army and won several battles against the Portuguese.

These women had courage and conviction a hundred years ago. Perhaps this was Mami's way of preparing me for what lay ahead.

Amba stretched her hands over her head and stood on her tippy toes to gaze at the temple spire. Her mother had once told her that Goddess Parvati's creative energy grew stronger with every calamity she faced in her many lives.

Destruction had occurred, but creation had to arise from those ashes. If she could create once, she could create again.

Ayya visited her that evening. Deep lines ran from both sides of his nose to his jaw. His cheeks sagged with the weight of his worries. Ageless Ayya had aged. He sat down heavily on the smooth wooden bench, the only piece of furniture in the house. *She should get one of those new chairs from Ove for Ayya to sit on.*

Amba spread out a bamboo mat, arranged a few cushions against the wall and sat facing Ayya.

Ayya said, 'I can't believe that someone's jealousy could be so intense. What caused the queen to destroy your work?'

'Misfortune seeks me out, Ayya. This would not have happened if I had not stepped out of the courtesan's palace.'

Amba scratched the mat with her fingers. A thin splinter poked her finger. 'I was impulsive. I was tempted to see how the street theatre transformed my Telugu poem into a visual story of our king.'

A tiny frown appeared between Ayya's eyebrows. 'I thought you wrote devotional songs? What sparked your interest in street theatre?'

Amba's hands twisted and untwisted the loose corner of her *sari*. How could she explain to puritan Ayya that street music was in no way inferior to devotional music? That ordinary folks preferred visual entertainment to pious music.

'As I got involved with political affairs, I maintained a diary of events that were happening around me. I thought someday I would write a scholarly biography of the king in Sanskrit as my contribution to future generations. But then I realised people like gardener Muthu, Shanta, maid Kamala and many others like them would never be able to read a biography written in Sanskrit. I wanted common folks to know their king. A man who chose music over mayhem and concord over conflict. I was in love with the king when I wrote that play. Little did I realise....' Amba swallowed the tears that threatened to erupt again.

Ayya was silent, his head hung low. Was Ayya disappointed with his spineless protégé, whom he had groomed to be a wise king?

Amba said, 'I wrote the epic poem in the *Yakshagana* style of music popular in folk theatre. The verses have a rhythm to invoke visual imagery. I read the verses out to the king, and he loved those songs when he first heard them.'

She had done what she thought was best for the king and his subjects. As a composer, she saw no boundaries between classical and folk music. It was up to Ayya to either condemn her for deviating from classical music or condone her actions.

Finally, Ayya's face relaxed. 'Few people think like you, Amba.

Oral history is the basis for folk theatre, but you have turned it upside down. Now your written verses will influence oral history!'

'I never thought of it that way. Is that wrong?' asked Amba.

Ayya thought about it and then answered. 'No. There's nothing right or wrong in poetry and music. People prefer to stick to one genre, one mode of communication, to tell their story. You have embraced all genres.'

'It is easy to touch the hearts of ordinary people with folk music. They listen, watch and get immersed in the story.' Amba added after a pause, 'Unlike connoisseurs, who sit in judgement, criticising the musician, the music and the composer. Their aim is to find a flaw rather than allow the music touch them on an emotional level.'

Ayya rubbed the back of his tuft. 'Amba, you trained in classical music for years. Rules around music composition are stringent, and we are expected to adhere to those rules. Naturally, connoisseurs expect musicians to conform to the *raga* and *tala* system. Imagine how it would sound if you broke away from the notes of the *raga* or skipped the beats of a *tala*.'

Amba blurted out. 'Folk music has its own rhythm and structure. My guru used to say that in Tanjore even trees know how to sing. Music is in their blood.'

Unfortunately, music, like people, had succumbed to class hierarchy. Educated *Brahmins* claimed that Carnatic music was superior to folk music. But since Ayya was a high-caste *Brahmin*, Amba kept these thoughts to herself.

Her new maid Kanchana brought a cane tray with a bunch of finger bananas and two silver cups of sugar cane juice. Amba took the cup from Kanchana and handed it to Ayya. She waited until he had his drink, and then she had hers. Paru Ma had drilled it into her head that guests had to be served first. The zing of ginger tickled her throat, and the edible camphor, cooled her tongue.

Ayya drank the juice and handed the cup back to Kanchana. With a shy smile, she disappeared into the kitchen.

'Is Kanchana looking after your needs?' Ayya asked. 'Her mother works in our house. Nagamma has a soft spot for Kanchana.'

Amba said, 'True to her name, Kanchana is bright and beautiful. Her smile makes up for her silence. Was she born with this disability?'

'The poor girl was born deaf. She can't talk and is terrified of strangers. Nagamma thought it would be good for her to be with you in a safe place until she gains confidence.'

Amba moved her fingers rapidly to show her new skill in communicating.

'Kanchana is teaching me her sign language, and I'll teach her to read and write Telugu. Kanchana is intelligent. She'll be a fast learner.'

Ayya's tone matched his smile, warm and tender. 'Don't forget your own writing while you teach her to write.'

The following week, Ayya turned up with a fresh batch of palm leaves.

'Remember, you were to write some new compositions for Venkata's new *raga* framework? That didn't happen because of the fire. But now there's another opportunity.'

Ayya paused and continued. '*Navaratri*, the nine-day festival, starts on the new moon day, three moons from now. Every year, on the tenth day, we have a tradition where Carnatic musicians present their compositions at the music palace. This year, I would like you to present some new songs on new *ragas* drawn from Venkata's *raga* framework. This will be the highlight of this music season.'

Amba acknowledged the invitation with folded hands. No matter how far and how frequently she strayed, Ayya steered her back on track to follow her calling. But would the male composers be open to her music? She could never forget her first performance at the music palace all those years ago when Venkata had rejected her music.

Amba brushed a palm leaf frond with a rag dipped in neem oil and waited for it to dry. Shanta had taught her that trick. 'You don't want insects to eat up your work,' she had said when she applied the bitter oil on the palm fronds.

Amba gently pressed her forefinger and thumb on the thin end of the gold stylus to etch the Sanskrit words on the palm leaf. Too much pressure made holes in the writing surface, and too little pressure prevented the words from showing up. She sat back and reviewed the script; a bit of charcoal dust brought it to life.

Life at the farmhouse was not as erratic as it used to be in the palace. Amba was not at the beck and call of the king nor a victim of the queen's mood swings. While she did not miss the daily commotion of royal life, she missed her garden, Muthu and Shanta, and her frequent visitor, Ove. Did he get the resources to build the fort as they had planned? Was it a year ago that she had visited Tranquebar with Ove? It felt like another world in another time. But no matter what life threw at her, music drew her back to her reality.

Humming the notes of *raga 'Malahari'* Amba scribed a song in two verses, four lines each, four phrases per line, so as to fit into a rhythmic *tala* of sixteen beats. She hummed the first four lines and adjusted a couple of syllables till the rhythm was perfect. Eight lines fit perfectly on one frond.

Amba dipped a narrow cotton ribbon in fine charcoal powder stored in a coconut shell, and gently brushed the rag along the palm leaf's light brown surface until the letters were dark and bold.

Kanchana made it her business to arrange Amba's writing accessories around her desk every morning. A fresh stack of palm leaves, cotton ribbons of different widths and a coconut shell filled with fine dark charcoal powder filtered from kitchen embers were always ready and waiting for her. She took great pains to clean and polish the gold stylus for Amba each morning until the tip was shiny and sharp. The stylus made deep imprints, and the letters were clean and crisp, but the leaves were never as smooth as the ones Shanta created.

A few moons later, Amba arrived at the garden hut unannounced.

Muthu's rheumy eyes grew moist. 'Amba Ma, welcome, welcome.' He brushed the dust away from the stone bench and waited for her to sit.

'My hands and feet are shaking with excitement,' Muthu said, plonking himself on the stone bench.

Shanta sat down near Amba and started massaging her hands. She spoke as though she had read Amba's thoughts, 'Do you have enough palm leaves to write on?'

Amba's eyes welled as she took Shanta's hands in hers, 'Shanta, every time I write I think of your thick, wide palm leaves. My maid Kanchana prepares the leaves for me, but the quality is never like yours.'

Shanta said, 'I'll prepare some fronds for you today.'

Muthu asked, 'Amba Ma, do you want to see your garden and talk to your flowers?' He pointed to a huge hibiscus. 'Every flower here remembers you. I told them you would be back one day.'

When Amba returned from a stroll in the garden, Shanta was ready with her customary buttermilk. Amba sat down on the stone bench on the veranda, feeling the cool breeze blow across her face.

'Shanta, can you please teach Kanchana your technique to strengthen and preserve the palm leaves? Kanchana does a fine job of cutting them to size, but she doesn't know your tricks to make them soft.'

'Yes, Amba Ma, I'll teach her. I will make sure your leaves have a long life.'

Amba turned around at the unexpected sound of bootsteps.

'*Ola*, Amba, what a pleasure! I didn't expect to see you here.'

'Neither did I! How are you, my friend?'

Ove stretched out both his hands. She hesitated for a moment, then allowed him to hold hers. Theirs was a friendship that bound kingdoms together.

'How's the fort coming along? Has your Danish architect arrived? Has King Raghu kept his promise with the supply of building materials?'

Ove nodded. 'It's all going as planned. We plan to call it the Dansborg Fort. I'll take you when it's complete, with your lighthouse,' he grinned,

Amba laughed. 'My lighthouse? When do you think it will be finished?'

'At the end of the year. We plan to have a grand celebration when its's finished.'

'I, too, have a plan. A plan to build a school for girls. Do you have schools for girls in Denmark?'

'No. They are taught at home if they have a liberal father. But like you, there are female scholars.'

Amba said, 'We have a formal system for boys, the *gurukul*. The boys live with the teacher and learn for a period of seven years before they return to the community. I want to start a *gurukul* for girls.'

A deep crease appeared between his eyebrows. 'Can you ensure their safety if they choose to stay with you?'

Amba let out a loud sigh. 'The king says he will keep us safe.'

Ove was quiet for a long time. 'Maybe the school will force him to act.'

Amba pretended not to hear Ove's words. He had picked the one weak link in her big plan. She asked, 'What do you remember about your school in Denmark?'

Ove's answer was spontaneous. 'A big playground.'

Amba burst into peals of laughter. 'My girls' school will be different. We'll have an art studio and a music hall instead of a playground. I am sure the girls will love that.'

Ove was thoughtful. 'If that's your plan, allow me to talk to my architect friend. He will have some good ideas.'

Muthu cleared his throat. Ove smiled. 'Yes, I'd love some coconut water.' Ove followed Muthu to the coconut grove.

The sun was setting down the horizon, and the temple shadows grew longer. It was time for Amba to head back to the farmhouse before it got dark. That was Ayya's strict instruction when she had asked for a palanquin to visit the garden.

Her chief palanquin bearer, Shama, came panting. 'Amba Ma, we have to leave NOW.'

Shama hustled Amba through the side gate of the garden into the waiting palanquin. The other three men stood ready. They each had a dagger peeking out of their waistbands, which Amba had never noticed before. They trotted off the moment she climbed in.

Shama steered the palanquin through the narrow side streets around the town square.

He whispered, 'The streets are chaotic today, but don't worry, Amba Ma, we'll keep you safe.' His hand patted the dagger at his waist. Though she did not know want they anticipated, the loyal men seemed prepared. Amba pulled her *sari* tight over her shoulders and crouched inside the palanquin as they scuttered through unlit streets. Her heart raced as a clop of hooves galloped past. She held her breath and pushed the memories of Thimma from the corners of her mind. Amidst the sounds of howling voices, a shrill scream pierced Amba's ears.

'Shama,' Amba whispered. 'A woman is injured. We must save her.'

'Amba Ma, it is not safe for us to stop now. You cannot step out of the palanquin.'

Amba stretched her hand out. 'Give me your dagger; I know you have one.'

Shama's voice quivered. 'Ayya will punish us if you come to harm.'

The scream grew louder. Amba hissed. 'Stop now, or I will jump out.'

The men lowered the palanquin, and Amba tiptoed to the corner of the narrow street before coming to a pause. Shama crouched by her side, his hand on his waist.

Handcarts lay toppled. Bananas, coconuts, metal pots, mud pots, bangles, and clay toys were scattered everywhere. Screaming women ran in all directions; some had babies tied to their backs. Men clutched their *dhotis* and turbans as they disappeared into alleyways. Hooded horsemen lashed their whips left and right. The air was dense with wails of pain and fear.

From where she was crouching, Amba saw a palanquin with a Nandi Bull emblem, the palace palanquin. But there were no palanquin bearers around. A shrill whistle pierced the air and the hooded horsemen disappeared as suddenly as they had appeared.

Amba whispered, 'Shama! Someone is trapped in the palace palanquin.'

Amba ran to the palanquin and parted the curtains. A woman lay crouched into the folds of her *sari*. Not wanting to startle her, Amba spoke in a soft voice. 'The gangsters have gone; you are safe now. Are you injured?'

'No.' The woman's fearful eyes darted around as she peeked through the folds of her silk *sari* embedded with gold sequins. The shimmering pearls around her neck and silky black hair were evidence she was from a royal family, but not from Tanjore. Her *sari pallu* was on her right shoulder, unlike Tanjore women, who wore theirs on the left. With her smooth skin and head bent, she looked like an inert marble statue.

Where was she from? Amba gently lifted her head and murmured.

'You are safe now. I'll ask my palanquin bearers to take you back to the palace.'

The young woman's body shivered like a leaf caught in a storm. 'Please don't take me back to the palace.' Her Tamil accent was not from Tanjore. In spite of the fearful eyes, her voice was firm and authoritative.

Amba said, 'I don't know who you are, but my palanquin is around the corner. I can take you to my place if you wish. Hurry, we have to run now.'

Amba hoisted her up, yanked her hand and ran to the side street and into her own waiting palanquin. Instantly, Shama and his men hoisted the palanquin on their shoulders and trotted along back lanes, avoiding the main street. The woman fell into a deep sleep, lulled by the rhythmic motion of the palanquin. Amba's spine stiffened at the sound of approaching hooves.

Shama must have sensed her fear. 'Amba, Ma, don't worry. They are Govinda's men. Our friends are here to escort us home.'

Amba held her breath and let her company rest until they reached the farmhouse. As soon as Shama and his men set down the palanquin, Amba stepped out, straightened her *sari*, took the woman's hand and led her to the house.

Amba hesitated at the unusual brightness emanating from the doorway, surely Kanchana didn't fear the shadows enough to light up all the lamps at once. Her feet stopped the moment she saw Ayya and Selvi waiting inside. Selvi had saved her once, and here she was again. *What was she doing here?*

Ayya let out a loud sigh of relief. His lacklustre eyes and deep worry lines along his nose betrayed his anxiety. Amba had never seen him in such a state. The palanquin woman ran to Ayya and collapsed at his feet. He patted her hair and remained silent, his eyes misty.

Turning to Amba, Ayya said, 'This is Chandrika, Princess of Jaffna, King Changili's sister.'

Ayya lifted the woman's shoulders, but Chandrika was in no condition to talk.

Amba's words came out in spurts. 'There were rioters on the streets. I found her huddled in a palace palanquin. Her palanquin bearers had disappeared. I didn't know what to do, so I brought her here with me.'

Everyone was silent. After a while, Ayya said, 'It's late. You all need to rest.'

Chandrika's brown eyes filled with fear. Ayya patted Chandrika's head reassuringly. 'Chandrika, we had assigned a bodyguard in the palace for your safety. Selvi's son, Govinda, was on guard. You were never meant to be alone without escorts.'

Selvi mopped her sweaty face with her *sari*. 'We had not expected rioters to be out on the streets today. Govinda and his men were caught off guard. The palace palanquin bearers should never have abandoned you, and we will deal with them later. By the strangest coincidence, Amba arrived on the scene and rescued you. None of us foresaw any of this. Goddess Shakti has her plans; she must have decided to bring you two together.'

Before departing Ayya said, 'Chandrika, this farmhouse is a haven, away from political turmoil. I suggest you stay here with Amba for now. I will let your brother know you are safer here than in the palace.'

Unaffected by the riots in town, birds around the farm chirped as they did every morning. Amba stepped out onto the veranda, inhaling the fragrance of *champas* wafting in with the dawn breeze. The sun rose over the horizon, splashing hues of red, purple and orange across the sky.

Kanchana was sweeping the muddy ground outside the porch with a coconut-frond broom. She sprinkled a layer of cow dung water over the swept area, which turned the muddy earth into a smooth, greenish surface.

A thin stream of white rice flour glided through Kanchana's thumb and forefinger, forming a continuous flow of lines around a central core of red earth. Like every morning, a unique symmetrical design emerged, though no two designs were ever identical. Kanchana completed the *kolam* motif and placed a yellow pumpkin flower at the geometrical centre of the design, a beautiful piece of art to welcome visitors.

Hearing footsteps approaching her from behind, Amba turned around.

'Princess Chandrika. I hope you had a good sleep. I know the pith mat here isn't as soft as the silk mattress in the palace.'

Chandrika raised her head to the sky and spread out her hands as if welcoming the morning sun. 'I didn't notice the mattress. I had the deepest sleep I've had in months, without any nightmares, too.'

Amba took Chandrika's hand, unwilling to pry into what tormented the princess. 'Let's go to the backyard well and freshen up.' She felt Chandrika's hand relax.

Selvi was already at the well, exchanging gestures with Kanchana.

Amba said, 'Selvi Akka, I was surprised to see you here with Ayya last night.'

Selvi's mouth twisted into a half smile. 'I too have a story, like all of us here.'

After they had all freshened up, Kanchana brought out a tray with three silver cups filled with fresh lime juice. Tiny shavings of grated ginger floated on the surface of the juice; the sweet-sour concoction was Kanchana's special recipe. She combined the flavours of ginger and lime to reduce the sweetness of jaggery, unlike Paru Ma's cardamom-infused juice, which was too sweet.

They sat down on a rough wooden bench under the neem tree overlooking the kitchen garden. A pumpkin vine scrambled around the tree, over the yard and past the lattice gate that separated the backyard from the farm.

Selvi reached out and stroked the edges of a pumpkin leaf.

'God wants us to see nature's bounty even when we live in a chaotic world. Look at the abundance of gourds and green fields as far as the eye can reach.

Chandrika murmured. 'What a peaceful spot for tired souls to rest their bodies and minds.' Her voice was wistful, longing for something that was no longer there.

The sun was up now, and hot beads of perspiration appeared on Selvi's forehead. Amba brought out three hand fans woven with aromatic vetiver grass. She kept one for herself and handed the other two to Chandrika and Selvi.

Selvi lifted her hair bunched up in a bun and fanned the back of her neck.

'I have never seen hand fans made of vetiver. The ones we get in the markets are made of date palm leaves.'

'There's a large field of vetiver grass on this farm. We have vetiver screens on the windows to keep flies and insects away. You'll feel their gentle fragrance when the breeze sets in at night.'

Amba moved her finger along the smooth red silk trimming stitched around the circular edge of the fan.

'This is Kanchana's creation. One night it was very hot, and the palm frond fan did nothing to ease my discomfort. Next day Kanchana braided this vetiver fan. She has made a few more since then, so I sent a couple to Ayya and Nagamma.'

Selvi took the fan to her nose and inhaled the fragrance.

Amba said, 'Selvi Akka, but for your help all those years ago, I would never have escaped from Thimma and his Portuguese crony.'

Selvi patted the beads of sweat on her brows with her *sari*. 'Amba, you once asked me what made me and my son Govinda rescue girls from street attackers. My daughter Chinni, Govinda's younger sister, was a beautiful and innocent girl. She used to collect flowers from nearby gardens, string them into garlands and take them to the temples, morning and evening. Everyone around loved her and knew her routine.'

Selvi's body heaved, and she hid her face in her hands. Amba waved the fan over Selvi's back, which was now drenched with sweat. Her voice came out amidst sobs and hiccups.

'One evening, a couple of men attacked Chinni. They raped her and left her to die on a side street. Govinda's friend, who happened to pass by, tried to defend her, but he was badly wounded. That poor boy limped home and told us that Thimma stood by watching as his friends raped her, not concerned in the least that Chinni was his niece.'

After a long pause, Selvi lifted her head. 'My biggest regret is that I did not train my daughter to defend herself against attackers.'

Chandrika hugged Selvi, and they stayed huddled together for some time. Chandrika's voice was tight when she finally spoke.

'In Jaffna, rebels went on a rampage inside our palace. They murdered everyone they could get hold of. Some rebels were our relatives; brothers fought brothers. People whom we thought were our friends turned out to be traitors. The blood bath went on for months. Finally, the Portuguese took control of Jaffna Fort and threw everyone out.'

Chandrika rocked her body back and forth. Amba held her close till Chandrika's body relaxed.

'In the end, my brother Changili had to leave his kingdom. Disguised as labourers, Changili, his trusted General Veerasena and I escaped from the palace and reached Jaffna Port. Veerasena knew the captain of the ship that was sailing to Nagore, near Tanjore. King Raghu was kind and welcomed us with open arms. My brother and Veerasena decided to stay in hiding near the ports surrounding Tanjore. They wanted to keep an eye on Portuguese ships arriving from Jaffna. They decided it was best I stay at the palace with Queen Kalyani.'

Chandrika has suffered much more than I have, thought Amba. Sorrow sees no difference between a princess and a courtesan.

Amba shook her head: ambitious men and tearful women. Women paid the price for men's follies. This is not how life was meant to be. Yet, there were women like Queen Kalyani, who could turn a king into a puppet. King Raghu was ready to sacrifice his entire kingdom for fear of annoying his queen. Was he foolish or ambitious? Amba could not tell.

Kanchana's shadow appeared behind the door; her fingers moved rapidly.

'Lunch is ready, with *payasam* for the princess.'

Amba responded with hand gestures. 'Thank you. We'll be there soon.'

Kanchana spread a long bamboo mat on the floor and invited Chandrika, Selvi, and Amba to sit down. In front of each of them she placed an oval-shaped banana leaf and a tall copper tumbler with water at the tip of each leaf. Selvi sprinkled a few drops of water on her banana leaf and cleaned the surface.

As hostess, Amba served the first dish: sweet *payasam*; rice boiled in coconut milk and *jaggery* and infused with the aroma of crushed cardamom and nutmeg. Kanchana served the rest of the meal for all three of them: steaming white rice, yellow lentil *kolambu*, and a side dish of tender green snake gourd and pumpkin tempered with mustard and garnished with freshly grated coconut.

Amba addressed Chandrika, while also using the sign language. 'Gourds and pumpkins are abundant in the garden. Kanchana uses them in a new recipe every day. She is an excellent cook.'

Kanchana's hands danced, 'Thank you, you are very kind.'

After they washed their hands in the backyard well, Amba said, 'You must both be tired; it's been a tough day. Later in the evening, we can go for a walk around the farm.'

The long, silent walk along the paddy fields in the cool evening breeze was a welcome diversion for all of them. After familiarising themselves with the farm's boundaries, they returned to the log under the neem tree.

Amba turned to Chandrika. 'Did Queen Kalyani treat you well?'

Chandrika fidgeted with her necklace. 'Life was peaceful in the palace for the first few days. The queens were nice to me, particularly the second queen, Tara. I spent more time with her, and soon, Queen

Kalyani's behaviour turned erratic. One day, she would be pleasant, and another day, she would fling silver plates and smash beautiful vases. Perhaps she resented my presence in the palace.'

Amba asked, 'But how did you end up in the town square?'

'Queen Kalyani was in a good mood that morning. She said, "I'll ask my maid to take you to the temple markets." The perfumers' stalls enamoured me, and I readily agreed. When we reached the market, I asked the palanquin bearers to set me down in front of a perfume shop. As I inhaled a vial of rose perfume, someone covered my eyes and mouth.'

Chandrika's eyes welled with tears. 'When I opened my eyes, you were in front of me, Amba.'

Selvi continued the rest of the story.

'Ayya had warned his informer, Muruga, to be alert when Chandrika took asylum in the palace. My son Govinda and I work with Muruga.'

Selvi glanced at Chandrika. 'Govinda's strategy is to have his men mingle with Thimma's men. They roam around freely, and no one knows who works for whom. But, unknown to us, your palanquin bearers were switched at the last moment. The moment you were made unconscious, Govinda's men went into action, and your attacker was wounded, perhaps killed.'

Chandrika said, 'I don't understand why King Raghu has ignored the plight of women in his own kingdom. My brother mentioned that during past wars, King Raghu ensured that women from both sides were treated with respect and escorted to a safe place. But he is spineless in his own kingdom.'

A sudden thought flashed across Amba's mind. 'I am sure Queen Kalyani planned this! She's got both Thimma and the king under her thumb. She is a festering wound eating away the king's body and mind.'

Selvi said, 'Ayya is the only person who is not driven by personal ambition. That's the reason why Govinda and I work for him.'

Amba took Selvi's hands. 'Does the king know that you and Govinda are doing what his security guards have failed to do? You two shouldn't have to take on this burden alone. The king must act.'

There was much to learn from Selvi. Despite being born into the same family as Thimma, Selvi had made it her life's mission to protect women snared by men like him.

A couple of days later, a palanquin was at the door for Selvi. She let out a loud sigh. 'That cousin of mine is out and about. I have to go.'

Kanchana packed a tiffin of steamed *idlis*, lentil crispies and some finger bananas for Selvi. She indicated rapidly with her fingers. 'For your journey.'

Selvi spoke and gestured with her hands. 'I'll see you all again in a few days.'

Amba gave her a big hug. 'Like a protective older sister, you turn up whenever I am in trouble. Stay safe, Selvi Akka.'

CHAPTER 27

MAYA
Sydney, 2015

I composed sixteen new bars of melody to add to the climax scene for *La Bayadere*. Dave wrote the chords to harmonise the melody and transcribed the notes into a formal music score. Over the last three months, I had learnt to read Western music notation though I still play by ear. My head has an automatic music translator that converts Western music into notes of a Carnatic *raga*. It seems my Indian ear training is too deeply ingrained in my genes.

Through an amazing set of circumstances, my thoughts outside of office hours were hijacked by either a temple dancer or a temple musician. As my practice sessions with the quartet grew more frequent, Deepak's frown lines found a permanent home between his eyebrows.

After a long day of work and music, I ordered pizza one night.

Deepak scowled at the Dominos carton. 'Have you stopped cooking altogether?'

I raised my eyebrows. 'I have a life outside the kitchen too.'

Deepak's tone rose a pitch. 'Well, that life is making you shirk your duties as a wife.'

I sneered. 'What about your duties as a husband? Your crankiness creeps out every time you see me happy outside your world.'

After dinner, Deepak tuned into his sports channel, and I turned to Amba's manuscript.

Amba had described the scene as though she had watched the army's departure from the palace gates. The horses were mounted by soldiers who wore long turbans, and elephants were caparisoned with iron howdahs. Soldiers carried bows and arrows and a weapon with a long wick. Palanquins accompanied the king, carrying material for tents, provisions for the army, and followers with medicinal herbs for the soldiers. They crossed the territory occupied by the mercenary Solaga, captured him and marched forward towards the sea coast to reach Nepala.

In answer to my email with a single question, 'Where is Nepala?' Professor K had sent a long reply.

'Nepala refers to Jaffna, in Sri Lanka, formerly Ceylon. If you are interested in events that happened in Ceylon at that time, read *The Portuguese Chronicles* The Portuguese chroniclers of 1616 provided a colourful description of the events that took place. Elephant battalion with iron howdahs crossed the seas into Jaffna using a chain of boats and wooden floats. As the Portuguese soldiers had never encountered an elephant battalion, they fled the scene.'

There was a link to the documents underlined and in bright blue text.

I had had a tough day at work with a new client. The large health services provider wanted to compare the quality of care across different private hospitals, but the parameters required for the analysis weren't available in the data they provided. I spent the whole day making a list of the missing attributes, a tedious task that was not part of my role.

I was tired, but I cooked a simple meal to get my head out of work mode. I had already soaked the chickpeas in the morning. I cooked it in the pressure cooker with ginger-garlic paste and *garam masala*. I rolled out the *rotis*, toasted them on a hot griddle until they puffed up, splashed a blob of *ghee* on top and placed them in the hot-case. Deepak liked his *chapatis* hot.

My stomach rumbled, and my head throbbed as I waited for Deepak.

The improvisation segment I had promised Dave and the crew for *La Bayadere* needed more work, so I put my idle time to use. I took out my *veena* and played listlessly for a while. I was exhausted.

As the evening wore on, the splash of colours faded along the waterfront with every minute. November is a strange month in Sydney: warm and sunny one day, dark and gloomy the next--a lot like my moods lately. Even the purple jacarandas lining the streets, bright and beautiful one day, turned into hazy purple blotches on cloudy days.

It was 9pm, and there was no sign of Deepak. I ate my dinner, changed into a comfortable *salwar* and *kurta* and escaped to Amba's world. It was way more colourful than my miserable present with a husband who expected his wife to earn money, cook dinner and wait around hungry and tired.

I opened my laptop and selected a translated biography of *King Raghu Nayaka* by poet Yagna Narayana, who lived around the same period as Amba.

Poet Yagna Narayana had written about King Raghu Nayaka's monthly concerts at the Music Palace Indira Mandira with female scholars whom the king admired. Occasionally, if the king was pleased, he organised a *thulabraram,* rewarding them with gold and jewellery equal to their body weight. I couldn't suppress my chuckle. Today, most musicians needed a second job to sustain their music while back in 1600s they were showered with wealth.

Deepak walked in around 10pm , flung his backpack into a corner, washed his hands, and sat down in a dining chair. There was one plate on the table.

'What about you? Aren't you eating?' Deepak asked.

'I have had my dinner. I was hungry.'

Deepak grumbled, 'If you can't wait up for me, what's the point of us being a couple?'

It was late, and I was too tired to argue, but then he got louder. 'My mum waits for Dad, no matter how late he comes home, whether it's from work or his bridge game on Friday nights.'

What a thankless man! First his mum and now me: we were nothing but service providers in the guise of good wives.

'Shows how much you know your mum,' I sniggered. 'Neetu's way smarter than you and your dad realise. She eats her dinner when she is hungry and then serves herself a little something to peck at when she sits down with your dad. She has figured a way of staying sane and retaining the image of a model wife as you men expect.'

I shut my laptop with a thud. 'My regret is that your mum, a warm-hearted, caring soul, didn't bother to educate you. Now, a generation later, I have to deal with the same problem as your mother. Waiting on a husband who'll turn up whenever he pleases, expecting his wife to stay hungry until he comes home.'

Deepak glared, too shocked to respond. He tore a piece of

chapati, dipped it in chickpea curry and took a bite. He puffed out his cheeks and glared.

'This *chole* is too spicy; all your anger has been cooked into it. I can't eat this.'

'Last week, you ate a curry much hotter than this from that take-away place.'

Deepak rose from the table, grabbed the bowl of curry and tipped it into the bin under the kitchen sink. When he jerked back around, his palm hit the music triptych frame, shattering the glass of my favourite artwork. A shard pierced his thumb, and the blood-stained prints of a *veena*, didgeridoo and cello fell to the floor in a mangled heap. I fetched a plaster, and he snatched it from my hand before I could put it around his thumb.

Words flew out of my mouth with a force I never knew I possessed. 'I have tried to be a model wife, like your mum. I cooked the food you loved, washed your dirty linen, and hid my happiness under your armpits. Then *you* trashed the chickpea curry that took me two hours to cook after an exhausting day at work! I bet your father would never do anything like this to your mum.'

No tears, Maya, not now, hold it together.

'There was a time I admired you and the way you had blended into the Australian way of life. Now, I have a well-paying job to support my music and the mortgage *you* want to take out. Yes, you get paid more than me, and I am happy for you. But that is no reason for you to behave like old-fashioned Indian men, of a generation ago. That's not okay with me.'

Deepak's voice rose. 'How dare you? If not for me, you wouldn't have this cushy life hanging around with white men using music as an excuse. Why don't you stick to your Tamil crowd?'

'What of your wise words about integrating into this culture?' I sneered.

Deepak yelled, 'Integration does not mean you give up your values.'

I lowered my tone to cut through his crap. 'My principle is to lead a life that's meaningful to me. Music is an integral part of that life, and David's quartet has opened up a new world for me. You wanted me to earn a living and integrate, I have done both.'

I couldn't stop the torrent of words that flew out of my mouth. 'You know what your problem is? You are not broad-minded. My values are neither white nor brown and you can't handle that. You're jealous when I am cheerful around Dave, who appreciates my music. I don't respond to the colour of someone's skin the way you do. You're soft and gentle with white folks, but rough and tough with *desis* who come from where you come from.'

Deepak was stunned and his thumb continued bleeding. I snatched the plaster back from him and fastened it around his thumb. All the pleasures of lying in bed with him was not worth the pain of dealing with his jealous mind. I stormed out of the kitchen, went into the study and banged the door shut.

I couldn't hold the tears back any longer. I sat there rocking back and forth, wondering what my options were when the music festival was due to take place in two weeks.

Should I crawl back into bed with Deepak or not? Should I walk out or not?

I thought of my old Aunt Charu's life in Chennai. My aunt and uncle quarrelled frequently, and they often stopped talking to each other and slept in different rooms. Sometimes, their silence went on for months until one of them fell prey to the night and crept into the other's bed. She chuckled when she narrated that story. She was unconcerned with the flow of her life.

It may have worked for my aunt, but for me, it had to be unconditional love or nothing. Deepak was a tender lover at night but obnoxious by day. How did he perfect this game, and how did I not see this coming?

The time had come to find my own path. What would Viji Ma and Neetu Aunty say? Their generation's mantra was, "Be patient, and men will come around." In their world, it was the responsibility of the wife to exercise caution and patience, never the husband's.

My head collapsed on the table with the weight of my thoughts.

CHAPTER 28

AMBA

Tanjore, 1627

Amba and Chandrika settled into a routine at the farmhouse. Amba spent her time composing songs or recording events that had happened during her years at the palace. She wrote about the king's women, his queens and courtesans. She wrote about battles won and lost, about friends turned traitors and foreigners who came to trade but instead became looters. She wrote until her knuckles turned red and her fingers could no longer hold her stylus. Kanchana massaged her fingers every night with an unguent of coconut oil, camphor and sticky resin from myrrh trees.

Chandrika spent most of her time on the back veranda. At dawn and again at dusk, she painted the same landscape, the temple dome hanging over the green paddy fields, its shadows changing with the time of day. The shadows and changing hues of the sun created starkly different moods in the paintings. When she was not painting, Chandrika wandered around the farm collecting herbs, flowers, and soil from ant hills before grinding them into pigments for her paintings.

Kanchana fussed over them both, making sure they ate on time and drank her lime juice when the air became hot and humid. At times, she hovered around Amba, watching her write, and at other times, she observed Chandrika create her pigments.

Amba's fingers danced. 'You are soon going to be a writer and an artist.'

Kanchana's hands and fingers went up to her throat and mouth. 'But how can I write and paint if I am not able to speak?'

Amba signed, 'I'll teach you to read and write, which is better than speaking.'

Chandrika too started using her hands to talk to Kanchana. 'You are good at drawing; I'll teach you to paint.'

Amba smiled, 'We have two teachers and one keen student.'

At the end of the day, they sat on the veranda watching the changing colours of the temple dome. Amba hadn't visited the temple since she had moved to the farmhouse. *How was Paru Ma doing*, she wondered.

As if she had heard Amba's thoughts, Paru Ma turned up a few evenings later. She came bearing the temple *prasad*, sweet, puffed rice pancakes full of cardamom flavour that Amba loved. Paru Ma handed Amba the warm banana leaf cup.

'There was a special *puja* at the temple this morning. The head priest remembered your songs on Ganesha and sends you his blessings with this *prasad*.'

Kanchana drew a pot of water from the well, added some vetiver grass and mint leaves and invited Paru Ma to wash her hands and feet after her long palanquin ride.

Paru Ma touched Kanchana's head, a gesture of her blessing. 'You are a gem.'

Kanchana laughed and gestured. 'Your daughter is going to teach me to read and write.'

Chandrika, ever fearful of unexpected visitors, had disappeared when she heard the sound of a palanquin arriving. But listening to sounds of laughter, she peeped out of the room.

Amba said, 'Chandrika, come and meet my mother, Paru Ma.'

Chandrika immediately came forward and bowed. 'Amba is blessed, I grew up without a mother.'

Paru Ma was full of grace. 'You may think of me as your mother.'

Kanchana brought a tray with three glasses of lime juice and placed it on a wooden stool. She signed a tusk and a huge belly to symbolise Ganesha.

'How was the Ganesh *puja* at the temple?'

Paru Ma had no difficulty communicating with her hands as she had once been a dancer. 'Seven priests chanted the sacred texts. My students performed dances about God Ganesha set to Amba's compositions from when she used to sing for the temple.'

Kanchana signed, 'I want to paint a Ganesha and write poems about him.'

Amba spread out her left palm and moved her right forefinger and thumb over her open palm. 'We will start a school. You will be my first student.'

Paru Ma said, 'I can't dance anymore, but I can teach dance. Your friend Vani was at the temple this morning. She led a chorus with my students, who sang a beautiful Tamil song. I am sure Vani would love to teach music if you ask her.'

Chandrika's eyes sparkled as never before. 'What a great idea, Amba. I'd love to help you with the school. I'll teach art and painting.'

Amba laughed. 'Right, here we have three teachers and one student. We need a few more students and a safe location before we start a girls' school.'

Kanchana's hands moved rapidly. 'I'll talk to my mother and bring her nieces from the village to study.'

It was time for the evening meal. Kanchana went into the kitchen to get started preparing the food. Chandrika followed her, allowing mother and daughter to spend time together. Amba picked a few stray fibres from the vetiver fan as she waved it around.

'Society has no expectation of women. Men want nothing from women except their bodies. Will families send their daughters to a *gurukul* for girls?'

Paru Ma gently pressed Amba's sagging shoulders. 'I would have sent you if there was one when you were a child.'

After their meal of rice, pumpkin and lentil *koottu*, Amba came out to the veranda. Through the dark clouds, tiny stars winked like shy little girls ready to sparkle. Yes, her *gurukul* for girls would be a safe place, a home away from home, for girls to learn without being told their place was in a man's bed.

The next morning, when Amba came out to the veranda, Paru Ma and Chandrika were happily chatting about temples and paintings as they watched the sunrise. The slanting rays splashed shades of orange and yellow on the golden temple dome, changing its hue every minute as the sun rose over the horizon.

Chandrika described her childhood in Jaffna and the times she went out with her nurse to The Thousand-Pillared Temple dressed as a boy.

'Dressed as a boy?' queried Paru Ma.

'When I went dressed as a boy, I could observe the paintings at leisure. But if I went as a princess, I became an object for visitors to gawk at and gossip about. I hated going out as a princess.'

What irony! We have both been trying to escape from our reality, thought Amba. Amba would have loved to have been a princess instead of a temple musician or a courtesan, and here was a real princess who hid her identity to go unnoticed.

During their evening walk, Chandrika's hands unconsciously picked up a handful of paddy shoots, crushed the stems, crunched the leaves and threw them around. Her voice turned hoarse with worry.

'Something has happened to my brother. That's why Ayya has not come to visit us. Will King Raghu help Changili if the Portuguese try to capture him? I wish to meet with Ayya. I have to know if my brother is safe.'

Amba tried her best to cheer Chandrika up. 'Didn't King Raghu fight the Portuguese all those years ago to save your brother? I am sure he will protect him again if there is a problem from the Portuguese.'

Kanchana had her own way of cheering Chandrika up. She picked large yellow pumpkin flowers from the garden, crushed them with turmeric, and created a new golden hue for Chandrika's artwork.

Ayya turned up a few days later. His smile was warm, but his cheeks and shoulders sagged from the weight of his burdens.

Amba touched Ayya's feet and paid her respects. 'Ayya, what's worrying you?'

As Chandrika bent her head to take Ayya's blessings, there was a tremor in her voice. 'Is my brother safe?'

Ayya placed his hand on Chandrika's head in a gesture of blessing.

'Yes, your brother is safe in Nagore. King Raghu's trusted soldiers are guarding the whole area where your brother is housed.'

Ayya let out a heavy sigh. 'Everyone is safe, including those who have no right to be.'

What did Ayya mean? Was there anyone who had no right to be safe, Amba wondered.

Suddenly, she blurted out, 'Thimma!'

Ayya's voice was gruff. 'Pandya Varma's men went after Thimma. They chased him to the footbridge. Soldiers were stationed on either side of the bridge to prevent his escape. They caught his men, but Thimma jumped from the bridge and disappeared into the river.'

Amba's eyes flared. 'Did King Raghu really believe that Pandya Varma would capture Thimma? The general is the queen's cousin, isn't he? When it comes to Thimma, the general will follow the queen's orders over the king's. Even I sensed that, but...' Amba's voice trailed off.

Ayya hung his head as if he, too, had failed.

Kanchana brought a bowl of cut mangoes and handed Ayya a cup of warm milk infused with cardamom. Ayya took a sip of the milk and placed the silver cup back on the tray. He did not touch the fruit.

Amba said, 'Ayya, you should not feel guilty for the king's mistakes. You did everything you could. You appointed Selvi and Govinda to cover the king's blindside.'

Ayya patted his tufted hair as he got up. 'Raghu can no longer stay a sleeping tiger. The time to pounce has come.'

Amba had never heard that kind of cold determination in Ayya's voice.

The following week, Nagamma came with Ayya, who was back to his cheerful self. She had that effect on him.

Nagamma said, 'Chandrika, we hear it's your birthday on Friday. We would like to invite you and Amba to our house to celebrate. I'll cook some Jaffna dishes for you.'

Chandrika's face lit up. 'Thank you, Mami. I feel blessed. My brother will be happy to know that I am with affectionate people.'

Ayya had a wide grin. 'Amba, Nagamma has found another reason to celebrate. She is thrilled that finally a woman has been invited to sing publicly at Indira Mandira.'

Amba looked from one to the other. What did Ayya mean? Nagamma turned to Amba with a smile that lit up her entire face. 'You are that musician.'

Nagamma's voice was soft, reticent. 'The music palace has heard nothing but male voices. It is time the walls hear a woman's voice.'

Did Nagamma too crave recognition when she was young, Amba wondered.

Nagamma said, 'We will see you both on Friday.'

Amba and Chandrika were in Nagamma's kitchen, helping her with *puttu*, a favourite rice flour and coconut dish in Jaffna. Amba twisted the saw-toothed scraper around the fresh coconut kernel and scooped the tender shavings into a bowl. Chandrika crushed cardamom pods using a small wooden mortar and pestle. The aroma of cardamom and coconut milk engulfed the kitchen.

Nagamma pressed a thick layer of steamed rice flour to the bottom of the narrow earthenware tube, then topped it with a layer of freshly shredded coconut shavings and a pinch of cardamom powder. She continued alternately layering rice flour and coconut until the cylinder was full, then placed it in a brass steamer pot.

Ayya was in the hall on his swing, rocking back and forth, humming a song in *raga 'Hindolam'*. The brass chains of the swing clanked with a slow rhythm that accompanied his music.

The distant sound of hooves shattered the peaceful ambience of the house. As it grew closer, it turned into a trot and finally came to an abrupt halt at the front of Ayya's house.

Amba peeped from the kitchen as she watched the agile man jump down from his horse. A large red turban covered his forehead; he had thick arms and a rotund belly.

Too much good food. A merchant, perhaps, she thought to herself.

Ayya went out and welcomed the visitor. He invited him to sit on a chair and went back to his seat on the swing.

'That chair is a gift from the king and is for his use when he visits me,' Ayya had laughed when Amba had first visited.

Nagamma called, 'Amba, can you churn the buttermilk? Add a pinch of salt and crushed cumin and pour it into two silver cups. The visitor might be tired from his ride. The cold buttermilk will quench his thirst.'

Nagamma walked to the hall door and cleared her throat, and in response, Ayya came into the kitchen. Amba smiled at their wordless communication. The custom was that married women did not go to the front hall to welcome male visitors. Men entertained men, and women cooked for men. Amba handed the silver tray with the two silver tumblers of buttermilk to Ayya.

Ayya said, 'Amba, come and meet the visitor.'

Amba signed rapidly with her hands, indicating she did not want to meet the pot-bellied visitor.

Ayya laughed and handed the tray back to Amba, insisting she take it to the visitor. When he stretched his hand to take the tumbler, deep callouses were visible on the fingertips of his left hand. Signs of playing the *veena*! The base of the ring finger bore the marks of a missing ring. Amba froze, clutching the tray so it wouldn't crash.

What was the king doing here? Why was he in the garb of a merchant?

Amba abruptly turned her back to the visitor, pretending she did not know who he was. She had no feelings left for this weak king.

'Amba, please stay for a minute,' said Ayya. 'Sometimes the king has to go out in disguise to escape his bodyguards.'

She could feel his intense gaze from the corner of her eye. The king placed the silver cup on the side stool. He spoke with the same endearing voice she had once loved.

'Amba, I have missed you immensely.' His eyes were tender with a love she had once shared. 'My music has gone mute without you; I need you back in my life.'

Amba's face turned hot. 'Raja Nayaka, how can you expect me to come back?' She heard her voice crack. 'When you invited me as your musical consort, I willingly accepted. I thought music would be a permanent bond that would connect us forever. I enjoyed the days we created music together. All my actions and my involvement in political affairs were to keep you happy so your music could flow and not flounder.'

She had no control over the torrent of words that poured out. 'Your Majesty, you are bound to your queen. I am not and never will be. I would rather be a temple musician, a *devadasi* serving God. But I became a *rajadasi*, serving a king who could neither protect me nor my music.'

The king lowered his eyes. Ayya stiffened like a statue. Amba could not tell what was going on in their minds.

The king cleared his throat.

'Amba, you do not have to be a *rajadasi*. Be my queen. A queen who can rule alongside me and not against me. You don't have to live with the other three queens. The summer palace will be yours. You can write your music and poetry without any disturbance. I'll ensure the palace is protected.' The king's eyes were pleading.

'Your Highness, I do not want to be the queen of a kingdom where women are not safe.'

Amba stormed into the kitchen, caught hold of Chandrika's hand and dragged her in front of the king. 'This is Chandrika, the princess of a foreign country and sister of your close friend. She was abducted by Thimma's men when she was under your roof. Could you protect her?'

The king stuttered, 'General Pandya Varma...'

Amba's voice came out cold and sharp. 'Yes, you sent the general after Thimma, and Thimma escaped. Is that a surprise?'

She hissed. 'Raja Nayaka, Pandya Varma is Queen Kalyani's cousin, is he not? Did you expect him to act on your instructions?'

Ayya's face wore a worried expression. Had she gone too far?

The king got up. His voice was gruff, deep and heavy. 'I will capture Thimma and come back to claim your hand.'

Amba stormed out of the room, Chandrika close on her heels.

A few moons later, Ayya came to the farmhouse with Selvi. Ayya's ageless face no longer hid his years; his jowls sagged as never before. Selvi's eyes had dark pouches, too, as if she had not slept for days.

Amba welcomed them and brought two cups of cool water from the earthen pot. The evening was in no hurry to shed its heat, and the vetiver *punkah* high up in the ceiling provided little respite as hot air turned into wisps of steam. She then brought out the hand fans and waved them around Ayya's shoulders.

Ayya cleared his throat, patted his tuft, and cleared his throat again. 'The king received information about Thimma's whereabouts from two sources, his own intelligence team and from the Danish Captain. Both these trusted sources pointed to an island near the port of Nagore as the place where Thimma was hiding. General

Pandya Varma insisted that Thimma was holed up somewhere else, far away from Nagore. That's when King Raghu finally realised he could no longer trust his general.'

Ayya took a sip of water and continued. 'Last week, the king set out with his trusted band of soldiers towards Port Nagore. They had to cross a bridge to reach the island where Thimma was hiding. Meanwhile, the General's men had reached the bridge ahead of the king's battalion. Under the pretext of helping the king cross the bridge, they separated him from his trusted bodyguards.'

Ayya was too exhausted, and Selvi continued. 'The moment the king was separated from his men, General Pandya Varma was close on his heels. That's when my son Govinda and his men sprang into action. They captured Pandya Varma and shoved him into the nearby catacomb of caves from where he can never escape.'

'In the meantime, Changili's men kept Thimma's men engaged in a skirmish, and King Raghu took on Thimma himself.'

Chandrika's face came alive; her eyes glistened at the mention of her brother.

Ayya continued as Selvi wearily sipped at her water. 'King Raghu and Thimma had a sword fight. The king stabbed Thimma, who is badly wounded and imprisoned in a highly guarded prison.'

Amba exclaimed, 'The king should have killed Thimma! Why did he spare his life?'

Ayya said, 'Thimma will die in prison in due course. But for now, Thimma being alive and captive will be more useful to the king than him being dead.'

Ayya's voice conveyed a sense of relief. 'Thimma will never get out. All his men have been rounded up and thrown in prison. Finally, women will be safe in Tanjore. You should be happy with that.'

Amba was dismayed that Ayya, too, supported the king's decision to spare Thimma's life. Men and their muddled motivations made no sense to her.

As he got up to leave, Ayya said, 'We need music to restore us and bring a sense of peace. Nagamma wants to listen to your *Navaratri* compositions, the ones you plan to sing at the music palace.'

Amba touched Ayya's feet and took his blessings.

'Ayya, I will come a day before the concert and sing for Nagamma. She is the silent force who has inspired me to stay focused and direct all my energies to music.'

CHAPTER 29

MAYA
Sydney, 2015

I woke up startled when my neck rubbed against the rough edge of the table. Tears streamed down my cheeks. My body rocked with silent sobs as I remembered the events of the night before. There was no option but to move my body and mind away from the unhappy place my home had become.

I freshened up, packed a small bag and called an Uber.

I left Deepak a brief message, 'Need peace and space,' and left home.

With my *veena* tucked precariously under one arm and the other clutching the rough handle of my wheely bag, I arrived at Meena's front door, shivering. I was not sure if the tremor was caused by the cool mist of dawn or a deep fear of the unknown.

My hand hovered around the doorbell. What was I doing? Good Indian wives did not leave home. Was I foolish? Stubborn?

When I messaged Meena that I needed a quiet place for a few days, her reply was a simple thumbs-up emoji. I knew she wouldn't drill me with questions, and she lived alone. Her only son was an investment banker all the way in New York.

Meena's house was nestled in a quiet cul-de-sac, tucked behind Australian native trees and bushes in Killara, an upmarket suburb in northern Sydney. Meena had once mentioned that her house was heritage listed, which meant that changing even a tiny brass latch on the front gate was an expensive and complicated affair.

'*Ulla Va*. Come in.' Meena's warm smile reminded me of my mother. She took my carry bag and led me through the living room which looked like an art gallery. Ancient Indian bronze lamps and Aboriginal paintings blended as though they were meant to be together. The guest bedroom was tucked in the far corner of the house, with semi-circular windows facing a row of bottlebrush trees dotted with red flowers.

'Thank you,' my eyes glistened. 'What a peaceful home. I can start my day here with meditation as I used to in Chennai.'

'You won't need an alarm here,' Meena smiled. 'There are no temple bells like Chennai, but lorikeets and wrens will wake you up every morning when they come to feast on the bottlebrush blooms.'

I emailed my manager at work and took the next week off, devoting every ounce of my energy to music practice. The music festival was in two weeks, and I refused to let Deepak taint the last good thing I had. Meena gave me a set of house keys and left me alone to go about her day. Although retired, she had a busy schedule. She was involved in community activities, both Indian and Australian. The peaceful ambience of the house calmed my tumultuous mind. I breathed a heavy sigh of relief. When I found several text messages from Deepak, I deleted them, unread.

Meditation in the morning, *veena* practice between breakfast and lunch, a jog around the block at 4pm and then it was time to head out for the practice sessions with the quartet. Dave picked me up every evening, and we drove to the Ryde Civic Centre for our rehearsals. We took a pizza break at 7pm and then continued practising until 10pm. Dave dropped me off at Meena's place and again picked me up the following evening. Music was the security blanket that cocooned me from the realities of a harsh world I did not want to face.

Coming from all corners of the globe, our quartet members were at ease with world music. The Chamber Music Festival was spread out in multiple venues around Sydney over the October long weekend. We had a thirty-minute slot at the Manly Arts Centre.

In my hurry, I had forgotten to pack clothes for the performance. Gita, who had a similar build, suggested that I borrow a *sari* and a matching blouse from her wardrobe. On the day of the concert, Dave and Gita came to pick me up from Meena's place early in the afternoon. Meena was planning to arrive later to be there for the 6pm start.

When Gita arrived, Meena said, 'Maya needs to sit down to play the veena, not stand like the other musicians. Have you folks planned for that?'

Gita had a beaming smile. 'That's the first thing Dave organised. Maya will have a small, raised platform to sit on.'

Meena turned around to me. 'What are you going to wear?'

I said, 'Gita is lending me a *sari* and blouse.'

Meena went in and brought out a pair of dangling gold earrings. 'Here, wear these. The ones you are wearing are too small for the stage.'

I cringed. 'Meena, I can't. That's too kind of you.'

Meena was not the one to be deterred. 'Return the kindness to someone else when you get a chance.'

She pressed the earrings in my hand. 'Here, wear them today and return them after the concert.'

How was I ever going to repay her? How would I repay Gita and Dave? If not for them, I would be frying *puris* and crying over my fate. Instead, here they stood cheering and leading me to follow my passion, as I had once hoped Deepak would.

With my *veena* tucked under my arm, I walked along the Manly esplanade with Dave and Gita to the auditorium. The swish of Norfolk Pines on either side of the winding pathway and the sound of waves lashing against the sand provided me with a sense of serenity. It reminded me of the ambience I felt around Kalakshetra in Chennai when I used to sing and play the *veena* for their dance troupe.

But here I was in another part of the world with these lovely folks on the ancient land of the Guringai people. Dave and the quartet members had accepted me and embraced my music as an integral part of their ensemble, something I would have missed if I had never come to Australia.

Inspired by the huge encore we had received when we performed *The Temple Dancer*, Dave had suggested using variations of dance music as our theme for this Chamber Music Festival.

When I casually remarked that the Hindu God Shiva was a dancing god, Miguel said, 'Let's have a dancing Shiva on our program brochure.'

His sister designed cards and brochures and made sure they reflected everything our music encompassed. As we walked up to the stage, I saw several people in the audience holding our program brochure, which had a dancing Shiva as an elegant watermark background—nothing like the overwhelming bright blue god of an Indian calendar.

We took our positions on stage, and Dave, Alex, Eiko and Miguel set up their music score on a stand in front of them. I patted the pleats of my yellow silk *sari*, sat down cross-legged on the raised platform and arranged the *veena* on my lap. I placed my iPad in front of me, as I needed the score to know when I had to play although not for the actual melody, which I played by ear.

As soon as the cacophony of last-minute tuning subsided, Dave raised his hand for a minute of deep silence. With an energetic wave of his bow, the music sprang to life.

The first piece was a repeat of our 'High *Brahmin*' song from *La Bayadere*. I used the twang of the three rhythmic strings to imitate the humming voices of *Brahmins* chanting Vedic hymns. It was the same music we had performed for the school ballet, but with the audience being adults, the dynamics and the effect of the music were vastly different.

After the last note faded, there was a stunned silence. For a split second I thought they didn't like the music. In India I could sense the audience's sentiment while performing, because they responded with head nods and soft tapping to the rhythm of the music. But here, I had no visual clues to gauge the response of the classical music connoisseurs. Was the sound of the *veena* too foreign for the Western ear?

As I dabbed my temples, the audience broke into a loud, extended applause. With a huge sigh of relief, my hands automatically folded into a *namaste*. Dave nodded with a smile, and the others followed my gesture. How generous of them to embrace my *namaste*, respect my music, and not treat me like a freak foreigner.

The next piece was my all-time favourite: Tchaikovsky's 'Swan Lake'. The cello, violin, and viola took centre stage with Miguel's guitar and my *veena* providing the harmony with a few simple chords. The music was mellow and poignant, and I was lost in its haunting melody.

The third piece shifted into a fierce tango, showcasing the guitar as Miguel played Piazzolla's 'Libertango'. As the music conjured an image of a passionate dancer, I played the chords in first and second inversions––something I had not done before–– in an unexpected release of emotions. Miguel loved my impromptu response, and we repeated it to roaring applause.

Eiko chose the next piece, slow Japanese dance music played on a *shamisen*, the Japanese lute. Elko's interpretation of plucking her viola to make it sound like a shamisen had the audience mesmerised. Eiko took several bows as the audience loved the beautiful sounds she produced.

The finale was a fast-paced *tillana* popular with South Indian classical dancers. I chose a *raga* that lent itself to a smooth chord progression. All four of them improvised to the seven-beat tala, which is not common in Western classical music. The texture of the sound we collectively produced was beyond anything I had imagined. Our complete trust in each other, leading at times and blending into the background like a chameleon at other times, made for surreal dancing of musical minds.

The standing ovation and the shouts of 'bravo' uncoiled every taut nerve in my body. We clasped hands and took repeated bows. Finally, when the curtains closed, the five of us huddled and hugged and heaved and sighed, releasing the tension of relentless practice over many months.

We shared not only the highs and lows of musical notes but also of our personal lives. Deepak had so much to learn from my musical family.

CHAPTER 30

AMBA

Tanjore, 1630

Amba stepped out of the palanquin, extracted her tiny pouch tucked under the waist of her *sari* and handed out four silver coins to the palanquin bearers. She had asked the men to set her down at the rear door of the music palace, Indira Mandira. From there, it was a short walk to the narrow spiral staircase that led to the balcony above the stage.

As pre-arranged with Ayya, she waited, invisible to the audience below. Her nerves were taut like a tightly wound *veena* string, tuned at a pitch so high that it could snap at the slightest tug.

Amba drew the silk curtain aside and peered through the marble lattice window. Tufts of oiled hair tied behind thick necks, top knots piled on top of small heads, bald patches glistening with sweat, the *Brahmins* huddled together. The other side of the hall was filled with colourful turbans with gold borders; the wider the gold border, the richer the merchant. Amba's mouth twisted into a crooked smile. Men of knowledge and men of wealth sat apart, ignoring each other's presence.

The ministers, though, both *Brahmins* and merchants, united through power, sat next to each other and closer to the stage. They were here out of a sense of duty to Prime Minister Ayya.

Amba released her clenched fists and took a slow, deep breath. *One, two, three, four.* The fragrance of sandalwood filled her nostrils as she counted her inhale and exhale. Tall brass oil lamps flickered in alcoves partitioned by carved pillars. The gods and goddesses carved along the granite pillars danced to the rhythm of the flames. The five hundred year old gold figurine of Saraswati, the goddess of knowledge, regarded the assembled men from her carved sandalwood pedestal placed in a corner of the dais.

This was an assembly of people who shaped the story of Tanjore and it's culture. Her friend, Vani, the solitary female musician, sat in an invisible corner of the big hall, as they had done twenty years ago when they first participated in the competition. Vani was neither a *devadasi* bound to the temple like Paru Ma, nor a courtesan like Amba, nor a high caste *Brahmin* tied to her home like Nagamma. Yet, despite being recognised by the king at the *Shivaratri* Festival, she had never been allowed to perform at the music hall. Men had shaped their world by shutting out female talent, no matter where they belonged in the social order of Tanjore. No woman had been allowed to perform at Indira Mandira. She was here today at the mercy of these scholars, who could butcher her like a sacrificial goat.

A hush fell over the hall as Ayya walked in with musicologist Venkata in tow.

A few young *veena* players and musicians took their seats on the dais. There was a new female *veena* player Amba had not seen before.

Ayya was on a mission to bring in female musicians to penetrate the conservative clans that had previously denied them.

Ayya had discussed the program with Amba. It would start with young musicians performing a few songs. Next, Venkata would introduce the new *raga* structure and highlight the importance of a theoretical framework to represent the melodic variations of the traditional seven-note scale. Amba's performance would be the final event of the day, during which she would sing nine compositions in nine new *ragas*.

This was her chance to make men aware of the talents that lay outside their world, making them open the doors of the hallowed music hall to talented female musicians. Her shoulders sagged with the weight of responsibility she carried on behalf of all women.

Ayya's booming voice rang through the hall like a temple gong. 'Six hundred years ago, when the Chola kings constructed The Big Temple, poets and musicians thronged to Tanjore to experience the divine presence of God Shiva. But Shiva cannot function without Shakti, his divine consort, the female power essential to energise Shiva. *Navarathri* is the time to celebrate Shakti, the goddess who manifests herself in different forms to energise the world around us.

'This year, we have created a unique program for *Navarathri*. Nine new musicians, nine new songs, nine new *ragas* with a musical framework to support our music.'

Ayya's gaze fell on the young musicians. 'We want each of you to sing a song about the goddess, in any one of her forms that is dear to you.'

Following the well-practised performance of songs by the young-sters, Ayya introduced Venkata. 'Many of you have heard Venkata's concerts, but he is not here to sing today. Instead, he will talk about his new approach to systematically classifying *ragas*.'

After the turbulent years at the palace, the quiet stay at the farmhouse had changed Amba's perspective. All she wanted, all she cared about, was to compose lyrical poems and songs that touched people's hearts. As a young musician, blinded by ambition and conditioned by limited thinking, she had allowed her dislike of Venkata and scholars like him to inhibit the joy she derived from composing.

Venkata's emphatic voice dragged her thoughts back to the present.

'All these years, we have been singing songs that have pleasing melodies. Such songs are often guided by emotion without underlying theory.'

Ayya nodded with an indulgent smile. He was not bothered by Venkata's authoritative tone, even if it was bordering on arrogance.

After droning on for some time, Venkata concluded, 'The new framework is a theoretical construct of seventy-two *ragas*, based on the tonal variations of five notes within an octave.'

Ayya stood up and nodded; it was Amba's cue to go down to the stage.

The nine songs she had composed were etched in her memory. She didn't need her manuscripts; she had handed them over to Ayya. It was his vision to place her music in the context of the theoretical framework and establish Tanjore as the capital of Carnatic music.

Amba climbed down the spiral staircase and landed behind the stage. She gently pushed the door leading to the backstage, parted the thick curtains and walked in. Mouths flew open as a hundred eyes poked at her body. Perhaps they had not expected her to appear after the insults hurled at her all those years ago. The silence was louder than the chatter that abruptly stopped at her entrance.

Amba sat on the thick silk carpet, placed the *tanpura* on her lap, and strummed the drone's four strings. Male musicians often had their students sit behind them and strum the *tanpura* so the lead singer's importance would never be undermined.

When my school girls are ready, they will sit beside me and not behind me, she thought.

Amba adjusted her *sari* to cover her toes. She had chosen a simple yellow *sari* with a thin gold border, a short chain with a tiny gold pendant and matching gold bangles. Grand *saris* and jewellery were essential when she had lived in the palace. Queens, courtesans, and even palace maids respected appearance first and the person next. Right now, she wanted them to listen to her music and not gawk at her appearance.

Ayya cleared his throat, and people snapped to attention. 'Today, we are here to listen to Amba, a talented composer, who has composed many songs. Some years ago, King Raghu heard her devotional music at the temple and invited her to compose music for him to play on his *veena*. Her compositions inspired the king to modify the *veena* and add more frets to accommodate the nuances of her melodies.'

Ayya paused at the shuffle of dusty feet rubbing against the marble floor. The principal court musician, the *Dikshita,* hoisted himself from his high cushion. His rotund belly heaved and jiggled as he thrust his chest forward.

'Revered Govinda Ayya, Tanjore scholars have the highest regard for you and your music, but...'

The *Dikshita's* eyes swept around the hall, a crooked smile crawling like a worm along his lips. The *Brahmins* nodded like grinning puppets as the *Dikshita* acknowledged their compliance.

'With due respect to Ayya, we cannot allow a temple *devadasi,* who turned into a *rajadasi* and pampered the king, to dilute the sanctity of Tanjore music. Until we read her manuscript, review and validate her compositions, she cannot be allowed to perform in this music palace.'

The puppets' heads nodded in unison.

The *Dikshita's* words felt like sharp stones hurled at her body. Amba's breath felt trapped in her lungs, and bitter bile burnt the back of her throat.

How dare he, she thought scornfully.

The *Dikshita* and his cronies never had to work to fill their bulging bellies. They lived in comfortable houses with granite floors, tiled roofs, and plastered walls in the *Agraharam,* the township donated by the king to the *Brahmins.* Devoted *devadasis* like her mother, Paru Ma, had no such perks. Living in tiny houses with thatched roofs, sharing a common well around the temple, and toiling night and day, they sang and danced with devotion at every temple festival to earn their keep.

Amba took a deep breath, offered a silent prayer to her goddess, and turned towards Ayya. She folded her hands in a *namaste,* bent her head, and sought permission to speak. Ayya nodded his approval. She steadied her hands on the soundboard of the *tanpura* and directed her gaze on the *Dikshita.*

'With due respect to *Sri Dikshita* and other scholars gathered here, yes, I was born to a *devadasi* who offered her services to the temple. It was my good fortune that our musician king recognised my talents and asked me to be his consort. If composing music for a musician king makes me a *rajadasi,* so be it.'

Amba placed the *tanpura* back on the carpet and glanced at the ministers in the front row. She knew many of them from her time in court during the negotiations with Danish traders.

'When my music and poetry could no longer flourish in the palace, I discarded the mantel of *rajadasi.'*

Even after all these months, her voice choked at the memory of the burnt manuscripts that had left her with a sharp pain every time she took a deep breath.

'*Devadasi, rajadasi...*they were mere garments I wore at different times. Those labels mean nothing to me anymore. I am not here to seek recognition from the people assembled here. My songs are offered to the goddess and not meant for men of letters to validate.'

Amba clenched her fists. She could walk out this instant, but that would be giving up and letting down Ayya, who believed in her. Her heart melted when she saw Ayya's hunched shoulders and sagging cheeks.

Amba took a deep breath, sat erect, and cleared her throat, willing the men to listen. 'I have dedicated my life to music. My songs are a garland of prayers to the goddess. If you are true scholars in pursuit of knowledge or musicians who seek divinity through music, focus on the goddess addressed in my songs and *not* on who I am. *She* has given me the knowledge to compose, and I pray that *She* gives you the wisdom to hear her voice through my music.'

Amba paused. 'If it is her intention to mask your minds, I shall walk out and go to her temple to offer my songs on this special day of *Navarathri.*'

The men lowered their heads in total silence.

The *Dikshita* shuffled his feet and collapsed into his seat. Ayya glared at Venkata, who hung his head low, unable to face Ayya.

Had Venkata instigated the Dikshita? Amba thought for a moment before pushing the betrayal from her mind.

There was a hush, and nothing more was said.

Amba recited a silent prayer. This was not the time to allow pride and anger to rule her heart. She placed the round hollow base of the *tanpura* on the right side of her lap, held the long soundboard vertically close to her ears, closed her eyes and surrounded herself with the calming drone of the *tanpura* strings.

Amba sang the notes of the first *raga*, 'Kanakangi', and followed it with a brief improvisation segment to highlight the nuances of the *raga*. She composed the first three songs in Sanskrit, as the language allowed her to create the rhythmic prosody required to project Goddess Durga's vitality and energy. The first song dealt with inner reflection when the pride, anger, jealousy, hatred, selfishness, and wickedness of our inner demon––the *ahankara*––are demolished. The second song proclaimed the symbolic victory of good over evil, and the third song focussed on a new awakening inspired by Shakti, the vital force of creativity.

'Aaha, aaha,' the *Brahmins* cheered. Their eyes glistened with devotion. An elderly *Brahmin* raised his hand in a gesture of blessing, 'May you live long.'

She sang the next three songs in Telugu about Goddess Lakshmi, the giver of wealth. The silk-turbaned merchants understood Telugu, and their wide smiles revealed a mouthful of betel-stained teeth as they responded to the music.

The last three songs were in Tamil, the ancient language of the Tanjore kings. They addressed Goddess Saraswati, whose knowledge and wisdom enabled God Brahma to create the world.

Amba closed her eyes and stretched the final note until it faded into a peaceful silence. If it had been performed in the temple, she would have extended the peace with a soft chanting of OM. But these scholars had no time or space for that deep silence.

Amba opened her eyes and set the *tanpura* down. The murmur of 'Aaha' grew louder.

As she was about to get up, Venkata and poet Yagna stood up and clapped their hands in a slow rhythm that echoed through the hall. Soon, more scholars stood up and joined the rhythmic applause. Several voices echoed in unison, '*Pramadam, arpudam,* brilliant.' A rare and spontaneous outburst of appreciation acknowledging her performance, a woman's performance, filled the air. These men rarely complimented each other, let alone a woman, as they firmly believed that compliments made a person arrogant.

Ayya gestured with his hand and asked her to remain seated. Venkata walked up to the dais amid muffled whispers. His gaze swept over the audience, and his unspoken authority silenced the voices.

Now, what was he going to spout, Amba thought, exasperated.

'We Tanjore scholars are proud of our musical heritage, which has come to us over centuries. In our goal to reach perfection, we have created rigid boundaries about what this means. Such self-inflicted boundaries limit our thoughts.'

Wide smiles lit up the faces of ministers in the front row.

Venkata's tone became sombre. 'When I closed my eyes and allowed my mind to focus on the music, the lyrics and the rhythm, I had a glimpse of the devotion Amba expressed in her music.'

A shiver ran through Amba's body as though a fountain had erupted in the core of her heart, its cool spray coursing through her veins. Not for a minute had she expected Venkata to acknowledge her work. She blinked away the tears that threatened to gush out.

Ayya came over and gently patted her head. Even his eyes were moist as he waited for the hum from the crowd to subside.

'This is the beginning of Amba's journey. Her vision is to nurture other girls and young women who do not get the opportunities they deserve. I hope and pray that Amba's vision of bringing women's compositions to life translates into reality in my lifetime.'

Tears of joy, tears for the lost years, and tears of gratitude poured out of her eyes. Her heart felt light, shedding its heavy burden. It was a long-held burden of unfulfilled desires that had taken her on a tumultuous journey out of the temple and into the palace, then out of the palace and into a new world where men did not define her boundaries.

Amba thanked the audience and hurried out of the hall and through the side door. She staggered across the veranda, collapsed under a pillar and surrendered to the moment she had waited so long for.

A gentle hand stroked her head, a hand that had woken her up every morning, all those years ago, propelling her to start her music practice.

Paru Ma!

Her mother's face lit up with the brightest smile Amba had ever seen. At that moment, Amba knew that by fulfilling her own dream, she had fulfilled her mother's as well. All along Amba had believed that Paru Ma wanted her to follow in her footsteps and become a *devadasi*. Only now could Amba get a glimpse of a mother, who had neither the means nor the dreams to cross the boundaries she had just crossed. Paru Ma had accepted life as it was offered to her. A life of devotion to the temple, which she had tried to pass on to her daughter.

Amba rested her head on Paru Ma's shoulders, unable to stop the sobs that rocked her body.

Finally, after the tears subsided, Paru Ma said, 'The palanquin is waiting for you. I'll accompany you to the farmhouse.'

They stayed quiet on the ride back home. Paru Ma never spoke while travelling in the palanquin. She cautioned, 'Eight ears listen to you when you are in a palanquin.'

The noise of the city receded as the bearers trotted to a rhythmic pattern, swaying and humming as they carried them home. The moment the palanquin touched the ground, Kanchana was out the front door with one big hop and a skip across the porch steps. A huge pot of aromatic water stood ready for Amba to wash her face, hands and feet, a habit she followed every time she returned from an outing. Amba signed a thank you to the ever-attentive Kanchana, who drew another pot of water from the well. She added some vetiver grass and mint leaves to the water and invited Paru Ma with her hands. Soon Chandrika joined them.

Kanchana brought out three glasses of lime juice and a semolina pudding, fragrant with cardamom and glistening with *ghee*. She was eager to hear about the concert.

She signed. 'How was it?' She took her finger across think?'

Paru Ma's hands and fingers moved rapidly, and her eyes expressed a range of emotions. 'The big scholars were impressed; they called her the Queen of Composition, and Ayya called her a woman with a vision because she wants to start a school for girls.'

Amba gestured, folding her hands into a *namaste*. 'Blessings of the goddess.'

Life is strange; you seek recognition, and it's hidden, but once you stop, it turns up at your doorstep, Amba thought peacefully.

CHAPTER 31

MAYA
Sydney, 2015

The roaring applause and encore following the concert continued to echo in my ears as I exited the stage. Gita drew me into a bear hug. 'What a star!'

Neetu and Vikram were right behind her. 'So proud of you Beti!' uncle and aunty repeated a few times.

Behind all of them stood Deepak! He held a large bouquet in his hands, standing slightly apart from the others, with that same smile that had dazzled me all those years ago. My heart raced, but my feet refused to move. *Why was Meena standing next to him? Had she dragged him along?* Deepak's parents knew about the music festival, and Neetu Aunty had bought tickets a long time back. But with me walking out on Deepak, I hadn't expected his parents to turn up. During the final weeks of practice, Meena, my pillar of strength, had hinted that my resilience and passion would pay off, but I had never expected this.

The next few moments were like a slow-motion movie. Deepak walked towards me with the flowers and embraced me in front of his parents. Neetu and Meena exchanged smiles of unspoken gratitude. Was this a second chance for both of us or was this another phase of compromise?

When we reached home that night, Deepak held me tight as sobs rocked my body. He kept whispering, 'Shhh, shh, I love you. I love you, my darling.' I crumbled into his arms like a broken Tanjore bobble doll. He kissed my neck, my face, and my eyes as he wiped away my tears.

As they always did, the birds chirped at the crack of dawn. *Don't they ever feel sad?* I didn't want to open my eyes. The aroma of strong coffee nudged me awake as Deepak stood gingerly at the end of the bed with a steaming coffee in my favourite mug.

When I finally stirred, Deepak sat next to me on the bed and handed me the mug. He knew how to make good coffee!

Deepak said, 'Let's take the day off and go for a drive.'

I showered and lit a tiny oil lamp in front of the picture of Ganesha and mumbled a silent prayer. 'Remove the obstacles in my path and from Deepak's mind.'

Deepak stood beside me; quiet, contemplative. He said, 'Let's visit the Helensburgh Temple and then go to Kiama from there.'

The last time we had visited the temple was during the crowded Ganesha festival with Deepak's parents, that first year when we were besotted with each other.

Being a weekday morning, the temple was quiet. Soft chanting of mantras from the speakers greeted us as we walked into the main hall. The fragrance of incense and flowers filled the air. We spent a few minutes in front of each shrine: Shiva, Parvathi, and their sons,

Ganesha and Kartikeya, all of whom are gods who destroyed evil egos.

A priest in a white *dhoti*, his forehead smeared with three horizontal lines of holy ash *vibhuthi*, led us to the Ganesha shrine.

'Newly marriedaa?' Thanglish, even in Sydney. Deepak grinned as he nodded his head up and down, allowing the priest to come to his own conclusion. The priest performed a *puja* for us and gave us a *prasad* of half a coconut and two bananas, the standard offering for the elephant god in most temples. We thanked the priest and went around the shrines.

In a corner room, a few women were chatting happily while stringing garlands for the deities. One of them looked familiar, her *sari* pinned, and her hair bunched low.

I tugged Deepak's hand. 'Wait a moment, let me say hello to Radha.'

Radha turned around before I even reached her. 'Maya! What a surprise to see the two of you on a weekday!' Her eyes twinkled, 'Any special news?'

Deepak and I both knew what she was hinting at. He couldn't hide his grin.

I chuckled. 'No, Radha Aunty, it's not what you think. We've both been working hard and needed a break.'

Radha asked, 'How's your experiment going with Western classical?'

Before I could answer, she turned to Deepak. 'We are lucky to have a musician of Maya's calibre in Sydney. I don't know how she manages to work during the day, spend evenings with the Australian quartet, and have the energy to teach Carnatic music to our kids on weekends.'

She added after a pause. 'Maya's lucky to have a supportive husband like you. It's impossible otherwise.' *Little did she know.*

Deepak folded his hands. 'We need your blessings, Aunty.'

Radha said, 'Wait a minute, I'll give you some special *prasad*. Our garland group have made some *laddus* for God Venkateshwara.'

She led us to the Vishnu wing of the temple. If Shiva destroyed egos, then Vishnu fostered love. We paid our respects to the deities there, thanked Radha for the sweets and headed to Kiama.

When we arrived, we watched the unruly waves erupting one moment before rippling through the rugged rocks in the next. We held hands and waited for the blowhole to erupt again.

Deepak kissed my ear. 'That's a bit like us.'

I squeezed his hand. 'We don't have to be that way.'

Deepak kissed me again. 'I hear you.'

After lunch at a local cafe, we headed to the Minnamurra Rainforest. Under ancient trees in a land that had been around forever, our skirmishes seemed petty and insignificant.

Deepak settled on a rock under a giant gum tree. He said, 'These ancient trees and rocks have been around for centuries, weathering the obstacles nature throws at them. But we humans can't handle even the smallest change.'

His hand reached out for mine. 'I struggled when you wanted us to move out of my parents' home. It was the right thing to do, but it took me a while to adjust.'

He held me tight and kissed me deeply.

'I love your passion. I love you more than ever before. Yet, I find it hard to keep up with the pace of change you have ushered into our lives.'

I took his hand to my lips. 'I have loved you from the moment I set eyes on you that evening after my concert in Chennai. In a matter of months, I moved countries to be with you. Think about that. I realise it's difficult to make money as a musician. But music is in my blood and in every breath. Amidst all the changes, music is the bedrock of stability for me. I will crumble if you snatch that away from me, and I do not want to crumble.'

Deepak held me in a passionate hug as if he didn't want to let me get away from him again. 'I will never let you crumble. I promise.'

I gently extricated myself. 'I need space to be who I want to be. I love you, but things have to change. You cannot be another Vikram but with an Australian accent. You have to change your attitude. I enjoy playing music with Dave, but I don't love him. You must understand that. I'm not going to stop playing music with Dave or with anyone else.'

I changed my voice to a lighter tone. 'You grew up here. Why didn't you marry an Aussie girl? I'm sure Neetu would have accepted that.'

Deepak kissed my ears. 'I met you instead.'

'Seriously? Were you scared an Aussie girl wouldn't put up with your tantrums or cook for you?'

'Not all Indian girls can cook. Take Gita, for instance, Dave's the cook in their house.'

'But I'm sure she washes the dishes and does other chores around the house instead.'

Deepak kissed my neck. 'I'll wash the dishes for you and order takeout on Tuesdays and Thursdays when you're out practising.'

It was hard not to kiss him back. 'Those days might change too. Can you handle that?'

Deepak kissed another part of my neck. 'I'll try.'

Would he really try? Or would he be like that mythical Prince Dushyanta who forgot his promise to his wife?

'You have to embrace my music all the time and not think of it as something you have to put up with. I'll keep my side of the bargain and hold on to the paying job, but it'll be for four days a week instead of five.'

Deepak stepped back in surprise. 'They'll ignore you when it comes to giving you a promotion. Won't that bother you?'

'I don't care. Four days of work is enough to give us those extra savings to buy a home, and I can pursue my passion without a sense of guilt.'

I shrugged my shoulders. 'But you need to accept that your wife's goals and dreams are different from yours. I have no interest in being a hotshot manager; I want to be a musician.'

For a moment, Deepak was quiet, but the next instant, he caught me in a bear hug. 'You are a hotshot musician. I was blown away when I heard you perform with your group at the music festival. I had no clue that's what you were working on.'

As we were driving back home, Deepak said, 'Let's invite Gita and Dave over for dinner tonight. There will be no shop talk today. I need to make amends with Dave.'

I called Gita from Deepak's phone, and her voice came over the car speaker.

Deepak said, 'Maya and I are planning to go out for dinner. Want to join us?'

Gita said, 'Come over to our place instead. Dave has made a chicken korma using Maya's vegetable korma recipe.'

Over dinner, Gita's eyes oozed love when she glanced at Dave, and Dave could barely keep his hands off her whenever she was around. How could Deepak be so blind to their love to think there was ever anything other than friendship between Dave and me?

Gita said, 'Deepak, you and I are both lucky to have musicians as partners. They are gentler souls than us techies hell-bent on proving our worth.'

Gita gave me a friendly hug and glanced at Deepak. 'Dave wants to produce a new album, *The Veena Quintet*. He wants to add a few more pieces to their festival repertoire and take it to a record producer or ABC Radio.

Dave grinned. 'And Gita wants to be the hard-nosed business and marketing manager.'

Was this real? I said, 'You think we can do this?'

Deepak said, 'I'll create a website to promote your music.' I squeezed Deepak's hand. How hard he was trying to support my passion. My eyes grew moist.

I didn't miss the grin Gita and Dave exchanged. Dave took out a bottle of prosecco from the fridge and poured the amber liquid into four champagne flutes.

In off-key unison, we all cheered, 'To The *Veena* Quintet!'

CHAPTER 32

AMBA

Tanjore, 1640

Never did Amba dream that one day she would be sitting at a vantage point on the raised platform of the music palace, witnessing her desires being fulfilled. Was it thirty years ago that she sat invisible behind one of those distant pillars, her heart laden with dreams and ambitions? Ambitions of taking her music beyond the temple into the hallowed halls of Tanjore.

Amba was one of the three judges at this year's music competition. Venkata and Tanjore's court poet, Kaviraya, were the other two. The panel selection was Ayya's idea.

'Amba, your presence as a judge at the Tanjore competition will inspire young women to excel and become recognised scholars. It is time men realised music is not their exclusive domain.'

Three of the four women at this year's competition were students from her *gurukul*. After their basic training, they received advanced training in music from Nagamma. Nagamma never stepped out of her house but agreed to take on Amba's *gurukul* girls who were keen to devote their lives to music. She trained one of the girls to sing and play the *veena* simultaneously, as Ayya had done for Amba all those years ago.

Over the last few years, the barren land behind the summer palace had been transformed into a beautiful semicircular building. It had beautiful, curved verandas supported by teak pillars and vetiver curtains separating the classrooms. Music, dance, languages, and even the art of self-defence were part of the curriculum for her students. Selvi made sure that every girl was trained in *silambam*, a form of martial arts to defend herself against the likes of Thimma.

Young faces with stars in their eyes gazed at the mythical creatures twirling along the giant pillars of Indira Mandira. Six men, hair tied in top knots, and four women in half-*saris* sat in the front rows on either side of the big hall. No girl had to hide her face, and no man dared shun them from participating.

Ayya had retired from active court duties. 'My old bones need to rest now. I want to finish writing the musical treatise before my eyes fully go blind.'

Amba visited him every week, and they chatted about the events that had launched Tanjore as the cultural capital of South India. After a relaxed lunch, Amba sat with Ayya and Nagamma, mulling over the past.

'Ayya, I have wondered for a long time if you knew I was listening when you and King Raghu were talking about the Danish ship when it first arrived?'

Ayya threw his head back and laughed. 'Your curiosity had no limits, Amba.

'Nagamma, do you know what Amba did once? She hid behind a cupboard and overheard the conversation the king and I had about the Danish ship. But that wasn't all; she went after that Danish captain and extracted a lot of information that helped us form a cordial relationship with the Danish king.'

Amba chuckled. 'My language teacher had taught me a bit of Portuguese, and I wanted to test my skills on our new visitor. Little did I realise that Captain Ove didn't speak Portuguese. He spoke Danish instead, but we managed to communicate anyway. Ove loved my garden and helped me grow new types of flowers that had never existed in Tanjore.'

'But that friendship got you into more trouble, did it not?' Ayya asked with a grin.

Amba flicked her hand as if she was swotting a fly. 'Best not to talk about Queen Kalyani.'

Amba opened her large hessian bag. 'Ayya, I have a surprise for you.'

Amba unwrapped the white cotton cloth and delicately lifted her manuscript as if it were a baby. Twelve bundles, each with seventy-five palm leaves tied together by silk chords. Each leaf carried one verse of eight lines, each line delicately etched with her gold stylus. It was her life's work, and she wanted Ayya to have it.

'*The Life and Times of King Raghu Nayaka* in twelve cantos, seventy-five verses per canto. I wrote it in Sanskrit.' She stressed the word Sanskrit and smiled.

A bright smile lit up his rheumy eyes as Amba placed her manuscript in Ayya's hands.

'King Raghu Nayaka's ancestry, military success, cultural and artistic achievements, trade pacts...they are all here. This is my offering for future generations.'

Ayya touched her head with his palm and blessed her. 'May you live long and create works that shine like the brilliant sun.'

Ayya squinted through the first page of the first canto and then the last page of the last canto.

He held the last page of the manuscript close to his eyes. Turning to Nagamma, he said, 'Can you read the colophon aloud?'

Nagamma read out the last leaf. 'Goddess Parvati has blessed me with the art of composing four types of poetry in eight languages. I, Amba, was installed on the throne of Sahitya Samrajya, Empress among poets.'

CHAPTER 33

That massive argument was a much-needed catharsis for both of us and our relationship. I no longer craved Deepak's validation. 'Market worth' was his problem, not mine. For me, my own validation was vital.

It was a huge relief to drop down to four days of work a week. Deepak came home on time, exhausted but cheerful. He cleaned up after dinner and loaded the dishwasher. When he slumped down in front of the TV or brought back work, I worked on my music. We had finally found a way to live for ourselves and each other.

Frequent chats with Viji Ma and email exchanges with Professor Krishnamurthy kept Amba's world alive in my thoughts. We talked about Govinda Ayya, who was the mentor for three generations of Nayakas, and his son, Venkata, whose music theory became the basis of Carnatic *ragas*. Separated by continents and centuries, Amba drew me into her world. The same chord of music and melodies bound us.

Over dinner with Deepak, I talked about Amba's life, her remarkable contribution to music and poetry, and how she had established the first school for girls. Deepak served himself another helping of pumpkin soup, a new Thai-inspired recipe I had discovered on YouTube.

'Flavoursome soup.' He slurped the last spoonful and said, 'You are so passionate when you talk about Amba. I think you should write about her.'

My hand stopped buttering the bread. 'What? I have never written a story, let alone a biography. But yes, Amba and I are connected.'

A few evenings later, when we were clearing up after dinner, Deepak said, 'Remember my colleague, Susan? She casually mentioned that she was taking a creative writing course through the Australian Writer's Centre at Milson's Point.'

I stopped wiping the bench top and turned around. 'Susan, your software developer?'

Deepak nodded. 'Yep. I asked her for more details, and she messaged me their link.'

He wiped his hands on a tea towel and reached for his phone. 'I've forwarded you the link. You should trawl through their site.'

I mumbled, 'Too hard, no time.'

A few weeks later, I browsed through their courses on creative writing. They had an online course for total novices like me, and I could fit it in on my day off.

That evening, I asked in a soft voice that even I couldn't hear. 'Do you really think I could write?'

Deepak paused the TV and kissed my forehead. 'About Amba?

Of course you can. If I had recorded your words every time you talked about her, you would have half the book by now.'

The next evening, Deepak could barely hide his wide grin. 'Here's a special gift for you.'

As I untied the gold ribbon around the slim black leather case, I asked, 'Jewellery?'

Deepak's grin burst out of his face. 'Open it.'

My jaws dropped. 'A Montblanc pen!' I squealed. 'Are you crazy? It costs an arm and a leg. It was my father's dream, but he could never afford one.'

Deepak gave me a bear hug. 'I thought your Amba will like this: a rollerball with a gold tip. Didn't you say she wrote with a gold stylus?'

I guffawed. 'Possibly, the archivist said there were traces of gold dust on her palm leaf manuscript.'

I rotated my fingers over the shiny tip of the pen. 'Can I really write?' My stomach churned in rebellion.

Deepak said, 'Sleep on it. Don't let it become a point of stress.'

We slept on it alright, a night when mind and body came together.

The next morning, I called the Australian Writers' Centre, and by evening, I had enrolled in an online creative writing course.

My first assignment was a five-hundred-word synopsis. I decided that my novel would be a conversation with Amba. I rapidly typed the story outline, my excitement overflowing to the top.

Yes, Amba. I hear you loud and clear. You claim you are the Empress among poets, and I have verified that, indeed, you are.

Scholars write PhD theses about your biography of King Raghu Nayaka. Indians, Danish, British, Portuguese: everyone who is remotely connected to Tanjore cites your biography as an authentic source of Tanjore history.

Ove Gjedde, the captain of the first Danish ship that landed near the Coromandel Coast in 1618, has written a diary of his years in Tanjore and Tranquebar. He has mentioned you, by name, as one of the most distinguished scholars of the Nayaka's court. Did you get to meet him?

Perhaps Prime Minister Govinda Ayya deposited your palm-leaf manuscript at the Saraswati Mahal Library. A library that he created with Sevappa Nayaka, King' Raghu's grandfather. But the Tanjore professor mentioned that your manuscript had disappeared when the British historians catalogued the books of the library in 1800. Maybe that's why the British Museum Catalogue of Saraswati Mahal Library does not list your manuscript. But then, you are not the one to stay hidden, are you? An Indian scholar from Madras University found your manuscript tucked away in a gunny bag in 1910. Today. your work is the centrepiece of the largest ancient manuscript museum in the southern hemisphere––the Saraswati Mahal Library Museum in Tanjore. That is where I found you.

Now, Amba, you are not going anywhere until I tell your story— my story of your story.

ACKNOWLEDGMENTS

Like me, this book owes its birth to my mother Mangalam Ramamoorthi; a Tamil writer, a storyteller, and my first inspiration. Amma, my deepest *Namaskarams*. You're not here to see where you have taken me, but every page is lit with your spirit.

Back in 2009, a month before passing away, Amma asked me to translate her Tamil novel *Nandinayakan*, set in 16th-century Tanjore. I knew next to nothing about Tanjore then. While translating *Nandinayakan: The Temple Builder*, I began to wander across temples, streets, and archives of Tanjore. That's when I came across a palm-leaf manuscript dated 1630 CE written by a female scholar preserved at the Tanjore Saraswati Mahal Library.

When I began my creative writing journey in 2010, I quickly realised how different it was from the academic writing I was used to. That led me to the Australian Writers' Centre, which became my *gurukul*—my learning space. I owe so much to the people I met there.

To Cathie Tasker—my first creative writing teacher, a gifted editor, and now a treasured mentor. You showed me how to shape a story, how to chisel a character. You nudged me forward when I stalled, celebrated the breakthroughs, and pointed out where I needed to grow. I'm immensely grateful for your belief in me and this story.

To Pamela Freeman—what a gift you've been! Award-winning

author, teacher, mentor, magician with words. You taught me to examine every scene with care, precision, and honesty. Each session with you was like unearthing a new nugget of wisdom. I truly wouldn't be holding this book today without your generous guidance every step of the way. *Mikka Nanri*, heartfelt thanks.

To award-winning writers/teachers Kate Forsyth and Tracie Skuce. Your courses helped me discover and polish that elusive voice inside me. I thank you for the voice you have given me. I extend my gratitude to Writing NSW and the Australian Society of Authors for their ongoing support to writers like me.

As the old saying goes—it takes a village to raise a child. This book too, has been nurtured by a community of kind, wise, funny, brilliant, and generous people.

My brothers, Bhaskar and Ashok—you're my energy boosters. Bhaskar, those endless book recommendations came just when I needed a fresh perspective. When I doubted myself, "it'll be good in ten years," you counselled. You were right! This story began its long walk in 2015. Ashok, you've been my loudest cheerleader. From the first draft, you championed my story and encouraged its publication. Without you, I'd still be carrying this book around in my head.

My supportive siblings Meera, Mahzarin, Radhakrishnan— thank you for reading the early, messy drafts, for your nuggets of wisdom and for your unwavering belief in me.

My daughters, Supriya and Soumya—you've been my light and laughter. You pushed me forward when I was tired, held me up when I faltered, spurred me on towards the finishing line. The book is in your hands because you were there every step of the way.

My generous beta readers—Alastair Pennycook, Bhuvana Venkataramani, Cecile Paris, Christine Allman, Kalpana Rao, and Sashi Prasad—you gave me your time, your thoughts, your kind and sharp suggestions. You helped make this story stronger.

My ever-present writing group—Anne Farrell, Alex Gibson, Jenny Wilson, Louise Hayes, Michelle Bryceland, Vanessa Andean—you've become my writing family. With you, I've felt seen, heard, and held. You helped me navigate the highs and lows of writing life with courage and joy. Thank you for always being there. A special thanks to Christine Allman for drawing me into the self-publishing world where I met amazing writers like Maria P Frino and Lisa Creffield, who generously shared their knowledge of the self-publishing world.

And to the wonderful team who helped bring this book into the world: To my editors—Cathie Tasker (again!) for your special touch, Robyn Hooper (Blurb and Her Writing Services) for making me dig deeper, Laura Boon (It's All Write Editing) for that final polish — thank you all for shaping this book with such care and skill. Special thanks to my dear friend Suresh Rao for editing the raw edges around the novel. To Kavitha Amarnath, thank you for the stunning cover design. You understood the soul of the story and turned it into a beautiful piece of art. To Aparna C P for creating an attractive author platform and a home-base for my creativity to emerge.

Finally, to all my writer friends who've encouraged me, laughed and cried with me, and walked beside me on this long road—I haven't listed every name, but you know who you are. I carry your kindness with me.

AUTHOR'S NOTE

Etched in Gold is inspired by people who lived in Tanjore during a dynamic period—between 1600 and 1630 CE. This period marks a crucial transition in South Indian history, connecting the waning Chola empire (9th-13th centuries), the 1565 Vijayanagar collapse, and the subsequent British ascendancy in 1858. The fall of Vijayanagar, once a formidable South Indian empire, led to the rise of local powers like the Tanjore Nayakas, shaping the region's political and cultural landscape in the years that followed.

Tanjore, known as Thanjavur in Tamil, is home to a majestic Shiva Temple constructed in the eleventh century, under the patronage of the mighty Chola kings. Fondly referred to as the Big Temple by the locals, the massive *gopuram* tower carved with intricate sculptures and frescoes, pre-dates the Taj Mahal. This magnificent UNESCO heritage temple has remained mysteriously shielded from casual tourists. The imposing Nandi sculpture in the temple complex is a subsequent addition introduced by the Nayaka dynasty

(1530-1670), who transformed Tanjore into a vibrant cultural and trading hub.

This novel is set in the period of King Raghunatha Nayaka (1600-1634), considered the gem among the Nayakas.

The protagonist of this novel, Amba, is a fictional character inspired by the real-life scholar and poet Ramabhadramba. Historical records confirm her presence in the court of King Raghunatha Nayaka. Ramabhadramba's epic work, *Raghunathabhyudayam*, is a twelve-canto Sanskrit *mahākāvya* epic poem with 897 verses. It celebrates King Raghu Nayaka as a heroic figure, drawing rich parallels with Rama and Krishna, divine incarnations of God Vishnu. Her verses highlight the king's valour, lineage, patronage of the arts, and her own extraordinary talents—including her command over eight languages. This led some scholars to label her work as hagiography. This epic work written on palm leaves is preserved at the ancient Saraswati Mahal Library in Tanjore.

However, Ramabhadramba's childhood before she became the voice of a king's legend remains unknown. That mystery opened up the creative space for me to imagine her formative years. Was she a temple musician, a devadasi, a courtesan, a queen, or a self-made scholar? *Etched in Gold* is a re-imagination of her journey through the voice of a fictional character, Amba.

THE TRANQUEBAR TREATY OF 1620

In 1620, while the Portuguese and Dutch had already made their presence felt in South India, a quieter but significant event unfolded: the signing of the Tranquebar Treaty between King Raghu Nayaka and King Christian IV of Denmark.

This landmark agreement granted the Danes: The right to trade in the Thanjavur kingdom; Control over the coastal village of

Tharangambadi (renamed as Tranquebar), initially for two years; for an annual rent of 3,111 rupees, giving the Danes permission to build a fortified settlement, which became Fort Dansborg. When it was built and to this day, this remains the second largest Danish castle in the world after Kronberg, the setting for Shakespeare's Hamlet.

The treaty, inscribed on a gold foil, symbolized Tanjore's wealth and prestige. Copies of the original treaty are preserved at the Danish National Museum and displayed at Fort Dansborg in Tranquebar. This Danish foothold lasted over 225 years. In 1845, the Tranquebar assets were sold to the British for 1.25 million rupees.

WOMEN, WISDOM, AND WEALTH

The Nayaka period is distinguished by the rulers' active recognition and celebration of scholars, highlighting their patronage for intellectual and cultural achievements. There are recorded accounts of poetesses being honoured with pearls and gems equal to their body weight—a tradition that speaks volumes about the respect accorded to intellectual and artistic brilliance, regardless of gender.

Ramabhadramba was one among many such torchbearers. Her poetry is studied by scholars and PhD candidates both in India and abroad. Her legacy lives on as a symbol of female intellect thriving in a patriarchal age.

STANDARDISATION OF CARNATIC MUSIC

Simultaneously during the Nayakas period, the arts were undergoing a dramatic transformation. Carnatic music as we know it today took formal shape during this period. The foundational concept of 72 *Melakarta* ragas—parent scales from which all other ragas descend—

was codified by Venkata Makhi, son of the renowned minister and musicologist Govinda Dikshita, who served three Nayaka rulers.

King Raghunatha Nayaka himself was an accomplished veena player and is credited with standardizing the number of frets on the instrument. Music wasn't just entertainment; it was an intellectual and spiritual pursuit, deeply intertwined with temple culture.

The story imagines the subtle tensions and power dynamics between figures like Venkata, a Brahmin scholar, and Amba, a woman of uncertain social standing but immense intellect. Through this lens, it also explores the life of temple musicians and Devadasis, who were once revered as the custodians of sacred music and dance—only to be marginalized in later colonial times.

FROM PAST TO PRESENT

17th century Tanjore was a hub of commerce caught between tradition and transformation. It pulsed with foreign ships, twang of veena strings, and voices of women scholars. It was a cultural crucible—and that legacy echoes even today.

To bring this magnificent past into the present, I introduced Maya, a modern-day protagonist who stumbles upon Amba's lost manuscript in the Tanjore library. Maya's own search for identity and freedom mirrors Amba's, weaving together an eternal quest that resonates across centuries into the present day.

I consulted several scholarly essays, numerous websites, newspaper and journal articles in Tamil and English, in Chennai and Sydney, before and during the writing of this novel. My sincere gratitude to libraries and librarians of Tanjore, Sydney, Chennai, and Copenhagen for their invaluable help in providing research materials for my novel. If I were to list all the Tamil and English books and journal articles I read during the last ten years, it will fill several pages.

For want of space, I have listed only a few books that I consulted repeatedly while writing this novel. If I have omitted an important reference, the fault is entirely mine.

The Nayakas of Tanjore, Vridhagirisan, University of Annamalai Press, 1942.

A History of South India, K. A. Nilakanta Sastri, First published in 1955.

The Vijayanagar Empire, Chronicles of Paes and Nunez, written around 1535-37.

The Story of Tanjavur Nayakas (Tamil), Saraswati Mahal Library, 1999.

Martyn's Notes on Jaffna, Chronological, Historical, Biographical, 1922.

The Trials and Travels of Willem Leyel 1639-1648, Denmark Museum Press, 2009.

A Southern Music, T.M. Krishna, Harper Collins, India, 2013.

About the Author

Uma Srinivasan writes from the land of the Wangal people in Sydney, Australia. Born in the temple town of Chidambaram and raised in the royal city of Mysore, she had a long career as a Computer Scientist in India and Australia and now devotes all her time to writing. Her journey into historical fiction began with the translation of her mother's Tamil novel, *Nandinayakan: A Temple Builder*, published in 2015. In 2024, Uma co-authored the delightful children's book *Chaos in the Gym* with her granddaughter, Anika Kuber.

Etched in Gold, her first major work of fiction, brings forgotten pieces of history to life in a modern global context. The manuscript was shortlisted for the 2023 *Write It* Fellowship by Penguin Random House Australia.

umasrinivasanbooks.com

facebook.com/uma.srinivasan.1441

instagram.com/umasrinivasanbooks

linkedin.com/in/uma-srinivasan-b451a71

www.ingramcontent.com/pod-product-compliance
Lightning Source LLC
Chambersburg PA
CBHW040215170726

48295CB00014B/677